"I'd be well wi...
you apart for crossing the line."

"What are you up to?" Jaden drew even closer. "What are you running from, Lyra?"

It didn't matter what she said. There would be no help for her here, not now that her presence had been discovered.

"Where I go and what I do are none of your business," she said. "But you're welcome to *your* territory. There's nothing here I want."

She started to spin away, and only caught the dangerous flash of his eyes too late. His hand closed around her arm. He pulled her back hard, and she wound up plastered against him. For a brief, heated instant their bodies connected, and she could feel every hard knot of muscle in his long, lean form. Her body wanted to curve against it, fitting itself so that they were fused together, two pieces formed to connect with the other.

"You didn't answer my question, Lyra. What are you running from?" he breathed against her ear. She felt herself tremble with need.

Fear, anger, and helpless lust tangled together inside of her. And he was so still, watching her as poised and inscrutable as the sphinx.

But she could feel his want, the beast half of her sensing it and demanding she respond...

Praise for **DARK AWAKENING**

"Rising star Castle is sure to please with an exciting new series…Castle does a good job of laying out the bloodlines that distinguish her differing clans. Passion and loyalty collide as the hero is forced to reevaluate the choices that have driven his life."
—*RT Book Reviews*

"5 stars! I'm so glad this is the beginning of a series… While the world-building is rich and layered, its complexities are seamlessly incorporated into the story and contribute to making it a satisfying read…Ty is everything I love in a hero…The secondary characters were fleshed-out and interesting. And frankly, I want more."
—GoodReads.com

"A superb, fast-paced tale that grips the audience from the moment the lead couple meets in New England and never slows down until the final confrontation. Kendra Leigh Castle cleverly transports the Highlander historical clan disputes into modern age vampire clan disputes."
—GenreGoRoundReviews.blogspot.com

"I loved the new breed of shapeshifting vampire Ms. Castle introduced, and this is one of the few books that I finished with the thought of 'Wow, I bet this would make an incredible movie!'…Jaden's book is next and can I just say 'swoon'?…Recommended for fans of vampires and shapeshifters, political machinations, betrayals, and forbidden relationships, all with a touch of magick."
—Romanceaholic.com

Also by Kendra Leigh Castle

Dark Awakening

MIDNIGHT
RECKONING

A Tale of the Dark Dynasties

KENDRA LEIGH CASTLE

FOREVER

NEW YORK   BOSTON

Grand Central Publishing
Hachette Book Group
237 Park Avenue
New York, NY 10017

www.HachetteBookGroup.com

Printed in the United States of America

First Edition: January 2012
10 9 8 7 6 5 4 3 2 1

Grand Central Publishing is a division of Hachette Book Group, Inc. The Grand Central Publishing name and logo is a trademark of Hachette Book Group, Inc.

The Hachette Speakers Bureau provides a wide range of authors for speaking events. To find out more, go to www.hachettespeakersbureau.com or call (866) 376-6591.

The publisher is not responsible for websites (or their content) that are not owned by the publisher.

For my Gramma Hager
The heart of the family
Beloved giver of books, hugs, and cookies
Thanks for always being there for me

MIDNIGHT
RECKONING

THE DARK DYNASTIES
Known Bloodlines of the United States

THE PTOLEMY

LEADER: Queen Arsinöe

ORIGIN: Ancient Egypt and the goddess Sekhmet

STRONGHOLDS: Cities of the Eastern US, concentrated in the Mid-Atlantic

ABILITIES: Lightning speed

THE CAIT SITH

LEADER: Lily-Quinn MacGillivray

ORIGIN: A Celtic line originating with the Fae

STRONGHOLDS: United with the reborn Lilim in the Northern United States

ABILITIES: Can take the form of a cat

THE DRACUL

LEADER: Vlad Dracul

ORIGIN: The goddess Nyx

STRONGHOLDS: Cities of the
Northern US and Chicago
(shared with the Empusae)

ABILITIES: Can take the form
of a bat

THE GRIGORI

LEADER: Sariel

ORIGIN: Unknown

STRONGHOLDS: The deserts of the
West

ABILITIES: Flight is rumored due to
their mark, but no proof

THE EMPUSAE

LEADER: Empusa

ORIGIN: The goddess Hecate

STRONGHOLDS: Southern United
States; Chicago (shared with the
Dracul)

ABILITIES: Can take the form of
smoke

THE REBORN LILIM

Leader: Lily Quinn-MacGillivray

Origin: Lilith, the first vampire, now merged with the blood of the Cait Sith

Strongholds: Northern United States

Abilities: Lethal bursts of psychic energy; can take the form of a cat

chapter ONE

Tipton, Massachusetts

O N A NIGHT when only the thinnest sliver of a crescent moon rode the sky, at a time when even the most adventurous humans had fallen into bed and succumbed to sleep, a solitary cat padded in and out of pooled shadow as he made his way across the deserted square in the middle of town. He was large, the size of a bobcat, with sleek fur the color of jet. His coat shimmered as he moved, gleaming in the dull glow of streetlights in between shadows, and he moved with speed and grace, if not purpose. Eyes that burned like blue embers stayed focused on the path ahead of him.

The cat had gone by several names in his long life. For more than a century now, he had been simply Jaden, or even more simply, "cat." If pressed, he would answer to either, and neither if he could get away with it.

Tonight, in the night's seductive and silent embrace, Jaden answered to no one but himself.

Jaden took his time as he made his way through town, savoring the stillness of the blessed lack of humanity with all its noise and emotion and complication. He paused in front of the darkened windows of a beauty salon, letting his gaze drift over the sign that read, CHARMED, I'M SURE, and then lifted his head higher to catch the scent of air that was heavy with moisture and ripe with the promise of rain. Jaden could sense that summer was making its way to this little corner of New England, while aware that even in early May the frost could arrive on any given night to give the season's fresh blooms a deadly kiss.

Deadly kisses, Jaden thought, lashing his tail. Yeah, he knew all about those. When you were a vampire, especially a lowly shape-shifting cat of a vampire, deadly kisses were sort of your stock in trade.

Damn it. So much for a late-night walk to clear his head.

The shift came as easily as breathing to him, and in a single heartbeat Jaden stood on two feet instead of four, his clothes firmly in place by some magic he had never understood but always appreciated. He stuffed his hands deeply into the pockets of his coat and continued on down the street, glaring at the ground in front of him as he moved. Though he'd spent years seething silently at the Ptolemy, his highblood masters who had treated "pets" like him with little mercy and even less respect, these days he didn't seem to have much anger for anyone but himself.

Jaden now had what he'd always thought he wanted: friends, a home, and most important, his freedom. The Ptolemy were not gone, but they were cowed for the time being, and his kind, the much-maligned Cait Sith, had been chosen for an incredible honor. They were to be the foundation for the rebirth of a dynasty of highbloods that had vanished ages ago but had now resurfaced in the form of a single mortal woman who carried the blood.

The seven months since Jaden had helped that woman, Lily, make a stand against the Ptolemy had passed like nothing. And though it had been considerably less time since the Vampiric Council had given Lily's plan its grudging blessing, Jaden was now really and truly free. Whether it had been a wise decision, Jaden couldn't say. The Cait Sith were an unruly lot at best.

But he was grateful, as were the rest, which had to count for something.

Jaden rubbed at his collarbone without really being aware that he was doing it. There, beneath layers of clothing, was his mark, the symbol of his bloodline. Until recently, the mark had been a coiling knot of black cats. But a drink of Lily's powerful blood had changed it, adding the pentagram and snake of the Lilim. It meant new abilities he was still exploring, newfound standing in a world where he had always been beneath notice. It should have meant hope, Jaden knew. After all, for the first time in his long life, he was not a pariah. He could be his own master. It should be everything. And yet...

The empty places inside him still ached like open wounds. Something was missing. He just wished he knew what it was.

A soft breath of wind ruffled through his hair, and Jaden caught a whiff of something both familiar and unfamiliar.

Then he heard the voices.

"There's no place to run to now, is there?" That was a gravelly male voice, reeking of self-satisfaction. Its owner gave a low and vicious chuckle. "You're going to have to accept me. I've caught you. It's my right."

A female voice responded, and a pleasant shiver rippled through Jaden's body at the low, melodious sound of it.

"You have no rights with me. And chasing me down like prey isn't going to get you what you want."

He was almost certain he'd heard that voice before, though he couldn't place it. What Jaden *could* place, however, was the scent that had his hackles rising and the adrenaline flooding his system.

Werewolves.

Jaden's lips curled, and he had to fight the instinctive urge to hiss. Not only were the wolves vilified by vampires as savages, banned from their cities under penalty of death, but the smell of their musk caused a physical reaction in him that was difficult to control. He had two options: fight or flight. It was less trouble to run. But this was his territory now, vampire territory. And these wolves had a hell of a lot of nerve coming into it.

Jaden was moving before he could think better of it. His feet made no sound on the pavement as he headed for the parking lot behind the building. And as he slipped into shadow, he listened.

"You can make this easy or hard, honey. But you're going to have me one way or the other. And there's not a damn thing you can do about it."

A low growl from the female. A warning. "I'm not about to take a backseat to some social-climbing stray. I don't want a mate."

The male's voice went thick and rough, as though he

was fighting a losing battle with the beast within. "My family is plenty good enough to mate with an Alpha. You should be glad it's me, Lyra. I won't be as rough as some. And you and I both know there's no way the pack is ever going to have a female Alpha. There's too much at stake to let the weak lead."

Lyra... The pieces clicked into place, and Jaden's stomach sank like a stone.

He did know her. And that brief meeting had put him in one of the fouler moods of his unnatural life.

Memories surfaced of a Chicago safe house, full of vampires in hiding, in trouble, or on the run. And on the occasion he remembered, it had also been a hiding place for a female werewolf with a sharp tongue and a nasty attitude. Rogan, the owner of the safe house, had mentioned something about Lyra being a future Alpha... right after Jaden had demanded she leave the room.

Lyra had gone, though she hadn't taken the slight quietly. And now, she was here, in the seat of the Lilim. It was almost inconceivable. Jaden wondered briefly if Lyra hadn't hunted him here to finish their brief altercation with blood. That would be like a werewolf, brutish and nonsensical. But no, Jaden realized as she and the male who was accosting her came into view. Lyra seemed to have bigger problems than any grudge she bore him.

Jaden kept to the shadows, melting into darkness as effectively as he did in his feline form. He now had a clear view of a tall, over-muscled Neanderthal who was wearing the expected smug sneer. A predator. Being one himself, Jaden had gotten very good at identifying others. Lyra he saw only from behind, but he would have known her anywhere. Long, lean, and tall, with a wild tangle of dark hair shot through with platinum and tumbling halfway down her back. He let his eyes skim the length of her, suddenly apprehensive...hoping that his reaction to her the last time had been some kind of sick fluke. It had been easy enough to dismiss then. Being under constant threat of annihilation could do strange things to a man. But he knew it had fueled his anger at her presence in the safe house.

And now, just as before, the sight of her sent desire cascading through him in a wild rush like no other woman had provoked in him.

Jaden's sudden arousal mingled with a punch of blood-lust, creating a tangled mix of wants and needs that had his breath beginning to hitch in his chest. He moved slowly, walking the increasingly fine edge between man and beast as he struggled to stay concealed. He remembered more than just his brief meeting with her, no matter how he'd tried to block it all out. He'd had dreams...bodies tangled together, biting, clawing...licking...

Appalled, Jaden told himself he couldn't truly want a werewolf. Apart from being forbidden by both races, it was just *wrong*. Wasn't he screwed up enough?

It was a relief when the Neanderthal provided a distraction from his thoughts. The male moved like lightning, and far more gracefully than his bulky form would suggest. A hand shot out, snatching something from around Lyra's neck. The werewolf dangled the item in front of her, and Jaden could see it was a silver pendant hanging from a leather cord. She tried to snatch the pendant back, but the male held it high above his head like a schoolyard bully.

"How *dare* you?"

"It's just an old necklace," he said with a smirk. "If you want it that badly, come and get it."

Jaden could hear the helpless outrage in her voice when she spoke.

"My father—"

"Isn't here right now, is he? No one is." The Neanderthal shifted, crooked a finger at her. His stance said he knew he'd won. "I've got a hotel room. Or we can do it right here. Your choice."

His grin was foul. She seemed to think so too.

"Like hell, Mark."

Lyra's muscles tensed. She was going to run. What choice did she have? But the other man knew it. And while she might be fast, there was no way she would be able to match his strength.

Jaden hissed out a breath through gritted teeth. He was no hero. He might be nothing more than a lowblood vampire, a gutter cat with a gift for the hunt, but even among his kind, there were unspoken rules. And something in Lyra's voice, the hopeless outrage of someone railing against a fate they knew was inevitable, struck a chord deep within him. He had spent centuries being pushed and pulled by forces he couldn't fight. No one had ever given a damn what *he* had wanted, not from the first.

Gods help him with what he was about to get tangled up in.

Lyra spun, leaping away with a startling amount of grace. The man she'd called Mark lunged almost as quickly. His hand caught in all the glorious hair, fisting so that her head snapped back. Jaden heard her pained cry, heard the man's roar of victory. Then Mark's hands were on her, grabbing, tearing...

One look at Lyra's eyes, wild and afraid, and nothing on earth could have prevented Jaden from stepping in. He sprang from the shadows with a vicious snarl, fury hazing the darkness with bloodred. He landed directly in front of the grappling pair, fangs elongated and bared. The shock of his appearance gave Lyra the opening he'd hoped for. She twisted away, but not quickly enough. Mark took her down with a quick clout to the side of the head before whipping back around. Jaden watched, an odd twist of pain in his chest, as Lyra gave a single, shocked sob and collapsed to her knees.

Still, Jaden had gotten part of what he wanted. Lyra could no longer be used as a shield.

Recognition dawned in Mark's eyes a split-second before the instinctive hatred did.

Then another set of fangs were bared. Eyes flashed hot gold. The werewolf gave a guttural growl and reached for Jaden, long claws already extended from his fingertips. Jaden hissed as he stepped out of reach and waited for his chance. Jaden knew from experience that a wolf would always go for brute force over finesse. And against a vampire, it was almost always the wolf's downfall.

This time was no different.

Mark lunged, swiped. Jaden ducked easily and extended claws of his own, drawing first blood across the vulnerable belly. The thin ribbons of blood darkening his opponent's T-shirt seemed to incense his adversary, and he launched himself at Jaden only to find himself with a face full of asphalt. Unable to control himself, Jaden laughed, though it sounded nasty and hollow to his own ears.

"Hmm. I think someone's going home alone tonight."

Face bloodied, the werewolf dragged himself off the ground and growled at his tormentor.

"Get out of here, bloodsucker. This is wolf business."

"Really? Looks like garden-variety jackassery to me," Jaden said, watching Lyra out of the corner of his eye. She had shifted to a sitting position, and was holding her head in her hands staying very still. How badly she was hurt, Jaden didn't know. It was so like a wolf to try to win a woman by damaging her. Regardless, it was time to run this bastard off and give Lyra what care she needed.

He tried to ignore the way his heart began to stutter in his chest at the thought.

"Leave now," Jaden said, his voice soft, deadly. "Or I kill you."

Mark snorted. "Skinny piece of shit bloodsucker like you? I don't think—"

His words were cut off abruptly by two kicks, one to his gut and one across his thick head. At that, he went down like a ton of bricks with only a soft grunt for a response. This time, he stayed down. Jaden glared down at him for a moment, only barely denying himself the extra kick he wanted to give the wolf for good measure. But the stupid bastard should feel lousy enough when he awakened face-down in the parking lot in the morning. Although it might be momentarily satisfying, killing him would be nothing more than a messy waste of time.

And despite his disturbing interest in Lyra, Jaden had no interest in getting the Lilim into a pissing match with whatever scruffy pack of werewolves this loser belonged to.

Satisfied that they were now, for all practical purposes, alone, Jaden moved to Lyra's side and crouched down beside her. A light, intoxicating scent drifted from her, making his mouth water. Apples, he remembered. Sweet, tart apples, with something earthier beneath. Strangely enough, he felt no urge to run, to hiss and spit. He realized now it was a good thing he hadn't gotten this close the last time. He might have done something really stupid.

Though he supposed his current actions qualified.

"Lyra?" he asked, trying to keep his voice low and soothing. He wasn't sure how successful he was... he was way out of practice at damage control. Usually, he *was* the damage. "Are you all right? Do you need a doctor?" Wolves were self-healers, he knew, but it could take a while, which was dangerous when the wound was severe.

She said nothing, moved not a muscle, and Jaden's concern deepened. He reached for her, momentarily overcome by the urge to make even the simplest physical connection. But his hand stilled in midair when she finally lifted her head to look at him. And whatever he'd expected to see—fear, confusion, even a little gratitude— none of it was in evidence as he looked into Lyra's burning, furious eyes glowing fire-bright in the dark.

"Don't even think about touching me, *cat*," she said. "I can take care of myself."

chapter TWO

AND SHE'D THOUGHT her night couldn't get any worse.

Lyra Black glared into the face of her would-be savior. He looked comically surprised that she wasn't already batting her eyes and breathlessly thanking him. That was what all vamps expected: mindless adoration. And thanks to their talents with manipulating human minds, they tended to get it. Especially vamps as pretty as this one, she thought, seeing big, almost innocent blue eyes set in a face made for sin. Fortunately, werewolves were immune to the bloodsuckers' brand of "charm."

Not that this one had tried very hard the last time they'd met. Of all the vamps who could have interfered tonight, did it have to be *him*?

He drew back his hand as though she'd burned him. Lyra felt a fleeting instant of shame when his expression, so open and filled with what appeared to be genuine concern, shifted into a narrow-eyed glare. But it was no more than he deserved, she reminded herself. When she'd been holed up at that rat-infested vampire safe house all those months ago, he'd all but announced she was unfit to be in the same room with him. She'd quickly gathered that the other people in residence were his refugee friends—some other cat vamp and a human woman who'd seemed nice enough, despite her questionable taste in companions, as Lyra remembered.

But *this* one. This one was a Grade A, certified cat vamp asshole.

Knowing it made it easier to say what she needed to, easier to look into those big baby blues and tell him where to go, and she was glad. Because a non-vamp who looked as good as he did might have tempted her to trouble, and the gods knew she had enough of that in her life already.

"I can see you're as sweet as ever," he muttered, getting to his feet in a single graceful movement that left Lyra, normally so confident, feeling awkward as she regained her own footing.

Stupid vampires.

"Yeah, I have a lot of reason to be sweet to you," she sniffed. "First throwing me out of your super secret vampire meeting because I'm not the right species, and now cold-cocking some idiot I could have taken out myself." She crossed her arms over her chest, disconcerted by the way his eyes darted to her breasts and then away. She could almost think—but that was stupid. Vamps didn't check weres out. They *took* them out, and that was always going to be the way of it.

Still, beholden to her own morbid curiosity, she shifted so that her folded arms pushed her breasts up and together, displaying them attractively beneath her cami. Sure enough, his eyes flickered back and then away a couple more times, as though he wanted not to look but couldn't quite help himself. Lyra tipped her head to regard him, stunned to realize that not only was her erstwhile savior most definitely checking her out, he was flushed. His nostrils flared ever so slightly, as though he were scenting something. Prey, maybe.

And when she caught his eye again, he looked both miserable and so hungry it took her breath away. Lyra let her arms fall back to her sides, suddenly very uncomfortable with the game she'd just played. Every lesson she'd ever learned, everything she'd been taught by her pack, filled her head at once, admonishing her.

To toy with a vamp, even a lone and seemingly well-intentioned one like this, was to play with fire. Nothing would ever come from mixing wolves and vampires but blood. And more often than not, fair or not, it was the wolves who would shed most of it.

It was small consolation, but the vampire looked just as uncomfortable as she felt all of a sudden. He turned his head to look down at Mark sprawled out on the pavement, sleeping the sleep of the deservedly unconscious. She watched the sharp flicker of his movement and felt a momentary pang of . . . something . . . as she allowed herself the barest of moments to take in the lithe perfection of his form encased in slim-fitting black jeans, scuffed black boots, and a high-collared military-style coat. His chin-length hair was black as night and tucked behind his ears, making his features that much more sharply appealing.

He could have been a sullen young rock star instead of a centuries-old vampire. And Lyra found, with no small amount of horror, that her mouth watered either way.

"You could have taken him, huh?" The vamp prodded

Mark's prone body with the toe of his boot, and Lyra finally remembered his name. Actually, she remembered the human woman saying it in a tone usually reserved for small and badly behaving children, which nearly brought a smile to her face.

"Yes, I could have, *Jaden*," she said, enjoying the startle it gave him to hear his name fall from her lips. A strange name for one as old as he must be, she decided. Very modern. But he'd probably renamed himself at some point. Lyra had heard they did that, living so long they got sick of the name they were born with. She might... but then again, she enjoyed being the only Lyra she knew.

"Guess I did make an impression that night," he remarked. "Since you feel the need to bitch me out, by name, instead of thanking me. But there was no way you were going to take this guy down. I was watching. It was over the second he got his fist in your hair."

Whatever oddball fantasy she had been entertaining about him up to this point crumbled into dust. Just another arrogant vamp, Lyra decided. It didn't matter that he was right, that she *knew* he was right about Mark. What mattered was that he and the rest of his ilk had no respect for either her or her kind.

"I would have found a way," she growled, stepping closer to Jaden. "I don't need some cat vamp rescuer who expects me to lick his paws for gracing me with his presence."

His brows lifted, mocking her subtly. He knew she'd needed him...needed someone, anyway...and that was the thing Lyra hated most. She was already considered unfit to lead because of her sex. Her entire life had been about projecting strength, about watching what the males of the pack did and then doing it better. To have to be rescued from a single wolf who'd caught her off guard was humiliating. The only silver lining that she could see was that the story of it would never reach her pack. Or Mark's, Lyra thought, shooting another glance at his unconscious form and barely restraining herself from curling her lip at the sight. She wasn't the only one who wouldn't want word of this encounter getting out.

"I'll take that as your thank-you, I guess," Jaden said, "since it's obviously all I'm going to get."

"Take it however you want," Lyra replied. "As long as you take it and go. I'm not interested in chatting right now and lucky for you, not in the mood for cat chasing either. But I might change my mind." When her words seemed to amuse him for some perverse reason, Lyra narrowed her eyes and added, "Go *away*."

She thought, and hoped, he would leave now that his heroics were finished. Instead, he surprised her by lingering. And she surprised herself by not turning and walking away, which is what she knew she should have done. Now that she had stepped closer to him, she was unable to avoid his scent. He smelled unmistakably of vampire, the faint whiff of some rare and ancient spice that Lyra doubted he could even smell himself, just as she'd been told (snarled at, more like) on several memorable occasions that her breed stank of wild animal musk. She had never seen anyone but a vamp react to her as though she'd rolled in garbage, and she certainly saw nothing wrong with the wolf scent.

But Jaden wasn't reacting normally to her, wasn't cringing and backing off as though she had some dread disease. He simply acted…interested. And it had affected her, Lyra realized, because she didn't find him to be an assault on her senses either. He smelled good to her. Really good. Good enough to make her want to roll over on her back and—

She took a quick step back, sucking in a breath as she realized what was happening to her. Her skin had warmed, her heart rate had increased, and she was greedily drinking in Jaden's vampire musk. Beneath her shirt, her nipples had pebbled into tight little buds, and it had nothing to do with the cold. Her sex was swollen and slick already, demanding she accept him, bare her neck to him, get him behind her and let him . . . let him . . .

Lyra exhaled harshly and stared at Jaden as though he were the Hellhound himself, a mythical beast come to drag her to the underworld for her disloyalty to the pack. He watched her steadily, his eyes still blue but grown decidedly more feline. The pupils were long, dilated, the irises a glowing blaze of blue. And she knew she was in trouble when he took two steps toward her, closing the distance until he was only inches from her, his breath fanning her face.

Only pride kept her from backing away again. Lyra stood her ground, even when those unusual eyes dropped to her lips. She licked them nervously, saw his jaw tighten. She decided it was not to her advantage that Jaden was only perhaps an inch taller than she. She'd always hated the way the males of her kind used their height and brawn to try to intimidate her, though at five feet eight she was tall for a woman. But she saw now that there had been one good thing. When those men had tried to move in on her, their mouths hadn't been so very close, so evenly matched with the position of her own. If Jaden leaned in just a bit, he would have her.

Lyra couldn't let that happen. But the thought of it was so much more tempting than it should have been. Her skin tingled pleasurably. Her fingers flexed, itching to grab him by the shoulders, the hair, and plunge.

"You're something," he said softly, his British accent doing terrible, forbidden things to the muscles deep in her belly. "Telling me where to go on my own territory. You shouldn't even be here, Lyra. You know the wolves are banned from our cities, and this place belongs to the Lilim now. So this is twice I've met you when I'd be well within my rights to tear you apart for crossing the line."

It was a threat, but she knew instinctively it wasn't a real one. Killing her was the last thing on Jaden's mind, just as fighting him was the last thing on hers. Still, she knew the reality of the situation would intrude soon enough, and at that point she was going to have to get away from him, no matter what it took. Sure enough, his next words set her already frayed nerves on edge.

He tilted his head, putting her in mind of a curious and not altogether benevolent cat.

"What are you up to, here? First it was hiding in that safe house in Chicago, and now you've turned up in a small town in Massachusetts that just happens to be the home of the newest vampire dynasty. What are you looking for?" He drew even closer. "Spying so you can run back and tell your leader what a dynasty full of cats looks like, are you? Or were you thinking we wouldn't notice if you holed up here for a while? What are you running from, Lyra?"

Lyra swallowed with a dry click, and the words wouldn't come. He would think what he would think, she knew. It didn't matter what she said. His kind didn't understand hers, and never would. And he would never understand the desperation she'd been grappling with, looking for ideas, or even scraps of ideas, that might save her.

It was a shame she couldn't have stayed, seen more. She'd really hoped to find a way to see Lily, without Lily seeing her, of course, and study how a woman with so much power and responsibility conducted herself. Was there some secret to the way she walked, moved, talked? Why had they allowed her to claim so much so easily, with no males fighting for dominance? The whispers she'd heard of the human woman's ascendance to the upper echelons of vampire society had been true. But as insane as it had sounded to all the wolves who had heard the rumors, Lyra now knew the rest was true as well. This was now a dynasty of Cait Sith, the vampire cat-shifters, no matter the new name they had taken. And if there was a more poisonous relationship than the one between that bloodline and her kind, she'd never heard of it.

There would be no help for her here, not now that her presence had been discovered by both a Cait and one of her many unwanted suitors. If Mark had sniffed her out, others would too. They were getting better at it, especially with the Proving so close at hand. So she would run again. Run home, this time, where she would have to begin preparations in earnest. Alone.

Defiantly, Lyra raised her chin and glared into Jaden's searching eyes. "Where I go and what I do are none of your business," she said. "But you're welcome to *your* territory. There's nothing here I want."

She started to spin away, and as she did caught the dangerous flash of his eyes too late. His hand closed around her arm, and Lyra could feel the incredible, tightly controlled strength in his grip. He pulled her back hard, and she wound up plastered against him. For a brief, heated instant their bodies connected, and she could feel every hard knot of muscle in his long, lean form. Her body wanted to curve against it, fitting itself so that they were fused together, two pieces formed to connect with the other.

Jaden pressed his mouth to her ear, and she could feel the briefest rub of his head against her hair, like a cat marking a possession with its scent. She tried to struggle: she was no man's to possess, and certainly not *his*! But with the slightest flex of deceptively strong muscle, she was forced to be still.

"You didn't answer my question, Lyra. What are you running from?" he breathed against her ear. Such a simple question from a stranger, and still she felt herself tremble with the need to pour it out to him, to plead for help from a man who would doubtless laugh at her before turning away. It was the stress, she knew. The knowledge of what was building against her back at home, from both within the pack and without.

Finally, she found the strength to wrench away from him, and this time he let her go. She bared her teeth and growled at him, the only warning Lyra could give now since words had failed her. Fear, anger, and helpless lust tangled together inside her, threatening to push her back toward Jaden and make her do something she would later regret. And he was so still, standing there watching her, as poised and inscrutable as the sphinx with his eyes glowing like blue flames. But she could feel his want, the beast half of her sensing it and demanding she respond.

There was only one response she could give that she wouldn't regret.

"Stay away from me, cat," she snapped, her voice rough as it began to morph into a wolf's snarl. "I have enough problems."

She turned from him, surprised by how hard it was to leave him standing there. She was losing it, Lyra feared. Losing it from the pressure of being hunted, ridiculed, and discounted for so long. But it would be over soon, one way or another.

Lyra took off at a sprint, her muscles coiling and responding like a well-oiled machine. Her heeled black boots were no impediment to speed. She didn't give a damn how she looked, running away from him. He was nothing to her. Just like any vampire. She felt her limbs burn and change, pulling her toward the ground and into a four-legged lope, clothing vanishing as fur bristled over her skin. As the wolf, she could breathe again. Never looking back, Lyra raced away from where Jaden stood watching and let the seductive embrace of the night be her freedom, if only for a little while.

It was time to go home.

Jaden watched the wolf, her silvery fur the color of smoke, vanish around the corner and into the darkness. Lyra was as long limbed and graceful in this form as she was in the other, the very picture of deadly beauty. And she was beautiful, even if his nature stood in dangerous opposition to her own.

There were a few drawn-out moments when he didn't trust himself to move, worried that he'd wind up chasing after the wolf. He had no doubt now that Lyra was still in some sort of trouble, still running, and that the unfortunate suitor lying on the ground was only a piece of the problem.

"It's no concern of mine," he said out loud, hoping the sound of his own voice would bring him back to reality and lift whatever spell he'd fallen under. But nothing was going to remove the memory of how Lyra had felt against him, as if she'd been burned into his skin. Silently, he cursed himself for having touched her. Impulse control wasn't an area where he usually failed. But something about Lyra Black—yes, that had been her last name, he remembered—had made it impossible to resist. Her hair had been like silk against his cheek, and the scent of her skin...

"Enough," he growled, and turned his head away from the direction she had gone. She had let it go, walked away. He needed to do the same. Jaden didn't know where this interest in the ornery she-wolf had come from, but he knew nothing good could possibly come of it. *Time to get out of here.* The sun would be up before long, and at that point he could brood about it in his dreams and hopefully wake up refreshed and past this madness.

He was just turning to go when his eyes caught a glint of something. Inside him, some voice of self-preservation began screaming at him to leave it, to just keep going. Although he had ample control over most of his impulses, curiosity, like all cats eventually discovered, had often been his downfall. Jaden walked to the locket, glittering atop its length of broken chain, and picked it up.

Jaden let it dangle from his fist for a moment, examining what Mark had torn from Lyra's neck. What caught his eye first was the stone; it was large, about the size of a silver dollar, and worn so long that the surface was perfectly smooth. The shimmering silver-blue was familiar to him: moonstone. The gem was set into a larger disc of white gold that framed the stone in scrollwork. The design put him in mind of his years spent in Scotland. Not a particularly feminine piece, but strong, and for no reason Jaden could really pinpoint it seemed to him that it suited the woman who had left it behind.

Lyra would no doubt be angry when she discovered her talisman had been forgotten. Before he could think better of it, Jaden closed his hand around the pendant and pocketed it, feeling the faint hum of power given off by the moonstone. He'd been around long enough to know that a powerful artifact such as this should be treated with respect.

She was going to want it back. Perhaps he could send it to her, if he could discover where she was from. Or maybe she would come find him, though Jaden didn't think that was likely. Lyra had made it very clear that she didn't want to see him again, and considering his reaction to her, maybe that was best.

No, *definitely* that was best, he qualified, stroking a thumb over the stone before removing his hand from his pocket and setting off in the opposite direction from Lyra, heading back toward the mansion. Not really home, but a fine place to stay...for now. He would sleep, Jaden decided, and figure out what to do with the she-wolf's pendant when he awoke. Until then, he would put her out of his mind. His life was troubled enough. He didn't need to fixate on an unimportant woman who would as soon tear his head off as look at him.

But he dreamed of her eyes.

And of the wild, uncontrollable hunger of beasts in the dark.

chapter THREE

LYRA AWAKENED around noon, sprawled on her bed with the blankets and sheets twisted around her waist. Her head was turned to the side as she lay on her stomach, her arms curled beneath the pillow her head rested on. For a brief instant, she was pleased to greet the day, late though she was. It was justified: yesterday had been spent in a car as she'd headed home, and the night before that had taken a lot out of her.

But as she recalled, for the millionth time, what exactly that late night had involved, her pleasure at the warm spring sunlight died.

Her necklace had been on the ground. And she would bet, she'd just *bet* that vampire bastard had picked it up.

Lyra gave an irritated little groan and buried her face in her pillow. One hand went instinctively to her throat, hoping against hope to feel the smooth metal of her mother's talisman. But no. Her birthright, a symbol of her position and full of warm memories of her mother, was back in Massachusetts, probably displayed prominently in Jaden's bedroom or coffin or whatever vamps like him used for a sleep space. And once her father realized she'd lost it, she was in for an ass-kicking of epic proportions.

A soft knock at her door had her cringing. He was checking on her. Of course he was. Dorien Black seemed to think his only child was headed right over the edge of the Cliffs of Insanity, especially once he'd figured out she'd thrown her hat in the ring for the Proving. She knew he was waiting for her to back off and withdraw, to either find a mate who would fight in her stead or to throw her support behind one of the other "viable" candidates. Like her cousin.

Lyra gritted her teeth. Her father had made it very clear, along with just about everyone else in the pack, that she'd thrown a major wrench in the works by refusing to step back. *Too damn bad.* The way she figured it, the position was hers to lose. And if things kept going so badly, she knew she very well might. But nothing worth fighting for was easy.

His voice, warm, familiar, and still beloved despite everything, came through a crack he opened in the door.

"Lyra? You feeling all right, kiddo?"

"I'm fine, Dad," Lyra said, clearing her throat when she heard how ragged her voice sounded. "You might as well come in."

The door opened, and Dorien walked in to sit at the edge of her bed while Lyra scooted up into a sitting position and pulled her knees into her chest. In that moment, she felt like she was eight years old again, waiting to be scolded for misbehaving…likely for fighting with the boys again. Remembering that she'd usually won brought a soft smile to her face, but it was gone as quickly as it had come.

She was not a child anymore. She was twenty-three, and the ensuing years had been etched onto Dorien's handsome face. He was still larger than life to her... but no longer infallible. And she would be caught in the ancient, and very sticky, web of werewolf succession unless she figured out a way to tear free. To prove that worthiness didn't always go hand in hand with a massive *male* body.

So far, she wasn't exactly doing a bang-up job.

Dorien's eyes, the same burnished gold as her own, searched her face.

"So? You plan on telling me where you were this time?" he finally asked, his voice gruff.

Lyra tried for a smile, but she only half succeeded. "Do I ever?"

Instead of finding it funny, Dorien heaved a sigh so long-suffering that Lyra felt the prickle of guilt. This was partially his fault, she reminded herself. As much as she loved him, he would never take a stand for her and buck tradition. He was a Black, and he was in far too deep to go against what that name meant. And it definitely did *not* mean training your daughters as warriors.

"At least you don't stink of vampires this time," he said. "I hope you were smart enough, after all we talked about, not to risk so much again."

Now it was Lyra's turn to sigh, but the sound was far more irritated coming from her. "*You* talked," she pointed out. "Every time I tried, you cut me off. Do you honestly think I would have holed up at a vampire safe house if I'd felt I had any other choice? I needed to get out of here, to get away from all the macho BS. Guys I've known my whole life were just about taking one another's heads off to get near me, Dad! I'm not stupid. They weren't nearly as interested back before I hit twenty-two and could be mated."

"You're a beautiful girl—er, woman, Lyra," Dorien said, patting her awkwardly. "There's no chance they didn't notice before."

She snorted. "Whatever. Explain to me why I had to go away to college to get a date."

"You're very confident, sweetheart. You can be a little intimidating."

That made Lyra grin. "You mean I'm bitchy. Sweet, Dad."

He chuckled. "No, confident. With a sharp tongue sometimes. You get both from me, so I'm not calling it anything but good." His humor, which she'd always loved, subsided far too quickly.

"It wouldn't hurt you to give them a chance, Lyra. They're not boys anymore. But you've managed to send them running in the other direction all on your own; they all think you've lost your damned mind."

Lyra dug her fingers into her hair and glowered at her father. "Oh yes. I want to fight in the Proving, so obviously I'm nuts. I'd like a shot at my birthright, but going for it makes me a weak, stupid little she-wolf. You do realize how sexist you sound, right? I'm actually surprised you haven't tried to shove an arranged marriage down my throat."

She saw the mulish expression and knew immediately that he'd thought about it. She growled and threw her head back in exasperation.

"Seriously? You really think I'd go for that?"

"No, which is why it hasn't happened. In some packs, it would have happened as soon as you were of age, so consider yourself lucky. I want you to be able to choose, but you're not making it easy."

Lyra tried hard not to bristle. She loved her father dearly. But once she'd hit her twenty-second year and all hell had broken loose where male werewolves were concerned, it seemed like every conversation had turned into a battle. He wouldn't get off her case until she had done what was expected of her. Yet there was no way she could in good conscience *do* what was expected of her.

"I'm a grown woman," she said, trying to keep the bitterness from her voice. "You're lucky I haven't run. I've heard of *that* happening in some of the other packs too."

But not often, Lyra thought as her father's eyes reflected the misery he felt she was putting him through. It wasn't often that an Alpha male had only a single, female child. A strong male son would still have had to go through a Proving, but he would have been trained, prepared, and generally accepted as his father's Second even before he had to go through the motions. But a daughter... in a patriarchal system like the wolves', there was no place for a female Alpha.

Especially when the males were mostly built like linebackers and would sometimes fight to the death to become Alpha.

"If you'd wanted to leave, you would have left already," Dorien said. He sighed again, this time wistfully. "I'd almost rather you'd chosen that, Lyra, instead of the mess you've gotten yourself into. But you can't leave the Thorn any more than I can. This is your place, just like it is mine."

She hated that he was right, but he knew her better than anyone. She loved Silver Falls, loved the forest and the hidden clearings, the sound of the running waters deep in the trees. She loved the way the town and the surrounding landscape wore each season, and the way it felt to run on four legs here when the moon was high.

Moreover, she loved her pack. They were her blood, true relations or no. A number of the women had had a hand in raising her after her mother was killed, women she could still go to with problems when her crusty father just wouldn't do. Most of the pack loved her, as well, Lyra knew.

Even if a lot of them now thought she must be crazy, suicidal, or both.

She looked down, plucking at the comforter. "I don't want to go, Dad."

"Then stay here! You keep running off the way you do, you're going to get hurt. I try to keep things sane here, Lyra. The Thorn have worked very hard at not being the savages our kind is seen as. But some of your suitors are going to use any means to get at you, and you know that!"

She rolled her eyes, recognizing the riff from so many of their arguments lately. "Dad, I've got *suitors* from every pack in the eastern US sniffing at my heels. Some of whom, I will have you know, have gotten plenty aggressive on our own territory. And off of it," she added, thinking of Mark. His pack was neighbor to her own, and the two groups congregated from time to time. She hoped she wouldn't have to see him again, but the chances of that sort of luck were slim to none.

Dorien's expression turned thunderous as his protective instinct kicked in. "Who—"

"It doesn't matter," Lyra interjected, cutting him off. Dorien's face said that it damn well did matter, but Lyra didn't really want to get into it. Instead, she continued, "I have no intention of picking up some stray loser who wants me just because I'm an Alpha's daughter, Dad. I don't like being the way in. Especially because when it comes to being your Second, I'm the best candidate this pack has. I learned from you, even if you weren't trying to teach me."

Dorien reached out, tucking a wild curl behind her ear with a tenderness that made Lyra want to weep. She knew this was killing him. But if she didn't step up, Eric would surely become the new Alpha to the pack. If her father was traditional with welcome little dashes of forward thinking—a little old-fashioned but beloved—her cousin was conservative with a capital "C," an authoritarian puritan isolationist with a massive stick up his ass. Sideways.

Not only would he not move the Thorn forward, he seemed destined to push the pack back at least a hundred years. It was something Lyra couldn't bear to endure. Not when she had so many ideas to bring the Thorn into the twenty-first century...even if they came kicking and screaming. It was adapt or die out. Sadly, with the pack shrinking in recent years, the latter had begun to be whispered about as a possibility.

There would have to be a female Alpha somewhere eventually, she reasoned. A new voice, a new point of view. Why not here?

Why not her?

Her father seemed to have plenty of ideas on that subject himself.

"I'm asking you one last time, Lyra. Step back. There's no shame in withdrawing from the Proving. Hell, I don't even know if the other males will consent to fight you."

"They have to," Lyra replied. "I looked it up in the histories. I'm to be treated just like the male candidates."

Dorien's brows went up. "I don't recall that in the histories, though it's been a while since I had to look to them. When was this?"

Lyra felt her shoulders beginning to hunch defensively and forced herself to straighten. "In 1759. Pack of the Broken Arrow. There was a female wolf in that Proving."

"And?"

"And...well, she didn't succeed, but she made it pretty far."

He zeroed in immediately on what she wasn't saying. "How was she treated when she fell, then?"

"Um. I...I think it was something like being torn apart by the remaining candidates once she'd fallen." Lyra mumbled it as quickly as she could, but Dorien's sharp intake of breath indicated he'd heard her just fine.

"Damn it, Lyra!" he snapped, his patience for her obviously already exhausted for the day. "This can't end well. You'll get that, or worse, especially with your cousin likely to lead the pack! I'm not going to be able to save you either. Do you understand that? No one will!"

Lyra did understand, better than he knew. She thought of Mark, the determination in his eyes, his strength. A single wolf, and she couldn't even manage *him*. No amount of bravado was going to make up for her limitations in strength and size, and Lyra knew it. But there had to be a way. Jaden appeared in her mind's eye, taking Mark out in a series of quick moves that looked effortless. It wasn't exactly inspiring, considering she couldn't move like a vampire and likely never would. But Jaden had used something other than raw power to win, and that was encouraging...if she could find a way to emulate it.

Lyra was tough. No one in the pack would argue that. But she hadn't been trained to fight like the males. She'd had to pick that up herself. Dorien's refusal to teach her still cut deep.

"I'll figure it out. I always do," Lyra said. What else could she say? She had no plan, and she certainly had no one willing to help her. But every time she considered backing down from what seemed an increasingly untenable position, she thought of the silent, humorless figure of her cousin. His stark view of right and wrong, his unnerving ability to quote whole passages from the histories of any given year and then apply it to a given situation made her nervous, to say the least. Hell, he made a lot of people nervous. To be born without a sense of humor wasn't normal. And then there were the things Simon had told her he'd heard about him. If even a small amount of those rumors were true, her quiet, creepy cousin had plenty of ugliness lurking just beneath the surface.

Eric Black had always put her hackles up. But as it stood, he would be Second unless she found a way to stop it. And he would be the ruin of the pack.

Dorien dragged a hand through russet-colored waves of hair only slightly touched with gray and looked upward, as though the mystical wolf gods themselves might descend from on high to help with his unruly daughter.

"I know it seems unfair to you," he said, and Lyra could hear the way he tried to modulate his tone, to hide the fear and anger running beneath them. "But like it or not, we survive through strength and ferocity. The vampires have it in for us, and half the damned time we have it in for each other. The pack looks to the Alpha to be the strongest of all. You're plenty strong, and very clever,

Lyra. But physically, you couldn't take down even the larger males in our own pack. That matters."

"I could learn if you'd train me properly. Any human would think this is bullshit. They treat their women as equals," Lyra snapped, hating the old argument, the one that always seemed to poison their conversations anymore.

"The humans don't have to live by fang and claw the way we do!" Dorien snarled. "And my training you wouldn't have done a bit of good. You versus a two-hundred-pound wolf, each of you fighting the same, is never going to come out in your favor. *Never.*"

"You don't know that," Lyra snapped. Dorien dug his fingers into his hair and looked like he wanted to bite something.

"Damn it, Lyra, why can't you just accept the way things are instead of fighting so hard?" He stopped, closed his eyes, and collected himself. It was an action Lyra had seen plenty of times when she was the subject of his discussion. She knew he was counting to ten so he didn't blow. Sure enough, when his eyes opened, his voice had softened, though it was thick with emotion.

"You've never seen a Proving, sweetheart. You think you can be ready for it, but no one ever is. All you'll have is your wits and brute strength. You've got the first in spades, but the other..." He trailed off for a moment.

"I already lost your mother. Don't you leave me too."

It hurt her. And it made Lyra angry, because he *knew* it hurt her, even though he meant it. When she focused on the latter, Lyra managed to cool off a little. But as far as bending, she just couldn't.

"Female or not, tradition or not, Alpha is my birthright," she said quietly. "It's in my blood. If I give up, the Thorn will get Eric. You know it, Dad."

Dorien exhaled loudly through his nose. He looked at her, and the bleakness in his eyes brought on a fresh wave of guilt despite her best efforts. "You haven't heard a word I said, have you? *You can't win.* Rules are rules, and if Eric wins the Proving I'll take him. He's a Black, and he's got the strength to prove it. I know he's a bit…dour. It's hard to believe he's my brother's boy sometimes…Gerik would be sad, I think, to know how he came up with Mara's family. But I can work with him, mold him—"

"He's a waste of a werewolf, and there'll be no changing him," Lyra burst out. "He's so obsessed with rules that he can't see the benefit of change. He wants everything to stay the same, harsh punishment for anyone who bucks the system…and besides that, he's twisted."

Dorien looked at her sharply. "You don't know that. I've heard whisperings, same as you, Lyra, but there's never been any proof."

"By the time you have proof that he enjoys hunting human women in his spare time, the humans will be on our doorstep," Lyra snapped. "And if you want to talk about running off, he's made himself pretty scarce lately too. So the solution is to hand him the pack on a silver platter? At least I still care, even if I've had to put my life on hold because of these stupid *traditions*!"

"I didn't make the Thorn; I only keep it, Lyra. You've heard it for enough years to know how it works. Eric will win the Proving on his own merits or not," Dorien said, rising from the bed. "And as for you, better a life on hold than over."

He headed for the door, but Lyra's question stopped

him in his tracks. She knew Dorien had been hoping that
her signing up for the Proving had been a stunt, a way
of expressing her anger with pack tradition when it came
to the relentless marginalizing of their women. So she
decided to let him know she meant it.

No matter what.

"Do you plan to try and stop me from competing?" she
asked. A simple question, but a loaded one. Lyra tensed in
anticipation of his answer. A great deal rode on this. And
if he said yes, then she knew she might have no options
but leaving. The very idea was like a knife in her heart.
Still, if she couldn't be free to choose her destiny here,
then life was too short to stay encased in amber.

His shoulders slumped, making Dorien look every one
of his forty-five years.

"No," he said without turning around. "I won't stop
you, Lyra. Just know that if you do this, I won't be able to
save you. No matter what happens. At the Proving, I have
to be Alpha first and a father second. I must uphold the
law. Some traditions really can't be broken."

"I'm going to prove I can do this," Lyra replied, feeling
a little desperate to gain even a bit of support. He was her
father. It would mean everything to know he was root-
ing for her, if only silently. "Have some faith in me. Just a
little. Please?" she asked.

He turned his head to the side, and the small smile he
gave her was sad.

"It's not about faith," he said. Then he left the room
without another word. Lyra watched him go, watched the
door shut behind him, and then put her head in her hands
and closed her eyes.

"Yes, it is."

chapter FOUR

JADEN? WHAT ARE YOU DOING in here all by yourself? Hiding?"

Jaden looked up, startled by the warm female voice that cut smoothly through the silence he'd been sitting in for the better part of an hour. His first thought was to hide the necklace he'd been toying with, but it was already too late for that. He'd assumed no one would bother him, since apart from the fact that he wasn't known for being a particularly friendly cat, this was one of the rooms in the mansion that hadn't been renovated yet. No television, and nothing of interest except for some hideous floral furniture, meant solitude. Usually.

He should have known better.

"Uh-oh. You're brooding," Lily said, narrowing her eyes when she leaned into the room to look at him.

"I'm not brooding," Jaden grumbled, curling his fingers around the pendant and pulling it in toward his body. "Your husband broods. I'm just...thinking."

She raised her eyebrows at the necklace disappearing into his fist, but didn't seem inclined to say anything about it. Yet. Instead, she walked in, settled herself on the ugly couch across from his chair, and smiled at him. That smile went a long way toward smoothing his ruffled fur, Jaden had to admit. And of course, she knew it would.

He wasn't at all sure he liked how quickly she'd figured him out.

"Deflection, hmm? Interesting. Yes, Ty broods. But he's usually got a good reason for it. And it's fun to tease him out of his moods." She cocked her head. "You're cute, Jaden, but I don't think the methods that work with Ty are really appropriate for this situation, so you're going to have to just tell me what's wrong."

It would be so easy to lean on her, Jaden thought. He'd liked her from the start, and the ever-increasing numbers of Cait Sith showing up on her doorstep to become a part of her dynasty seemed to agree. In the past, there were a few moments when Jaden had wished she'd been meant for him, that he'd been the one sent to find her. Lily was a beauty, and as strong as they came. But she and Ty were perfectly matched, and Jaden had never seen his old friend so disgustingly happy.

He was glad for them. He should be happy here too, but instead he felt a gnawing ache in his gut. Why couldn't he just be happy?

Lily frowned suddenly as something occurred to her. "It's not the Ptolemy again, is it? I've got Ty recruiting more guards, but it's a slower process than I'd like, and the Council seems determined not to help."

"They're not helping because they would like you, and all of us, to go away. We don't belong in the club, Lily. It's easier for them if the Lilim are smothered in their infancy while they're turning a blind eye."

Lily swore softly, making Jaden smile. Such a sweet thing shouldn't have such a foul vocabulary. He was sure that he and Ty had been bad influences.

"You're right. I know you're right," Lily said, shaking her head. "I didn't think this would be easy, but I never imagined that the Council would be so..."

"Hostile?" Jaden supplied. "These are men and women who've actively participated in the suppression of mixed bloods for centuries. They may not go out of their way to hurt us—most of them—but they certainly won't help us if we're sinking." He leaned back and looked at Lily. She looked very young, and very vulnerable, in that moment. It made him wish he hadn't just used his dagger on that traitor Nero's head.

He should have taken Arsinöe that night, and saved all of them this trouble. Whatever Ptolemy might have taken her place, there would be no threat anywhere near as great as the ancient queen. Arsinöe's grudge wasn't about her dynasty's liberated slaves anymore. She'd been humiliated. And she would make the Lilim pay until she was satisfied.

Lily rubbed one hand restlessly over the frayed fabric on the arm of the couch.

"Well, whatever anyone thinks, if we catch any more Ptolemy slinking around here, I swear I'm dragging Arsinöe's ass before the Council. I may be new, but that doesn't mean she gets to pick off my people because she's angry and down a few hundred slaves."

"I've been out looking nights," Jaden said, "and I haven't seen anything. It's been a month since the last sighting. Maybe they've knocked it off."

But he didn't believe it, and he saw Lily didn't either.

"I wish you'd stick closer to the house and not go wandering around alone," Lily said. "I worry."

He understood her concern, and it touched him. But Ptolemy scouts would keep circling Tipton like the vultures they were, and Cait Sith would keep disappearing, one by one. At some point, there would be another confrontation. He just hoped it wasn't soon. Lily, powerful though she was, wasn't ready. And Jaden, though he hadn't said anything to anyone, was concerned that he'd escaped one prison only to find himself in a more comfortable one of his own making.

The scars they'd left him with were never going to be enough. Was there a list of defectors to be hauled back or destroyed? He would guess there was. Arsinöe was focused about her grudges. And Jaden was quite sure that the Ptolemy queen wanted his death.

It would likely get a lot messier before things settled down.

"I can take care of myself, Lily. You shouldn't worry. But for what it's worth, I appreciate the sentiment."

"I'd rather know you were safe than appreciative," Lily said, then heaved a frustrated sigh. "I swear the Council wants to see me and Arsinöe in some kind of steel-cage death match and just solve it that way. Two-thousand-year-old bitch."

Jaden couldn't help his smile. "I'd pay to see it. My money would be on you."

"I wish I was as confident about that," she said with a wry smile. "I never thought this would be easy, but… well, it's definitely not easy. Anyway, enough of my complaining. I'm glad this isn't about the Ptolemy." She tucked her hair behind her ear, and Jaden could actually feel her honing in on him. Inwardly, he cursed. She was like a dog with a bone over things she wanted, or wanted to know.

It was funny when he wasn't the target.

"Okay, you've stumped me. What is it? What's making you look like you're staring into the face of impending doom?" She drew the last word out dramatically, trying to soften him up, Jaden knew. But it wasn't going to work.

"Nothing." He hedged. "Since when does me wanting to be by myself mean anything's wrong?"

"Jaden," Lily said, angling her head at him, "I know you. You have degrees of unapproachable, and you've been way above baseline for two nights running. Does this have something to do with that necklace you're doing a lousy job of hiding?"

Jaden felt his jaw tighten, his muscles tense. She knew. Of course she knew; this was Lily. But how could he talk about it when he didn't even understand exactly how he felt?

"I'm not hiding it. It's just…something I found."

"Uh-huh." Lily considered him, and he fought the urge to squirm under the scrutiny. She was an unnervingly perceptive creature, and becoming a vampire only seemed to have intensified the fact. "Can I see it?"

"No."

"Did you find it in the house?"

"No."

Lily exhaled loudly, her patience with him finally strained. "James Dennis Harrison," she said irritably. "Just tell me where you got the damned necklace or I'll come over there and get it. And don't think I can't do it."

Jaden cringed at the sound of his given name and rued the day she'd wheedled it out of him. He'd left that name behind with his old life. Its stodginess had never suited him anyway.

"I don't remember where I picked it up. Off the *ground*, I suppose," Jaden said, his voice taking on a growly edge. When Lily simply arched one slim brow, he hunched reflexively, feeling like a child who'd been caught doing something naughty. She tapped long fingernails on the arm of the couch and waited silently. Jaden was slightly ashamed at how quickly he broke.

"Oh, for the love of—I helped a woman out of a tight spot last night. This got left behind, and I picked it up. Happy now?"

Her knowing smile was almost worse than the prying.

"Oh," she said. "It's *that* kind of brooding. Never mind, then." She stood, surprising him. He'd figured she would stick around to harass him for a while longer. He found it a sign of how twisted he'd become when he realized he didn't actually feel like being left alone after all.

"What kind of brooding?" Jaden asked, puzzled. "Do you think you might enlighten me before you wander off? Because I don't see anything out of the ordinary here."

Lily rolled her eyes, hand on her hip, looking for a moment like an irritated teenager. "Jaden. Helping out humans isn't a habit of yours, not that I've noticed. So you save this woman, she drops a necklace, I find you sitting up here mooning over it, and you think your rotten mood is…mysterious to me?"

He opened his mouth to give her a smart reply, but nothing came. Instead, he had to settle for a chagrined, "Well, but—"

"Ah, there you are. I was looking for both of you."

Jaden took one look at Ty MacGillivray's long, rangy form striding in the door and had to bite back a groan. Instead of solitude, he now had a party. If he decided to stick around Tipton for much longer . . . and that was still a big *if* in his mind . . . he was really going to have to get his own place.

Naturally, Ty didn't seem bothered at all by the extra company. Being with Lily had changed him from the solitary, humorless man he'd been for so long, consumed only with survival and staying indispensible to the Ptolemy queen. His natural intensity had remained, but Lily had softened him and brought out a good humor and playfulness that still amazed Jaden.

"Not interrupting an illicit tryst or anything, am I?" he asked.

Lily's smile was slow and warm as she looked at her husband. "Pretty much." She strolled over and wrapped her arms around his waist. "Go away, you're killing the mood."

Jaden watched the two of them, the way they fit together. He'd never had that. Nothing even close after two hundred years of living. Some of it was being a Cait Sith, of course . . . female vampires weren't exactly clamoring to hook up with Ptolemy slaves . . . but some of it was just him. He'd never had a woman he was so hungry for, never met one he couldn't walk away from.

Until that night at Rogan's. But that couldn't possibly be the same thing—

"Hell, you're brooding," Ty remarked when he finally turned his attention to Jaden, his musical Scottish burr rolling out the last word and making Jaden seriously consider walking out of the room and leaving Ty and Lily to make love on the ugly furniture or whatever they did when they were alone.

Actually, he was pretty positive about what they did when they were alone, and that didn't make him feel any better right this second.

Jaden started to say something snide, but Lily cut him off.

"We've been through that already. Jaden isn't brooding. He's *thinking*. And since I already told him I'd leave him to it, I've got to go make a few phone calls. If we're going to petition the Council for our own territory any time in the near future, we've got to get a little more organized." She wrinkled her nose. "If it weren't for the Dracul, I'd have to ask the Shades for help. That'd look good... not that it probably matters at this point."

"Damien could probably set that up for you," Jaden said with a smile, referring to his blood brother who had eschewed slavery to the Ptolemy in favor of a career as a thief and assassin with the notorious House of Shadows. "He's in good with the Shade Master. And they know all sorts of things about the highbloods you could use."

"All the *wrong* things," Lily replied. "I'm not into blackmail. And I'd hate to have to start checking our blood supply for poison. Anyway, duty calls. Later." She gave Ty a quick kiss, waved at Jaden, and headed to her office downstairs.

Ty watched her go, his heart in his silver eyes.

"She's tired," he said quietly. "Damn Arsinöe. Lily saving her life wasn't enough. She's still got to prove hers is the only dynasty that matters."

"It'll get taken care of," Jaden replied. "One way or another. We both know it."

Ty gave a short nod, then turned back to look at Jaden. Jaden saw immediately that Lily wasn't the only one who looked a little tired, and for a vampire, that was a feat. He shouldn't be here causing them more worry, Jaden thought. Out of sight, out of mind. Or further from their minds, at least. They had enough to deal with, and everyone expected he was high up on Arsinöe's hit list.

Maybe it would be best to skip town for a while.

"So whose ass do we need to kick?" Ty asked, relaxing a little as he sauntered further into the room.

Jaden looked at the ceiling and chuckled.

"No one's. Though you and your wife are so ready for it, I ought to just make something up so you can run off and fight for my honor."

Jaden was slightly more comfortable talking with Ty about this, only because the man was as good as a real brother to him. Ty had taken Jaden under his wing early on in Jaden's days with the Ptolemy. He would understand the difficulties inherent in the situation, where Lily, still so new to their world, would not. There were such deep divisions between night races. He was almost sorry Lily would have to learn them and then try to navigate the minefield they presented. She had enough minefields right now. Maybe it was better she not learn the truth of the necklace's origins. The truth would only bring her trouble, and trouble was the last thing Jaden wanted for her.

She and Ty were family to him, Jaden realized. He'd forgotten what a blessing and a curse having such a thing could be.

Jaden looked back at Ty, at his earnest concern, and began to relent. "If I tell you, will you leave me be?"

Ty's answer was succinct. "Not bloody likely."

Jaden didn't bother to hide his smile, though he was certain it looked as weary as he felt these past two nights. "At least you're honest about it. Fine, then. When I was out last night I ran into a woman who was being given a...bit of a rough time by a man she didn't want anything to do with. I took care of the problem for her, and she was, let's say, less than appreciative. She left in a huff and forgot the stupid bastard had thrown her necklace on the ground. So now I have it."

Ty held out his hand. "Hmm. Let's have a look at it."

Reluctantly, he handed over the disc and chain, wondering whether Ty might recognize it. His friend studied it, turning it over in his hands.

"It's quite old. Older than I am, at any rate, and probably valuable. Not the kind of thing you'd see someone wearing every day. And you already know all of this, of course." He lifted his eyes to meet Jaden's, and Jaden could see the question in them. "Moonstone, I see."

"Yes, and with good reason."

Jaden was relieved to find that his fears about revealing what sort of woman the necklace had come from had been unfounded. Ty might be a dangerous man, but he wasn't judgmental, even in this. Mainly, he looked puzzled.

"You took it upon yourself to help a werewolf?"

Jaden nodded. "For some ungodly reason."

"No wonder she didn't appreciate it. Brutish lot, even the women. I'm surprised she hadn't ripped the male's throat out herself. I'm not going to bother asking what you were thinking, but what the hell was she doing here? There isn't a wolf pack that I'm aware of for miles."

Ty handed the necklace back, and Jaden was ashamed at the rush of relief he felt to have it in his hands again.

The metal warmed against his palm quickly. The fact that the pendant had rested against Lyra's skin, probably many times, fascinated him. Holding on to it was as close as he might ever get to touching her again. She was so warm... and he was so cold...

"As you might imagine, she wasn't in the mood for conversation. I think she was a little embarrassed that she hadn't managed to deal with her admirer herself, actually." He paused, wondering whether to reveal the rest of the story. At this point, it could hardly hurt, and Ty would keep it to himself. "I recognized her," Jaden continued. "From Rogan's, when you and I were there with Lily."

Ty's dark brows winged up, and he sank down to perch on the arm of the couch.

"That pretty she-wolf? The one you hated on sight?" To Jaden's surprise, Ty started laughing. "No wonder she was angry. That would have been adding insult to injury. You've got a sick sense of humor, brother. Now I understand why you helped her. Though there has to be a better way of entertaining yourself around here."

Jaden forced a chuckle, unsure whether he was glad to have kept the heart of his secret. He wished he could have spoken to someone with a similar experience, but one didn't just wander around asking random vampires whether they'd ever been possessed by the desire to get naked with a werewolf.

He'd had his ass kicked a time or two for lesser offenses. That one would find his head and his body residing in different parts of the country.

"I wonder why she was here, though. It's possible her pack doesn't know that the Lilim are set up here, at least for now. Then again, she could still just be running from . . . whatever it was that had her at Rogan's, I suppose."

Jaden nodded. "It definitely looked like she was here on her own. Whatever problems had her holed up at a vampire safe house last October seem to have followed her right along. Annoying her was an amusing side benefit, but trust me, I wouldn't have jumped in if Lyra hadn't been in serious danger of losing more than her pride."

"Lyra," Ty murmured. "That's right, I remember Rogan mentioning her name at some point. And he was pissed off about you giving her a hard time too. I think he said she was an Alpha's daughter or something like that. Mentioned she was a probable pack leader too, though I don't see how. The wolves aren't much on female Alphas. Or female anything." He looked in the direction Lily had gone. "They're missing out. Not that they'd know it, bunch of hairy savages that they are. It should scare everyone that there are places in this country where they blend in so well, since those attitudes don't change in their human skin."

"They've always found refuges," Jaden replied with a shrug. "Just as we have. And I agree, I'm not keen on running into a wolf pack. From what I saw with Lyra, things are just as backward among them as they ever were. Still, I don't feel right hanging on to this. I do think she's an Alpha's daughter. Actually, that seemed to be the attraction where the other furry bastard was concerned. But this is something important to her family. She didn't lose it on purpose, and considering that she might get in serious trouble over it, it just seems like . . ." He trailed off, frowning at the necklace in his hand. "I don't know. Maybe I can mail it to her."

That wasn't what he wanted, though. He wanted to see her again. Everything he'd thought about werewolves, everything he'd been told, didn't seem to mesh with the tough, confident beauty he'd saved against her will. And in the back of his mind, the memories of a couple of centuries of being thought a veritable savage because of his own bloodline were very fresh. Werewolves and vampires were apples and oranges, of course, but he couldn't shake the parallels. Nor could he forget the way she had melted against him, vulnerable for just a moment, only a breath away from tasting.

It was a few moments before he realized Ty was watching him closely with an odd expression on his face.

"Are you sure you're all right? That there isn't something more to this?"

"What more could there be?" Jaden replied, a bit more gruffly than he normally would have. He tucked the necklace into the back pocket of his jeans, hoping that having it out of his hands would improve his mental state a little.

"I don't know. You just seem . . . odd over this."

Jaden reached for an explanation and found one that was actually part of the truth. "I was whipped simply for being what I am, Ty," Jaden said, referring to the long scars that still scored the length of his back. "I'll carry the marks for the rest of my life, or forever, whichever comes first. I don't like to think of Lyra Black being punished this way, or possibly some worse way, for losing something that was torn off her while she was being threatened in the worst possible way. You know what her father probably is."

Ty's lip curled in disgust, and Jaden saw that he did indeed remember. The two of them had taken down an

Alpha just once, when Arsinöe had grown tired of the Alpha's pack's constant encroachment on her territory. The leader of the Pack of the Nine Trees had been a beast in both forms, a slobbering hulk with several unhappy wives and, if the rumors were true, a taste for human flesh. Jaden had never forgotten the eyes of the ragged women of the pack.

In sharp contrast, Lyra's eyes had been full of fire. But that meant nothing. Her spirit would obviously be a hard one to break.

"Well, then." Ty reached over and gave Jaden a rough pat on the shoulder. "If you're that worried about her well-being, Jaden, go deliver it in person. Even if she's got two black eyes, she'll probably spit in your face when you hand it to her. You can't change what she is or how her kind lives. But go. I can see you won't rest until you've done it, and you're no help to anyone here when you're this miserable."

Jaden cocked his head, catching the insinuation beneath Ty's words.

"Do you *need* my help for something?" Jaden asked.

Ty sighed and rubbed at the back of his neck. "Lily needs to assemble an actual court, and a good guard. She's been putting it off, but we can't keep running this place like a boarding house, and no matter how much she wants the Lilim to be modern and free and easy, there are certain things that need to be in place. Not only for her to be taken seriously, but also to keep her safe. Vlad and I have both been working on her, and she's finally started to relent."

Jaden tensed. "Because of the Ptolemy?"

"That, and Damien let her know that there are a lot of

highbloods asking the House of Shadows for information on her weaknesses. At this point, she has plenty."

Jaden sighed. He had worried about this. Lily was on a steep learning curve, even with the help of Ty and him, as well as the support of the Dracul. Every house would be looking for an angle to exploit to chip away at the legitimacy of what they were making. Highbloods weren't fond of making room for others in their rarified little world.

"What did you need from me?" Jaden asked. Had he really thought he was being freed? He had just traded one set of responsibilities for another. Though at least with the Lilim, he didn't run quite as high a risk of being killed for screwing up.

"Lily wants you to help choose the guard," Ty said. "You and me both. I'm not comfortable without extra input anyway, and it's what we both know. Vlad has a better eye for loyal courtiers, so he'll help her on that end. And...don't run screaming, but I think she has an idea you'd do quite a job as her Captain of the Guard."

Jaden winced, though he was flattered along with the horror of such a proposition. "Captain? Is she crazy?"

"If she is, then so am I. I agreed with her when she brought it up, as it's something I'd considered as well. You've got a hell of a lot of talent as a hunter, as a fighter, and you know how to train others."

"Can't I just be a lazy courtier and sit around here on my ass?"

Ty angled his head and gave him a knowing look. "That's basically what you've been doing, and you're miserable. You like having a job. This would be a good one."

"I...I don't know," Jaden stammered, taken a little aback by the revelation. Everything Ty had said was true, but Jaden wasn't sure he ever wanted to be tethered to a dynasty again. Even one he respected. Moreover, being responsible for Lily's safety when he knew damn well the long knives would be out for her was a daunting thought. Still, he couldn't bring himself to reject it outright.

Ty, at least, seemed to understand his quandary. He stood up, preparing to leave.

"You don't have to decide right now. I'm telling you so you can think it over while you're gone."

Jaden frowned. "While I'm gone?"

Ty nodded with a half smile. "The guard can wait a few days. Go deliver your necklace, satisfy your curiosity about this woman, and then come home. You can tell me what you want to do then."

"I'm not curious—"

"Oh, the hell you're not," Ty snorted. "But you need to see that Lyra Black is a typical werewolf from a typical pack, for whatever reason. And after that you'll be begging to meet the trio of pretty Cait Sith who just came into town. So go. The Blacks have always led the Pack of the Thorn. I can tell you how to get to them."

"Thanks," was all Jaden could say. Inside, however, his slow-beating heart had assumed a rhythm that was almost human. He would see Lyra again, come what may. And then maybe, hopefully, he could work out why his head had been full of nothing but her for months.

"I'll leave tomorrow night."

"That works. You can spend the rest of the evening figuring out how to see her without the rest of the pack tearing you apart," Ty said. "You didn't ask how I knew where they were. I had a nasty run-in with the Thorn in last year's travels. A tip: I would avoid being a cat among them as much as possible. That crew has a high prey drive no matter what form they're in."

"Got it," Jaden replied, already feeling a little uneasy about the wisdom of a lone vampire heading into a pack's stronghold. Ty was right, however. Jaden would never be happy unless he followed his instincts.

"I certainly hope so. Come on. We can butt in and use Lily's computer. She likes the company."

Jaden rose to follow without another word, grateful that he had friends who would help him even in this, and hoping that his curiosity wasn't finally going to do him in after all.

chapter FIVE

J ADEN DIDN'T KNOW what he'd expected as he drove into Silver Falls, New York, but it wasn't what he was seeing so far. He'd imagined an off-the-beaten-path hillbilly haven, full of rusted-out pickups on blocks, trailers with tires on the roofs, and the occasional sad-looking specimen of livestock hanging out in someone's front yard. Instead, he'd driven through a quaint downtown and navigated streets lined with mostly well-kept homes dating from the Victorian era all the way up to the present. There were no grizzled locals giving he and his 'Vette the stink eye, no roving bands of barely human werewolves patrolling for intruders like himself. And best of all, he hadn't caught so much as a hint of wolf musk as he'd driven around.

Maybe it was a smaller pack than Ty thought, Jaden reasoned as he made the final turn onto what the GPS told him was Lyra's street. Maybe it was just a handful of mangy stragglers bound together and trying to hang on to their only item of value. He'd never heard of werewolves taking up residence in such pretty environs, at least. Silver Falls wasn't terribly far from Syracuse, nestled more in the middle of the state among the Finger Lakes. Like many of the towns in the area, it was picturesque and surrounded by beautiful landscape that was just awakening from another long New York winter. The town did sit by itself, probably fifteen miles in any direction from another one. That part made sense.

But the charming Craftsman with the inviting front porch he pulled up in front of didn't make any sense at all.

The Alpha wolf of the Pack of the Thorn, a pack that according to Ty was known for its ferocity, lived *here*?

Jaden killed the engine and sat for a moment, trying to absorb the fact that not only was the house immaculate, but someone who lived there obviously liked to garden. He had a hard time picturing Lyra as that person. Her mother, maybe? And what sort of woman would have given birth to a fiery thing like Lyra? He supposed he was about to find out, if he could work up the nerve.

"Damn it. I could outfight a pack of werewolves if I needed to," Jaden grumbled. He hated the way he felt, all twisted up with nerves like some pathetic teenager. He hadn't been one of those in over two hundred years, and he had no intention of revisiting his adolescence. Jaden jerked the keys from the ignition and got out of the car.

Immediately, he realized his mistake, but it was far too late to do anything but stand there and try desperately to acclimate before he lost his mind.

The scent of werewolf was everywhere.

Jaden had no idea how he had missed it. Maybe he'd had the air in the car set to recirculate. Certainly he should have rolled down a window a while ago to acclimate slowly, because this was a shock to his system. The air he breathed, the breeze that ruffled his hair, everything in this place smelled of wolf. And the cat inside of him wanted, no, *demanded* that he dive back into the car and get out of town as fast as possible. Jaden only barely swallowed back a pained yowl. His muscles seemed frozen, and beads of sweat broke out on his brow. His breath came in shallow little sips. All his senses screamed that he was surrounded by the enemy.

He might have run for it, might not have been able to help it, except that at that moment he saw Lyra through one of the front windows. She paid no attention to the outside, instead looking lost in her own thoughts as she wandered into the room, stooped to pick something up, and then left.

Instantly, Jaden was transfixed. The smell, the fear, all faded away into the background, then vanished. He didn't stop to question why. All he could think about was Lyra, her wild hair tumbling around her shoulders, her face drawn and tight, as though she had a great deal to worry about.

Maybe he could help relieve some small part of that worry.

Jaden reached into his jacket pocket, gave her necklace a quick squeeze for luck, and with a deep breath, headed up the stone steps.

"You're perfect for one another. Damn it, Simon, tell her!"

Lyra stopped pacing to glare at her father. It was lost on him, however. He was too busy begging Simon to marry her. She would have been embarrassed, but Simon looked mortified enough for both of them.

"I can hear you just fine, thanks," Lyra said finally. "And I'm not getting married. Not now, and possibly not ever," she added pointedly, shooting a warning look at the friend who sat stiffly on the couch, looking as though he would rather be anywhere but here. Simon Dale had been her closest friend since they were children, and she knew that if push came to shove and her father leaned hard enough, he would give in and try whatever facsimile of wooing Simon was capable of.

She tried to stay away from that part of his life, but she'd caught glimpses. What she'd seen didn't bode well. What some girls called "awkwardly charming" usually just looked awkward to her, and Simon was the poster boy. Cute...but clueless. And damn it, he was wavering already.

Gods, she was tired of overbearing males.

Simon scrubbed a hand through his already tousled crop of chocolate-brown hair and looked at her with big, soulful eyes of gold-flecked green hazel. As friends, they had always been an excellent match: he was calm where she was fiery; he was thoughtful where she was brash. They'd decided long ago, however, that they were unsuited to be anything more.

She had the sudden urge to plug her ears.

"Look, Lyra," Simon said, "he has a point. It doesn't have to be some stranger. There are plenty of guys right here who would be happy to protect you, and it's not like Eric already has a lock on the Proving."

"Mmm," was all Lyra said, turning away to pace a different part of the room and hoping, very strongly, that Simon would stop there. Naturally, he didn't. When Simon had something to say, he usually finished.

"Maybe we should think about it. We're already friends. It could work."

"Of course it would work!" her father cried happily. "Problem solved!"

Lyra stopped, tipped her head back, and closed her eyes, wishing for patience she currently didn't have. "Simon," she said, trying not to sound as frustrated with him as she felt. "I think I'm going to have to remind you that we don't actually *like* each other that way. And as a couple, we would make one another really unhappy. Trust me."

She looked over at him and saw she'd managed to hurt his feelings despite the fact that she'd spoken nothing but the truth. Lyra blew out an exasperated breath. She didn't know why he had to be the one who was more sensitive. It was so backward.

"*What?*" she asked. "You think I'm wrong?"

"No. I just think you could have toyed with my emotions a little longer before shooting me down," Simon said. "Especially since I was lured here with free pizza and got a free rejection instead." His dimples winked for a moment, then vanished as his expression once more turned serious. He hesitated for a moment, then glanced at Dorien like he wished the man would leave. Since that didn't seem likely, he murmured, "It's not the world's worst idea, though. I could take Eric—especially with your father's help beforehand. He could back me fully if I was yours. And friendship isn't such an awful way to start…"

Lyra looked at him, full of as much affection as exasperation. He looked so adorably disgruntled about the whole thing. She wished, as she often had, that she could have wanted Simon as a lover along with their friendship. Life would have been easier in a lot of ways, and she knew very well that if Simon became the Alpha through their marriage, he would be more than happy to let her run things behind the scenes. But the necessary feeling just wasn't there.

And besides, though she had a lot of faith in Simon as a fighter, he had a sense of honor. He wouldn't fight dirty . . . Eric would. Meaning Simon would lose.

"No," Lyra said firmly, shaking her head. "No way. I can do this. I want to do this. The Proving's not exactly Mortal Kombat, right? It's speed, stealth, agility—"

"Beating and slashing one another to a bloody pulp in the dark," Simon added quietly. Lyra decided to ignore him.

"What I need is a month of the most intensive training you two can give me. Every technique, every dirty trick, I want to know it and practice it. We go to the course, we train, we work out a way for me to take out the big boys."

Her father and Simon shared a look, and Dorien opened his mouth to speak. Lyra was quite sure she wasn't going to like what he had to say. More excuses, probably. She was a she-wolf, she wouldn't understand, it would upset the other candidates, blah blah blah. She moved to cut him off.

"Don't tell me—"

The sudden knock at the door startled her. Lyra turned her head sharply toward the sound, as did the men. The three werewolves stood frozen in silence for a long moment. She shot a quick look at the clock. It was a little past eight, and with the moon just recently begun to wane again, visitors were unexpected. It took most pack members a full week to recover from a Full Moon's Feast, and this last one had been as wild as ever. Wilder, since she'd caused such a stir by stepping forward when the Proving candidates were asked to announce themselves.

Another knock. When no one moved, Lyra rolled her eyes. "Okay, I guess I'll get that," she grumbled, stalking from the room. "Maybe someone else wants to marry me and save me from my own crushing stupidity."

She moved into the foyer, already dreading what she expected to find on the steps. It likely wasn't another wannabe mate, but since an entire week had passed and she hadn't yet pulled out of the Proving, it probably *was* an elder pack member come to dispense some comforting wisdom along the same lines as what her father had been spouting all day. *"Find a strong mate to fight for you, put an end to this nonsense... and by the way, do you remember that my daughter married into the Pack of the Black Tree? Well, she has the nicest boy about your age..."*

She didn't even bother to look through the crackle glass sidelights, catching only the vaguest impression of a single human shape standing outside. She had already decided that if her guess was correct, whoever this was would quickly find him- or herself with a door slammed in their face.

Lyra pulled the door open with an angry jerk, ready to verbally carve up her nosy visitor.

When she saw who it was, her mouth dropped open, but whatever words she'd had in her head blew away like dead leaves in the wind.

He was everything she remembered, everything she'd replayed in her head a thousand times. Slim and pale and preternaturally beautiful, with that shaggy black hair that looked as though it would feel like silk against her skin.

His eyes, an impossible blue that her memory had insistently dimmed simply because eyes couldn't truly be a shade so vibrant, were fixed on her.

Words finally appeared in Lyra's head. Sadly, they didn't make any sense when put together. The shock of seeing Jaden here, as though he'd wandered out of one of her fevered dreams to find himself smack in the middle of werewolf country, was just a little too much for her.

It was some small consolation that Jaden seemed as startled as she was. He had his hands stuffed into the pockets of the same black military-style jacket he'd been wearing the other night, and stood very, very still, as though moving might provoke her into attacking him.

At the moment, she was in no shape to do that.

Finally, he spoke.

"Hi." One word, in that soft, sultry voice, and he never let his eyes leave hers. She would almost have thought he was trying to thrall her, except that sort of thing didn't work on her kind and he knew it. So his wide-eyed, hopeful, slightly terrified stare meant... what, exactly?

"Lyra? Who is it?" Her father's voice called from the other room, bringing Lyra back to reality with an unpleasant jolt.

"It's... nothing, be right back," she called, hoping her father and Simon didn't hear how strange her voice sounded. Then she took a deep breath, catching a whiff of Jaden's cologne. Gods, he smelled good. Why did he have to smell good? She needed to get him the hell out of here, now, before something awful happened. She had enough shit to deal with right now without trying to prevent her pack from dismembering a stray cat vamp.

She leaned in close to talk to him but immediately

wished she hadn't. The memory of being pressed against him was still too raw, and it hadn't stopped haunting her, both in her sleep and in her unguarded waking moments.

She steeled herself. This was too important to lose her head over. And she sure wasn't going to get ridiculous over a vampire.

"What are you doing here?" she hissed. "Are you nuts? The other wolves will kill you the second they smell you!"

Incredibly, Jaden shrugged. "Yeah, well, I can take care of myself. I brought you something."

From his pocket, he pulled out a disc hanging from a long chain, one Lyra knew immediately. She exhaled a shaky breath, hardly able to believe her luck. Her father had thus far been too upset to notice she wasn't wearing it. Now he didn't ever have to know it had been gone. And all because Jaden had decided to bring it back to her.

All this way back to her.

Jaden frowned as he held it out to her, not understanding.

"You hunted me down just to give this back?" she asked. "Why?" There had to be some kind of angle. But what a vampire could want from her, apart from verbal abuse, was completely beyond her. Lyra felt strangely off-balance, just as she had when Jaden had saved her from Mark. She couldn't think of a good reason why he might have done that either, apart from some twisted enjoyment he might have received from making her angry.

Unless Jaden was just kind of…sweet. Which was a possibility she had no interest in considering. Trying to figure out vampires was an exercise in futility.

"It looked important," Jaden replied, keeping his voice quiet, eyes darting quickly over her shoulder. Lyra noted that her father and Simon had fallen suspiciously silent, and she knew it was only a matter of time before they came out to where she and Jaden stood. That wouldn't be good.

"Anyway, you seemed pretty protective of it when that guy—Mark, was it?—ripped it off of your neck. So I figured I would bring it back."

It would be so easy to believe it, to take Jaden and his soothing, melodious British accent at face value. But Lyra was too used to being bitten, literally and figuratively, when she let her guard down.

"It isn't that easy and you know it," Lyra replied, keeping her own voice down, though she had a feeling that it was no longer making any difference. Wolves' hearing was impeccable. She quickly took the necklace, feeling a burst of relief as her fingers closed around the metal disc. Lyra noticed that Jaden let his hand linger against hers, cool and smooth against her own vital warmth. She should have been repulsed. But like everything else about this vampire, she found it strangely compelling.

"How did you even find me?" she whispered. "What do you want, Jaden?"

To her surprise, he seemed unsure how to answer.

"I—"

He was cut off by the sound of an animal's snarl, accompanied by her father's voice.

"What the hell is *this*? Get away from my daughter, you piece of—"

Dorien's curse was drowned out by Lyra's startled cry as an enormous red wolf leaped from behind her and landed on top of Jaden. She was knocked to the side and quickly felt her father's hands on her, steadying her. Just as quickly she shook him off. Lyra turned to look at him. Her stomach sank. He had murder in his eyes.

"I don't know what that bloodsucker thinks he's after, coming into my town, but Simon will make sure he understands what it means to come onto our territory. There," he growled, jerking his head toward the scene. "That's how you fight, Lyra. No mercy."

Dorien jerked his head toward the fiasco unfolding in the front yard, urging her to look. Vampire or not, she really didn't want to see Jaden being torn apart. It was a good thing it was dark, and that all their neighbors were part of the pack. A scene like this would have merited plenty of calls to both the police and Animal Control in a normal town.

Still, after a few seconds of listening to vicious snarling, Lyra couldn't help herself. She looked out, expecting to see Simon with one of Jaden's limbs in his mouth and one or two others littering the ground around them. Instead, she ended up watching, wide-eyed, as Jaden proved himself more than a match for the brute strength of a werewolf. With a series of moves that were almost balletic in their grace, he extracted himself from Simon's claws, extended his own, and with bared fangs proceeded to open Simon up, *slash-slash-slash*. When Simon roared in anger, blood coursing down both sides and his nose sliced open, Lyra saw him make what would, she knew, be a fatal mistake.

He let the anger drive him.

The anger made Simon sloppy, whereas Jaden's cold focus seemed only to intensify. Every time Simon lunged, Jaden avoided him with a simple quick feint. His shoulders were hunched, almost like a threatened cat. Without taking his eyes from his opponent, Jaden addressed Dorien.

Lyra realized she'd moved from terror to fascination. The man wasn't even winded.

"Sir, I only came to return something to your daughter. If you have a problem with that, fine, but I don't think it merits killing me. I came alone."

Dorien didn't even look at Lyra to confirm this. "I don't give a damn what you say. Why should I trust one of your kind? You've banned us from your cities. Maybe you're looking to take the countryside too, and that isn't going to happen. We'll send you back in pieces. That should take care of the problem for a while."

Lyra knew she wasn't imagining Jaden's exasperated groan, as though he was engaging in a polite disagreement instead of a life-or-death battle. Simon threw himself at Jaden again, and Jaden spun away, opening up Simon's left flank. The wolf reacted with a roar that was now far more pain than fury. Simon, Lyra saw even by the dim light in the front yard, was bleeding heavily now. Her kind healed quickly, but in a battle like this, not quickly enough. He would need to rest, to sleep.

If this kept up he wasn't going to get that chance.

She stopped worrying about Jaden dying and started worrying that he was going to kill Simon.

"Dad," Lyra said, beginning to panic as she saw Simon had no intention of stopping, "he's telling the truth. He brought me Mom's necklace. I...I lost it the other night, and he brought it back to me." When her father looked back at her like she'd suddenly grown another head, she raised her voice to a shout, hoping it would get through his thick skull.

"Tell Simon to stop! Damn it, he's going to get killed, and Jaden didn't come here to fight! This is my fault, okay? Make him *stop*!"

She saw the instant of understanding, then reproach mixed with disgust. It settled like a rock in the pit of her stomach, but there was nothing for it now. Lyra wasn't about to cause the death of her dear friend by stubbornly refusing to tell the truth.

Dorien moved like lightning, staying in human form but leaping with the sort of controlled power that a human could only dream of having. He landed squarely in between Jaden and Simon, who were circling one another again. Jaden's eyes glittered like blue fire, and Simon staggered stubbornly along, though obviously he was very wounded.

"Enough!" Dorien bellowed, his voice so loud the very air seemed to vibrate. Lyra stepped into the night, noticing that curious faces looked out at the scene from windows of houses all around them. Inwardly, she groaned. It wouldn't be long before the neighbors came out for a closer look, and there would be no restraining them once they caught a whiff of vampire. Lyra doubted her father would try very hard to stop them.

Dorien's voice dropped to a harsh growl as he addressed first Simon, then Jaden.

"You, get inside. Those wounds will need tending. Lyra can take care of that…it's the least she can do."

Simon complied immediately, remaining in wolf form as he limped past Lyra and into the house. He didn't spare her a glance. Ashamed, Lyra supposed. And later, he would be angry when he learned what had brought the vampire here to begin with. She started to follow, but slowly, wanting to hear what her father had to say to Jaden. Dorien saw what she was up to, however, and the glare he fixed her with would have caused ice to burst into flame.

"Go with Simon," Dorien snapped. "If you're really responsible for this vamp being here, I won't harm him.

He may be a bloodsucker, but he isn't the one who told you to go running unprotected all over the country. And I'm guessing the necklace didn't leave you willingly, did it?"

Lyra said nothing. What could she say? She had no defense. Even for Mark. Her father would no doubt lay the blame for that squarely at her feet because she had left the protection of the pack. And now this...bringing a vampire onto pack territory...

She nodded and spared a final look at Jaden, whom she was quite sure she would never see again. Her only consolation was that Dorien Black was a man of his word. If he said he wouldn't harm Jaden, he meant it. Jaden's eyes met hers in the half light, beautiful and strange, so different from the wolf eyes she had grown up around. Her anger at him had fled, replaced by confusion and a strange longing that seemed to come from deep within...a thing she knew she needed to deny at all costs, lest it take root and grow.

Wanting things she couldn't have was standard operating procedure. Wanting Jaden would not only be pointless, but also an incredibly stupid waste of energy. Still, he deserved some thanks. Even if he'd brought her as much trouble as relief.

"For what it's worth," she said to him, "thanks for bringing it back to me."

Jaden gave a curt nod, his expression deadly serious. "You're welcome."

She hesitated only a moment longer, feeling like there was more to be said, though she wasn't quite sure what it was. But in the end, she had to turn away, go inside.

Running again. But this time, for whatever reason, she felt like she was running in the exact wrong direction.

chapter SIX

·

JADEN WATCHED LYRA turn to go inside, allowing himself a second or two to admire the sensual sway of her hips. She was abrasive enough that he doubted she was fully aware of her own appeal. He supposed it was for the best that her father was now going to get around to throwing him out of town.

Or trying to kill him.

Or both.

Now that he finally had a moment to size the man up, Jaden turned a cautious eye to Dorien Black. Lyra didn't favor him in looks particularly, Jaden thought. Dorien's hair was reddish-brown instead of Lyra's deep chocolate color, and his features were rough and blocky. She most definitely had his eyes, however. Hot gold, with a wild glitter and a slight upward tilt.

It was small comfort, that little reminder of the woman who'd drawn him here. But above all, Dorien Black was a werewolf, and an Alpha wolf at that. Which meant he was too damned big for his own good. Simon had been young, easy to defeat. This one, one-on-one, might pose a few problems if he decided to give chase.

The Alpha's gruff tone was far from reassuring.

"You bolt, and I'll run you down until you drop. I want some answers."

Jaden didn't move. He knew he ought to—the wolf was probably bluffing—but if all it took to leave were a few simple questions, that was preferable to running for his life.

"That depends on what the questions are," Jaden said.

Dorien snorted dismissively. "You're on my territory now, boy. Why you thought setting foot in it was a good idea is beyond me, but here you are. My territory, my rules."

The words were typical wolf posturing, but generally best heeded. Jaden hadn't yet met a wolf without a short fuse, Lyra included. He suspected she came by it honestly.

"All right," Jaden replied. "Let's get this over with. What do you want to know?"

"That should be obvious." Dorien's eyes glittered in the semidarkness. "Why did you have my daughter's necklace? How do you know Lyra? And again . . . what the hell are you doing in the middle of my pack's territory?"

Jaden shifted, then raised an eyebrow. "Just passing through?"

The attempt at humor fell flat as Dorien bared his teeth. His incisors were as sharp as any vampire's. "This is a joke to you, then. My family, our honor, our kind . . . a *joke*."

Jaden felt his hackles rising and had to swallow a hiss. His eyes saw a man, but his senses were screaming wolf . . . his natural enemy. Dorien likely fought much the same battle as he stood there, a low growl giving Jaden fair warning that the situation was deteriorating rapidly.

He might have fought the Alpha after all, had he not glanced up and caught a glimpse of Lyra's face at one of the upstairs windows. Their eyes locked for the barest of seconds, but it was long enough for Jaden to see worry, fear…and the same strange longing that had pulled him here. The last sensation shook him to his core. He knew he was probably imagining it, just like he knew he was the only one reliving their last meeting over and over in strange, heated dreams.

But that glimpse of interest, of faintest possibility, was enough to pull him back from the edge.

Lyra's face vanished. Time sped back up. And Jaden put his hands before him in a sign of truce.

"It's not a joke, sir. I might be a vampire, but since I was a slave up until not very long ago, poking fun at other races isn't all that appealing as entertainment."

There was a moment where Dorien looked like he could go either way, and Jaden half expected to see the claws start to lengthen, the fur begin to sprout. Instead, with a deep breath, Dorien, too, stepped back from the edge.

"Yet," Dorien said flatly. "We do hear things out here, from time to time. It's in our best interest to keep an eye on your kind, just in case they decide the cities aren't for them and that they like what we have even better. You're one of the Cait Sith. I smell cat all over you. So I guess that means you're newly respectable these days."

Jaden knew he was skating on thin ice. "You could say that," he hedged, unsure of just how much the wolves had heard.

The Alpha snorted contemptuously. "Yes, I could.

Your kind has joined up with that demon bloodline. I'm not surprised, considering."

"Lily MacGillivray is not a demon," Jaden snapped, defensive at the first mention of his friend, the woman who had saved his bloodline from the gutter. "And I might not know much about the wolf definition of honor, but you obviously don't know shit about my bloodline."

For some strange reason, Jaden's outburst seemed to please Dorien. His lips slowly lifted into a grin.

"Nope. Don't want to either. But I'm glad to see you've got some loyalty, and some spine...for a vampire. It's not the sort of thing we expect."

"Yeah, well...I don't expect to be standing here talking to an Alpha wolf after I've just torn one of his young wolves to ribbons, so I'd call this a new experience for us both." He paused, then threw caution to the wind when he saw the calculating gleam in Dorien's eyes.

"What do you *want*, Black? You want something, or I wouldn't still be standing here."

Dorien chuckled at that, and Jaden could see he'd been right: there was more. Dorien stepped closer to Jaden, shooting a look around them to ensure they were still alone. Jaden glanced around too, curious. The faces were gone from the windows, and all was quiet. He imagined the occasional tussle was the norm around here. To the casual observer, it likely hadn't looked like any big deal. Still, he knew full well someone could be lurking in shadows, trying to figure out what was going on. There were so many wolves here...he wondered whether there were even any humans in this town. The air was thick with werewolf musk, though he'd acclimated to it somewhat by now. It surprised Jaden that he could manage to stand it so well. But then, he'd never been interested in finding out if he could desensitize himself at all. His nerves were still on edge—that was to be expected when you were continuously inhaling the scent of a natural enemy—but he could stand here and breathe normally, speak normally, without swinging between fight and flight.

The distraction of Simon's attack seemed to have done Jaden a world of good after all.

After a moment, Dorien seemed satisfied that they weren't being listened to. "What do you know about werewolf Provings?"

Jaden thought the question was an odd one, but he tried to be accommodating.

"Hmm. Bunch of wolves ripping one another apart while the pack cheers? Winner takes all?"

"That's…an interesting simplification," Dorien said blandly. "It's how the pack chooses who will be the next Alpha. It's a test of strength, of skill, of wits. And the winner has the honor of becoming the current Alpha's apprentice, what we call a Second."

"So you're telling me it doesn't involve tearing one another to shreds?"

Dorien exhaled loudly, looking annoyed. "That's sometimes a part of it. Think what you like about it. Vamps are plenty vicious in their own way."

Jaden thought about the long scars on his back from the Ptolemy's whip. "You won't get an argument from me on that."

The wolf looked slightly surprised at Jaden's response. "Well. Good."

"So what does this Proving have to do with anything?" Jaden asked, shoving his hands in his pockets against a chilly breath of wind. Maybe it was because his natural temperature was already cooler than a mortal's, but he preferred the warmer weather.

"We have one coming up, actually. At the next full moon. There, I'll choose my Second."

"Exciting," Jaden replied in a tone that indicated he thought it was anything but. His life had been full of violence, but it had always been something he'd considered necessary, not something to be enjoyed. Werewolves, on the other hand, were known to draw one another's blood for the slightest things, just for the hell of it. The line between animal and man was very thin there, at least with some. There were reasons why they'd been hunted so fiercely in the Dark Ages.

"Lyra has declared herself."

It took Jaden a moment to process what Dorien was saying. "Lyra has…" Then he realized what the Alpha meant. He looked at Dorien, typically big and bulky as the males of his kind tended to be, and then thought of Lyra, who was long and lean as both a woman and a wolf. He tried to picture her throwing herself into some bloody fray with a bunch of enormous beasts, but he found it was too disturbing to think about in any detail. Maybe he was wrong about these Provings…maybe there was more to them than he'd thought, that she felt she had enough of a chance at winning to enter.

And hell if he knew what to say.

"She's ambitious," was all he could think of.

"She'll be killed," Dorien replied flatly. "It's as simple as that. Most would just hurt her badly enough to take her out of the running early. But her cousin, my brother's boy, has been waiting for an excuse to get his teeth in her throat.

He'll win. And then I'll have to train the wolf who killed my only child, and who I'll always know *enjoyed* doing it."

Jaden stared at Dorien, stunned at the man's blunt assessment of the likely outcome. Finally, he noticed how tired the wolf looked, the faint smudges beneath his eyes that told the tale of plenty of sleepless nights. And though Jaden had no children of his own, or many people he cared enough to worry like that about, he felt something surprising for the wolf.

Sympathy.

"Can't you get her to see reason? Lyra doesn't seem like a stupid woman. Stubborn, but not stupid. She must know what the chances are—"

"Of course she knows," Dorien interjected. "I think if she thought there were a better candidate here than Eric—that's my nephew—she might consider throwing her support behind whoever that was. She doesn't have a death wish...or at least, she didn't used to. I don't blame her for being angry about the way women in the packs have always been shunted aside for leadership. But I didn't make our ways, and I can't change them. We rule by fang and claw, we follow the strongest...and it doesn't get much stronger than a full grown male werewolf." He sighed and shook his head, looking away. "She's afraid of what Eric will do to the pack. Besides, so many look to Lyra for advice, for leadership, that I think she has an idea they'd accept her if she managed to pull out a victory in the Proving. Maybe they would. But she'll never get that far." He looked back at Jaden wearily. "This would be a lot easier if she'd just find a mate to fight for her. But she's never done what she was told. I shouldn't have expected she'd start now."

Thinking about Lyra's stubbornness made Jaden smile a little, despite the pall that had been cast over the night. The shame was that someone so spirited had to be born into a race that would likely never appreciate her. She would have made a hell of a vampiress, Jaden thought, and then pushed the tantalizing image aside as his smile faded. Thoughts like that were stupid. She wasn't, she wouldn't be. And the reception she'd given him here hadn't exactly been warm.

He wondered for the umpteenth time what had possessed him to come here. And what he had gotten himself into by staying.

"Why are you telling me all this?" Jaden asked quietly. All the tension had left the air with Dorien's confession, leaving behind it nothing but a faint sense that he was about to ask something of Jaden. Something he should stay hundreds of miles away from, if he had any sense. Yet Jaden felt glued to the spot. Over a couple hundred years of life, he'd rarely had any sense that his destiny was unfolding before his eyes. Mostly he'd just tried to get by, saving his own skin and lending a hand if anyone else's skin seemed worth saving without much trouble. But this was...different.

Sort of like knowing a piano was about to fall on your head and being unable to get out of the way. But if he bolted, Jaden thought, as he should, then he would be haunted by the image of Lyra's golden eyes, so full of life, closing forever.

Gods, he was losing it.

"I'm telling you this because I'm desperate, of course," Dorien said with a dry little chuckle, his small smile humorless. "You were interested enough in Lyra's welfare to bring her necklace—my late wife's necklace—back to her. Maybe you'll be interested enough to listen to my proposition. You seem to be an odd one, for a vamp. And frankly, I've got nothing to lose."

"Except your daughter," Jaden said.

Dorien's expression turned grim. "If I do nothing, I'll lose her anyway. Better to take a leap of faith, I think. At least then I will have tried everything I can think of."

He hated to admit it, but Jaden was inclined to agree. The chances of him even being alive right now had been slim, and yet here he was... because he and his friends had taken a huge risk and taken on an entire dynasty.

Realizing that he had any of this in common with a creature he would normally have considered a big, worthless, violent beast was uncomfortable, to say the least.

"You may as well tell me what I've stumbled into," Jaden said. "I have no idea how I can help with your problem, but I guess you've thought of something."

Dorien's gaze was unnervingly direct. "I have. While you were dealing with Simon's... welcome... in fact. You made short work of him, and he's a hell of a fighter."

"He's young," Jaden said with a shrug. "He let his anger get ahead of him. He'll learn. Hopefully."

"You also danced circles around him," Dorien said. "I'm no expert about vamp fights, and I'll deny I said this to my dying day, but you've got impressive skill, boy. I can't say I've ever paid much attention to one of your kind in battle... usually too busy trying to take his or her head off... but I expected you to fight dirty. You didn't need to." He paused. "I don't suppose that says much for Simon, though."

Jaden lifted an eyebrow, bemused. He hadn't been

called "boy" in a very long time, and then certainly not by a man who was a good two hundred years younger. Still, he appreciated the compliment, even though he was well aware he was being buttered up. It was funny. Dorien looked like a prizefighter, not a negotiator, but looks, it seemed, were deceiving.

Jaden found it hard to be anything but gracious in return.

"He's just young, like I said. I've had a few years to work on my technique, if you want to call it that. And you still haven't told me—"

"Teach her to fight like you do. I'll pay you anything you like."

Jaden blinked, not sure he'd heard the man correctly. "Teach her?"

Dorien's gaze was direct, completely confident. "Lyra. She's built more like you...not that you're built like a woman or anything, but size-wise, you're more in line. She's strong, quicker than most of the males in the pack. And if you want grace, she's got that too. I can't help her. You could."

For the first time in ages, Jaden found himself caught completely off guard. He'd expected a request to maybe watch Lyra's back. This, however...hadn't even crossed his mind. Probably because it was completely insane.

"I don't know if that would work, Dorien. I mean, even setting aside the fact that I've never taught anyone to fight before, she and I aren't exactly the same species."

Dorien waved his hand dismissively. "So she's not a vampire. Wolves are fighters. And she's sharp, she'll pick up quickly. You're telling me you knew how to move like that the moment you were sired? You turned into a vamp and could miraculously take out random wolves in under five minutes?"

"I...no. No, I guess I was shown a few things," Jaden admitted, trying to remember. "I think most of it was on-the-job training, though. I wanted to stay alive. So I watched the others, picked up the skills I needed. And when the Ptolemy grabbed me, I got better at everything."

"So you could teach her, like you were taught," Dorien said with a nod. "She hasn't had a sparring partner in quite a long time. The males wouldn't spar once she got older. But I know she stays in shape. Lyra will get it. Or get whatever she can out of it as a wolf. What do you say?"

Jaden had a sudden mental image of sparring with Lyra. Except they weren't fighting. And they were both naked. He shuffled his feet, trying to come up with an answer that would make some sense. The process was incredibly frustrating, since there didn't appear to be an answer for him that made any sense.

"You're as crazy as your daughter," Jaden finally said, his voice carrying plenty of bite. "You honestly think I can just...just magically turn her into a fighter who can take on wolves twice her size? This is insanity! Just tell this nephew of yours he can't be Alpha, then pick someone else!"

Dorien's frown returned with a vengeance. "That isn't how it's done. And outwardly, he's fit. As far as taking down a big wolf...you did it just now when you sliced up one of my men. Be grateful you're not hearing my offer while I've got you pinned to the ground by the neck."

It was Jaden's turn to bare his teeth. "You're not going to railroad me into this. I don't know how to teach someone to fight."

"You'll figure it out."

"Your daughter doesn't even like me!"

"Last I checked that wasn't necessary to teach some-one. I hated most of my teachers."

Jaden shoved his hands into his hair and growled at the indifferent moon. "Damn it, Black, you're asking me to set up camp here, in a town full of wolves who are going to try to kill me on sight just like Simon did, to try and show Lyra how to win a contest of brute strength that I'm completely unfamiliar with! I don't care how much you want to pay me, what about any of that sounds like a good idea?"

"The part where what you teach her saves her life."

Dorien said it so calmly, but he must have known his words would take all the wind out of Jaden's sails in an instant.

"I don't have any idea if it would even come close," Jaden replied. He hadn't had to pull out any of his real tricks to take Simon down, it was true. If he had, Lyra would have been out of luck. No wolf could toss around psychic energy, for instance. But to teach her how to move, how to use her smaller size to her advantage...he wasn't sure if that was possible. He had memories of being banged around a fair bit before he'd really come into his own. The natural ability had been there, but it was raw, much like Lyra's probably was. He'd had to hone his skill, learn to fight well.

But he was a vampire. And he'd had a hell of a lot longer than a month to prepare.

Dorien stared at him, *into* him, it seemed. His eyes were so wolflike in that instant, full of pride, power, and an instinctive intelligence that vampires tended to pre-tend didn't exist in their bestial counterparts. They were

the eyes of a being that demanded respect. Jaden had the
queerest sensation, like a rush of cool wind over his skin.
He knew, suddenly and without any doubt, he wasn't
going to walk away from this. Maybe it was because he'd
always been told to do things, and this was completely his
decision. Maybe it was because he knew what it was to be
in a desperate fight you were unlikely to win. Or maybe it
was simply because, for whatever reason, he couldn't bear
the thought of walking away from Lyra and letting her
sacrifice herself for nothing more than a bunch of stupid
werewolves.

Whatever kept him glued in place, Jaden knew that if
he left now, Dorien's request would haunt him. With an
eternity ahead of him, that wasn't a prospect he relished.
He heard his own voice speaking as though he were hearing himself over a great distance.

"What are you offering me, here?"

Dorien gave a curt nod, and Jaden didn't miss the
flash of relief in the Alpha's eyes. The wolf knew he had
Jaden…though Jaden hoped he didn't understand exactly
why. If the father had any idea that Jaden had entertained
some enjoyably impure thoughts about the very daughter
he was supposed to teach, Jaden thought Dorien might try
to take him apart regardless, Proving or no.

Fortunately, the man seemed more concerned with
money.

"I don't know what a creature like you needs or wants. I
can't give you blood, but there is some money. You'd have
complete safety while you were here, of course. I'll come
up with something to tell the others." His voice hardened
and grew intense, vibrating in his rich baritone. "Look.
She won't budge and I'm out of options. I won't have my

daughter die for this. Even if it doesn't look good at the end, I'll...well, we'll talk about that. But I'd rather have her hating me and alive than dead proving me right. I'll give you whatever is in my power to give if you'll teach my Lyra. Give her a chance. She might surprise you."

And that, thought Jaden, was exactly what he was worried about. Still, the acceptance was right on the tip of his tongue.

Anything it was in his power to give. Such a rash and generous offer. How could Dorien know that he wouldn't ask for some exorbitant sum or maybe a piece of the pack's territory? The answer was simple: he couldn't. And it made Lyra's situation seem that much more desperate. So much could go wrong...in fact, it was likely to. And the thought of Dorien's contingency plan, whatever it was, already gave him the creeping horrors. In the end, Jaden could only think to ask one question, simple and yet encompassing everything.

"Why?"

Dorien gave Jaden a look that was equal parts mystified and pitying. "She's my girl. I love her. Haven't you ever had someone you'd give everything up for?"

Jaden could give only a single negative shake of his head. No. But that didn't mean that he couldn't—that he didn't want to—understand.

"I'll do it," Jaden said.

Dorien's expression turned deadly serious, full of wariness and cautious hope. "And...in return, what are you asking?"

"It's very simple," Jaden replied. "I want a boon from your pack, to be decided later, which means when I need it. Anything I ask. No refusals. One thing."

The wolf frowned. "I don't much like the sound of that."

"And I don't much care. That's my price." He knew the value of a promise tucked in the back pocket. One never knew when it would be needed most.

Finally, after a minute, Dorien nodded. "Gods forgive me, but all right. A promise for later. But I'm warning you now, cat: hurt her, or break faith with me in any way, and I'll have you rent limb from limb. Your fancy footwork won't save you from the wrath of my pack. Got it?" He stretched out his hand, a gesture that Jaden had never seen extended from a wolf to a vampire.

"Fancy," Jaden grumbled, but he gripped Dorien's hand with his own, feeling the iron strength in the clasp. "You'd think I was going to teach her dancing."

When they broke the connection, Dorien beckoned him along and turned for the house. "Come on. We've got a lot to talk about. And then we'll need to speak to Lyra, get that screaming out of the way."

Jaden felt his lips curve into a smile despite himself, watching as Dorien made his way up the steps, muttering incoherently. Slowly, Jaden started after him, toward the welcoming glow of the house. He should have been appalled with himself, should have at least felt some sense of misgiving. But he felt better than he had in a long time.

If nothing else, his life, or what passed for it, was about to get a lot more interesting. For the first time in a long time, he didn't know what was going to happen next. And though a wolf would never understand the interminable sameness of forever, Jaden recognized this uncertainty as the gift it was.

He'd spent years enslaved, been tortured, escaped, and

helped to defeat one dynasty in order to begin another. No one could say his long life hadn't been eventful. But it now seemed possible, even probable, that he was embarking on something like an adventure.

Lyra Black might be bad news in every way imaginable. But she, and this, might be just what he needed.

chapter SEVEN

IT WAS LATE by the time Simon left, slinking home in a foul mood that Lyra hadn't been able to tease him out of. She'd doctored him in the upstairs bathroom as best she could, and put up with as much surly growling as she had patience for, but in the end she knew it would take him a good night's sleep and possibly a couple days more of wound licking to straighten up. She might love him like a brother, but Lyra was more than happy to send him on his way when he was ready.

She took some time to work up to going downstairs. Normally she didn't suffer from a lack of nerve, but then, normally she wasn't the cause of a vampire showing up on her doorstep. She had an idea that it might take her father some time to get over that, and that there might be shouting involved.

The week had been a long one. Lyra really wanted to postpone the shouting part.

In the end, she decided to get comfortable and take

her chances. She put on a pair of cotton pajama shorts, pulled on a hooded sweatshirt, swirled her hair up into a messy bun, and then headed downstairs in her bare feet. The house was quiet. She had no idea if that was a good sign, because Dorien was fully capable of fuming quietly.

If he was laying in wait somewhere, Lyra just hoped he'd let her grab a snack before he really started in on her. Her stomach was growling, and there was a bag of Cheetos stashed in the cupboard calling her name.

There wasn't a sound as she headed through the foyer, then back to the kitchen. When she rounded the corner, it didn't surprise her to see a figure seated at the table.

The shock came when she realized who it was.

Jaden's bright blue eyes flashed when they met her own. He straightened where he'd been slouched at the heavy wooden table, and Lyra watched him quickly look her over, seeming to take her measure while she tried to process the fact that he was still here. Not just in her town, but in her house. With her father nowhere to be found. Surprise quickly gave way to dark suspicion.

"Why are *you* still here? What did you do with my father?" she asked.

A ghost of a smile hovered at the corners of his mouth. "You have a knack," he said, "for thinking the absolute worst of my intentions. You realize that, don't you?"

She crossed her arms over her chest, standing her ground. "Don't play harmless with me. There's no way in hell he would have invited you in. Where is he?"

Jaden sighed, looking slightly uncomfortable. "Out. He had a few things to deal with. I was...kind of hoping he'd be back by the time you came down."

"Right, he's sharing his social schedule with you too. I don't remember him having anything to do tonight."

"He does now, if he wants to keep me around long enough to help you. From what he said, he's busy putting out the alert that I'm here, and that I'm not to be chased, dismembered, or eaten if spotted."

"*Help* me? Is this some kind of joke?" Lyra asked incredulously, narrowing her eyes. That he'd brought her the family talisman was a welcome surprise, and made her think he might even have a few redeeming qualities... for a vamp, at least. She'd even worried a little when she'd left him alone with her father, stupid though she knew it was. What did she care about what happened to him? It wasn't like they ran in the same circles, and with things coming to a head with the Proving so soon, she wasn't likely to bump into him again.

The necklace should have been the end of it. He should be long gone.

And yet here he still was, tying her insides up in knots just by hanging out in her kitchen like he belonged there. Did such annoying creatures *have* to be so ridiculously beautiful? Lyra wondered. And this one had a face that was way too innocent. It had messed with her head from the beginning. Apparently, even now, she wasn't over it.

She remembered how he had spoken so softly in her ear, how silky his hair had felt when he'd rubbed his cheek against her...

"Your father," Jaden said calmly, snapping her back to the situation at hand, "has hired me to do a job. And since I currently have nothing better to do, and am apparently a glutton for punishment besides, I agreed."

"Bull."

His placid expression quickly became irritated. Lyra was glad. It was a lot easier when she could tell what Jaden was feeling. He seemed sincere...but she knew from experience that vampires excelled at manipulation. Still, she'd thought it was odd to look out the window earlier, expecting to see some sort of a confrontation between Jaden and her father, only to find them engrossed in an apparently nonviolent conversation.

But no Alpha would ever invite a vampire into his home...ask for his help, when it went against everything the pack stood for...

Unless he were completely desperate. Unless he had a daughter who'd finally driven him over the edge.

Her eyes widened.

"Lyra, I haven't killed your father. He's not stashed in a closet around here. I'm not sitting here waiting for the right moment to go all Hannibal Lecter on you. Would you please just sit down or something? If either of us ought to be nervous, it's me. This entire town smells like a kennel."

His beleaguered tone sealed it for her. He was here with her father's blessing. For a moment, Lyra wasn't sure whether to laugh or scream. If it had been any other vamp, she might have been intrigued. She might even have been excited to see that Dorien could think beyond the very limiting confines of pack tradition. But of all the vampires he might have approached, it had to be the one whose ass she wanted to bite.

He lifted one dark brow. "Afraid of me now, are you?"

Lyra decided she could be grateful, at least, that Jaden made it impossible to moon over him when he started running his mouth.

"You wish." She sauntered into the kitchen, taking her time while she opened the pantry and found the Cheetos. Jaden sat watching her with an inscrutable expression that she found irritatingly catlike while he waited for her to sit down. Just to be contrary, she stopped to dig in the fridge for a soda.

"I think Dorien left you a note on the refrigerator," Jaden said. "If you're interested."

Curious, Lyra looked at the new yellow Post-it stuck to the fridge door. Scrawled on it in permanent marker was a message:

Don't eat the cat. Be back soon.

—Dad

She turned her head to glare at Jaden.

"Pointing this out earlier would have saved you some time trying to convince me, you know."

He shrugged. "It was more interesting the other way."

Lyra snorted as she headed for the table, decidedly more comfortable in her own house now that the last of her doubts had been removed.

"Oh, you enjoy seeing me pissed off?"

"Could be."

She grinned despite herself. "You're in for a treat then."

Lyra tossed herself into the chair opposite Jaden, tucked one leg up against her chest, and dug into her bag of artificial cheese powder heaven. Her taste buds thanked her immediately. Jaden's presence here was still unnerving, and she couldn't think of a single reason why her father would have allowed him to stay, but at least now she was on her own turf. Being in familiar surroundings helped soothe the nerves he seemed to awaken in her, at least enough that she could appear comfortable.

Lyra doubted it would ever be possible to be really comfortable around Jaden. And not only because he was a vampire.

The attraction was deeply annoying to her.

"All right," she said. "Why are you still here?"

"You know," Jaden said, "now that I've met your father I can see where you get your charm from. That's disgusting, by the way," he said, gesturing at the bag of Cheetos.

Lyra lifted her eyebrows. "You really want to discuss who has the more disgusting eating habits? Deal with it," she said. "And you still haven't explained this ultra-helpful job you seem to have conned my father into giving you. Apart from being bait, there's nothing we need a vampire for." She paused. "Though having some extra bait around could come in handy for me."

"Actually," Jaden said, looking smug, "your father seems to think I'm *just* what you need."

His wording, or maybe the way he said it, had her stomach suddenly feeling like it was full of caged butterflies, flustering her. Almost immediately, he seemed to realize the other way his words could be taken and surprised her by flushing slightly. She hadn't even known vampires could blush. For the first time, Jaden looked away, finding something on the far wall worthy of glaring at.

Lyra tried to brush off his reaction. She didn't need this. Not now, not ever.

"My father," Lyra snapped out, fighting to regain her footing in the conversation, "has a lot of ideas I don't necessarily agree with. And if he thinks I need anything you can give me, I'd say he's lost it."

Jaden seemed more than ready to rise to the bait. It was a relief. Anger was far easier to deal with than...

whatever else was festering beneath the surface here. Maybe for both of them.

"If wanting you to live through this fight you've got coming is insane, then yes, he might be. And if you'd rather find a kickboxing class to take instead of having me as a teacher, then go for it. You might entertain everyone for a few minutes before your cousin takes you apart."

Lyra inhaled sharply, sucked in a bit of junk food with the air, and began coughing furiously. She managed to get out only a single word, but it was enough to convey the source of her shock.

"*Teacher?*"

She had to have misheard him. *Had to have.* Because there was no way in hell her father would ever have come up with such a crazy scheme. Lyra fought to regain control over her windpipe and registered that Jaden still looked very defensive. His next words confirmed that he was.

"You know, I get that it's unconventional, but choking to death over it still seems like an overreaction."

She finally got the coughing mostly under control. To fix what lingered, she popped the top of her soda. Lyra took a long swig, savoring the coolness running down her irritated throat, and then returned her attention to Jaden. Her voice sounded strained when she spoke, and it wasn't all from the coughing fit.

"You honestly expect me to believe that my father—a man who I have never heard say a good or even a neutral word about your kind—has decided you need to stick around to be some kind of vampire version of Mr. Miyagi?"

"He laid it out for me," Jaden said evenly, though his eyes burned blue. "He can't teach you."

"Won't teach me, is more like it," Lyra shot back. "Not him, not any of them. I mean, did he explain *why* he can't teach me?"

"He said it wouldn't do you any good," Jaden replied. "He thinks if you go in trying to do the same thing as the rest, you'll be knocked out pretty quickly."

Lyra rolled her eyes. "Yeah, well, he wouldn't know, since he's never even given me a chance to prove myself." She took another swig of the soda, knowing she shouldn't even be getting into this with Jaden. It was wolf business, *her* business, and he had no part in it. But except for Simon, she didn't really have anyone to unload on... and Simon, for all his kindness, wasn't exactly a neutral party. He wouldn't help her either.

As a reasonably neutral party, Jaden would do.

"Did you know there have only ever been three female Alphas in the entire history of werewolves? Three. That's pathetic. And those were some really unusual, really specific circumstances. We're years past women's suffrage and women's lib, but here, it's still whoever has the biggest muscles wins the day." She knew she was bitching, knew her voice was heating up, but Lyra couldn't help it. All this had been building for the longest time. And oddly enough, it seemed like Jaden was actually listening to her.

"At least if I'd been born into one of the other pack families I would have been able to make my own life. Leave if I wanted, mate with who I wanted, get a job, a house, a *life* of my own! But no. I'm Dorien Black's daughter, so here I am, living with Daddy at twenty-three, no job because no one here will hire me until I find a mate and quit drawing all sorts of strays into town, and locked out of what should be my birthright because I don't have the right plumbing.

Gods forbid they train a lowly female as a warrior. I could fight just as well as they can. It's asinine!"

To punctuate the end of her rant, she slammed her fist on the table and pulverized an unsuspecting Cheeto. Lyra heard the crunch, lifted her fist, and saw the mess. She sighed heavily.

"Damn it." She lifted her eyes back to Jaden's, feeling a little sheepish. Her nerves might be ragged at this point, her tolerance stretched to its limits, but she realized that ranting to a stranger was probably not the solution.

"Sorry. I get...um...wound up. It's been a little rough lately." He was watching her with the strangest expression, Lyra thought. Well, she'd wanted to get rid of him. Looking like an escaped mental patient was as good a method as any. Except that didn't seem to be the reason he was looking at her so closely. Lyra thought she saw... could she really see...sympathy?

"Don't be sorry. I agree."

"You—"

"No, I listened to you. Now it's your turn," Jaden said. Lyra had to marvel at his ability to change gears. Just minutes ago he'd been an uncomfortable vampire. Now he was all business.

"You heard me right. I agree with you. That is, I would agree under normal circumstances. But these aren't. According to your father, who is definitely desperate by the way, you've got less than a month to figure out how to overcome not only the bigger males in your pack, but also some hulking murderous cousin in a fight that is unlikely to be fair. Whether or not you'll be able to use what I can teach you, I think you should have been trained from the beginning just for practicality, but I'm not even going to touch the weird gender issues your kind has. The point is that as of now, you don't have time to learn to beat these wolves the way one of your males would, even if you could."

Lyra huffed out a surprised breath that was almost a laugh. "The conventional wisdom around here is that I couldn't. I'm too small and *female*." She knew she growled out the last word, but she couldn't help it. Her sex wouldn't have been an impediment to her if her interests had been different. That is, anything other than leading her pack. But in her case, her gender had been tossed at her as a backhanded insult for years.

It would have cowed a lot of women, Lyra knew, or at least sent them looking for something else to do. In her case, it had just made her mad. And even more determined.

Jaden's calm and slightly disdainful reaction to all this was what she would have expected from a vampire, but she found it strangely reassuring. She wasn't the only one who found the werewolves' system unfair, outdated, and flat-out stupid. It surprised her to find him, just like that night in Massachusetts, an ally.

Hell if she knew quite what to do with that knowledge though.

Jaden waved away her comment. "Size isn't everything. Talent is more important. But considering the constraints you've got on you now, it's going to take more than anything a wolf could teach you."

"And that's where you come in." Lyra shook her head disbelievingly and popped another Cheeto in her mouth. "This is insane. Seriously, seriously insane." She tilted her head at Jaden. "What, was my father that impressed with the way you kicked Simon's ass?"

Jaden nodded. "Guess so. It wasn't the reaction I was expecting either, but there you go."

Lyra sighed, tucking an errant curl behind her ear. She'd been impressed too. He moved with so much grace, so much power. Simon fought well for a wolf, but it was all claws and teeth and muscle with her kind. It worked... but watching Jaden fight was like watching the master of some deadly dance. It was kind of beautiful. And unnervingly sexy, Lyra realized, as the mere memory of Jaden leaping and slashing got her motor running all over again.

"He loves to watch a good fighter do his thing," she said, trying to get her mind back on more practical things. "Simon's going to want to kill you, though. That was ugly."

"For *him*, maybe." Jaden smiled, a sultry little lift of the lips that made his eyes glitter with humor. "He can try. He won't like what happens."

"You can't kill him. Or hurt him again."

The smile vanished as quickly as it had come. "Oh. I didn't realize you had a...boyfriend? Lover? That might make things more difficult. Especially if he's been lobbying to stand for you."

Lyra gave an impatient little growl. "Yes, he has, but not because he's any of those things. Simon is one of my closest friends, ever since we were kids. And if you don't like me jumping to conclusions about you, I suggest you give me the same courtesy."

Jaden shifted in his chair, looking disgruntled. "Oh," he said again.

Lyra rolled her eyes back into her head. "Yes, *oh*. And back on the topic before we got sidetracked by your weird ideas about my love life, what I was going to say is that while my father might have gotten some wild idea that you can teach me to fight dirty to win, you are both missing one very simple point."

"Which is?"

"I'm not a vamp. I'm a wolf."

Jaden angled his head at her. "This is . . . not news."

Lyra threw her hands up, narrowly missing knocking the bag of junk food to the floor. "But it's relevant! I can't move like you. I don't have all the different funky abilities that your kind has. I can only work with what I have. And that is *very* different from what you started with."

"You've got a point," Jaden agreed. "But I took out Mark and then Simon without a lot of effort, and using very little of the ability I have at my disposal. Trust me." He leaned forward, and Lyra was struck again by his natural intensity, an interesting contrast to the glimmers of humor, and even of kindness, that she'd now seen beneath. Interesting, puzzling, and slightly unwelcome. She wasn't big on surprises.

"I'm not saying I can make sure you win, Lyra. But I can teach you to compensate for your smaller size, and to attack in ways the others won't expect. You've got plenty of natural grace and strength. There are more effective ways for you to use it than throwing yourself at another beast and biting and slashing away."

"How would you know? You haven't seen me fight."

"I—can tell." Blushing again, Lyra noted. It was probably wrong to be entertained by this reaction, but she couldn't help herself. It was cute. Dangerously cute.

"It's the way you move," Jaden said. "I can just tell. A couple hundred years of scrapping will give you a pretty good eye, you know."

"Uh-huh." Lyra played it off like she didn't care, but

knowing that he'd been watching her move—closely watching her—had her belly immediately tangled up in knots again. The memory of his hands on her, of the heat between them, tried to surface. Lyra pushed it away with all the force she could muster. Even if she was willing to consider this insanity, which was still a big "if," she needed to consider the effect Jaden had on her. This feeling wasn't healthy, it couldn't go anywhere, and if anyone found out about it, she'd be run out of town with her tail between her legs. So the question was not only whether she could handle training with a vamp, but whether she could handle that much alone time with this *particular* vamp.

It bothered her that she really didn't know.

"So, what, you're going to just hang out and teach me how to fight like a vampire? That's the whole plan?"

"Basically, yeah." He moved his head just a little, and a lock of his hair slipped out from behind his ear and swung into his face. He didn't bother to put it back, but Lyra's fingers itched to. She lifted a hand to toy with a curl that had escaped her bun instead.

"And you're going to hide out . . ."

"In your basement. Dorien said he'd figure out some excuse for my being here, though, so it's not exactly hiding out."

Lyra laughed then, a real laugh, and the loud and lusty roll of it seemed to surprise Jaden. But the entire situation, so completely strange and ridiculous, struck her all at once. He raised an eyebrow while he watched her, but he didn't seem offended, just curious.

She shook her head, amused all over again at how confident he was in his ability to stay alive for any length of time in a town full of werewolves.

"You're a cocky bastard, aren't you?"

"I may have heard that a time or two," he replied. "Why?"

"You realize that people around here are going to get one whiff of you, smell vamp and cat, and go ballistic, right? And you don't see that as a problem?"

"You haven't gone ballistic, and you've been sitting here a while. Nor have you ever grown fangs and chased me around," he pointed out. The thought of it made her grin despite the fact that she didn't think he grasped the seriousness of his situation.

"Yeah, well, I guess I'm used to your particular stink by now. And I love my pack, but not everyone here is a model of self-restraint."

Jaden shrugged. "Dorien assured me he would work something out. Since I would assume he's remained Alpha for so long for a reason, I'm giving him the benefit of the doubt."

She looked at him, sitting there so calm and collected, and realized two things: one, Jaden didn't understand a damned thing about werewolves, and two, he was completely serious about helping her win her rightful position in the pack. The first was strangely charming, even if it was probably going to get him killed. The second was a puzzle she couldn't begin to figure out, and that bothered her. She was pretty good at sizing people up. But Jaden was completely outside her realm of experience. Since he was determined that a vampire walking around in the heart of the Pack of the Thorn was totally hunky-dory, Lyra asked him the only question she really had remaining.

"Why?"

"Why what?"

She narrowed her eyes at the guarded expression that returned so quickly. "Why any of this? Why show up with my family's talisman? Why stick around to help me? I'm assuming Dad is paying you, but it wouldn't be anything that would rock your world. You've got to have better things to do than get involved in werewolf politics, and it's not like you and I hit it off right off the bat or anything. I just...don't get it."

Jaden's forehead creased with a small frown. Lyra toyed with her snack, turning her fingers orange while she poked at it. Her appetite had evaporated, an unusual occurrence. But it suddenly seemed very important to understand exactly what Jaden was doing here. Even if she had a suspicion that there were a lot of things about him she would never understand.

Finally, he said, "I'm well over two hundred years old, Lyra. For most of it, I had to do as I was told instead of doing things that interested me. But things are different now, and this interests me. I don't know why. Does it matter? You'll have my help if you want it, regardless."

"And what if I don't?"

"Then I'll go find something else to do," Jaden replied. The words were casual, but he looked deadly serious. Lyra watched him, seeing the tension in the line of his shoulders, the set of his jaw. For whatever reason, it seemed he really wanted to be here. To be with her, in some capacity. Despite her own reaction to him, she could hardly fathom why.

"So what's it going to be?" Jaden asked softly. "I don't think Dorien was really listening when I told him this was up to you, but obviously it is. This is your fight, your decision. I can be out of here, and out of town, before he gets back if you'd rather. And if you want me to stay, we can get started as soon as we have a safe place to work."

Lyra shifted uncomfortably, busying herself rolling up and clipping the top of the Cheetos bag so she didn't have to look at him. She *hated* being put on the spot, and this was an awfully big deal. Too big to make a snap decision about. Apart from that, the fact that she couldn't get a good read on Jaden's motivations, and that she might not ever, was tough to swallow. She knew a little about his bloodline—or at least, the bloodline he'd been sired into before he'd hooked up with the Lilim. But all that dynastic crap, with the aristocracy and the weird medieval way the vamps governed their own, was not her world and not her concern.

Jaden was a big unknown. And she wasn't sure she was in a position to be taking a risk with him. Then again… she wasn't sure she could afford to refuse.

Frustrated, and not really thinking about what she was doing, Lyra stuck a finger in her mouth to suck off a last bit of cheese. After a moment she realized that Jaden's attention had become completely fixed on her mouth. His expression, in the instant before his eyes met hers, was one that Lyra didn't think she would ever forget. He looked hungry in a way she'd never experienced, plagued by a longing so deep that it was unlikely anything could ever assuage it.

In that instant, he looked every bit the vampire: ancient, and lost, and nearly consumed by need.

Then he lifted his gaze to meet hers, and Lyra felt the hot punch of all that fathomless hunger blow right through her. He might be a vampire, she realized, but the animal in her responded frighteningly well to the animal in him. It was all she could do not to leap across the table, wrap her legs around him, and sink her teeth in.

She stiffened, folded her fingers together on the table, and crossed her legs. Jaden, too, seemed to withdraw a little. He leaned back in his chair, crossed his arms over his chest, and looked away as though bored, as though nothing had just passed between them.

Lyra realized he didn't want this either. It was a relief, in a way. But it was also no guarantee he would continue to behave himself. Or that she would.

Finally, she gave the only answer possible.

"It's late," she said. "I'm wiped, and this is a lot to take in. So why don't we do this: stick around for now. We'll give it a shot. If the whole idea crashes and burns, you go, and I come up with something else. No hard feelings."

Slowly, Jaden nodded. "Okay. Sounds reasonable."

"Good," Lyra said, trying to sound relaxed when she was anything but. She needed to get some air and some space, and wished she could get out for a four-legged run beneath the waning moon. But even that small pleasure had been denied her for some time. Too dangerous. Even here.

All she could do was head for another part of the house. It would have to be enough. And hopefully, a good night's sleep would provide her with perspective she currently lacked.

"Look, I need to, um, do a couple things before I hit the sack, and I have no idea when my father will show back up." She tried for a smile. "He's probably hiding from me. Anyway, I'm usually pretty nocturnal, but it's been kind of a rough week, so…" She trailed off, hoping he'd get the hint.

"Not a problem. I don't need a babysitter," Jaden said easily. "I'll find something to do until Dorien gets back. You go ahead."

Relief, and a desire to run from the room now that she'd been let off the hook, had Lyra rising too quickly. She didn't register that Jaden had risen with her until it was too late and she'd walked right into him. Which, she realized later, had almost certainly been by design.

"Oh, sorry," she blurted, her hands coming up instinctively to regain her balance. And of course she gripped the nearest available thing: him. She felt his hands at her waist, felt the taut muscle beneath her own hands. And whether it was her weariness that had shut her usual defenses down or something more subversive, Lyra found herself melting into him, against him, allowing herself just a few seconds of the wonderful sensation of simply being held.

She heard him breathe in, felt his arms go around her to hold her up, hold her against him. Lyra let herself linger, even though she knew it was dangerous. She sensed that Jaden felt it, too, this invisible thread that seemed determined to pull them together. She allowed herself only a moment to savor the way her body fit so perfectly against his, the feel of his breath on her skin.

Then she drew back and stood on her own two feet, trying to ignore the waves of longing and regret that swept over her the instant their connection was broken. It was a test, she told herself. To see whether she could handle being so close to Jaden without throwing herself at him or doing something stupid. And she'd passed, mostly.

But it was hard to feel much triumph when she looked at Jaden and saw the raw desire reflected back at her.

"Good night, Lyra," he said softly, his voice like darkest silk.

"Good night," she replied. And more shaken than she could have imagined, Lyra did the only thing she knew was safe, though it was the last thing she wanted. On unsteady legs, she turned and walked away.

And wondered whether it would be so easy the next time.

chapter EIGHT

H<small>E SLEPT LIKE THE DEAD</small> because he had no choice, but Jaden was haunted by dreams. He awoke agitated and disoriented, eyes darting around unfamiliar surroundings as he sat up with a jolt. He saw ugly wood paneling, a pool table, an older TV. Small windows that had had thick cloth tacked over them to keep out the light. A look down told him he'd been sleeping on an old brown plaid couch, comfortably sprung and made up with sheets, blankets, and a pillow.

Jaden had woken up in so many odd places during his lifetimes that panicking didn't even occur to him. Instead, he took a deep breath, closed his eyes, and collected thoughts that were always muddled upon waking at sundown. In that self-imposed darkness, he saw Lyra, her big golden eyes glowing softly as she looked up at him while he held her in his arms.

Then he remembered.

"Shit." Jaden groaned, drew his knees into his chest,

and dug his hands into his hair. All around him her scent rose, warm and spicy and singularly Lyra. The whole house was suffused with it. And he would be here, marinating in it, driving himself completely insane for a few more weeks.

Brilliant.

This had all seemed like a great idea last night. Amazing what a little sleep would do for perspective. Still, he was in it now, right up to his neck.

With a low groan, Jaden swung his feet onto the floor, gave his head a sleepy scratch, and yawned. He shoved the blankets aside and stood to stretch, exhaling with pleasure as his body awakened. The cool air of the basement swirled around his naked torso, over legs that were bare but for a pair of low-slung boxers.

He seemed to remember Dorien showing him a bathroom down here with a shower. Pouring water on his head for a while sounded like a great idea, Jaden decided. He turned his head to look around, knowing he'd brought in the duffel bag he always packed and carried with him in case of an extended stay anywhere.

Her voice, low and sultry, stopped him in his tracks.

"Hey, I brought you—oh, sorry."

Jaden turned to find Lyra, just three steps above the bottom of the stairs, staring at him wide-eyed in utter mortification. There was a small basket of toiletries dangling from one hand. She lifted it a little, almost apologetically.

"Brought some…um…bathroom stuff. For you. You're not dressed. Yeah, I'll go."

It struck Jaden as funny that all it took to embarrass the seemingly un-embarrassable Lyra Black was to strip down to your skivvies. She turned to flee, but he had no intention of letting her. The thought of tormenting her was way too entertaining.

"No, hang on, I can use all that," he said, walking very deliberately over and extending his hand. Intense color flooded her cheeks, and he didn't miss the way her eyes swept over every inch of him before they moved to the far wall.

She wanted him. He'd finally been sure of it when she'd fallen into his arms last night. Or rather, when she'd let herself fall into his arms. He'd felt the brief instant when she let go, felt the way her body responded to his. And if he'd needed more proof, the way she'd hightailed it out of the kitchen would have been more than enough.

Ordinarily, that knowledge would have been sufficient for him to make a move on her. He'd be rusty, but Jaden was pretty sure he could manage a seduction without too much trouble. Going there with Lyra, however, was a far more complicated matter. What she was…what she wanted to be…and that was to say nothing of the fact that her father would happily dismember him if he so much as touched her.

He knew it was better to keep this whole operation platonic. But that didn't mean he couldn't enjoy the simple things…like her reaction to finding him mostly undressed.

Jaden took the little basket by the handle and perused the contents, curious. Someone had been shopping—everything, including the basket, was new. He looked up at her, though she was still very pointedly not looking at him.

"You brought me dental floss."

Her eyes slid to meet his. "Yeah. And?"

"You brought me aftershave."

"I thought maybe you used it. Do vamps not grow facial hair? There's a razor in there too. Are you going to give me a laundry list of the stuff I bought? Jesus. I'm leaving now."

He grinned. He couldn't help it. He'd had no idea Lyra would be so appealing when she was caught off guard like this.

"Thanks. The poofy thing to go with the body wash is a little girly, but I'll live with it."

"Or I can give you some other ideas about where to shove it," grumbled Lyra. "You're welcome. Just...do what you have to do and come upstairs. It's been a long day already, so don't take forever."

"I won't. I don't know what your thoughts were, but I'd like to have a look at the area where you'll have the Proving before we do anything. You can give me an idea of how it works, and we'll go from there."

"Works for me. I'll be upstairs waiting." She turned to go, but Jaden couldn't resist one last poke.

"Lyra?"

She stopped, stiffened, and didn't turn around. Her voice sounded strained. "What?"

"Why was it a long day? Everything all right?"

She gave a short, humorless little laugh. "Oh sure. The whole pack knows I'm living with our very first vampire ambassador, and I spent the afternoon shopping and getting meowed at. Do days *get* any better than that?"

Without another word, she stomped up the stairs, and Jaden didn't have the heart to make her come back. She'd gotten herself into this mess, certainly...but even for as short a time as he'd known her, he was sure she had good reasons. And had she said "vampire ambassador"?

Jaden shook his head and carried the things she had bought for him into the bathroom, stupidly pleased that she'd taken the trouble. When was the last time a woman had bought him anything? Of course, this was just tooth-paste and shampoo, he reminded himself. Which Lyra would be quick to reiterate if he brought it up again. But once in the little bathroom, as Jaden ran the water and picked up the shampoo from the basket, he saw there was something he'd missed. It was just a small thing, a little sample of what he knew was expensive cologne, hooked into a paper card.

Intrigued, he removed the plastic tube, pulled the stop-per, and sniffed. It was subtle, but warm...exactly some-thing he would have chosen. And something he would use, as she'd taken the trouble to get it for him. He knew she would brush it off when he thanked her...but he was going to thank her anyway. In her own way, Lyra was try-ing to make him feel at home. Him, with his perpetual duffel bag, always ready to take off at a moment's notice.

The sweetness of her small gesture made him realize how very long he'd been running. How long it had been since he'd had a real place for his things, and things for a place, anywhere.

He didn't want to feel touched, but that's exactly what he was feeling. More when the realization hit him that he'd been turned around when Lyra had come downstairs: she'd seen his bare back, which meant she'd seen his whip scars. And he'd seen no evidence of it, no disgust, no judgment, and most of all, no pity when he'd turned to look at her.

Unexpected. Like everything else about the woman.

Jaden sighed and slid out of his boxers, then got into

the shower and closed the curtain. For a sharp-tongued, reasonably rude little she-wolf, Lyra seemed to have a disturbing number of attractive qualities. And that was before he took into account how she looked in those jeans she was wearing tonight.

All he could do was hope she kept the rest of her better nature under wraps so he could concentrate on teaching—instead of further unwrapping. He'd already decided not to pursue the attraction. It was tantalizing, but pointless. When this was over, he'd go back to drinking blood in Tipton, she'd go back to being an overgrown dog in her spare time, and that would be that. Maybe he'd ask after that trio of Cait Sith Ty had mentioned, Jaden decided. Which reminded him...he needed to send Ty a quick text to check in, since he had no doubt there was at least one message waiting for him already. And after that, the phone was getting turned off and stuffed in the bottom of his duffel bag for the duration of his stay here. They knew where he was. He wasn't a child who needed looking after.

And really, the less anyone back in Tipton knew about what he'd gotten up to out here, the better.

So thinking, Jaden tried to focus on the present, on the bloody Proving and where he should even begin with teaching Lyra.

But in the end, he still soaked his head.

He'd been tortured.

She'd tried like hell to get the image of Jaden's back out of her head all evening, but so far, no luck. It had stunned her. And then it had taken every ounce of her willpower not to ask him about it. Jaden seemed like a fairly private person. She doubted he'd open right up if she decided to push "Hey, who whipped you so badly you couldn't heal?" as the question of the evening.

Thinking of a vampire as oppressed was just strange, completely flipped from what she'd been raised with. But then, she wasn't shocked either. Lyra had spent a little time around vamps when she felt like she needed to blow Silver Falls for a while, much to her father's dismay. Not that any vampires had exactly wanted her around, but slinking into a "forbidden" city for shopping, fun, and cute guys who weren't any weirder at the full moon than they were any other time was an excellent way to take a break from the pressure and blow off a little steam. In her travels, she'd definitely noted that there was a large under-class of bloodsuckers. And the ones they called "high-bloods," though less numerous, were mostly not very sweet. No one wanted a wolf around... but it was usually only the highbloods you had to actively watch out for.

Mean suckers.

Lyra glanced over at Jaden when she pulled into a park-ing place and killed the engine of her little red pickup. He seemed relaxed enough. For him. Of course, he'd found plenty to occupy his attention out the window, so it wasn't that easy to tell.

"Okay, here we are." She glanced around the parking lot, which sat some distance from where the grass began and rolled off into the ever-encroaching trees. It was empty—but that didn't mean anything. They'd need to watch it.

"Good," he replied. "Let's have a look." And before she could warn him—again—about the fact that there might be other wolves hanging around here, he was out of the car and striding toward the green area as though he owned the place. Lyra pursed her lips, annoyed, but she did allow herself a moment, just one, to admire the way he moved. Wolves were built for power.

Jaden was built for grace and speed. And . . . other things.

She groaned and got out of the car, too, anxious to get as far away from these recurring thoughts as possible. If things went well, she'd be sparring with him before long. She needed to get in the mind-set of *not* wanting his hands on her body.

Lyra took the time Jaden hadn't, scenting the air, listening for the faintest sound of voices, or even paws treading softly. When she caught up to him, he was standing quietly, seeming to drink everything in. She figured it was worth a few quiet minutes to see if he came up with some miraculous insight she hadn't about this place, so she backed off. She walked a few paces away, tipped her head back, and enjoyed the stars dotting the night sky.

"So werewolves make their most important leadership decisions at . . . a playground."

He spoke as softly as he always did, but his voice carried in the still air. Lyra looked sharply at him, arms crossed over her chest to ward off the rapidly cooling temperature. She loved it up here, but man, she really wished summer would consider coming early once in a while instead of leaving winter and spring to play tug-of-war right up until June.

"It's not a playground. Grant Park is a large open space, genius," Lyra replied. "Live with it."

His mouth curved just a little with the humor Lyra was beginning to understand always lived just beneath the surface, even if he was good at hiding it.

"So where does everyone sit? On the jungle gym? Or maybe the swings. Or the bouncy pony."

Lyra gritted her teeth, and it took considerable effort to unclench them enough to respond. Jaden's cute almost-smile had turned into a cocky vamp smirk. She knew that look, the patented "Wolves are dumb, yuk yuk yuk" look she'd seen on plenty of his kind. It made her want to bite him—and not in a way he'd enjoy. Since she couldn't do that, she went with sarcasm.

"There's also a gazebo. And trees. And probably a Port-o-San somewhere, too, which I'm sure you'll find hysterical since you haven't mentally progressed since age five. Regardless, this is the place. Can we move on?"

That sexy little smile, Lyra decided, was awfully feline.

"Sure."

"Jackass," she muttered under her breath, but loud enough for him to catch it. It was at that moment, watching Jaden as he craned his neck and took another look around, that Lyra realized something strange: she was actually enjoying herself.

Lyra pretended to scuff at something interesting on the ground while looking at Jaden through half-lowered lashes. He didn't need to know how closely she was watching him. It was just that his reactions to everything out here were so interesting, she thought. He acted like all this was a novelty: parks, trees, even the night sky, which she was pretty sure Silver Falls didn't have a monopoly on. He'd even made some random comment about her father's flower beds on the way over. Nothing snarky, just interested . . . though Lyra imagined Jaden's reaction to the news that her father actually owned a garden center would be a little more cringe-worthy.

That information could remain under wraps for a while.

Lyra waited for him to say something, but when all he did was slowly wander around with wide eyes, she gave up.

"Jaden, seriously. They're trees. Thrillsville. Unless they have some bearing on my training as a vampire ninja, you might want to refocus."

Lyra found she actually looked forward to whatever biting response he would come up with. She didn't know many people who would engage her in verbal warfare except for Simon, and even he got tired of her sometimes. But when Jaden turned his head to look at her, she didn't get what she was hoping for. Instead, his expression was so full of honest wonderment that Lyra felt a suspicious fluttering in the pit of her stomach.

Butterflies, she thought, frustrated that she couldn't just banish them. Between this and the weirdness in the kitchen, she was starting to worry this was going to be a trend.

"Sorry, got a little sidetracked," he said, then grinned. It lit up his entire face, and what was already darkly compelling became completely enchanting.

"I hadn't realized how long I'd been away from places like this," he added.

Lyra's lips twitched. "Playgrounds? You want me to push you on the swing set?"

Jaden chuckled, a soft, warm sound that was completely at odds with everything Lyra associated with vampires. But then so far, so was Jaden.

"No," he said. "I'd just forgotten how nice it is not to be closed in. Cities can get claustrophobic. I mean, I'm used to it now, but it was hard at first. Before, I was just a—"

He stopped short, shook his head with a rueful smile. Lyra, her curiosity piqued, hoped he would finish. Why had it been hard at first? Where was he from? Who had he been? Not that it mattered, she told herself. But it was easy to forget that a couple hundred years ago, Jaden had been fully human, no doubt with a very different life planned than the one he had now.

"You were a country boy?" she asked. He hesitated, looking uncertain, but then nodded.

"Somerset. I'd never even been to London. Now, though...I've been everywhere." He shoved his hands in his jacket pockets and hunched slightly, what Lyra was already coming to recognize as his defensive position. He didn't seem to want to go into it. Maybe she wouldn't, either, Lyra thought, if she'd lost everything and had to start from scratch.

Soothing people was not a natural ability of hers. But Lyra found herself trying to put Jaden back at ease even before she really realized what she was doing.

"Well, this isn't the English countryside, but it's got its points. I wouldn't want to be anywhere but here," she said.

A ghost of a smile touched his lips then, so different from the irreverent grin he'd worn only minutes ago. He was a moody creature, Lyra decided. One minute teasing, the next wistful. He kept surprising her.

Yet another thing she liked when she shouldn't.

"I know the feeling," Jaden said simply, and then shifted gears completely. The subject of his origins seemed to be closed.

"All right. Why don't you start by explaining this mystical process to me so I can understand what, exactly, the Proving is about."

Lyra nodded, trying to be grateful that things had veered away from the personal and back to the professional ... if that's what this operation was.

"Okay. Walk with me." She closed the distance between them with a few steps, and the two of them made their way across the rolling landscape of the park. The young green of the trees and grass was vibrant even in the scattered light of the wrought-iron lampposts dotting the scenery. The air smelled of damp, rich earth and spring.

She pointed off to her right, where the ground sloped down into a long, flat area. White soccer goals rose, ghostly, from the ground. "There's the soccer field. We don't use it for the Full Moon Feast every month, since it would make things ... a little obvious. But it's always been used for Provings."

Jaden snorted. "Which isn't obvious at all. What do you plan to do with all the humans in town when all this is going on? Lock them in their closets?"

It was Lyra's turn to chuckle. "There *aren't* any humans in town, Jaden. When wolves set up shop, we do it right. Plus they can sense us. Subconsciously, I guess. But humanity's survival instinct seems to kick in pretty well when it comes to *not* moving into a town full of their natural predators. Hunting them may be outlawed now, but it wasn't always that way ... and something in them remembers."

The smile faded from her face as she thought of her cousin and his sycophants in the pack, wolves who wanted to turn the clock backward a few hundred years. He'd never said he wanted to hunt humans, of course ... that would be the kiss of death for his aspirations no matter how strong he was ... but his attitude about them was just short of disgusting.

The reign of Eric Black wouldn't exactly be a golden age if he managed to get what he wanted.

Troubled, Lyra tried to shake it off and continue. "Anyway, there's a huge farm field on the other side of town that works better for the full moon celebrations, and it's a much better place to do the bonfire. Here, the layout of the woods is better suited to the Proving. We're only a couple of miles from the falls too."

"Which is significant because..."

"Because that's where my father will place the talisman that will eventually belong to the next Alpha. See," Lyra explained, "it's actually very simple. All of us run into the woods, race to the falls, and try to sniff out the talisman. And then someone, eventually, will have to bring it back out. On two legs or four, doesn't matter. Anything goes."

"Ah," Jaden said, and Lyra didn't like the cast of doubt to his expression. "So what you're telling me is this is basically a free-for-all until someone delivers the talisman to your father."

She shifted her weight from foot to foot. "Well. Yes. I did tell you this was about strength, speed...and cleverness, supposedly, though I don't think that usually comes much into play." She laughed, but it sounded a little desperate. None of this had sounded quite so hopeless when she'd talked about it with her father and Simon. But she hadn't had to explain it...maybe that was the difference. She hadn't had to say it out loud and confront just how little chance she had of even surviving if she saw the matter through.

His eyes drifted back to the dark of the woods. "You, in there, with a bunch of enormous male werewolves ready to kill one another for the prize? Yes, Lyra, getting out alive is going to require some cleverness on your part. Being able to fight, sure, that'll come in handy if you end up one on one, but the rest…" He trailed off, muttering to himself, and wandered away from her in the direction of the woods. Watching his retreating back, Lyra let him go and hoped he was formulating some kind of strategy.

If there was even a plausible one to be had.

Doubt flooded her, as it did sometimes when she was alone. The pack wanted to force a destiny on her. But Lyra knew that if she accepted that fate she would die just as surely as she would if she failed at the Proving. It would just be on the inside, where no one could see.

So she would take a stand and make her own destiny. No mate to stand for her, in front of her, and hold her back. If she was fortunate enough to lead the pack she loved, she would make it there on her own merit…and there would be no questions about her fitness for the job.

"I can handle this," Lyra said quietly, watching Jaden move deeper into the darkness, away from her. "I can handle anything."

That was when she saw it, a fast-moving shadow flying over the ground toward Jaden, whose back was turned. It passed several feet from her, and the breeze it kicked up from its rapid movement carried with it the scent of ancient death—the scent of vampire. Lyra reacted instinctively. There was no thought as she sprang forward, her body shifting in midair to become the sleek, muscular form of the wolf. When her paws hit the ground, she leaped again, pushing forward with all her might to try to reach Jaden before this interloper did.

Though what followed happened in seconds, in her

memory Lyra would always see everything in slow motion: The way the shadow finally began to look like a man when it reached Jaden, the way Jaden turned, ready to fight, his coat flying around him and his eyes ablaze with unholy fire. She saw the blood burst from Jaden's chest, saw the shock and fury on his face, and then she slammed into the attacking vampire full force. They rolled together, Lyra snarling and snapping, looking for purchase with her teeth and claws.

She bit down hard on a fleshy upper arm, heard a banshee-like wail of pain just as a foul taste flooded her mouth. The vampire ripped the arm away and fled with a feral hiss, tossing Lyra aside as though she weighed nothing. She stayed loose, allowing herself to fall, to roll harmlessly when she hit the ground. Still, she was thrown with enough force to knock the wind out of her.

It took a few precious seconds for her to drag in a breath, longer to stagger to her feet and make sure that the new vampire was gone. But he was...though she could smell him on the light breeze, lingering. Fear, anger— retreat. Lyra showed her teeth in the direction it had gone, staking her claim on this territory—this man.

Then she was just a woman again, stumbling in her haste to get to Jaden. She found him lying on the ground, overly pale, spidery lashes twined shut. He wore a faded royal blue T-shirt beneath his coat, and she saw it was soaked with dark blood that spread out from a puncture wound in his chest like some malignant bloom. He was splayed at an odd angle, head turned to one side.

She switched gears from fury to worry almost instantly, falling to her knees beside him.

"Come on, Jaden," she breathed. "You can't be dead.

Your head's still attached, you can't be dead." But she remembered the sight of those vicious scars across his back. You weren't supposed to be able to scar a vampire, and yet someone had figured out how to do that. Who was to say that his torturers hadn't found a way to kill a vampire without separating the head from the body or burning him to a crisp in the sun?

Then he inhaled, a long, shuddering gasp like a man surfacing from the depths. She knew she shouldn't feel the relief that crashed through her system, so strong it would have taken her to her knees if she hadn't already been on them. But then, all of her reactions seemed outsized when it came to him.

Lyra realized now that she wasn't the only one whose life was on the line. And that was the last thing she'd expected to find in common with him. But she was beginning to see that nothing about Jaden was as it seemed. So she gave up thinking for the time being and simply went with what she felt. Lyra put her hands on his chest to find that amazingly slow vampire's pulse, and she waited for him to open his eyes and tell her he was all right.

chapter NINE

T HERE WERE WORSE THINGS than waking up with a beautiful woman's hands on you.

He surfaced, groggy but thankfully very much alive, and opened his eyes to see Lyra hovering over him. Her curls tumbled around her face, and even through his haze Jaden was struck by the concern in her bright golden eyes, twin sparks in the darkness. Her hands moved tentatively over his chest, searching for a wound he knew was no longer there.

He had no intention of stopping her examination though.

"Jaden," she said, her voice betraying her relief. "Are you all right? What *was* that?"

"Another vampire. But I don't think that's what you mean, is it?" His voice sounded too quiet, too shaken to his own ears. He didn't want her to know how the encounter had rattled him. It had to be the Ptolemy—had to be. The speed of the attack alone was a dead giveaway. How had they tracked him here? Was killing him, a nobody any way you looked at it no matter what mark he wore, *really* so important?

For once, Lyra didn't have a snide comeback. It was a shock to realize she was just as shaken as he was.

"You had a hole. Like halfway through your chest," she said, her hands continuing to roam and press and stroke. He didn't think she even knew she was doing it.

"I thought it was your heart. I mean, I know the whole stake through the heart thing isn't supposed to be true, but—"

"It's not," he said gently, catching her hands with his. He held them against his chest, letting her feel the slow and steady beat of the heart that had been keeping this rhythm for centuries. His hands warmed quickly to hers, and he felt another curl of unexpected pleasure when Lyra made no move to pull away from him.

"A stake through the heart wouldn't kill me," Jaden explained. "But it's a good way to incapacitate someone so you can finish the job the right way." He tried for a smile, but it felt tight and put on. "He missed, thanks to you. I guess we're even now."

If she hadn't been there, if her sudden transformation and attack hadn't startled his would-be assassin, Jaden knew he wouldn't still have his head attached to his shoulders. Lyra Black had saved his life. It was a difficult thing to wrap his mind around, but he knew it was something he'd be grappling with as the shock receded.

And she looked so bloody concerned about him. He wanted it—and he was afraid to want it. To want *her.* He gave a damn about very few people. Every single one he cared about had put him through hell once or twice by trying to get him- or herself killed, so he was glad it was a small group. But he had never expected to add Lyra to it. This was just supposed to be a one-off for him, a strange little physical fascination that burned itself out for him before too long.

With his hands tangled with hers, her breath warming his face, Jaden realized he'd been very, very wrong.

"I wasn't going to let some outside vamp come in here and take you down," Lyra said, looking flustered at his thanks. "While you're here, you're under pack protection. Which means no one kicks your ass, or stabs you with pointed sticks, but me."

She was coming around, he saw, and this time his smile was genuine. He'd caught enough tantalizing glimpses of what was beneath the tough, beautiful shell she wore to know there was a softer heart there than she let on. Jaden knew she would move soon, pull her hands away and break contact, ending the moment. He rubbed his thumb over her knuckles, willing her to stay. Her expression softened, changed.

Jaden slowly sat up, her hands still in his. He disentangled one hand, brushed his fingers down the silken softness of her cheek. She went very still but made no move to push him away. Instead, her eyes simply stayed locked with his, her expression open, waiting—longing. Before he could dwell on how many ways he might regret doing it, Jaden slid his hand into her hair and pulled her mouth to his.

She leaned in and met him halfway.

Her lips were soft, so incredibly soft. Jaden kept the pressure light, lingering against her mouth, savoring this first small taste of her. He heard her soft, startled intake of breath at the initial contact. For a moment, he thought she might shove him away, or slap him, or bite...and she would have been justified in any of those reactions. She wasn't his. He was taking advantage. He was taking an enormous chance.

Then he felt what she must have felt—hot sparks of pleasure where their lips touched that quickly spread to the rest of his body. It might have startled him if he'd been able to focus on anything but that incredible sensation. Jaden had never felt anything like it.

Lyra's arms slid up and around his neck, and her body curved into him, melting against him just as her mouth did. Her lips parted, her tongue flickered out to give his a tentative brush. The slow burn between them ignited with a wave of hot need that rolled through him like a summer storm. Jaden heard himself make a sound, some soft, longing sound that he knew gave away far too much of what he was feeling, what he wanted of her.

She seemed to know, to understand. They fell into one another at the same time.

Lyra's hand fisted in his shirt as the kiss began to turn hotter, hungrier. The initial sweetness of the moment vanished in the face of a desire that had been simmering beneath the surface ever since Jaden had first set eyes on her. When he felt her pushing him back to the ground, he allowed it, pulling her with him and then rolling her so that she was the one on her back. Jaden partially covered her, his weight on one hip, savoring the feeling of finally having her beneath him. Lyra didn't seem to mind: her kisses became insistent nips and licks while her hands roamed over his shirt, then slipped under it, seeking out bare skin. The muscles of his stomach jumped and twitched at the light glide of her fingers.

Jaden let out a shuddering breath. He cupped one small, perfect breast through her shirt, thumbing the taut pebble of her nipple. He was rewarded with an approving moan. Her hands grew more demanding, as did her mouth. Jaden was happy to urge her on, filling his hands with her, drawing out the wild thing that was the natural essence of her being.

Letting his own beast surface in response.

So this is what it's like with a wolf, he thought dazedly. *The vamps have been missing out…*

A thin sheen of perspiration began to appear on his normally cool skin. Lyra was making him hot, hotter than he ever remembered being. His heart picked up the rhythm of hers as they fumbled together on the ground in an eager tangle of hands and mouths and teeth. He could think of nothing but getting closer to her, of lying with her in the grass, skin to skin. It wasn't until Jaden moved to settle himself fully between her legs, throbbing hard and hot against the very center of her, that he realized how perilously close he was to embarrassing himself the way he hadn't since he was a young and awkward mortal. He pressed into her, a gentle, teasing thrust, and groaned. The sensation made his head swim. Her accompanying gasp only intensified the sensation.

He could imagine how she would look, spread beneath him, her skin tawny in the moonlight. How she would feel, so slick, so ready for him to move within her…

Lyra's fingers slipped beneath the waist of his jeans, seeking out the hottest part of him. His eyes slipped shut. Her fingers closed around him.

"Lyra," he whispered.

"Lyra!"

The unfamiliar voice sliced through the air, freezing the two of them in place. For a moment, neither of them moved, waiting to see if the disembodied voice was real or simply some kind of warning from whatever powers lurked behind the immortal veil, informing the two of them that the various vampire and werewolf deities did not find their performance amusing.

"Lyra!"

The second time, there was no question the voice belonged to a real person, and getting closer. Jaden opened his eyes to see the raw passion on Lyra's face vanish in favor of confusion and embarrassment. Her hand was quickly withdrawn, which sadly did nothing to quell his very obvious arousal. Jaden struggled to find something, anything to say that might bring back some of the heat she'd just allowed herself to feel for him. His entire body felt kissed by the sun.

Don't be ashamed of it, he willed her. Just don't be ashamed of me, of this...

"I...Jaden, that's Simon...crap, we need to...can you...?" She spoke breathlessly, wiggling a little to try to get him off her. Jaden had to grit his teeth to grant her fragmented request, since her wiggling had the opposite effect of what she'd intended. He managed to shift his weight, sliding off her to rest on one hip on the ground. Lyra slid up to a sitting position, her knees tucked close to her chest. He noted how quickly she scooted away from him, how she angled her body toward the approaching Simon instead of him.

He knew, on a rational level, they'd let it go too far. But he wasn't interested in rational right now. Not with his body screaming they hadn't gone nearly far enough.

Jealousy was quick to move in. And the young wolf now running toward them was a perfect target.

Simon's face was dark with concern and suspicion when he reached them, and when he spoke, it had the slightly breathless quality that indicated he'd come to find them in a hurry. Jaden watched the wolf's sharp gaze take in the picture he and Lyra presented, on the ground together in the dark and fairly rumpled besides. It was hard to suppress a smug smile when he saw the pieces click together.

"Well. I guess I don't need to ask if everything's all right out here," Simon said.

Out of the corner of his eye, Jaden saw Lyra flush. Fortunately, he had no similar shame to get in his way.

"No," Jaden said, rising to a sitting position from where he'd been resting on one arm. "You don't."

"We were…I was just…Jaden had some trouble," Lyra said, rushing out the words so that she sounded even guiltier. It didn't bother Jaden a bit, and he enjoyed watching Simon's expression darken even further.

"Uh-huh. So you were playing doctor. Got it."

Simon's tone was so dry that a single laugh escaped Jaden before he could swallow it. It didn't seem like the wolf wanted his sense of humor appreciated right then, though. When he turned his dark eyes on Jaden, they were hot and accusatory.

"You think that's funny, huh? You just waltz into town like you own it, set yourself up at the Alpha's house, have yourself a little sample of the local wares—"

"Simon, Jesus, I am not a *product*!" Lyra snapped. "And he's not sampling anything! Do you see the blood on his shirt? Some other vamp was out here and took a shot at him. I was making sure he was still alive—which is what most non-heartless people would be doing when the person they're with gets a stake through the chest!"

It was to Simon's credit, Jaden supposed, that he was able to put his anger aside so quickly. Even if most of his concern seemed to be for Lyra.

"So there was a vamp out here." He cursed colorfully, then extended a hand to Lyra. "Did he touch you, are you all right?"

Simon helped Lyra to her feet, his hands lingering on hers as he looked her over. Lyra's easy acceptance of Simon's assistance only fed the little green monster now perched on Jaden's shoulder. He watched silently and fumed as he got to his own feet.

"She's fine. Whoever it was, he was only interested in me," Jaden growled. "Lyra drove him off."

"Better safe than sorry," Simon said. He no longer looked angry, but the suspicion remained. Jaden glanced at Lyra, but she intentionally looked away from him. Frustration formed into a hard little knot in his gut, which only intensified when she focused her attention back on Simon.

"Really, I'm fine. Nearly took the guy's arm off, so there's that." She grimaced. "Not very tasty, but it worked."

Simon looked grim. "You got lucky," he said, and Jaden felt a smug satisfaction when Lyra stiffened, a murderous gleam coming into her eyes. It had been the exact wrong thing to say. He decided to add a little fuel to the fire.

"It wasn't luck. It's called courage and strength, both of which Lyra has. The vampire who attacked us wouldn't have run if he'd thought he could win easily." He paused. "You may not see it, but my kind has no problem recognizing those qualities in our women."

The knot in his gut eased a little when Lyra looked at him again. Some of the softness and warmth had returned to her eyes, and the tightness around her mouth eased a little to make way for a small smile.

"Thanks," she said.

Simon looked between them, suspicion written all over his face.

"What are you two doing out here anyway? Dorien said the vamp wanted a look at the site of the Proving, but it's not like there's anything to see." His tone sharpened when he focused on Lyra again. "You're lucky you didn't run into Eric. You won't be the only one out here getting ready this month."

"If we had, and if there had been a problem, I would have helped her take care of it," Jaden said flatly, meeting Simon's hostile glare with his own. "A better question is why you came running out here after her. Lyra doesn't need some sad little cub nipping at her heels."

Simon's eyes flashed, narrowed, and Jaden felt the return of a bit of pleasure, though of an uglier sort. His blood was still pounding through his veins. He was hungry, over-heated, and in desperate need of some sort of release. If that release came in the form of pounding the shit out of Simon again, so be it.

"Oh really? I know what she doesn't need. Some vamp who wants to take advantage while he's slumming it—"

"That's it," Lyra snapped. "I'm not interested in watching another one of these." She rounded on Simon. "If you're not going to tell me why you came after me out here, then I'll go get the information elsewhere."

She started to walk away, leaving both Jaden and Simon scrambling to go after her. They didn't have time, however, for more than a couple of ugly looks at one another. Lyra walked too fast for more.

"Wait! You can't just leave, Lyra!" Simon said.

"Watch me."

"I had a good reason for coming to find you."

"Sure you did," Jaden shot back. "You're a stalker."

Simon flashed his fangs at Jaden. When Lyra kept going, Simon cursed softly. "It was the vamp. Reed picked up the scent about a half hour ago. He called your father, who got a few of the wolves out tracking. And he sent me to find you." He slid an accusatory glance at Jaden. "We never get vamps here. Not until you. So I'm thinking you must have brought this one with you, one way or another."

"Simon," Lyra said, her tone warning. Jaden held up his hand, however, meeting Simon's glare head-on.

"You're right. Whoever he was, he seemed to be here for me. We don't usually attack one another just for the hell of it, and he was set to kill if it hadn't been for Lyra."

Simon blinked, as though trying to process the fact that Jaden had agreed with him.

"Well…oh. Did you, ah, did you get a look at him? Someone you know?"

Jaden recalled a split-second vision of fangs bared in a triumphant grin, eyes blazing dark blue. He shook his head. "No. I didn't get a very good look, but he was no one I know." Then he added blandly, "Contrary to what you seem to think, we don't actually all know one another."

Lyra, her arms wrapped around herself, pinned him with an equally intense look, though the concern in her eyes made it far easier for him to take.

"Who would do this?"

Jaden shrugged, suddenly uncomfortable with his

decision to keep his Ptolemy problems to himself. Still, what good would talking about it do? The prospect of assassins from an ancient and powerful vampire dynasty showing up here to take him out would only get him run off that much more quickly. And he needed to be sure that was the case before making his own decisions about the safety of being here—for him, and everyone else. He was no fan of werewolves, but he wasn't interested in getting a bunch of them killed on his account either.

"I ran a lot of errands back when I was a servant of the Ptolemy. Some of those errands could be classified as dirty work, but I had no choice. It's possible this is connected. But that could mean one of hundreds of things. I really don't know."

Lyra blew out a breath. "Well, that's just great," she said.

"No kidding. Whether this was intentional or not, you're going to get blamed for this," Simon warned him, his eyes cold. "We don't like vamps on our territory. One unwelcome visitor is enough. Two is going to get the pack up in arms, and you're going to hear about it if you've got the balls to stay here. Our kind hasn't forgotten what yours is capable of, what they did to us. Dorien can't protect you from everything ... or everyone."

Jaden gave him a small, humorless smile. "Now that I know there's an issue, I can take perfectly good care of myself. You don't need to play the victim card with me either. Wolves don't have the corner on the market for subjugation. Trust me."

"We'll need to go back. Dad will know if someone's picked up the trail again." She looked at him more closely, and Jaden found himself wanting to open up, to tell everything to the woman who belonged to those fathomless, burning eyes.

"Are you sure you have no idea who this could be?"

Suddenly it was all too much. Even the open air became claustrophobic. He didn't want questions, didn't want to feel beholden to this woman who tied him up in knots. He wanted to sink his teeth into her, wanted to feed, to kiss and soothe and lose himself in her. And most of all, he wanted freedom from the Ptolemy, freedom to be able to live whatever sort of life he wanted without the threat of recapture or death hanging over his head. Impossible things.

"I don't know who it is, but I'll have a look around. Tell Dorien I'll have a word with him about it when I get back."

Simon's eyes glittered in the dark. "Sure. Running off so soon?"

Jaden didn't give a damn what Simon thought. He did, however, care what Lyra thought of him, though to feel that way was setting them both up for disappointment. She looked as vulnerable as he'd ever seen her, watching him get ready to run away from her. He wondered if she already regretted the kiss. Did she think he'd brought some plague of vampires to her pack's sanctuary?

If she did... was she right?

"Are you coming back?" she asked. Such a simple question. A simple, loaded question. She tried to sound unconcerned, but he could already see through the cracks he'd made in her armor.

"I'll be back before sunrise. I need to... take care of a few things. Don't worry," he added, offering a small smile, hoping he could tease her back into a version of

Lyra he knew how to deal with. He'd started something that, for once, he had no idea how to finish.

"Whatever. I won't." Defensive. And a lie, but one he was glad for.

Jaden gave Lyra one last, lingering look, graced Simon with a small, mocking bow. Then he did the only thing he knew to do, the only thing he had ever done when the heat had gotten to be too much. He shifted into a sleek black cat, the form he often felt freer in than his own human skin.

And he ran.

chapter TEN

L YRA HAD HOPED to wake up feeling better.

Instead, she'd opened her eyes earlier this afternoon feeling like something someone scraped off the bottom of a shoe. Her dreams had been plagued with visions of herself and Jaden, back in the park. Except in her fantasies, they hadn't stopped at heated kisses. But no matter how he touched her, how he made her moan, some part of her had known it wasn't real. She'd known it would be so much better if she would just go to him and—

"Bullshit," Lyra muttered, glaring at the amber-colored bottle in front of her and ignoring all the music and pleasant chatter that surrounded her. Stupid damned vampire, she thought. Why couldn't he have just kept his hands—and that amazing mouth of his—to himself?

Of course, it might have helped if she hadn't been such a willing participant in his little cross-species experiment, testing the laws of attraction. But how could she spar with someone whose clothes she wanted to rip off?

Lyra trailed a finger down the condensation on the outside of the bottle, watching the water drip slowly onto the bar. At least she knew he'd come back last night. She'd checked. A couple times... or ten. When she'd headed here around dinnertime, Jaden was asleep and peaceful and obnoxiously carefree in her pitch-black basement. She'd never even heard him come in just before sunrise.

Not that she'd been upstairs waiting or anything.

Lyra propped her elbows on the bar and sighed heavily. She knew she was wallowing, and she planned to enjoy it for a while before she had to figure out what to do. She took a small sip of the beer she'd been nursing for the past half hour and managed to smile at Beth, the bartender, even though there was a nasty headache brewing at the periphery of her temples, beginning to throb with a distant but noticeably achy drumbeat.

"I still can't believe your father's letting him stay. And at your *house*," Simon said for what was possibly the hundredth time. His green hazel eyes were growing heavy lidded and bloodshot, and his wavy brown hair was standing up oddly in the places where he'd run his fingers through. After years of being the sweet, adorable boy-next-door without an enemy in the world, Simon had finally found a proper nemesis in Jaden. And all he could seem to think about was going full metal werewolf on his ass.

"You're making a big deal out of nothing, Simon," she muttered, which earned her a derisive snort. It bothered her to think all this overemotional posturing was on her behalf. This possessive/protective thing Simon had going on lately was both weird and unwelcome. She loved their friendship just the way it was. Why did he have to try to put kinks in it?

"Like he's so special," Simon continued, choosing to pretend he hadn't heard her. "He won't seem so special when this place is overrun with bloodsuckers. Vampire ambassador, my ass. I don't even know what that *is*."

Lyra sucked in a breath and scanned the area around them to see whether anyone was paying attention to her drunken friend. That a vampire had wandered onto their territory last night was now common knowledge—word traveled fast. But that it had attacked Jaden was supposed to stay between the four of them. Dorien didn't want the pack unnecessarily on edge.

Of course, it didn't seem to bother him that his only daughter was about as on edge as it got at the moment.

"Volume control, Simon," she growled softly, then assumed a more normal tone. "I told you why he's here. The Lilim's leader is so new she doesn't have all the usual vamp/wolf baggage. She's interested in knowing more about us, and I guess wanted to make a good impression, so . . . Jaden's here checking us out."

He looked at her balefully. "I noticed."

Lyra smacked Simon in the stomach with the back of her hand, making him grunt. "Shut *up*, Simon. I told you, it's not like that."

Fortunately, he didn't seem to want to discuss it any more than she did, but she did wonder just how much he really suspected about last night.

"Whatever. So what do we get out of this again? Besides 'not attacked by cat vamps offended that we killed their stupid ambassador'? Because the good impression thing isn't really working out so far, and I can't see that any of us are getting much out of this."

Lyra shrugged and took a sip of her beer. "He's only

been here a couple of days. Maybe things will turn around and we'll get an actual alliance. You never know."

It was complete BS, of course, but Lyra found herself wishing that part was true. The thought of added protection for her pack from such a powerful source had a lot of appeal. It always had, actually, for Alphas going way back before her time. The problem was the wolves' overtures toward the vampires had generally ended in bad blood and slaughter. Even if the Lilim's hand was extended, Lyra wasn't sure the members of her pack wouldn't just bite it off.

Simon rolled his eyes, unwittingly backing up her concerns.

"Oh, right. These vamps are just so different. They're probably scoping Silver Falls out for the Lilim's summer home or something. Maybe if we're lucky they'll let us stay and serve them drinks. Fan them with palms. The usual things they think they deserve. We're supposed to feel special because a dynasty is finally paying attention to us? They're either desperate or stupid." He paused. "I guess I'm a little curious about which, but not enough to want the cat vamp to stick around."

Lyra didn't bother to argue with him, watching his shoulders sag as he toyed with his glass. She hated having to lie to Simon about why Jaden was here. Just like she hated being at odds with him. They'd been each other's support for a long time. She gave him an affectionate nudge, and when he looked at her through his reddened eyes, she was surprised to find them sad.

"What's wrong?" she asked. "You're not yourself lately. Even before this mess with the Proving. And... everything." She decided mentioning Jaden by name would just make him shut down.

Simon lifted his eyebrows at her. He really was handsome, she thought. A little sloppy right this second, but really classically good looking. She'd always wondered why another girl hadn't snatched him up. She felt more than a little guilt at the thought that she might have scared those theoretical girls away...or that he'd simply been waiting for her.

"Well," he said, "you being determined to get yourself killed is kind of putting me out lately, Lyra. So there's that. And what do you mean I'm not myself? I'm not boring? Dependable? Always around because I have nothing better to do? That stuff never changes."

Lyra frowned at the edge in his voice. "I meant friendly, fun, and charming, none of which you are being right now. Or recently."

He looked at her for a long moment, as though trying to decide what to say. He didn't look hurt, at least. But this side of Simon was unfamiliar to her. It wasn't like him to be troubled and broody. She worried. Of course, lately, it felt like all she did was worry. She shouldn't have been surprised that Simon was getting in on the action. Finally, he spoke.

"I don't know, Lyra. I know you want all this. But I just keep thinking...there's a lot more out there than Silver Falls." He looked away. "Maybe you're not the only one who gets tired of being pigeonholed."

It hurt to hear him so down. She'd had no idea he was dissatisfied with pack life, and that hurt more...because he hadn't told her. Better late than never, she guessed. If she could only find the words to fix what ailed him.

"Simon," she said gently, "you're great. You're one of the most promising members of the pack guard, everyone says so. Not to mention you're one of the only people who's able to put up with me on a regular basis. You're like…" She searched for a good comparison. "Like the local knight in shining armor. Just werewolf style."

One side of his mouth curved up, but his eyes were full of melancholy. "For who, exactly?" With a deep breath, he got to his feet, swaying only slightly. "I think I'll take a page out of the cat vamp's book and go get some air. I'll see you later, Lyra."

Her next response wasn't something she usually did. Physical affection just wasn't her thing, and she'd never been one of those girls who couldn't let a friend go without some kind of gushy display. But before she could think better of it, Lyra rose and wrapped her arms around her friend. She felt like she was losing her grip on everything she cared about with no solution in sight, and something in her compelled her to reach out even though she knew damn well doing so would get the gossips going again.

She felt Simon stiffen, then relent for the briefest of moments as his arms went around her to give her a single, tight squeeze. Somewhere beside them, she heard Beth give an approving coo.

"Everything's changing," Lyra said unhappily, her head against Simon's broad chest.

"Yeah," he replied. "I guess things do." Then he disentangled himself and stepped back, leaving her just as surely as Jaden had last night. The difference was that she didn't even have Jaden to lose. Simon looked off to his left, toward the door to the bar, and frowned.

"Great. And he called *me* a stalker." Simon gave her a meaningful look. "Steer clear of him, if you know what's good for you, Lyra. Vamps are nothing but trouble. And that one's got more than his fair share. I'm going to be watching him."

She opened her mouth to protest, but he shook his head. "It's my job. I don't care how pretty he is, or how mysterious or whatever it is you see there. You'd better start thinking with your head, or you're not going to get what you want."

Simon leveled a hard glare across the room, where a commotion had kicked up in the form of growling, muttering wolves rapidly clearing from the path of a newcomer to the bar. Then he turned and headed for the back door, leaving her to deal with the situation all on her own. Lyra's stomach sank as she looked around and saw every wolf in the place tense, bristle, their eyes lighting like lamps in the dim room. And of course, she knew exactly why.

She could smell him: vamp, feline, and utterly male. Of course, the difference between her and the rest of the wolves seemed to be that while his scent made them want to attack, she sort of wanted to find the source and...roll around in it.

Her heart picked up its pace as soon as she caught sight of his dark head. He held it high, ignoring the hostile glares, the low growls, and the not-so-quiet epithets as he strode into the room with the sort of preternatural grace no human, or wolf, could possess. Jaden seemed to take in everything and yet look at nothing, avoiding the direct eye contact many of her pack would have taken as a challenge. She couldn't seem to move, drinking in the sight of him hungrily. His lean form was all in black, and his eyes glowed their bright blue as they swept the room. Assessing threat, she supposed. A wise move, considering the thinly veiled hatred with which most of the wolves were watching him.

When those eyes settled on her, she knew immediately that he'd seen her hugging Simon. He looked hot, bothered, and fixed on her with a raw possessiveness that knocked the breath right out of her. This was everything she'd feared, everything she'd sworn she didn't want even though it tempted her like nothing ever had.

Why him? she wondered. *Why me?*

Since bolting wasn't really an option, Lyra decided to take what control she could. She felt dozens of eyes on her, some curious, most suspicious, and a few outright hostile. The room had fallen strangely quiet, the only sounds coming from the jukebox and the electronic poker machine. Lyra shook her hair back behind her shoulders, straightened as though she hadn't a care in the world, and strolled as casually as she could to where Jaden was making his way toward her.

Lyra thought he stuck out like a sore thumb, but in the most appealing sort of way. She gave him credit for guts, or at least hardheadedness, for showing up here. No matter how firm her father had been in his edict that the cat vamp shouldn't be touched, however, some of the less restrained (and drunker) members of the pack were going to forget themselves before too long.

She needed to get him out of here.

"Jaden," she said coolly by way of greeting as she made her way toward him, coming to a stop within a couple of feet.

"Lyra," he returned. She could sense the caution in him, despite the hungry way he was still looking at her. No big bad wolf could have done it better. Once more, he looked around at the pack members, now openly gawking at him. How many had ever even seen a vampire? she wondered. The Thorn was a closed society. One the vamps had ignored for a very long time.

"Your father said that if I wanted to start meeting some of the pack, this is the place."

Lyra lifted her eyebrows as a wave of quiet laughter erupted around them.

"Uh, yeah. You could say that," she said. Gods, what was he *doing* here?

"Hey, vamp! You can turn into a kitty, right? Why don't you show us?"

More laughter, louder now. Lyra recognized the voice of Dan Marshall, one of her father's buddies, and barely suppressed a groan. This could go south quickly if Jaden got defensive. Fortunately, he seemed cool—so far. And she really needed to come up with an exit strategy that didn't look like she was getting too comfortable with him. Tightropes, she thought. Her life was walking them.

"I wouldn't want to shed in such a nice place," Jaden replied, looking directly at Dan with a twinkle in his eye. "And I like the odds better if I buy you all a round instead. What do you say?"

Lyra held her breath, expecting the worst. But Dan simply laughed in his ragged whiskey voice. "Sure. We're not that easy to butter up, vamp...but buying drinks is a start I'm fine with."

"Didn't expect you would be. Drinks on me, then," Jaden said, provoking several hoots and howls from the peanut gallery that, Lyra found, were a great deal friendlier than she'd expected just a few minutes ago. She let out the breath she'd been holding as activity resumed all around them, maybe a little quieter than it had been but minus some of the tension.

Jaden leaned in close now that he had the chance of not being overheard. "You're late. I've been up for over an hour."

She fought the urge to fidget as his breath fanned over her ear. "You're the one who took off last night. I didn't even know if we were still on."

He backed off a little, seeming to realize that whispering in Lyra's ear for too long was not going to create a picture she would want. Instead, he spoke in a low voice that she doubted anyone would hear but her over the resumed conversations.

"I didn't think you'd want to watch me eat. Was I wrong?"

The image in her head was immediate: Jaden, his arms around some attractive blonde, his teeth in her neck. She felt her claws bite into her palms when she closed her hands into fists. No, she realized. He wasn't wrong.

"It's not just that, and you know it," Lyra said, keeping her voice as low as his. "We need to talk."

"Yeah, I guess we do," he said. "Later, though. Your father—"

Lyra nodded. He didn't need to finish. She was well aware that her father was angry that last night had been a bust. He was focused on keeping his daughter alive. And Lyra knew she needed to focus on the important things too. Simon had been right about that: fixating on Jaden wasn't going to get her what she wanted. In fact, she could easily lose everything.

"I'll go give the bartender my credit card," Jaden said, looking a little glum as he watched Beth pull a bottle of what looked like expensive champagne from beneath the bar while two grinning wolves gave him a cheerful thumbs-up. "And then we can go."

Lyra nodded and watched him stride away, trying not to be amused at the free-for-all beginning at the bar. Beth was busy filling some very large glasses with some sort of concoction Lyra had never seen before. Looked like tonight was going to be a party. At least no one could say wolves didn't know how to have a good time. And the slaps Jaden got on the back from a few of the braver members of the pack gave her a little glimmer of hope. Even if the first one caught Jaden off guard and nearly knocked him over.

Which was undoubtedly by design.

As she watched him give that sardonic little smile to Beth, who looked suspiciously pink-cheeked, she found herself wishing, just a little, that things were different. Stupid, she knew, but true. It wasn't every guy who could walk into a den of werewolves and navigate it without a scratch.

Of course, he wasn't out of the Inn yet. And the sight of a very large, very familiar wolf making a beeline for Jaden made her feel like sinking through the floor. Looked like this was the night for baptism by fire. Lyra walked as quickly as she could on her long legs to get between Jaden and the one pack member she'd hoped he would never have to meet. She put her game face on before she got to them, knowing that to show any real interest in Jaden was to risk having him taken away from her as soon as Eric could manage it.

"Eric," she said smoothly when she reached the two of them, stepping casually (she hoped) in between. "I see you're introducing yourself. Jaden, this is my cousin, Eric Black."

Jaden raised one slim brow and very deliberately looked Eric's hulking form over. Finally, he extended his hand. "Pleasure."

As expected, Eric ignored the proffered hand in favor of simple intimidation. He didn't crack even an artificial smile—that wasn't his way. Tall and dark, with golden eyes like all the Blacks, he would have been handsome if he didn't always look like he was about to sentence someone to a painful execution.

"So you're our new guest," Eric said. "I heard there was a cat vamp in town, but I wasn't going to believe it until I saw you for myself." He looked Jaden over very deliberately. "I forgot how small you vamps can be."

Jaden smiled blandly. "Yes. Tiny. It's a wonder you noticed me."

"And of course, you're staying well off the territory to drink."

"Jaden is here to learn about us," Lyra said very deliberately. "Not to cause trouble. He's our guest, and the Alpha expects him to be treated that way."

Eric turned his bright gold gaze on her, and she saw the violence she'd heard so much about lurking just below the surface.

"He's already causing trouble. Everyone knows there was another vampire in town last night. Are you telling me that's a coincidence? Letting even one in is a mistake. First you get one, then another…then you're overrun. Like cockroaches. Those things live forever, too, seems like."

Lyra looked around at the faces of her pack, watching them. Waiting to see if she would stand up to Eric or back down, to see whether she would defend the vampire to a fellow wolf.

"I trust my father's judgment. If he accepts Jaden's presence, then so do I. So should we all. He's been a good Alpha." She looked around. "Change can be difficult, but it isn't always bad."

Eric's expression hardened amid the assenting murmurs and reluctant nods. His smile was humorless. "Then I guess we'll wait and see. Dorien is worthy of trust. But I doubt a vampire is, no matter how pretty his promises are."

He stalked away, leaving Lyra feeling shaken and unsure. She was very good at keeping those things to herself. But when she turned back to Jaden, he looked as though he could see everything she was feeling as plain as day.

Suddenly, everything about the Inn—the people, the music, the noise—was too much for her. The headache that had been threatening all day felt like it was coming in for a landing, and she wanted to be the hell out of here before she crumpled up into a ball. Her looking comfortable leaving with Jaden now seemed decidedly less important.

"Let's get out of here," she said.

He nodded, and his lack of commentary told her that he did see how close to her breaking point she was. "Lead the way," was all he said.

She didn't look at him again as she headed through the crowd, feeling him right behind her like a shadow. People moved out of her way, most offering friendly good-byes, a few goggling at Jaden as though he was some kind of sideshow freak. She heard him murmuring a few cordial good-byes of his own and wondered whether it would make any difference. It wouldn't if Eric, who already had a crowd around him at the bar, had his way. And no one would ultimately go against him, because despite everything, he was the strongest of them all.

She pushed the door open and walked out into the night, trying to convince herself that she could do what was needed, that she had a real chance to claim her birthright. But when she tried to imagine the Proving, all she could see was Eric's broad form, easily twice her size, and his cold, unblinking glare.

For the first time, she didn't feel a single shred of confidence that she would prevail.

All she had was tattered hopes, an unwanted vampire, and dull despair.

chapter ELEVEN

LYRA UNLOCKED her little pickup with her keychain, jerked open the driver's side door, and slid in. Jaden quickly got in on the passenger side. Once the doors slammed, they sat there silently for a moment in the dark. She'd felt awkward in the bar, but at least there had been people around as a buffer. Now, it felt a lot more... fraught.

Lyra began to fumble with getting the key in the ignition, uncomfortably reminded of her first make-out session. The car, the dark, the tension...

"Didn't you drive here?" she blurted out. It seemed better to fill the silence with words, even stupid words. She felt lousy enough. Uncomfortable silence wasn't going to fix anything. And since she knew what was coming, she really, really wanted to get it over with.

"Didn't need to drive. I think you're forgetting that you're not the only one who can get around pretty quickly on four feet," he said.

"Oh."

The silence returned with a vengeance. When she heard Jaden shift a little in his seat, it occurred to her that he was just as uncomfortable too. Lyra gritted her teeth, ready to plunge in. But as she opened her mouth, Jaden spoke.

"I didn't thank you," he said. "For saving my life last night."

She turned her head to look at him, startled into silence. He nodded.

"That's probably what you did, you know. I'm not saying I couldn't have managed to get out of it, but…" he trailed off, looking slightly embarrassed. "Yeah, probably not. I owe you one."

"Oh. Well. You're welcome," Lyra said, thrown off balance by the unexpected gratitude. In truth, she hadn't thought much about what had happened before they'd ended up on the ground together. Only then did she realize she'd taken Jaden's assertion that he didn't know who his attacker was at face value.

An odd thing, to put faith so easily in a vampire. But there was something about Jaden that made it easy. Probably too easy, she knew.

"You don't owe me anything," she added with a nervous laugh. "You saved my butt from Mark, so I'd say we're even."

"Fair enough," Jaden said. He looked relieved, like this was a burden he'd needed to get off his chest. Maybe he was like her, Lyra thought. She hated to be beholden to anyone. The idea that they might have that in common gave her an unexpected bit of pleasure. And that, she decided, was dangerous in her present mood. She felt weak right now, and far too inclined to share her burdens with anyone who seemed to care—with *him*.

"We should get going," he said. "After getting a look at Eric, I think you've got your work cut out for you. So we should swing by the house, you can change into something better suited to sweat in, and we can head out. Your father said you'd know where to go."

Lyra sat for a moment in stunned silence. That was it? She knew he'd said they would talk about it later, but... she didn't want to talk about it later. It had been festering since last night, and she wanted to talk about it *now*. Tired, frustrated, Lyra pushed the topic into confrontational waters in the hopes that dealing with it would clear her head a little.

"Okay, look," she said, turning her head to look at Jaden. "I'm still not sure what happened last night, but before we go any further, I think we need to sort a couple of things out."

He blew out a breath and slicked his hair back with his hands. "Does it really need to get sorted out?"

"Yeah, it does," Lyra replied, gripping the steering wheel hard enough that she was sure her hands would leave imprints. "If you're really sticking around to teach me, this is going to have to stay professional. Whatever it was—that thing last night—it can't happen again. Ever."

She was ashamed of the fact that she couldn't look him in the face when she said it, but it would have been too difficult to mean the words otherwise. Still, she could feel the heat of his eyes on her skin. What did he see in her? Even if she hadn't sworn off men, she didn't have anything to offer one right now. Especially not a bloodsucker.

"Just out of curiosity," Jaden asked, his voice mild, "is

your main objection to sleeping with me that I'm a vampire, or that you're an Alpha's daughter?"

She had to look at him then, because the question indicated he was losing his mind.

He looked perfectly sincere in his interest too. She wasn't sure whether to slap him for being an idiot, or to kiss him for the same exact reason.

"Both," she replied, astounded he'd even asked. "What kind of a question is that? You know very well our kinds don't...we don't..."

"Yes, I know it doesn't happen. But that certainly doesn't mean that it *can't* happen."

Lyra felt her mouth go dry and her face grow hot. How could he even act like there was a discussion to be had about this?

"It can't happen with *us*, Jaden. It would be...I mean...I would be an outcast if anyone found out! My father would disown me, and I—I..." She started to stammer, paused, and took a deep breath. "You're just supposed to teach me to fight! Why do you have to go and make this more complicated than it already is?"

He didn't move a muscle, watching her like an animal fixed on its prey. This new sensation for her, coming from him, was a lot more enjoyable than it should have been.

"You brought it up," he said. "And you didn't exactly push me away last night. I have a right to ask what you find so disgusting about it when it's obvious you don't object to me once I have my hands on you." His eyes began to glow, and it was a moment before Lyra realized that he was actually angry.

"It's that wolf, right? Simon. I saw you with your arms around each other." He shook his head, the anger gone as quickly as it had appeared. Jaden slumped into his seat and frowned at the dash, his voice dropping to a sullen mutter. "Forget it. You're better off with the wolf, I suppose. It won't happen again, okay? Let's just go."

Somehow, watching Jaden struggle openly with what she'd been wrestling with privately soothed her ragged nerves. This wasn't some joke for him. And Lyra knew she wasn't appealing just because of her position, which could do him no good. He just…wanted her. And was stupidly jealous to boot.

Lyra could only stare, wonderingly, as he sat brooding and looking like he wanted to kill someone.

"You're serious about this?" she finally asked.

He turned his head to give her a beleaguered look.

"I don't humiliate myself for fun, usually."

She opened her mouth, hoping a rational response would emerge. When one didn't, she decided she needed a minute to think about it. Jaden, for the moment, was a captive audience. Lyra jammed her key into the ignition, turned the car on, and pulled out of the parking space without saying a word. She'd left the radio on, and The Black Keys ground out a gritty, sexy, bluesy ode to attraction that did nothing to take Lyra's mind elsewhere.

She reached out to turn the volume down but didn't turn it off, which kept the current situation from feeling completely surreal.

"Okay, let's get a few things straight. For one thing, I'm not interested in Simon," she said. "He's been my best friend since we were kids. Not that it's any of your business, but thinking that is just…gross. Don't."

Jaden's response was little more than a growl. "Does it matter what I think about it?"

"Maybe," she allowed, and felt his attention return to her full force. She had to concentrate hard on what she wanted to say so she could stay on the road. He was being honest. And considering what they would have done last night if Simon hadn't shown up, she supposed she owed him the same courtesy.

"For another thing, what if I did want you in my bed, Jaden? It's not like it would do either of us any good. I don't want a mate, and you couldn't be one to me anyway. Apart from the fact that my pack would hunt and kill you for touching me, the bond doesn't happen if one person isn't a wolf."

"Bond?"

Oh gods, she didn't want to explain this. Lyra felt another rush of heat to her cheeks, but she pushed through it. She might as well get it all out.

"Yeah, the mate bond. Happens when two wolves, ah... you know. It's unbreakable. Wolves mate for life. Unfortunately, it's not a perfect system. You don't have to actually like the person you bond with."

She looked quickly at him and saw that he'd figured out the whole truth of it. His mouth thinned with distaste.

"Yes, I know," she said. "Welcome to my world."

"That's why you've been running. You don't have to *agree* to be mated to any of the wolves who want your hand. All it takes is being in the wrong place at the wrong time." He wrinkled his nose and shook his head. "Where's the appeal in marrying a woman who's been forced to accept you? I don't understand wolves at all."

"You don't have to. It's just biology," Lyra said. "I don't like it either. It's one of the things that have kept female werewolves in permanent second-class status for so long, and a big part of why packs are so insulated. One big raid by another pack, and boom, all of your breeding females belong to your rivals."

"That's disgusting."

Lyra shrugged, nodded. "It is. That really used to happen, a long time ago, and it wiped out more than one pack. Not so much anymore. But that doesn't mean it isn't still a hazard of being born a girl. Especially if you're the Alpha's daughter and your hand comes with so many benefits."

He seemed to be mulling this over. "And how does this bond affect you? Couldn't you just ignore it? Walk away, if you tried hard enough?"

"Heh. Your lack of werewolf knowledge is showing," she replied with a small smile. "We get marks too. Around the upper arm. Only upon mating, and the marks of the pair match. You can't remove them, and it's easy to check. But worse, I think, is that the bond makes it difficult to be apart from one another. Or at least, that's what I hear. There's some kind of freaky emotional component that's almost telepathic. I don't know exactly how that works, and I don't want to know. They say death breaks it. But my dad has never gotten over my mom, and that was years ago."

She didn't want to talk about her mother and wished she hadn't brought her up. But Jaden asked the question she knew he would, and his tone, quiet and nonjudgmental, had her speaking before she could think better of it.

"What happened?"

"Hunters," Lyra said. "She was alone in the woods when she shouldn't have been, too far from home. And a lot of humans don't much care what they shoot as long as it might look good on their walls. I—I don't remember much about that. I was just a toddler. And that's besides the matter," she said, ending that part of the discussion. He didn't need to know about all the tears she'd shed for a mother who was never coming home. The hole in her life that had never closed. She doubted he would understand anyway.

"The point," she said more firmly, "is that I just don't see what acting on this *thing* you and I seem to have between us does but muddy what I'm trying to accomplish. Like I said—I'm not interested in having a man. Any man. Even if you weren't a vampire, that would be true. A mate would just be an excuse for the pack to brush me aside, and I need to do this, win this, on my own."

"Since I don't want a mate either, and learned a long time ago not to get too emotionally involved with mortals, I'm not sure what the problem is."

She glanced at him, amused at his matter-of-fact tone. "So you're advocating for meaningless sex, then. Oh. Well that makes a huge difference."

His answering smile was faint, and in the near dark of the car his perfect face was both beautiful and sad, like that of a fallen angel. "Meaningless is the wrong word. Look, I've been either enslaved or on the run for longer than anyone in your pack has been alive. Now that I'm free, to be perfectly honest, I don't know what the hell I want anymore. But I've been around long enough to know that sometimes it's fine just to enjoy something in the moment. That's not meaningless. That's just realistic. That's life."

The statement was so unexpectedly honest that Lyra found herself touched by it, even if she didn't know exactly how to respond. She drove in silence while she gathered her muddled thoughts—trying to sort out what she wanted, what she needed. Until Jaden had made his offer, she hadn't quite realized how appealing such a thing would sound. If there were truly no strings...

Her heartbeat picked up at the mere possibility of saying yes. But there were other considerations—ones she would have to give a lot more thought to. And she had no intention of getting into those with him now when this was all still so fresh.

"This isn't exactly what I was expecting, Jaden," she said as she made the turn down her street. "Nothing is this easy, or free. There has to be a catch."

A soft chuckle. "So suspicious. No, there's enough to worry about without there being a catch."

But his words reminded her of one very large potential issue. "Oh? What about the vampire from last night?"

She could actually *feel* him shut down a little with the shift in the conversation, and it worried her. She knew there were plenty of things she didn't know about Jaden—would probably never know. But she needed to be sure that his secrets weren't going to put her pack in danger.

"I'll take care of it. That's nothing you, or your pack, need to worry about," he said in a clipped voice.

"Then you know who it was?" she asked.

"No," he replied, his voice turning cold. "But I'll find out. I have the resources to be able to, finally, and I plan to use them. If it turned into a problem, Lyra, I would go. Not without finding someone to replace me. I wouldn't abandon you like that, especially not after meeting your charming cousin. But I don't want you to worry about your pack. I was obviously the target. I've made a lot of enemies over the years, so I expect I'll stay the target. Whoever it is knows that no one here will mourn me if I suddenly disappear. Or my head does."

There was more to it. She was sure of it. But she also didn't think he was lying in his assessment of the danger. It wouldn't fit with the man she was slowly coming to know. He had a sense of honor about him. Not one she had completely figured out yet, but it was there.

"Is it one of the ones who put the scars on your back?"

He stiffened, and she knew she'd gone further than she should have.

"I don't want to talk about them."

Well, that was obvious. "I'm not asking you to. I'm asking if it might be—"

"I certainly hope not. But even if it is, it's no concern of yours."

Lyra recoiled a little at the coldness in his voice, something she hadn't heard since their very first meeting. She wondered again who had done that to him, what it meant. But that, it seemed, was off limits. He didn't seem to want to talk about the past. Which should have been fine.

Except that she wanted to know more about him, whether or not she ought to.

The car lapsed into silence as she pulled into the driveway, comforted by the familiarity of the house, the cheery lights against the dark. She'd had so many simpler, happier times here. It was a comfort, but it also made her sad. Everything was so complicated now . . . her *feelings* were complicated. She'd known that the path she'd started on would be a lonely one. But it surprised her how much Jaden's company made her crave the sort of connection she'd long denied herself.

The sort of connection he seemed to be offering, albeit temporarily.

He was so quiet, Lyra had almost forgotten Jaden was there with her, until he spoke up with a new hesitance in his voice.

"Will you give some thought to the rest of what I've said?" he asked as she pulled the keys from the ignition and put her hand on the door handle.

That was the big question, she supposed. And there would be no avoiding it, one way or another. Lyra took a deep breath, turning to look him in the eyes. "I think it's probably a bad idea," she said. "But I honestly don't know. I guess I need some time to think about it."

"Fair enough," Jaden said softly, and she didn't think she'd ever seen him look so serious despite the fact that he rarely smiled. "My offer stands for as long as I'm here. Just let me know."

Her heart, treacherous as ever, fluttered nervously in response.

"Deal," she said, and then, anxious to get her racing heart under control, changed the subject to something lighter. "Let me get changed, and we'll head out to the fields on the west side of town on four legs. Less conspicuous." She couldn't help a small jab. "As long as you think you can keep up."

"Don't worry about me," Jaden said. "I'm as anxious as you are. Your cousin may be lacking a personality, but he's made up for it in brawn. We've got work to do."

His grin was utterly wicked and full of sensuous promise...if she were brave enough to take him up on it. She would see.

• • •

The wolf padded silently through the underbrush, his massive paws barely making a sound as he headed for the falls. He'd needed a run, badly. But even that had failed to ease his mind tonight...so he would try to find his peace at the falls and hunt some of the wild things that hid from him in the underbrush. In that, he felt a strange kinship to the town's unwelcome visitor. Both he and the vampires found comfort in blood.

He hadn't been surprised to find Lyra playing bodyguard to the bloodsucker. She was prickly, but the sharp exterior hid her biggest weakness: a soft heart. He kept tabs on her. He knew full well where she ran off to on the occasions she decided to disappear. She'd hung around vamps before, and why not? That's where the power was. Where it would always be. He could understand the attraction to power.

But Lyra was never going to have the wherewithal to gain any for herself, or for the pack. That alone made her unfit to be Alpha, more important even than the fact that she was just a woman. That kill would be sweet, the wolf thought as he moved in and out of shadow like a ghost.

He hoped he would have time to savor it. The Proving didn't worry him. He'd have help if he needed it, which he wouldn't. The competition was pathetic, none more than Lyra.

But her new vampire pet was going to be a problem. This Jaden was no transient no-name lowblood. His connections could screw up everything, and yet the wolf had been told nothing about him, had had no advance warning of last night's attempt to deal with him. How was he supposed to manage the situation if he was being cut out of the loop?

He'd clawed his way in, and he'd worked his ass off to line everything up. The pieces were all in place. And he'd be damned if Lyra was going to screw it up at the last minute by making sad cow eyes at some freshly minted Lilim.

He would have killed the bitch already, if he'd thought he could get away with it.

The wolf leaped over a fallen tree and kept his pace steady, letting the scents of the forest at night calm his frayed nerves. He had a lot on his plate these days—more than anyone knew—and on some nights, like tonight, keeping it all together proved almost overwhelming.

Just three weeks, he told himself. *A little over three weeks, and I'm set.*

A shadow peeled off one of the trees up ahead, so quickly and silently that he didn't notice until he was almost on top of it. When he did see the shadow in his path, he jerked to a halt, too startled even to growl. There was an exasperated sigh as cool blue eyes gleamed at him in the darkness.

"Situational awareness," said a soft, cultured voice with a posh English accent. "Learn it, wolf. I could have killed you ten times over by now if I'd felt like it."

The wolf shifted quickly into a human to stand in front of the slim, elegant silhouette that the vampire presented and tried to hide his shock that a Shade, any Shade, would want to talk to him after cutting him off so completely. He'd met this one only once, but he hadn't forgotten the sharp tongue or the air of superiority. Maybe it was the cat vamp blood that made him so insufferable.

"What do you want, Damien?" he asked. "If the Shades want to talk to me, there are safer ways to do it."

There was a derisive snort. "I'm in no danger here. You, on the other hand, are in a lot more if you don't watch yourself."

"I don't know what you're talking about."

But inside, cold tendrils of fear began to wrap around his heart. He'd gone to the Shades because he'd wanted to spread his wings a little, to learn how the truly powerful conducted their business...and how they destroyed one another. The short time he'd spent with them had been very instructive.

And it had led to far greater things than a society of criminals.

"Oh, I think you do. So let me begin by saying that the House of Shadows doesn't take kindly to apprentices who use us to find better positions."

"I didn't use anyone," he snapped, imagining the pleasure he would get out of wringing Damien Tremaine's neck and then popping his head right off his shoulders. Vampires were pricks, by and large, but Damien was in a class by himself. "Anyway, what do you care if I made a useful contact? You let *me* go, remember? Drake said he didn't like my style."

"Very true," Damien replied blandly. "Since that style of yours involved a rather higher body count than what had been ordered. And there was that lowblood maid you left in pieces. In fact, that was the last straw, wasn't it?"

He wished he didn't know what the vampire was talking about, but it was hard to forget. "She got in the way," he growled. "I was just doing my job."

"Unacceptable. It was sloppy work, and the House of Shadows has a reputation for being quick, clean, and discreet. I don't know how many times Drake is going to have to beat his head against the wall with one of these grand ideas of his, but I warned him you weren't suited to be an apprentice."

"Because I'm a wolf?" He snorted. "You vamps are all alike. Think your shit doesn't stink."

"Actually, it's because you're an unreliable thug with sociopathic tendencies. You being a wolf is irritating, but not the issue. You were his first go at a wolf, but I doubt you'll be the last." A sigh. "I understand the need to keep his fingers in a lot of pies, but your kind isn't really suited to our needs. Next it'll be a pixie or some damned thing."

The wolf's blood heated to a slow boil. He'd thought long and hard before seeking out the famed House of Shadows, the guild of vampire assassins and thieves. And he'd managed to get Alistair Drake, the Shade Master, to give him a shot at an apprenticeship. So it hadn't worked out... it had been worthwhile regardless. Fortunately, he hadn't gotten far enough in to be considered a liability to the Shades. They didn't tend to let those go.

He flexed his fists, claws extending and retracting, and willed himself to hold it together.

"Did you come all the way out here just to tell me off?" he asked quietly. "Or did you have something useful to offer?"

Those blue eyes went ice cold, and the wolf actually felt uneasy. He hadn't worked with Damien. From what he'd heard, the vamp had refused to. But he had to be a favorite of Drake's for a reason. And the Shades were a lot more cold-blooded than he'd figured on. He doubted they'd get in his way once he was Alpha, or at least not openly. Wasn't their style. But he wasn't Alpha yet.

"I was sent to give you a message, from Drake. And

he's a man who's been watching the dynasties for centuries, not to mention meddling in them for pay, so I suggest you heed his advice."

The wolf rolled his shoulders impatiently. He wanted his run, he wanted to get through this month, and more than anything, he desperately wanted never to have to interact with a Cait Sith or a Lilim ever again. At least not to speak. Hunting them down would be a pleasure.

"Say what you have to, and then get out of here before I call out the guard."

Damien regarded him for a moment with something like pity in those cold eyes. Then he spoke, slowly and calmly, betraying no emotion at all.

"Drake wanted to tell you that you should be careful who you trust. That friends among the dynasties are rarely what they seem, and that no one, particularly your new...associates...ever does anything unless they know they will have the advantage. An offer of power is usually just an offer to be someone's puppet...or a glorified slave. If you want your pack to survive intact, you'll walk away."

The wolf's laugh was a short, sharp bark. "Are you joking? Maybe Drake is just concerned that the wolves are going to end up with more power and clout than his pissant little operation. And you know what? He's right. So you can tell him where to shove his advice. With my thanks, of course."

Damien hissed out a breath, narrowing his eyes. "That's exactly the response I told him he would get. Still, he wanted to try. I suppose he's sorry you didn't work out. There's always something to be said for dumb muscle and a willingness to eat the opposition."

The wolf smiled, deliberately showing his sharpened teeth. "You remember that you said that, cat. Remember it when your kind are all hiding in shadows, afraid of the big bad wolves. I know your scent, and I'll remember it when the time comes."

Damien didn't look intimidated in the least, and that, more than anything else, infuriated him. He was so sick of his kind being counted out, looked down upon. Finally, he had been sought out by creatures that could change all that. And they—*she*—would have his undying loyalty, and that of his pack. Once they understood what was at stake, that was. Which would happen soon.

"So predictable," Damien said. "So full of yourself. When someone puts a bounty on your foolish, furry head, I'll be first in line to take the job. It won't be long. You're too stupid to last. I doubt you'll even live to see your people in chains. Pity."

"You worthless ball of fur, why don't we settle this now if you're so eager to try and take me out?"

Damien laughed softly, a mocking sound drifting through the quiet night. "Because I only kill for money. And there'll be quite a bit to make if I wait."

With a hoarse snarl, he leaped at Damien, his form shifting in midair to become that of an enormous, muscular wolf. Bloodlust hazed his vision along with his anger, welling up from a source that never seemed to run dry. He had been made to hunt, to kill. Why fight it? Why, when he dreamed of tearing into flesh with his claws and feasting as the wolves had long ago.

But when he hit the ground, slashing out with his front claws, there was nothing but air and the hard, unforgiving earth. The wolf gave a loud grunt as the air rushed from his lungs, then lay there for a moment, panting with help-less fury and confusion. Gone. How?

Didn't matter, he decided. When the time came to begin the hunt, Damien Tremaine was first on his list. The mark of the cat would be washed away in a sea of blood. And he would stand at the head of the first wolf pack in centuries that would be truly respected, truly feared, by the rest of the world of night.

Slowly, he got to his feet, already knowing what he needed to do. He was the future Alpha of the Pack of the Thorn. He wouldn't just be shunted aside, no matter what Damien said.

The thought soothed him, and he quickened his pace again, ready to run beneath the waning moon.

To be free.

chapter TWELVE

T HE MAN WAS a sadist.

Lyra sat in her car, staring at the Shopway and wondering whether her legs would actually get her in and out of there. She hurt. Everywhere. In places she hadn't even been aware she had muscles. And tonight, after nearly a week of continuous torment, she and her aching muscles were going to go to that damn field and do it all again.

Another week of this and she'd be dead. Or lurching around like Quasimodo.

Pretty sad, when he was only barely sparring with her yet. Then again, she was a wolf, which she kept trying to explain him. Flipping through the air and slashing gracefully was not exactly her kind's stock in trade. Barrel rolling people and mauling them . . . that she could handle with her eyes closed.

Now she remembered why she'd been a ballet dropout.

She took a moment to enjoy the way the light had turned reddish gold as the sun began its long descent behind the Shopway. Then she groaned when she remembered what that sky meant. Jaden would be awake in a couple of hours. And the house would still be devoid of fuel for her abused body. Maybe she could hide out here tonight, huddled in the junk food aisle, munching. He'd never find her...

A rap at the window made her jump and let out an embarrassing squeak. Fortunately, the face she saw when she turned her head was friendly, if amused, and very familiar. Still uncertain enough of her throbbing legs that she didn't want to get out of the car, Lyra rolled down the window.

"Hey, Gerry. What's up?"

Gerry McFarlane grinned in at her, blue eyes twinkling. The stout, barrel-chested wolf was ostensibly the police chief in Silver Falls and in practice the head of the Thorn's guard. He was also one of her father's closest friends, and he never missed an opportunity to tease her.

Like now.

"I don't usually see you just sitting with your mind in outer space. I couldn't resist." He chuckled. "Hiding from your hostessing duties, I presume?"

Lyra laughed ruefully. She'd taken enough ribbing over having to entertain the Falls' newest visitor this week. The only good thing was that it provided her ample opportunity to demonstrate that she was most certainly *not* enamored of the handsome vampire in town. It was also a good way to try to convince herself of the same thing.

"Yeah, you could say that," she said with a wry smile. "He's all right, though, really. Nice... for a vamp."

That much, Lyra thought, was true, if odd. Being hot for him was one thing. Discovering she actually liked the guy was something else entirely. It warranted caution on her part, which was why she hadn't laid a finger on him since that very appealing offer.

Every time she got too close, she heard warning bells.

"Well, he bought a little goodwill at the Inn the other night, I'll give him that," Gerry replied. "And he's kept his fangs to himself. That's a start, even though I still can't figure out why his people would pick us out and try to make nice."

Lyra shrugged uncomfortably. That was one thing she hated about all of this—the lying to people who were her friends. Three more weeks of this and she'd be dying of guilt.

"We're well respected among our kind," Lyra said. "Why not us?"

"Well," Gerry said, leaning companionably against the car as he settled in for a chat, "we've bitched and moaned about being marginalized for long enough that actually getting some positive attention just feels odd. But who am I to question it, as long as the vamp behaves himself?"

"Jaden," Lyra reminded him. It bothered her to hear him referred to as a what and not a who. Gerry's brows lifted a little, but he nodded.

"Right. Jaden. Of course, your cousin isn't big on this whole idea."

Lyra angled her head to look up at Gerry. "No way. Really?" Gerry chuckled.

"Yeah. Well, he's at least not crazy about this *specific* vampire," he qualified, and Lyra couldn't help a smirk. No, after the other night, she was sure Eric wasn't big on this specific vampire.

"You're spending time with him. I've never exchanged pleasantries with a vamp myself. What's your take on it?"

Lyra flushed with pleasure. She might have known Gerry forever, and he was fond of picking her brains over things. But being asked about something so important when Eric, the presumptive heir, had already given his word from on high, felt...well, pretty good.

"I think it might be a good idea to re-engage, myself," Lyra said slowly, considering her response as she gave it. In truth, it had been on her mind as well. Jaden might not have seriously offered an alignment with his dynasty, but it had occurred to her that if she herself extended a hand to Lily it might not be simply dismissed. Especially because Lily had been human not long ago and wasn't carrying all the vampire-werewolf baggage the rest of them were.

It might work. And for all the wolves like herself and Simon, who had yearned to be able to broaden their horizons outside of werewolf territory, it could be a godsend.

"It would have to be the right dynasty, though," Lyra continued. "Jaden's dynasty is so young that I think it provides the best opportunity for us. The wolves have no history with them. They're building something new, and we could be a part of that." When she saw the way Gerry was looking at her, she had to smile. "I'm going to guess that Eric's take on it is nothing like mine."

"Ah, well, you know your cousin. Tradition and upholding pack law. He says he doesn't know what they'd want with us anyway, that the price might be too high. That would be my worry. We've warred with them all. I'd think that puts us at a disadvantage right off the bat, but..." He trailed off, then shrugged. "Well, we'll see which of you gets to help make the decision, I guess. Whoever it is, I know Dorien will listen."

The casual compliment touched Lyra. Part of her

wanted to hop out of the car and give Gerry a hug, just for speaking of her as an equal, and viable, candidate. It had never happened to her before. And she hadn't realized until just now how much such a simple thing would mean to her.

"My father's a smart man, and a good Alpha," Lyra said. "I'm sure he will listen."

Gerry grinned and touched a finger to the tip of her nose, the affectionate gesture taking her back to being an adoring five-year-old. The memory of such a pleasant, simple time made her heart ache, just a little.

"You've got a lot of him in you. I've always said it. Only Dorien Black's daughter could have a vampire eating out of the palm of her hand."

"Oh. Well, I—"

"Get your groceries, sweet pea. I'll see you later on."

Flustered by Gerry's description of the dynamic between her and Jaden, Lyra managed only a soft and perfunctory laugh. Was that really what people saw? Maybe Jaden seemed deferential toward her out in public. She had no idea. Or maybe it was just too dark for people to see him making faces at her.

"See you later," she murmured, wondering exactly what people *did* see on the rare occasion she and Jaden had been together among the pack. Was she missing something?

Gerry started away, and she thought she might actually need to pull her aching self out of the car, but he stopped short just a few feet away and turned back.

"Hey, I do have a favor to ask of you, if you're up for it. And if you want an excuse to get away from your charge for an evening."

"Sure," she said quickly. Having an actual job lined up

would be a lot better than admitting her muscles needed a night off. She was determined to keep up with Jaden. The worst thing it could do was kill her, and since death was already a strong possibility, she wasn't terribly worried.

But man, she would love to do something that didn't involve her trying to be Bruce Lee for the evening.

"Not that it's going to be very taxing for you. But it requires a certain...flair for diplomacy, let's say...that a lot of us are lacking, and—"

"You've got another werewolf nut you want me to get rid of."

Gerry's relieved smile was all the confirmation she needed. Lyra winced. This would be only marginally better than Jaden's brand of torture. Silver Falls was isolated, and the pack generally disciplined, but the same sense of danger that humans got about the place, the thing that prevented any of them from moving in, also sometimes attracted a different element. These types usually came armed with books on supernatural phenomena and video cameras, and often enjoyed skulking around in the woods after dark in the misguided belief they might surprise someone doing something paranormal.

They were annoying. They were also worrisome. If even the smallest bit of actual evidence got out, many more of these hunters would come. Fortunately, all that had ever emerged from here was the occasional wild story. Still, it was trouble no one wanted.

Getting rid of the overly curious was also a job no one wanted. Unfortunately, Lyra had been roped into it before, and she had a knack for the task. There were two ways to go about it: sweet talk, or scaring the person so badly they ended up right on the verge of a nervous breakdown.

She excelled at both.

"I know someone recommended the Lost Dog Café to him. That'd be a good place to look…don't see where else he can sit around giving everyone the stink eye."

Lyra sighed. "What does he look like?"

Gerry chuckled. "Black leather fedora and a Supernatural T-shirt. Very inconspicuous."

"Ha. Fabulous, another Indiana Jones of the Night. I'll take care of it. But only because I love you."

"Love you too, sweet pea. I owe you one."

"Mmm-hmm. I'll add it onto your tab. You currently owe me into infinity anyway."

Lyra watched Gerry saunter away, smiling despite herself. She supposed she was glad to have an excuse for a night off, even if it wasn't really a night off. Her father could entertain Jaden. Or he could wander off to…wherever Jaden wandered to when he needed to feed. He didn't say, and she didn't ask. But the thought of him with his teeth in some pretty young thing, his hands on her, made her smile evaporate all too quickly.

Yeah, maybe her father could entertain him.

With a muttered epithet, Lyra opened the door and slid out of the car. She felt about as bad as she'd expected. An actual injury would have healed long before now, but this pain wouldn't end without a full night to recover. And she'd be damned if she would let Jaden see her hobbling around like an old woman. Better to get the kinks out now.

Grimacing, and lamenting what now passed for a night off, she got to her feet, locked the car, and marched stiffly toward the Shopway.

chapter THIRTEEN

JADEN PULLED HIS CORVETTE into the small parking lot behind the row of shops that contained the Lost Dog Café, muttering under his breath about difficult women and their indulgent fathers.

He'd awakened looking forward to another evening of Lyra's undivided attention. He hated to admit it to himself, but that was one of his favorite things about instructing her. After all, there was much to like: she was an apt student, easy to teach and incredibly talented. Still, he mostly just liked having her to himself. For a vampire of his age and experience with women, that was sad.

Sadder still was how unhappy he'd found himself when Dorien, happily ensconced in the kitchen with a beer and a battered paperback, informed him that Lyra would be out for the evening on "pack business."

"Pack business my ass," Jaden grumbled, putting the car in park and killing the engine. A date, even a fake date with some idiotic werewolf hunter, was not business. Especially not when Dorien had gotten such a laugh over exactly how good Lyra was at running off unwanted visitors.

Actually, Jaden thought, remembering how charming she'd been on their first couple of meetings, he could see that.

He got out of the car, worried for a moment over whether anyone would decide to open a door into it, then locked it and headed around the building. There was a nip in the air tonight—the weather still couldn't quite decide to commit to being consistently pleasant. In the past week, the town had seen cold rain, wind, and then seventy-degree temperatures. It seemed to be working its way back to the latter, but the night wasn't without its bite.

His stomach rumbled at the thought, and he pushed it aside. Later. He would skip town for a bite *later.* Right now, he just wanted to see Lyra. And possibly throttle whoever this idiot human was, fake date or not.

He passed under a purposely shabby yellow sign featuring an abstract-looking dog. Jaden pushed open the door and walked into the café. He let his eyes sweep the room, absorbing the feel of the place. Velvet curtains framed the large windows looking out onto the sidewalk. The dimly lit interior was punctuated by the flickering lights of candles atop tall, spindly tables and the leather-upholstered booths that lined the walls. Pieces of art hung on the coffee-colored walls in bold colors, mostly Dali-esque dreamscapes with the occasional martini bar painting thrown in. A husky male voice sang over a sax, the music piped through the speakers.

Though the café was the opposite of the quaint, salty, charming Inn, it managed to be warm instead of pretentious. Jaden thought he might like to come check it out sometime when he could actually enjoy it.

Right now, however, all his attention was focused on the woman who sat with her back to him, and the loser in the black fedora who had drool just about leaking out of his mouth.

Lyra was wearing some sort of sweater that draped down in the back, exposing enough smooth, creamy skin and strong shoulder that Jaden found his own mouth watering. Her hair was tied back at the nape of her neck, left to coil downward in a long tail. She seemed casual, relaxed from the way she held herself. And as he watched, she tossed her head back and laughed. The sound was a loud, throaty roll that had his fangs lengthening, hunger for her beginning to rush through his system like wildfire.

He could smell her. He could damn near taste her. And if the fedora didn't stop looking at her like he wanted to take his own bite out of her, he was going to—

"Hell with this," Jaden growled, slapped what he hoped was a pleasant expression on his face, and headed for the table.

Fedora guy spotted him almost instantly. Jaden had to stop himself from smiling over the immediate wariness that came over the man's expression, inordinately pleased that he'd managed to suck all the fun out of whatever joke he and Lyra had been sharing. Lyra turned to see what the problem was, the curiosity in her eyes turning quickly to some odd combination of irritation and pleasure the instant she saw him.

Considering that pleasure was definitely in there some-where, he would take it.

"Lyra," Jaden purred, wondering whether she would play along. "Fancy meeting you here."

He saw one corner of her mouth twitch before she

answered. The look in her eyes was very plainly *I'm going to get you for this.*

"Jaden," she said. "What a nice . . . surprise." She turned her head to look at her companion, who was already looking suspiciously between them. Jaden thought he looked like the kind of guy who was considered decent looking now, but who had been hung by his underwear from lockers on a fairly regular basis in his youth. Lyra was a prize he didn't want to share.

"Blake, this is Jaden. Jaden," she paused, and he caught a warning flash of humor on her face before she fired her opening shot. "Finkleman. Jaden, this is my friend Blake Torrance."

Jaden slid her a fulminating glare from beneath his lashes when he went to shake the fedora wearer's hand. Her grin could have melted butter.

"Charmed," Jaden said, giving Blake's hand a quick, firm shake and then quickly letting go. The man had sweaty palms. Jaden hated that.

"Do you live in Silver Falls too?" Blake asked. He seemed suspicious. But then, Jaden was fairly sure he practiced his pseudo-intimidating suspicious face in the mirror every morning. He doubted it helped much in his travels, but he probably thought it would heighten his credibility when he eventually got a ghost-hunting TV show.

This sort, in Jaden's experience, always wanted a TV show. Considerably more than they wanted to know the truth behind the supernatural phenomena they chased around.

"Recent transplant," Jaden said. "How about you?"

He caught Blake's eyes and pushed a thought at him: *Ask me to stay for dinner.*

"I...I'm here on business. And some unexpected plea-sure," Blake said, his eyes clouding for a moment before clearing again. He looked up at Jaden, seeming slightly puzzled. Jaden smiled indulgently and waited.

"Would you like to join us?" Blake asked.

"Love to, thanks," Jaden said, and slid into an empty chair before Lyra could protest. Instead, she shot him a narrow-eyed glare before turning her attention back to Blake.

"So you were telling me about the rumors that brought you here?" she asked, and in a far sweeter voice than she'd ever used on Jaden. "Blake is a paranormal buff. He seems to think we've got some kind of phenomena around here. I'm just not sure what that would be, apart from the one time Billy Carmichael got so drunk he stripped and went running down Main Street in the middle of a snowstorm."

Jaden blinked. "I'm...not sorry I missed that."

She gave him a small smile. "Don't blame you. It was emotionally scarring."

"Um," Blake interjected, looking between them again with more than a hint of jealousy. "There are a lot more reported instances of supernatural occurrences around here than you two seem to think. Lycanthropy being the most common thread running through them. It's easy to dismiss and laugh at if you're not up on the research, but I assure you, this is no laughing matter."

He sounded so prissy and uptight that Jaden had to bite his tongue to keep from snickering. Then he made the mistake of catching Lyra's eye and realized she was hav-ing the exact same problem. Her lower lip quivered, and she bit it, very gently, before she pointedly looked away.

Jaden let his eyes linger on her profile a moment longer, wishing they were alone so he could run his own tongue and teeth over that entrancingly full lower lip of hers.

"You can't expect me to believe the two of you are ignorant of the stories about this place," Blake continued, sounding increasingly peevish at being ignored. "They've been covered up pretty well, I'll say that, but the truth is out there for those of us willing to dig deep enough."

Oh hell, there it was. Jaden managed to cover the laugh with a cough, but he doubted it was very convincing. Lyra grabbed her glass and took a long drink of water.

Taking a little pity on the man, Jaden turned his attention back to Blake. Yes, Jaden decided, he was pissed. His date had been ruined, and his life's passion was being laughed at. He might not be so mad if he'd realized he was being laughed at by a vampire and a werewolf, respectively, but still. Jaden decided to make a little effort to be civil, since he now knew there was no way in hell Lyra was going anywhere else with this guy.

"Look, Blake," he said, "there are a lot of unexplained things in the world. A lot of them, maybe most of them, are better left unexamined by the unwary."

"I'm plenty wary," Blake snapped. "And I'm obviously onto something, because I've never met anyone who liked playing vampire who chose to live in a normal town."

Jaden lifted his brows. "You think I...play vampire? That sounds like a pretty personal question, Blake. You'll have to at least buy me a drink for the answer."

Blake huffed out an angry little laugh. "Okay," he said, standing up. "This is going nowhere. I don't know why I asked you to stay...really...but if you're not going to help me, then I've got other leads to follow."

"Do you?"

"Damn right." He was fumbling in his wallet.

"No, Blake, don't go. Jaden can leave, or you and I can find someplace else to sit and talk. This was supposed to be just the two of us—"

"Blake."

Turning his gift, his power for controlling humans, on was as intuitive as breathing. Jaden's voice turned gentle but commanding, smooth and utterly irresistible. Even Lyra turned toward him, her head slightly tilted in response to the change in his voice. But he'd had his fun with the interloper—it was time to help him on his way so he and Lyra could have the table to themselves.

Blake stilled and turned to look at Jaden, as Jaden had known he would. Humans really had no choice about succumbing to a thrall. And once their eyes met, when Jaden saw them go hazy and confused, he knew he had him just where he wanted him.

"Are you listening to me, Blake?" he asked, his voice as calm as if he were about to discuss the weather. Blake nodded, his action slow and dreamlike.

"Yes . . . master."

He felt Lyra glaring at him, but he didn't want to break the connection, so he addressed her without looking.

"All right, I didn't mean to lay it on that thick. Don't call me master, Blake. I'm just your friend. Your buddy Jaden."

"Hey, buddy."

Jaden smirked despite his best efforts. "Hey, Blake. Listen, as your buddy, I have to tell you. You need to walk out of here, go get your things at the hotel, and leave town. Immediately."

"Leave town. Yeah," Blake murmured, swaying slightly on his feet where he stood. "But there are...lycans..."

"No, you've been watching too much Underworld," Jaden replied, calm but firm. He never blinked, feeling the power in the hold he had over the man. It made him hungry, unfortunately...a good thrall was wasted if you didn't get a drink out of it...but wasted this one would be. He doubted the patrons of the Lost Dog would appreciate the sight of him getting a snack.

"There are no werewolves here. No vampires. This is, in fact, the most boring place on earth, and you'll remember it that way. Get a girlfriend. Get a life. For the love of all that is holy, get rid of the stupid hat. And you will never come back here again. Is that understood?"

"Yes, master Jaden."

"Stop that," Jaden replied, frowning.

"Yes, Jaden Finkleman. My buddy."

Jaden sighed. "Better. Marginally. Go on now, Blake. Drinks were on me."

The ghost chaser glided off in a daze, bumping into a waitress as well as the door before he found his way out. Jaden turned to watch him go, amused. He hadn't done that in a while, really laid the suggestion on thick. Hopefully it would work. He was pretty sure it would in the short term at least.

Lyra was staring at him, and he couldn't read her expression at all. Finally, she said, "If he crashes his car, I will kick your ass."

"You won't," Jaden replied, "though you should be happy, because now that Blake the Flake has wandered away you've got plenty of time to try doing just that tonight. You look amazing, by the way."

He was deliberately casual about it because he knew that if he went heavy on the flattery she would just blow him off. Being told she was beautiful seemed to make Lyra uncomfortable, for some reason. He liked making her a little uncomfortable.

True to form, her cheeks flushed prettily. "Oh," she said. "Um, thanks." She hesitated a moment and then said, "You smell pretty good tonight."

"Must be that cologne you picked covered the cat smell," he teased. But he liked the compliment...a great deal. It was a small step toward him, but he would take it over the stalemate of the past week. He wanted her. He was going to keep wanting her.

He decided giving a few reminders didn't hurt, either, however subtle. Especially because she was gorgeous when she was flustered.

"Yeah, I hope you didn't mind that. You seemed like you might be a cologne guy. And I like to smell things that I like." She paused and shook her head. "You know what I mean. I'm a sense of smell girl. Wolf thing."

"Also a cat thing, so I can appreciate that. And I do like it, so thanks."

She smiled, a true smile this time. And as Jaden sat looking at her, at the candlelight flickering in her eyes, at the soft set of her mouth and the way the streaks in her hair glinted and shimmered, he felt a strange sensation in the center of his chest, a pulling from the seat of whatever he had for a soul. It drew him to Lyra, more powerfully than any blood had ever called him...though the scent of hers, dark and ripe and wild, enveloped him as he sat there, enchanted.

He had always known there was more than one way to

hunger for a woman. He had just never expected to find himself hungry in all those ways for a single woman. It filled him with a bottomless longing, the sort he would never be able to assuage with a simple bite or even a night in her bed.

He didn't know what it would take.

All he knew was . . . somehow, he had to find out.

The softness remained in her expression as she looked at him, and Jaden felt himself holding his breath, waiting to see what this new shift in his mercurial student would bring. Most of their interaction had been work, with (mostly) good-natured insults that passed as banter. He sensed the same guardedness in her nature as he had in his own, so he understood. But Jaden wanted, more and more, to see what was behind the shield she carried. Only she could decide to let him, though.

"The thrall thing is a handy trick," Lyra said. "You could rule the world with that."

Jaden shrugged. "I prefer just using it to get free stuff. And get the occasional power trip from being called master." He burst out laughing at the same time as she did. "Actually, the master thing is a new one. I think your new boyfriend has some deep-seated issues."

Lyra smacked him lightly on the arm. "While the hat was just dead sexy, not my type. I think I'd need to get into whips and chains, and I'm just not going there."

"Pity."

"You're a pig," she said, still grinning. "And . . . thanks."

Jaden feigned incredulity. "Seriously? You're *thanking* me for helping you?"

She rolled her eyes back into her head. "Bite me. I might have complained if I was enjoying myself, but listening to the walking encyclopedia of weird got old after ten minutes, and he was so dead set on this place it was going to take me a while. So yes, thank you."

The warmth between them lingered, invisible but palpable.

"You want to take a walk?" she asked suddenly. "I need to move. And it's finally not raining, so..."

He tipped his chin down to look at her. "Trying to skip out on practice?"

Her expression clouded with both guilt and irritation. Right then, he realized she didn't just want a night off... she probably *needed* a night off.

"Forget it. You've been working your tail off. Tonight, a walk works for me." He knew this was the right decision when he saw the relief. Lyra was a stoic, but she must have been hurting a little more than he realized. He wished she would tell him what was going on in that beautiful head once in a while. Her absolute refusal to ask for help worried him, along with her stubborn self-reliance...even as he knew these qualities were some of what attracted him.

"Great. I'll go grab the waitress and take care of the bill, and we'll head out."

Jaden watched her stride away and sighed to himself, enjoying the lingering scent of her perfume. He didn't know where they were headed, the two of them. Nowhere fast, probably.

But he wanted, very much, to try and enjoy the ride.

It might have been chilly, but Lyra loved being out in the open air. She breathed in deeply, tipping her head back to look at the night sky. Some of the clouds had cleared off, allowing the bright pinpoints of stars to shine down unobstructed.

Jaden walked beside her in companionable silence. She got the feeling he was waiting for her to speak. That was one thing about him: he was happy to engage when provoked, but he didn't seem to need to just chatter for no apparent reason. She was used to being talked at— whether it was because of her position in the pack or just because she looked like she might have answers, people tended to come to her with their problems, their concerns, their stories. No one, except maybe Simon, had ever been very interested in her own.

Now there was Jaden, waiting patiently for her to say something, or to say nothing, content in his own skin. It was . . . interesting.

And incredibly attractive. But hadn't she decided she wasn't going to think about that anymore?

Yeah, right. For tonight, Lyra supposed she would blame her weakness on the scent of his cologne. That fragrance really did smell great on him. And for now, a convenient explanation like that suited her just fine.

They left the square behind, ambling down the familiar streets of her hometown. Lyra stole glances at Jaden occasionally, enjoying the fact that he seemed to appreciate the beauty of her place, if not necessarily the inhabitants. Even there, though, she'd seen a change. People were getting used to seeing him. And the longer he went without freaking out and killing a bunch of wolves, the more comfortable her pack would probably become.

The two of them walked slowly over a little bridge that spanned Illoren Creek.

There were areas for pedestrians along the sides, and she stopped, leaning over to watch the water and enjoying the sound of it as it moved beneath.

She thought Jaden was watching the creek, too, but his words indicated he'd been looking at her instead. She found she didn't mind.

"You're wearing your necklace," he said. "The one I brought back to you. I haven't seen you wear it since then."

Lyra picked up the moonstone pendant from where it dangled between her breasts and looked at it, rubbing her thumb over the smooth stone out of habit. She'd once thought it brought her luck. Maybe it did, in its way.

"I don't wear it all the time," she said, lifting her eyes to meet Jaden's. The sight of him, watching her so intently and illuminated only by the faint glow of a streetlight farther back down the road, momentarily took her breath away. He was so perfectly suited to the night, she thought. So dark and beautiful. And having his undivided attention fixed on her, when he looked so very much like what he was, had lust unfurling like a dark and sensuous bloom deep in her belly.

Unsettled, she sought more words to fill the silence.

"When I'm away, I wear the necklace for luck, and because it reminds me of home. When I'm here, I usually just wear it if I'm doing some kind of pack business to let people know not to bother me unless it's important."

Jaden chuckled, then leaned against the railing beside her to look over. "I'm sure your Blake would be flattered to know he was deemed important by a pack of werewolves."

"He's not mine, because I don't want him. It is important that we run people like him off, though. Some of them are more astute than is safe for us. We don't want that kind of attention."

"No, I'm sure you don't." Jaden fell silent again, looking

out into the distance. She let her gaze linger on his profile, allowing her eyes to caress what her fingers longed to. There was so much she didn't know about him, and he offered very little freely. But here, alone, she felt emboldened to pry a little more.

"So how did you end up here?" she asked.

He gave her a sideways look. "I drove."

Lyra pursed her lips. "Hilarious. I didn't mean literally. I haven't ever talked much to vampires, except maybe Rogan back at that safe house where I met you. And I'm pretty sure at least half of everything he said was complete bullshit."

Jaden chuckled. "You would be right about that. Ty knew him better than I did, but that was the impression I got too. Sneaky bastard, but charming enough when he wanted something. Damien took his head off that night, you know. Right before sunrise."

Lyra winced. "Wow. I'm sorry."

"Don't be. Rogan had it coming from any number of directions. If it hadn't been Damien, it would have been someone else before too long."

"Who's Damien?" she asked. She didn't remember anyone by that name at the safe house, though in fairness, that whole episode had been unnerving. Fleeing there had been a last resort.

"He's a Cait Sith, like I am, or was, before I joined the Lilim. Never belonged to the Ptolemy, though. He's with the House of Shadows."

"Oh," Lyra replied, frowning. "I heard a lot about them while I was in Chicago. They're some kind of assassin's guild or something, aren't they?"

"Among other things," Jaden allowed. "Tangling with

Shades is usually ill advised. Damien's very good at what he does. Which means he's a useful friend to have."

"He's a good friend?"

Jaden gave her a half smile. "Well. More to Ty than me. They were turned around the same time, and knew one another way back. But he and I tolerate one another, even though I doubt I'll ever really trust him." He paused, then looked away. "I've done a lot of things I'm not proud of to survive, but living this long, having to make your way among the highbloods and the lowbloods and all the intrigue...it can kill some parts of you after a while. Your conscience. Your soul. Damien's missing a few pieces."

"And you're not?" she asked quietly. Not to tease, but because she really wanted to know.

He seemed to consider this for a moment. Finally, he looked at her, his eyes glowing softly in the dark. "I don't think so," he said. "I'm tired, of course. Tired of running, tired of never having a real place to call home. But I'm pretty sure all my pieces are intact."

Her mind raced directly into the gutter, and Lyra flushed. She was absolutely positive all his pieces were intact. Jaden read her face immediately and gave a low, warm laugh.

"See, that's what I like about you, Lyra. No putting on airs. You're very...earthy."

It was her turn to laugh. "I guess I'll take that as a compliment." Her smile lingered after the laughter died away as they stood, heads turned toward one another. The connection between them felt natural and comfortable right now. Maybe because it was no longer based on simple attraction...there was more.

Maybe a lot more, if she had the nerve to explore it. Here in the comfortable darkness, it didn't seem nearly as unwise.

"So now you *like* me, huh?" she asked, seeing no harm in flirting a little. What could happen? They were in public, sort of. She was safe enough. And the way he was watching her made her toes curl with pleasure.

"Of course I like you," he replied. "I thought I'd already made that clear." He surprised her by lifting his hand to tuck a stray curl behind her ear. His hand grazed her cheek lightly, and even that small amount of contact made her skin sizzle.

"Yeah, well, lust and like are two different things," Lyra said, hearing the slight quaver in her voice as she sought to hold back the instincts that rose so quickly to the surface whenever he touched her. So strange, that a cat would appeal so deeply to a wolf. But there it was. The wild thing in her wanted him just as badly as the rest of her did.

"Why can't it be both?" Jaden asked. "You're beautiful, Lyra. But I wouldn't be here if that's all there was to you."

"Ah, I see." Lyra laughed. "You like me for my ability to kick serious ass. Got it."

He smiled, but there was something soft in his expression that made her want to simply melt into him. No man had ever looked at her the way he did, she realized. She'd been wanted, and she'd had a few men enjoy her company. But never really both. Not like this.

This realization made her wish things were different. Because Jaden was special. She could accept that she felt that way, even though it would do her no good to admit it to him. It wouldn't change the way things had to be.

Yet she couldn't resist moving into him, watching his lashes lower in anticipation as he went very still, waiting. He allowed her to make the choice. He couldn't possibly know how much such a small thing meant to her. And it made it that much easier to lift her lips to his, pressing into the incredible softness of his mouth. Lyra felt him tremble, ever so slightly, and it was nearly her undoing.

Why did she always end up wanting the most impossible things?

She slid her arms around Jaden's neck, fitting herself against him. One of his hands curved around her waist, the other brushing over her hair to cup the back of her head. His mouth opened against hers, and she swept her tongue inside, deepening the kiss. Instead of climbing him, which a part of her always seemed inclined to do, Lyra held back, stroking the hair at the nape of Jaden's neck, savoring the taste of him, the feel of him. He was like nothing and no one she had ever known.

With great effort, she finally pulled away, though Lyra let her hands stay on him for a precious few more minutes. Part of her knew this was a slippery slope she was starting on. Wrong place, wrong time, wrong species—wrong everything. Maybe Jaden was right. Maybe they should just enjoy the now.

But she'd never been very good at living in the moment. She was always rushing headlong into a future that refused to let her shape it. Not that she would ever stop trying.

"You're sad," Jaden said, still only a breath away from her. It was so tempting to just give in, to let go with him. "I wish you wouldn't be."

Lyra managed a smile. "You're not the only one allowed to be moody. Don't worry. It's not you. You've got an incredible mouth."

She saw the heat flare in his eyes, felt it spark between them.

"I'd be happy to let you use it a little longer."

She had to muster everything she had to pull away, but that's what Lyra did, stepping back out of the protective circle of Jaden's arms.

"Maybe another night," she said. Not tonight. Tonight was for considering whether to further complicate her life.

He startled her when he gave her a quick, hard kiss that held more than a hint of possessiveness, then stepped back before she had a chance to react.

"I said I would leave it to you, Lyra," he said. "But you should remember that I'm not made of stone. Touch me like that again, and I won't let you walk away so easily."

She blew out a breath, then nodded. "Fair enough," she said. And she was suddenly glad he couldn't get into her head, couldn't know how hard it was for her to walk away this time. Testing herself, testing him, was at an end. She was going to have Jaden, because at some point, she wasn't going to be able to help herself.

"Come on, hot stuff," Lyra said, hoping to lighten the cloud of seriousness that had settled over them, as though whatever next move they made was going to be important no matter how she fought it. "You got your good-night kiss. Walk me home, and I might let you hold my hand."

"How could I resist?" he asked in a tone so full of dark promise it made her shiver. But he fell silent again as they moved off the bridge, walking back toward the house where a spontaneous tryst was, thankfully, impossible. But Lyra drew in a sharp breath, then turned her head with an amused smile when Jaden caught her hand in his.

"No welching," he said.

So Lyra left her fingers threaded through his, wishing it didn't feel quite so right, and headed for home.

chapter FOURTEEN

A<small>GAIN</small>."

Jaden tried to keep his amusement from showing as he watched Lyra hunch over panting, glaring at him from a few feet away. Her forehead was beaded with sweat, and a few curls had escaped from her ponytail to form a wild halo around her head.

Unlike her, he wasn't winded at all. But then, evading her attacks was an easier job than she had trying to launch them. Not that telling her that would do much to assuage her seething temper. She wanted to take him down. He planned to make her earn that right.

Channeling his sexual frustration into training Lyra had proven incredibly useful when it came to his focus, even if she didn't seem to appreciate it.

"What the hell do you mean, *again*?" she snapped, straightening and wiping her forehead with the back of her arm. "I've tried to do that move like ten times now, and all you do is step away! I don't think you showed me

right. That, or you're just making crap up to watch me fall
on my ass over and over."

That was an entertaining bonus, but he didn't plan
on telling her that. He shouldn't enjoy watching her get
mad, but Lyra's reactions to things were unfailingly honest. And when peppered with one of her profanity-laced
tirades, they were irresistible.

"I'm not making anything up. And you're getting it.
You just need to keep working at it," he said, keeping his
voice cool. She was coming along nicely. But if she didn't
learn to control that temper of hers, none of this would
be worth anything. He had a sneaking suspicion she was
grappling with just as much physical frustration as he
was, which likely wasn't helping matters.

Something had changed between them that night on
the bridge. The way she'd kissed him had been...unex-
pected, and as honest a thing as he'd experienced in a very
long time. Their interactions had become warmer since
then, more open, even as her training had become a lot
more fraught. He thought that probably the reason was
because the wolf in her was so close to the surface during these sessions. The animal in her was all instinct and
feeling—and it wanted him. He knew the feeling, Jaden
thought darkly.

But he wasn't going to beg, damn it. That kiss had
been three nights ago, and he'd behaved. Though knowing the itch was getting to her was kind of satisfying, in a
nasty sort of way.

He saw Lyra's eyes flash hot gold, and his body began
to respond accordingly. Jaden thought frantically of
images to halt his body's reaction.

Ice cubes...Antarctica...Dorien in a dress...

The last one worked—sort of.

"Keep working at it, keep working at it," Lyra mimicked in a sing-song voice. "Is that all you can say? I could have gotten a parrot and gotten as much help!"

"I resent that," Jaden said smoothly. "I have a much nicer voice than a parrot."

Lyra bared her teeth at him instead of laughing. "Oh, you think this is funny, huh? Watching me flail around while you just stand there directing. I'm not going to beat Eric like this, unless I can make him die laughing."

"You have to adjust your way of thinking about the movement," Jaden said, trying to stay patient while she railed at him. The woman herself had *no* patience, not that he was surprised. "Less wolf, more cat. Concentrate!"

Lyra threw back her head and let out something that sounded like a roar.

"How many times do we have to go over this? I am not a cat! I'm a wolf! I can't change that, so *make adjustments!*"

"You're going to have to make the adjustments, if you really want to learn," Jaden replied, hearing the heat enter his own voice. "Not everything revolves around you. Not everything can be tailored to you. I wasn't under the impression you were the sort of woman who needed coddling. You learn the right way, or you don't learn at all. It's as simple as that."

He could handle Lyra's anger for quite a while, since he realized a lot of it was self-directed despite what came out of her mouth. But when it started to really spill over onto him, he quit being so tolerant.

True to form, she put a hand on one hip and glared at him. He knew the look—insult time.

"You're a jackass."

"And you're acting like a spoiled child. If this were easy, you wouldn't need me at all," he snapped.

"Then maybe you should do more than just stand there if you want me to learn the right way, O Exalted Master of Kitty Fu," Lyra growled, beginning to circle him slowly. There was no light but the stars and the moon, still bright though past its fullness, but with his hunter's eyes Jaden could see Lyra as clear as day. She stood out to him against the dark backdrop of towering pines and maples, looking like some ancient goddess of bounty with the tall grass and wildflowers brushing against her legs. Her eyes glowed like embers.

All around was silence, broken only by chirping crickets and the occasional call of an owl. It was a perfect night, a perfect spot here in a hidden field long left for the woods to reclaim.

It was also an excellent place to fight, if one was so inclined. And Lyra certainly seemed to be. Jaden decided battle was as good an outlet as any.

"I might move more," he said in a voice both soft and deadly, "if I was in any danger of actually being taken down by you. As it is, this is almost…" he trailed off, watching her eyes narrow, enjoying her anticipation of his insult.

"Relaxing," he finally finished, and all the raw nerves Lyra seemed to be in possession of seemed to burst into flame at once.

"That's it." She gave a feral snarl and lunged for him. And because he was a masochistic bastard, he didn't even try to get out of her way. If this was what she needed, for tonight, they'd do it her way. Jaden caught her against him, grunting at the force with which she'd launched herself. He stumbled backward, and they fell to the ground together. They rolled as soon as they hit, a frenzy of claws and snapping teeth, each trying to gain the upper hand. Lyra made it a lot harder than he'd anticipated. But then, he might have expected it if he hadn't been so busy trying to keep his hands off of her up until now.

Her strength was incredible. Heat pumped off her in waves, heating his cool skin. They grappled together, hands hooked into claws, teeth bared. Jaden wanted to go easy on her. He was no sexist, but a certain sense of chivalry had never left him and he disliked having to hurt a woman. However, Lyra wouldn't let him give an inch. Her snapping teeth, snarling, and attempts at kneeing him in some very delicate places made it impossible to let down his guard.

"Damn it Lyra," he panted, rolling her beneath him only to have her flip him once again and snap her teeth together inches from his nose. "I'm not the enemy!"

"Close enough," she growled, then gave an outraged shriek as Jaden finally pinned her beneath him, her arms over her head. Lyra thrashed from side to side, and Jaden could only stare at the display of raw, powerful fury. She was less woman than animal in this moment, and he knew that he hadn't truly appreciated what Lyra was, what her powers meant, until right now.

He had her—but only barely.

"Calm down! You've got to get it under control," he ordered her, but all Lyra did was writhe and buck beneath him. He knew it wasn't her goal, but despite his own anger, and despite the blood pumping hot and fast in his veins—or the combination—Lyra's display had quite the opposite effect of her intention. And having her captive beneath him only compounded the problem. All he could think of was the dreams he'd had of her, bare skin like silk beneath his hands.

Flustered, and pushed nearly to his limit, he tried to instruct instead of giving in.

"You should try shifting back and forth during the fight," he panted, slamming her hands back down to the ground.

"*What*?" she asked through gritted teeth, which he noted had become awfully sharp.

He growled as she nearly threw him off again. "I mean be a wolf, be a human, be a wolf...mix it up, it throws off your enemies."

She stopped thrashing all at once. The sudden stillness was disconcerting, and all he could hear was the sound of labored breathing. Hers. His. Lyra's eyes blazed up at him, the brightest things in the darkness.

She was too tempting...irresistible. Their eyes locked, and he began to lower his mouth to hers, his eyes slipping shut.

He should have known that's when she would strike. The form beneath him changed shape in an instant, flesh becoming fur, snout in place of inviting lips. In the split second he was able to focus on them, her teeth were bared in what looked like an evil grin. He lost his grip and his balance at the same time, finding himself rolled and pinned by large paws before he could correct himself. His defensive instincts kicked in, overriding emotion.

Jaden slid into his cat form like water, his change in size making it easier to flip and scramble from beneath Lyra. He was the size of a wildcat, large enough to be intimidating, but smaller than a full-grown wolf. She snarled when she realized what had happened, but she was already behind him as he raced into the tall grass of the field, vanishing swift and silent into the dark.

She had been on hunts before, but never one as exhilarating as this.

Lyra raced through the field, the grass brushing against her legs, her flanks. Her heart pumped steadily in her chest as she put on speed, chasing the whispers in the grass just ahead where Jaden thought he would escape her. She could smell him, the seductive musk of man and vampire and cat all entwined.

Jaden would never know the effect that scent had on her, especially in her wolf form where all her senses were intensified. But he was about to discover that running from her was an excellent way to lose, and quickly.

Jaden was fast. She would give him that. He was also going to be responsible for his own downfall, considering he was the one who'd told her to shape-shift.

She could hear him, sense him, racing just ahead of her, darting back and forth through the field and trying to get far enough ahead to lose her. Wasn't going to happen, Lyra thought, so in tune with his movement that for a moment it felt almost like she and Jaden were extensions of the same creature. She was so close to him... almost there...

He darted to the side, then bunched his muscles to spring away. Lyra leaped at the same time, and with barely a thought shifted again in midair, stretching out her arms to grasp handfuls of sleek black fur. Beneath her fingers, Jaden changed, too, and this time when she hit the ground with him to roll in the soft grass anger was hopelessly tangled with lust. Lyra realized she'd pushed it too far tonight. Time to either kiss or kill, and the choice, once made, was an overwhelming relief.

Though she did slam him to the ground, just for fun.

His eyes were wide and startled, and a little admiring. "Well done," he said slightly short of breath. "You should always do what I tell you."

"Shut up," Lyra growled, grabbing fistfuls of his shirt and dragging her mouth to his for a kiss that was at least half wild.

One of her last rational thoughts was how good it felt to get her hands on him, to feel all his tightly coiled strength thrumming beneath her fingers. Then she couldn't think at all as their bodies came together, her curves molding instantly against Jaden's hard, lean form. Lyra slid her arms around him as he rose against her, letting her fingers finally slide up into all that dark, shining hair. His scent, masculine, appealing, and, oddly, deliciously *other*, swamped her. She crushed her mouth against his, sliding against him, into him, until she felt herself being drawn down into some dark and blissful heaven.

Seeing Jaden's hunger for her was one thing. Tasting it was something very different.

Lyra gasped against Jaden's mouth as his tongue swept inside, coaxing her own into a wild and primal rhythm. His hands were in her hair, tugging it so that it tumbled down her back. She only dimly realized that while she might have initiated this, he had quickly taken control. Jaden rolled her beneath him, effectively capturing her. This time, she allowed it.

Lyra's fingers hooked into claws and dug into his shoulders. His kisses grew deeper, his mouth more insistent. She could feel the prick of his fangs against her tongue, and it only stoked the heat growing inside of her. His hands slid over her body as though he couldn't get enough of her, coasting over her back, her breasts, his touch just light enough to have her writhing against him, demanding more.

Still, she could feel him holding back, and the wolf now snapping at the end of its own tether would have none of it. Lyra growled softly, beginning to play rough. She nipped at Jaden's lower lip, just hard enough to draw blood. She heard his soft hiss, knew it had excited him when he kissed her again, hard. She drew his lip into her mouth to suckle it. In response, Jaden gripped her hips, fingers digging in, and pressed into her.

Lyra moaned thickly in the back of her throat at the feel of him, hard where she was hot and throbbing. She arched into him, wrapping her legs around his waist, opening for him. Reality, sanity, everything slipped away. All she knew was that she wanted the man driving her mad with his mouth, his hands. Hot. Hard. *Now*.

"Lyra," he breathed, her name like a prayer on his lips. "I want—"

"Yes," she said. She had waited, unsure, wondering whether there would be a right time for this. But she knew it was now.

They tore at each other's clothing, grasping and pulling until there was nothing but skin on skin, the heat between them threatening to set fire to the grass around them. His mouth seemed to be everywhere at once: her mouth, her neck, and then lower to suckle the tight buds of her nipples.

Lyra gave a hoarse cry. The sensation was exquisite

when he trailed his hot tongue over her chest, kindling a delicious burn at her core. Then his mouth was on hers again, demanding and yet somehow soft enough that she sank into every kiss, never wanting to surface. He broke the kiss unexpectedly and rose above her in the darkness, bracing himself on his hands. His eyes were like blue fire. Lyra felt her breath catch in her throat. With only the night sky and the stars behind him, his pale skin shone like alabaster. He looked more god than man, unspeakably beautiful. Her hands trailed down his chest while her heart pounded within her own. Jaden's eyes slipped shut when she stroked him, and he made a sound that was half moan, half purr.

Lyra let out a shuddering breath. Gods, she wanted him so badly, it frightened her. But she couldn't turn away from him, not now. She reached between them and took him in her hand, stroking the throbbing length of him. Jaden's head dropped forward, and his hair hid his face from view. But his hips moved in time with her increasingly bold strokes, and his breathing was as ragged as her own. Finally, he reached down to pull her hand away, and he raised his head to look at her.

The raw need she saw written there sent shock waves of pleasure rippling through her.

"Much more of that and we'll be finished before we start," he said hoarsely. "Slower," he continued, lowering himself over her, his chest brushing her skin. "I've been thinking about this for months. I damn well plan to enjoy it."

Her eyes widened. "Mon—"

But her question, and the thoughts that went with it, were swept away on another rising wave of desire when his fingers slipped inside her and began a slow, deliberate rhythm that made all thoughts vanish. She tightened around his fingers, grinding against his hand, wanting something she no longer knew how to articulate.

"So beautiful," he murmured. Her entire being felt as though it was lifting, rising toward some shimmering climax just beyond reach. He played her body masterfully, those eyes missing nothing as he coaxed broken moans and gasps from her lips.

When he withdrew his hand and settled himself between her legs, Lyra knew she should speak up, divulge the secret she'd kept from him, one of the many things that had held her back. But his mouth claimed hers again in a long, drugging kiss, his tongue mimicking what his hips were doing with every press of the hard tip of his erection against her flesh. It was bliss. She didn't want to think, she just wanted to feel.

Then Jaden entered her in a single thrust, tearing through her maidenhead with a sharp burst of pain that drew a startled cry from Lyra. The pain was bright, intense—and then gone, the first clue their joining would not be usual in any way. She caught a split-second look at Jaden's wide eyes before the first orgasm shot through her like white hot lightning. Her body arched sharply upward, her mouth opening in a silent scream. The initial pain of penetration vanished in the face of pleasure so intense she could do nothing but give herself over to it. Lyra's legs locked around Jaden's waist, and she squeezed as the first wave crested, then began to ebb.

The instinct to move was primal, irresistible. Lyra opened her eyes, wrapped in a sensual haze that was like nothing she'd ever imagined could be possible. Jaden looked horrified. Fortunately, the bliss made it hard to care.

"Lyra, I—I'm so sorry, I didn't know you were a—why didn't you *tell* me?" he stammered. She heard his words, registered his concern. But more important was the flush suffusing his pale skin, the way she could still feel him hard and pulsing deep inside her. He thought he had done something wrong.

But he was everything right.

The shimmering haze that Lyra felt enveloping her only seemed to thicken. All she could see, feel, want was the man pressed against her, inside her. All her worries and misgivings fell away, replaced by a certainty that Jaden was right. The one. The only one. And she was so close to making him hers. To being his.

No! You don't want this, don't want to belong to anyone! Whatever is going on, you can't undo it once it's done, STOP!

But the warning bells sounding in the back of her mind were distant and easy to ignore. She slid her hands down Jaden's back, feeling him shiver at her touch, and brought them to his hips.

"Don't stop," she said softly, her voice breathy and unrecognizable to her own ears. "Please. What's done is done. I want this."

And she did, so much that in that moment it seemed to be all there was, all that mattered. Relief surged through her when she saw Jaden relax, desire replacing the fear now fading from his eyes.

"If you're sure," he said.

Lyra nodded. "I want this," she repeated, lifting her hips into him to make her point. The sensation had her head falling back, her eyes closing. Her breath escaped on a sigh.

So he began to move in her, slower thrusts at first, then stronger as the sparks between them once again lit and quickly turned to flames. The pace quickened, intensified, punctuated by Jaden's guttural moans as Lyra drove him beyond his control. She could feel everything inside of her gathering again, readying for a burst far greater than the one she'd only just experienced. Her desire coiled within, tighter, ever tighter. She opened her eyes again when she was close to the edge, gripping Jaden's hips tightly in her hands as she urged him on. When their eyes locked, his full of more passion than she'd ever imagined he might possess, Lyra felt something open up inside, unfurling like a night-blooming flower and stretching toward him as though he were the life-giving moon. He began to shudder, his own climax upon him, and with one small gesture made all that had built inside of Lyra break loose.

He threaded his fingers through hers to hold her hand.

When the dam burst this time, Lyra heard herself cry out as though from far away. Her body slammed upward, stiffening against him, tightening around him like a fist. A sensation almost too intense to be called something as simple as pleasure swept her away on dark and beautiful currents. Emotions she had never experienced, things that she could name but had never known, washed over her in wave after wave while he pulsed and throbbed within her.

She heard him cry out her name as he poured himself into her, and she did as instinct demanded. Without thought, without anything but feeling, Lyra raised up.

And sank her teeth into his neck.

chapter FIFTEEN

H<small>E FELT AS THOUGH</small> he had been run over by a semi. Several times. And then it had backed over him for good measure.

Fortunately, Jaden was far too happy to care.

Actually, happy wasn't quite the word for it, Jaden thought as he lay in the tall grass, his arms around the most unusual woman fate might have picked for him. Euphoric, maybe. Blissed out of his mind, even.

Words didn't matter. If that was the last time he ever had sex in his life, he knew he would die a happy man, even centuries from now.

"Mmm," Lyra said, the sound vibrating against his throat where she'd tucked her head. Her lips were still against his skin, and if he wasn't careful, he knew he would get worked up all over again. The certainty he felt about this amazed him, since by rights he shouldn't even be able to move.

Actually, whether he really could yet was debatable. His limbs felt like Jell-o. In a good way.

As a test, he stroked one hand along Lyra's back, over her silken curls, across warm skin, and down to cup her backside. Jaden gave a lazy smile. Yes, he could move.

From the position of the stars, Jaden thought it must be somewhere around two in the morning. Not even close to sunrise. Which was lovely, because he was perfectly awake and very content to lay here with Lyra for as long as possible. She was soft and warm, and smelled fantastic. And she was finally his.

For now, whispered a treacherous voice in the back of his mind, and he pushed it away quickly. He was great at spoiling his better moments with worry—this would not be one of those. Still, he pulled her just a little closer, resting his chin on top of her head. How long had it been since he'd held a woman like this? Ages. But he had never come anywhere near what he'd experienced tonight with anyone. He wondered if it was because she was a were-wolf...or because she was simply Lyra.

She sighed, her breath warming his neck. "I l—" she started, then paused abruptly. "I like lying here with you," she said quietly. For whatever reason, the muscles in her back tensed slightly, and Jaden began rubbing that area in gentle circles. Slowly, he felt her relax back into him, though perhaps a little more stiffly than before.

"I like lying here with you too," he replied. After a moment of consideration, he added, "You're not...hurt, or anything, are you? If I'd known, I would have tried to be a little gentler."

He wondered whether that was the source of her sudden tension. She hadn't so much as hinted she was a virgin, and she certainly didn't kiss like any virgin he'd ever known. But the evidence had been a little hard to ignore.

He hoped she didn't feel strange about their union. Jaden was honored that she'd chosen him...more than he knew how to express. Though it shouldn't matter to him, and though he knew the sentiment was archaic at best, knowing that he had been the only man to possess her that way thrilled him in some deep and buried part of his soul.

Of all the men she could have had, and with her beauty he knew there were many, she had chosen him. The simple truth of that filled him with wonder.

"No, I'm fine," Lyra said, and he could hear the smile in her voice when she added, "And no you wouldn't have. Which is also fine. It hasn't been a conscious choice or anything. I guess I'm just picky."

"You have interesting taste," he remarked. "Not that I'm complaining. Thank you."

He heard her amused exhalation. But she shifted in his arms, drawing away from him to rise to a sitting position, her arms curled around herself. The loss of her warmth made him shiver a little in the cool night air. Suddenly unsure of himself, Jaden lifted a hand to place it gently on her back.

"Lyra? What's wrong?"

"Hmm? Nothing," she said, turning her head to regard him. She offered a small smile, but Jaden felt the change in her as deeply as if she'd simply stood up and walked away. One minute she'd been very much with him. The next, she'd retreated into herself, effectively shutting him out.

Frustrated at this sudden shift between them, Jaden rose to sit beside her, his body curved into hers. He leaned over to kiss her shoulder, letting his lips linger, enjoying her warmth. He felt her slight shiver, and he was relieved to find she wasn't unaffected by what they'd shared.

"We should go back," she said quietly. "It's late."

"That's what you get for consorting with vampires," Jaden teased her. "Stay with me. It's a beautiful night. We're naked in a field. Enjoy it."

That, at least, got half a laugh. "We've done plenty of enjoying it."

"Then a little more won't hurt. I spent long enough fantasizing about this. It's cruel to cut the reality short. I'll be emotionally scarred."

Lyra's smile was warmer this time, though he still felt as though she had decided to distance herself from him in a way that she hadn't during their lovemaking. She was a difficult woman, he reminded himself. And he wouldn't be half as fascinated by her if she wasn't. Still, he wished he knew why her guard had gone back up so quickly.

"Cute," she said.

"Did you...not like it?" He hated how vulnerable he sounded, how pathetic. But he hoped she had enjoyed it even half as much as he had. He was a bit rusty. Perhaps that was it...

"It was amazing," Lyra said, with a brook-no-refusals tone in her voice that settled him instantly. "You were amazing. I didn't— I never thought—" She shook her head, then laughed softly. "There aren't words, I guess."

Tentatively, Jaden shifted, lifting his hand to stroke her cheek, then down her arm. He worried she would bolt if he moved too quickly, and he so badly wanted her to stay with him, stay here. To make what was left of the night last, in case this chance never came again. Jaden felt her respond to his touch, saw her resolve weakening. He decided to press the advantage and claimed her mouth in a soft, lingering, and very thorough kiss.

Lyra's need rose so quickly it seemed to burn right through him, a blast of heat that sparked every dark desire he'd ever had. His arms went around her, and he felt the pinpricks of her claws in his shoulders. Gods, he hoped she bit him again...that had been one of the most singularly erotic experiences of his life. And this time, he planned to return the favor.

Lyra abruptly broke the kiss with a sharp gasp, pushing herself back with such force that she kicked up a cloud of pollen from the ground.

"Lyra? What is it, love, what's wrong?"

Her eyes were wide, frightened. He'd never seen that look of pure terror on her face before and had no idea what had put it there. For a long moment, she stared at him as though she'd never seen him before, but then her look quickly faded into worry and confusion—simpler things to deal with, and far less concerning. Still, what had happened?

"Do you..." Lyra began, her voice shaking. She stopped, took a breath, then pressed on. "You don't feel... funny...do you?"

"Not any funnier than I would normally feel lying around naked outside," Jaden replied, frowning a little. "Lyra, what on earth is wrong? Are you hurt?" Even in the darkness, she looked a little pale, he thought.

She surprised him when she dropped her eyes, confirming to him that something more was bothering her. But her refusal to tell him what it was wasn't surprising at all. Just frustrating, and something he'd hoped they'd now gotten past.

"No. I don't know. Maybe I'm getting sick. I think I'm just tired, honestly. Between the training and...after... it was quite a night. I just feel kind of off all of a sudden."

"It was an incredible night. But if you feel like you should rest, then you should," Jaden said. "We can't afford you getting sick right now."

"No," she replied. "We can't." Something in the way she said it lingered with him, and not in a pleasant way.

Lyra got tentatively to her feet and began to collect the scattered bits of clothing strewn on the ground. At least she wasn't angry, Jaden thought. The boxer briefs that hit him in the head were a testament to that. And stepping away from him seemed to have restored a portion of Lyra's usual spirit.

"Get dressed, hot stuff. If I bring you back naked we'll give my father a heart attack."

Jaden forced a chuckle and got to his own feet. He began to dress, but the meaning behind Lyra's words hit him harder than he might have imagined. It was a reminder, and not too subtle, that however much they enjoyed each other, an actual relationship was impossible. Forbidden, if not explicitly by his kind, then very much so by hers. He hadn't thought he would care. In fact, he'd convinced himself otherwise—before.

Now, though, having touched her, tasted her, Jaden was having a hard time imagining just walking away. She was…important to him.

He knew it was a problem.

He just didn't know what the hell to do about it.

The hair on his neck prickled an instant before the familiar scent hit him. It was only then, too late, that he realized the night had gone dead silent around them. Jaden's eyes widened.

"Lyra," he said, a hoarse and urgent whisper.

She whirled around, eyes alight, body suddenly tense.

Her gaze connected with his, and he felt something pass between them, a brilliant flash of understanding that was both bizarre and completely unexpected. He's told her...something. But how? What had she just picked up from him?

There was no time to dwell on it, though. Four shadowy figures appeared around them, seeming to have pulled away from the fabric of the night itself. Jaden moved to Lyra, trying to shield her from what he knew was coming.

And Lyra, true to form, very deftly moved to his side.

"Jaden. Long time no see."

That voice was unpleasantly familiar. He recognized it quickly as LaSalle, one of the Ptolemy court's hangers-on. He'd always been looking for ways to curry favor with Arsinöe. It seemed he'd found a new one.

"I would have preferred it had been longer," Jaden said.

He heard a soft chuckle. LaSalle stepped forward, and Jaden's eyes, so well adjusted to the darkness, skimmed a face he had hoped never to see again. A quick glance at the other three was much the same story. Vampires he recognized, who would never mean him and his kind anything but harm. He and Lyra were far too exposed out here. He should have known better after the other night. But he hadn't wanted to believe these adversaries would be so bold...not here, of all places.

"You know the song. You can't always get what you want. And for you, in particular, there's a nice reward to be had." LaSalle's eyes, shrewd and cold, gleaming a dark green, flickered over Lyra. "An interesting place to hide. And even more interesting company you've decided to keep. Stooping a little low, even for you."

"If you're the company he *used* to keep, you can color me just as unimpressed," Lyra growled beside him. Jaden's heart sank, even as LaSalle's lip curled.

"You'll be sorry for that, bitch. This cat is the property of the Ptolemy dynasty. There's a big reward on his head for his return...and a slightly smaller reward for just returning his head. If you force me into the latter, I'm bringing yours along as a bonus."

"Try it," she snapped. "This is my pack's territory. Once they find out you've been here, you'll be hunted down. And we don't take prisoners."

"She's the Alpha's daughter," Jaden said, torn between admiring Lyra's bravado and wishing that for once she would step back and not come off as quite so sure she could destroy every enemy. "Killing her would be a bad move."

LaSalle snorted. "Like we give a damn what a bunch of wolves thinks. You think we're afraid of your kind, *chere*?" he asked Lyra. "The wolves only live because we let them. Now step away from the cat, or share what he has coming to him."

"Lyra, go home. I'll deal with this," Jaden growled, his claws already curling from his fingertips. This was his fight, and Lyra didn't deserve to be hurt because of it. These were no lazy courtiers. These were the sort of vampires who enjoyed hunting and killing his kind, and others, for sport. But he wouldn't be taken without a fight, and there was no way he was going back to Arsinoë alive.

Naturally, Lyra did the opposite of what he wished.

"The hell with that," she said, glaring at LaSalle. "This place belongs to the Pack of the Thorn. And Jaden is under our protection."

Jaden winced, knowing how that would sound, and LaSalle burst into laughter.

"Oh?" he asked, barely able to catch his breath when he could finally speak. "The cat needs a bunch of mongrels to protect him, eh? My. How far the mighty have fallen, Jaden."

"I am also under the protection of the Lilim," Jaden said, curling his lip. He pulled aside the collar of his shirt to bare the mark. "Lily is well aware that the Ptolemy have taken some of the Cait Sith who have come to us. Move against me, and you'll have the full wrath of the dynasty upon you. Our leader is not afraid of Arsinöe... or war."

He hoped it didn't come to that, though. Lily wasn't ready for what the Ptolemy could rain down upon her, even in their weakened state. And the Council would always side with what they knew. She would find little help there.

LaSalle glared at Jaden's mark, his eyes flashing bright red for an instant before he turned his head and spat on the ground.

"The Lilim are no dynasty. They're an aberration, and they need to be stamped out. The Ptolemy do not recognize you as legitimate, cat. And the war you seek will come soon enough. Until then, Arsinöe has us find and return her property. You, especially, she would like to see."

"Lyra," Jaden said softly, trying not to sound like he was pleading even though he was. "You need to get out of here."

"No. You need my help."

He knew there would be no budging her, so he offered all the advice he could muster as the four Ptolemy began to look at one another and shuffle on their feet, getting ready to pounce.

"Go for the kill as soon as you get a clear shot," he said. "They're fast."

LaSalle reached into a pocket and withdrew what looked like a length of thick silver chain. He grinned and dangled it in front of Jaden, whose blood went cold. He remembered the collars. All too well.

"I found your old collar, Jaden. I've brought it as a present."

Memories stirred in the depths of his mind, things he would rather keep buried: the burn of the enchanted metal around his neck, being forced into his cat form with no hope of returning to the human one until his punishment was ended and the collar removed; the kicks and food and objects hurled at him while he was forced to belly-crawl across the floor; the vicious, mindless laughter.

"No," he snarled, knowing his fury was exactly what LaSalle wanted but unable to control it. Jaden leaped at him, knocking the collar out of the other vampire's hand but missing the man himself, who stepped easily out of the way.

"You'll have to do better than that," LaSalle taunted him. "Or have you lost your touch?" Jaden couldn't miss the eagerness written all over the vampire's face. He wanted his kill. And so, Jaden discovered, did he. A small compensation for all the wrongs the Ptolemy had done, and were still doing, to his kind.

Jaden leaped again, this time catching LaSalle's arm as he tried to flicker out of the way. He heard his own furious roar, almost as if it were coming from someone else. And dimly, somewhere behind him, he heard Lyra's fierce shout, a scream of anger that quickly shifted into a howl.

He hoped to the gods she remembered what he'd been teaching her.

The frenzy as all four Ptolemy came at them was quick and brutal. The night turned bloody as claws tore into flesh; claws slashed and blows strong enough to send a mortal flying pummeled Jaden. He fought as a man, as a cat, hoping to gain some sort of upper hand. But the fight was difficult when he was so outnumbered, though he caught glimpses of Lyra fighting like hell.

She was holding her own, though thin rivulets of blood streamed down one side of her face as she fought a creature who was making it as hard as he could to land a hit. Fear and anger coiled inside Jaden, a toxic combination that had him striking out and opening up one Ptolemy's throat, the vampire's grin freezing as blood sprayed Jaden's face and chest. A furious snarl sounded behind him, and Jaden spun to see LaSalle leaping into the air, his moves so lightning fast he was little more than a flicker. Speed was the gift of the Ptolemy and the curse of their enemies.

LaSalle caught Jaden's eye and smiled. Then he vanished into a blur as he streamed right at Lyra.

"No!" Jaden shouted, knocking another Ptolemy to the ground as if he weighed nothing at all. He knew what was coming, knew he wouldn't reach her in time. Time seemed to slow to a crawl and he lunged toward Lyra, who was fending off a vampire just a few feet from him. He saw every tiny nuance of her movement as she looked to her left, the slight widening of her eyes when she realized what was coming for her.

Then, to his amazement, he watched LaSalle slam to the ground and roll as Lyra sprang from the balls of her feet, graceful as an acrobat, and back-flipped out of reach. Jaden had to shake off his surprise quickly, seizing the opportunity to jump onto LaSalle while he was down. Jaden's hands were around the vampire's throat in an instant, squeezing, his claws digging in. Fury that came from one of the darkest places in his soul, a place that they had created, quickly pulsed through his entire system.

LaSalle looked up at him, his eyes bright and gleaming and full of shock. It was clear he had not expected this turn of events. Behind them, Jaden heard Lyra engage the remaining two Ptolemy again, and he knew he had to be quick. They would not flag simply because their leader was down.

"*She*," gurgled LaSalle.

"Yes," Jaden sneered, baring his fangs. "She can outfight you, because I taught her to. I'm never going back, LaSalle. And neither are you."

Without his knife, the decapitation was quick but gruesome. Necessary, though, to end any vampire. Later, he would burn the body if he had time. A strange sound behind him slowly penetrated the bloody haze in which he was ensconced, crouching over LaSalle's body and drinking in shallow little sips of air. The rage was as dark as anything he'd ever experienced, fueled as it was by the memories of his torment. The scars on his back burned as if fresh.

Lyra. I have to help Lyra. This isn't finished.

Jaden rose and turned, and was greeted by an unexpected sight. Lyra stood over the corpses of the other Ptolemy, a bloodied dagger in her hand. She was a little battered, but there was something incredibly triumphant about her, like a pagan goddess of war. The oddity of her even having a dagger was quickly explained when he realized that they were no longer alone. A small group of werewolves had joined them, Simon and Dorien among them.

All the wolves were looking at him.

Jaden said nothing, simply walked to Lyra and held out his hand. She placed the dagger in it without a single question, and he turned to finish severing the head of the Ptolemy whose throat he had torn out, just to be sure.

"The bodies should be burned," he said flatly as he returned, handing the dagger to Dorien. The fury receded, leaving an odd numbness in its place. It was hard to fathom that a short time ago, he'd been as happy as he could remember being. The Ptolemy had managed to spoil even that. It seemed they were destined to ruin everything good in Jaden's life no matter what he did.

"We know. We'll take care of it," Dorien said. He was as somber as Jaden had seen the man, and he wondered, dully, if the wolves would use the attack as an excuse to run him off. He would have to let them. Right now, he had no fight left in him. But when one of the other wolves spoke, a shorter, barrel-chested man who looked as though he'd seen plenty of fights, his words were far from anything Jaden expected.

"You didn't run. You defended Lyra," he said. The man had the audacity to sound surprised. Jaden wanted to snap, but he managed to hold back. That was the anger still in his system, not what was called for now.

"I did," Jaden said. "But she did a hell of a job defending herself."

He saw the smile, small but unmistakable, that curved

her lips. It went a long way toward calming what remained of his rage. The rest vanished the moment the wolf who had addressed him stepped forward with his hand extended. It took Jaden a moment to register the expression the man wore, since it was one he saw so rarely.

Gratitude.

Jaden, dumbfounded for one of the few times in his long life, accepted the hand being offered and shook it.

"I was wrong about you. You defended a fellow wolf, and our home. For that, you have my thanks."

"I—you're welcome," Jaden stammered, even more shocked when the other wolves came forward to repeat the gesture. Simon was the last in line, and he gave a curt nod before shaking hands too.

"I told Lyra I'd be watching you. Looks like not all vampires are without honor. From now on, as far as we're concerned, you're welcome here."

Jaden looked around at each of their faces, seeing the simple truth echoed over and over again. He had shed blood for them. He had acted in defense of Lyra, and of their home. So they, in turn, had decided to accept him. Jaden couldn't help but feel the weight of the honor. These wolves must think poorly of his kind indeed to assume he would leave Lyra to the mercy of these vampire killers.

But since plenty of vampires were much like these Ptolemy, he supposed he couldn't blame Simon and the others for the bad impression.

"What the hell were they doing here?" Dorien wondered aloud, prodding one of them with his toe. "All these years, we've barely seen a one of your kind. Now we're some kind of tourist attraction."

Lyra caught his eye, gave a barely perceptible shake

of her head. She was right—it might not go over as well if they knew he was the one who had drawn the Ptolemy here, however unwittingly. Still, he thought it was odd the intruders had found him deep in werewolf country, of all places. Had he been followed from Tipton? That prospect didn't seem likely, and he'd been careful.

A puzzle, and one he needed to sort out. Putting innocents in danger because the Ptolemy refused to give up their claim on an entire bloodline was unacceptable to him. Just as lying about the danger was no longer acceptable, no matter whether the truth hurt him or not.

"They were here because of me," he admitted. "I was a slave of their queen for a very long time. She hasn't quite gotten over the fact that I, and my blood brothers and sisters, are no longer under her purview."

"Will there be more of them, do you think?" Simon asked, his expression unreadable.

Jaden shrugged. "Not sure. This lot won't be reporting back, at least. Beyond that, I couldn't say." He looked at Dorien. "I'm sorry I seem to have brought them here. I had no idea I was being tracked."

Dorien looked at his colleagues and grunted. "Not worried. A few stragglers here and there is just good practice for my men. Not often we get to rip into actual vamps. These don't seem to have caused much trouble, even with you outnumbered." He paused, looked at his daughter who seemed no worse for wear despite the blood. Then he shook his head wonderingly.

"Never thought I'd tell a wolf and a vamp that they make a good team, but you two are going to prove me wrong. This is some *carnage*. And I mean that in a good way."

"You're not kidding," the stocky one said, dropping a wink at Lyra. "I may have to conscript the both of you into the guard. That'd cause a stir!"

You have no idea, Jaden thought. He caught Lyra's eye, hoping to see a smile. But instead, she looked troubled and turned her head away. Still, Jaden gave a short laugh as the men chuckled. He suddenly realized that nothing about them was what he had expected. He was used to subversion, secrecy, and vampires who were more interested in covering their own asses than being heroes, though his experience being mainly with the Ptolemy had a lot to do with that, he supposed. The philosophy, the attitude of these wolves was...different.

They might be as rough as they'd been painted among vampires. But that was not all they were. Of course, expecting them to bless the romantic pairing of a wolf and a vampire was probably a bridge too far. Probably.

Wasn't it?

"Come on. We'll light these bastards up and then all go back to my house for a drink," Dorien said. There were nods of agreement as Dorien retrieved a lighter from his pocket. "I want to hear the story from the two of you, and no leaving out any of the gore. This should be a good one."

The barrel-chested one grinned at Jaden. "It'll be a dry evening for you, Jaden, unless you can stomach a beer. I might be impressed, but I'm still not volunteering to open a vein."

"I'll manage with a beer," Jaden said with a smile, feeling off-balance, but in a surprisingly pleasant way.

Lyra sidled up beside him as the burning began, the vampire corpses vanishing seconds after they were lit. The flames danced in her troubled eyes.

"What do you know?" she said. "Kill a few Ptolemy and you're golden." She sounded more weary than happy, which surprised him. Jaden thought she'd be pleased that they'd done so well. And from what he had been able to see, her technique was excellent. If she kept that kind of focus, she would already be a surprise that most werewolves wouldn't see coming. For Eric, it would take more, simply because of his size and particular fixation on killing her, but Jaden was encouraged. Taking down Ptolemy was no small thing.

Here she stood, however, looking defeated. He wondered if he would ever understand her.

"If only everything in life were so easy," he said. She knew what he meant, and he saw any sign of emotion in her eyes quickly shuttered.

"I'm impressed. You fought well," he added, low enough that only she could hear it. "They know it too," he added, jerking his head toward the other wolves.

"Yeah, that's…that's good, I'm glad." She sounded anything but, but Jaden hardly knew how to respond. Something was wrong, that much was obvious.

"You're going to join everyone, right? Stay up and share our tale of bloody derring-do?"

It was no surprise when Lyra shook her head no. He took a deep breath, frustrated by his inability to see what was truly wrong. Mind-reading mortals was often annoying, but the gift would have come in handy here among the wolves.

"Look, Lyra, don't be a hero. If you're sick or hurt, we need to get you to a doctor. Your pack must have one of those."

"No, I'm neither. I swear," she said firmly. Then she

seemed to deflate a little, slumping as though all the fight had gone out of her. "I think I just need some sleep. I don't...I really just don't feel well." She put a hand to her head and closed her eyes for a moment. "I'm going to head back. You have fun with the boys. You've earned it. I'm glad they've decided to like you, though. I really am." She looked so tired, and so uncharacteristically defeated, that Jaden barely restrained himself from putting his arms around her.

Instead, he had to stand there and watch her walk away, knowing it wouldn't be the last time.

chapter SIXTEEN

THE END of the night was bad.

Morning was worse.

Lyra stood beneath the spray, feeling more like a ghost than a werewolf. Last night had been a rough one, a swing from one extreme to the other. Today, she felt colorless, washed out. It shouldn't be that way. She and Jaden had had mind-blowing, earth-shattering sex! Awesome! Her father and the higher-ups of the pack guard thought she and Jaden made a great team, and had actually acknowledged that she'd kicked some vampire ass! Super-duper!

And yet somehow, she felt as though she was stuck in the pit staring up at the pendulum as its gleaming blade swung lower...and lower...

Lyra poured vanilla citrus soap on her bath puff and lathered up, barely paying attention to what she was doing. She decided that wallowing for a little longer was therapeutic. Lyra's lips lifted in a cynical half smile. Usually it was Jaden's job to brood, not hers.

Jaden. There was no residual soreness from last night, nothing but the memory of his hands on her body, the way he had almost worshipped her as he'd made love to her. She sighed, glad to at least have those memories as one hell of a distraction from her horrible mood. If there were such a thing as perfection, joining with him had come very close. Imagining the act hadn't done the reality justice at all. She only wished the night had ended better. Like, without a vampire ambush.

Of course, even if the Ptolemy hadn't shown up, she'd been rattled. The lovemaking had been almost *too* intense, solidifying a connection with Jaden that was far more potent than anything she'd expected to feel. Moving inside her, Jaden had seemed more like an extension of herself than a separate being. Even the aftermath had been charged, hazy and full of jumbled thoughts and feelings that all boiled down to the same impossible thing.

She was falling in love with him.

Worse, she'd almost said so.

She'd realized it as they lay there afterward, feeling the rhythm their heartbeats made together. She'd been too euphoric, too content to fight it any longer. And as she'd thought it, there the words had been, right on the tip of her tongue, along with the deep certainty that she should always be near him, that she never wanted to be anywhere she couldn't see his face.

Unfortunately, along with that had come another feeling, an unfamiliar sense that she *belonged* to him. Lyra grimaced at the thought. Ownership was a lot of what wolf matehood was all about, one of the reasons she had every intention of avoiding it. If she could feel like this from sleeping with a guy she couldn't actually bond with, how much worse must it be between wolves? No one was ever going to possess her. The best solution would be to never fall in love at all, she knew. So she would just have to deal with this, try to stop the slide before she was in way over her head.

Of course, that was presuming she wasn't already. But she had to believe she could make it stop, push back whatever this was turning into. Because not doing so would throw everything she wanted in doubt.

Lyra rinsed the soap off, brushing her hands over her skin to get rid of the last of the suds. She was barely paying attention, lost in her own thoughts. As she passed the puff over her arm, however, something registered as different. Lyra nearly managed to ignore it, through the distant warning bells going off in the back of her mind. But her eyes were drawn back, much against her better judgment. There, faint but unmistakable, she saw the intricate band encircling her right arm at mid-bicep.

The bath puff fell to the floor unnoticed. She stared. Tentatively, as though touching it might burn her, she raised her left hand and rubbed at the new mark with a finger. First lightly, then harder.

"No," she said softly, her skin turning red as she scrubbed roughly. "No, seriously, come on, *no*."

But no amount of begging removed it, and after a few minutes of fruitless effort, Lyra simply stood there under the running water staring at what she had done. What *they* had done.

It's not possible. It's NOT.

The numbness vanished quickly, replaced by an intense pressure in her chest that seemed to build and build, until it felt as though she might suffocate. Tiny starbursts appeared in front of her eyes, and Lyra knew she was going to pass out if she didn't sit down and get a hold of herself. Bracing herself against the wall, she turned off the water and slowly sank to the floor of the tub, wrapping her arms around her legs.

Cats. She had cats wrapped around her arm. Stretching forward, lolling on their backs, each connected to the other by catching the tail. Cute, apart from the bared fangs of some and the fierce eyes of others. Not housecats. Cats like Jaden.

Anyone who saw this would know what had happened in a heartbeat.

"Oh no," she said in a soft moan, and she hiccupped back the tears that wanted to come. She did not cry. Not ever. And certainly not about damn fool things she'd done to herself, even if they ruined...everything.

Had she really thought she wasn't in over her head? Somehow, she'd bonded with Jaden.

With a *vampire*.

She sat there, stunned, for minutes that could have been hours. Finally, Lyra forced herself to go through the motions, standing up and toweling off. Her eyes, gazing back at her from the mirror, were dull with shock. It shouldn't have been possible. But then...perhaps no one had ever been stupid enough to test the theory that wolves and vampires were incompatible. Until now, that was.

Did he have one too? Or would it just be her, bearing a singular mark as punishment for foolishly giving in to taking something she couldn't, and shouldn't, truly have?

She touched the band on her skin again, lighter than most marks of bonding she had seen but still very much there. Even as she did, the memory of Jaden filled her mind—the look in his eyes when he moved inside her, the way he touched her, as though she were some fragile, precious thing. His smiles, rare and beautiful and just for her. The longing that flooded her nearly took her back to her knees.

One of the few choices she'd had, now taken away forever. A forbidden mate.

What the hell was she supposed to do now?

A treacherous tear slipped down one cheek, and for once, Lyra gave over to the impulse.

She leaned against the counter and wept.

Once she'd collected herself, Lyra put on a little bit of concealer, sucked it up, and did what always got her through in the past: kept moving.

She hopped in her little pickup, peeled out of the driveway, and drove straight for the one place that might help her. She was at the Larison Silver Memorial Library in five minutes, and headed down into the basement in another five, her boot heels clicking and echoing on the wooden stairs. This was the part of the library that was only open to a certain subset of the public. The stairs themselves were hidden, and the basement musty enough to be a deterrent to anyone with a decent nose. But Lyra had an excellent nose, and she still pressed on.

She didn't know why she hadn't thought of it before. If there was an answer to her problem, it was here, in the Thorn Histories.

Teresa McFarlane sat at a scarred old desk at the foot of the stairs, utterly absorbed in what looked like a torrid novel. Lyra slowed to look at the cover, her curiosity piqued.

"Hey Teresa. How's the ménage?"

Teresa, a plump and pretty woman in her early fifties who looked as though the word *ménage* might send her into palpitations, looked up, startled. When she spotted Lyra, however, her quick grin said it all.

"It's just getting good. And I can't decide whether I want Rafe to end up with the sexy biker boy who's been worshipping him from afar, or the beautiful seductress who keeps coming between them. Literally."

Lyra burst out laughing, glad to find she was still capable of such a reaction. She could always count on Teresa, who was the opposite of what she used to think a Keeper of the Histories should be, to lighten the mood. She was also pretty sure that Teresa had taken the job because it gave her hours every day to read without interruption. And some of the Keeper's favorite subjects had introduced Lyra to a whole new literary world.

A multiple-partnered, very unclothed literary world. She wondered sometimes what Gerry thought of his wife's active imagination and then decided he probably wasn't complaining. Some of that stuff could just about set the pages on fire.

"Maybe he won't have to pick," Lyra said.

"That's what I'm hoping," Teresa said, sliding off her reading glasses to look at Lyra. "What's up, honey? What can I help you with?"

"I'm, um, interested in bonding," Lyra said. She'd tried to come up with a way to beat around the bush, but there simply wasn't one. Fortunately, Teresa preferred blunt, and Lyra doubted there would be too many questions if she played this right.

"Aren't we all?" Teresa said with a dramatic sigh,

fanning herself. "So what's the occasion? You finally find a wolf who can handle you? Or just one you want to handle?" She wiggled her eyebrows.

Lyra's smile felt slightly more pasted on. Of course Teresa assumed she'd be looking for a nice wolf. Why not? Anything else for a woman in her position wasn't *done*. Unless it was, and you wound up wearing a cat tattoo...

"Sadly no," Lyra replied. "I was actually wondering about, ah, interspecies bonding. Sort of."

Teresa's eyebrows lifted so high they nearly shot past her hairline. "Interspecies? You mean like human and werewolf? I've got quite a bit on that. Honey, tell me you didn't meet a human. It would break your father's heart." She pursed her lips. "It would make your aunt's day, though. I swear that woman's the biggest tightass in three counties."

Lyra blew out a breath, exasperated and amused all at the same time. "No, honestly, Teresa, this isn't for me. You know we've got the vamp staying with us."

"Mmm-hmm. Couldn't miss him," she replied. "Got that dangerous bad boy thing going on. It's a shame he smells like cat."

"Well, I've been stuck kind of squiring him around, and he's insistent that vampires and werewolves used to hook up. Like, actually bond. I bet him fifty bucks he's wrong, but I don't know how to prove it. I figured you would."

Teresa relaxed immediately, and the relief nearly took Lyra down. She bought it. Of course she would. Why else could she want to know such a crazy thing? She was a vamp hater just like everyone else here, after all, a nice Alpha's girl. Right?

Right.

"Good one, honey. And I'd love to see you fleece the vamp, but I'm afraid he actually has a point."

"Oh?" Lyra asked, trying to ignore the adrenaline now coursing through her blood. "No way. That's too weird."

"Oh, I don't know. They can be pretty enough." Teresa chuckled. "It's the rest of them that's the problem, personality especially." She stood, stretching a little. "Come on, I'll show you. At least then you'll know where to look it up the next time you decide to fleece somebody else with that bet."

Teresa led her into the interior of the Room of Histories, a dimly lit cave of a place filled with tall bookshelves that were stuffed with enormous, parchment-filled tomes. They were meticulously organized, and Lyra had come to learn, over the years, that Teresa's encyclopedic knowledge encompassed the contents of every single volume of the pack's history. It had saved her butt on a school paper a time or two.

She hoped that knowledge would do the same now.

They headed down the third row, which contained tomes that were quite old. The bindings, though kept oiled, were dull, and the parchment within had grown stiff and brittle over the years. Only Teresa was allowed to touch these, Lyra knew. It would be too detrimental to the tomes to allow any other hands on them. They stopped in the middle of the row, and Teresa scanned the shelves, murmuring to herself. After a few seconds, she selected a book, more ragged than some, that looked singed as if from a fire on the lower right corner.

"Here we are," she said. "Fourteen ninety-five. Not a happy year, as you might guess from the burn marks. Our camp was burned, half the pack was slaughtered when we were blamed for an outbreak of plague, and the Thorn was introduced to the concept of vampire-werewolf mating." She set the tome down on one of the long, low reading tables set in the wide middle row and opened to a place about three-quarters of the way through. Her hands, small and quick, turned pages with infinite care. Lyra watched, fascinated. She'd always loved to watch Teresa work, even though she knew that, in her own hands, this job would be a disaster. She could just see herself accidentally crunching up page after page...

"So...how did it go?" Lyra asked, moving beside Teresa to scan the pages of flowing script. The wolves, unlike nobility at the time, had always written in the vernacular, and Lyra could read the writing well enough, even if many of the words and wording were odd.

Teresa shot her an arch look. "About as well as you'd expect, since it's still forbidden. This was the root of it, here. A she-wolf of the Thorn, Elizabeth Thatcher, got involved with a vamp from the Rakshasa. Those were lion-shifters, actually," she said, considering. "Think I heard they'd been hunted to extinction by some dynasty or other, but who knows? And they think *we're* violent. Anyway, they went off together, tripped the night fantastic, and discovered that you can, indeed, hitch a wolf and a vamp together. There's a little poem about it here, see?" She chuckled. "Always had wolves who enjoyed writing in verse back then."

Lyra leaned in to read the section that Teresa tapped with her finger.

"When werewolf's bite the vampire takes," she murmured, eyes skimming the short passage. It was a short rhyme, rather pretty...and immensely informative. At least now she understood why she had only a faint mark and Jaden, at least as far as she knew, had none. They hadn't finished the ritual. And if she had anything to say about it they weren't going to...though the words describing the simple process of attaching to a vampire forever caused a strange fluttering in her stomach, and what felt like fireworks shimmering their way through her blood.

It *was* possible. The pairing had been done.

It could be done again, if it was allowed. Which of course it wasn't. In fact, *not allowed* was a kind way to put it. But...but...

Her mind spun as she tried to absorb it. She wasn't the first! There had been others like her, falling into the arms of a vampire, only to find—

"Shame what happened. The vamp had drained ten wolves before they caught him, and then they took him and his mate and..." She trailed off, made a face, and closed the book.

"Never mind," Teresa said. "They also never spared the gory details. And on that note, I think I need to get back to my ménage. My brain needs cleaning. What was it with medieval times and metal spikes?"

Lyra blanched, trying not to imagine what had been done to the ill-fated lovers. "Yeah. My question's answered. I do *not* want to know."

"Fair enough," Teresa said with a gentle smile. Uh-oh, Lyra thought. She knew what was coming.

"You know, Gerry and I have been talking a lot about you lately. And I don't mean to poke at you, Lyra, but... are you sure you want to go through with the Proving, honey? I know you and your cousin don't get along, but I was saying to Gerry, my cousin is in the Pack of the Shadowed Path, and her son would be *perfect* for you... a born leader, I always said, and what a match you'd make, running the Thorn!"

I'm backing away slowly, Lyra thought, trying not to give Teresa her patented Death Glare. She knew the woman meant well. She really did. But one more of these conversations and her head was going to burst into flames. Probably while she was shouting, "Actually, I've already got a mate, kinda sorta! He's a vampire! Talk about leadership qualities, right?"

Instead, she managed a smile as she headed for the stairs as quickly as she could walking backward. She found it funny, in a sick sort of way, when she realized that all of Jaden's instruction had helped her in that department.

"I appreciate it, Teresa, but I've got to go. Thanks for the help, even if I'm still out fifty bucks!"

"Okay, honey. You just let me know if you change your mind," Teresa called, heading back to her desk and the smoking-hot book.

Not likely, Lyra thought. But along with the continuing fear that her mark would be seen, she felt some measure of relief. This was only a half mark, really, another burden she could, and would, bear alone. All was not lost as long as she kept her hands to herself the rest of the time Jaden was there. More importantly, as long as he kept his teeth to himself.

She only wished she didn't feel regret... not from having been with Jaden, but because she had tasted something with him she would never forget, and would never be able to have again.

chapter SEVENTEEN

O KAY, NORMALLY I wouldn't ask, but... is everything okay? I mean, as okay as it gets for a vampire. I'm not sure what your baseline is, but you just seem... off."

Jaden turned his head from watching a raucous game of what looked like full-body contact pool to look at his unlikely companion. He was glad for the invitation, if surprised. Lyra had begged off training with him tonight. He'd found it hard to argue—she didn't look well at all. Her eyes, especially, had seemed glassy and almost haunted. She'd pleaded a headache.

But from the way she'd shied from his touch, he wondered. He could deal with almost anything it might be, unless she'd decided that touching him had been a mistake. Because rather than slaking his thirst for her, being with Lyra had increased it a thousand-fold. The prickly she-wolf had gotten under his skin, inside his head. Whatever she had done to him, he wanted more.

He forced himself to focus on the man speaking to

him, instead of the ghost of the woman prowling rest-lessly through his mind.

"You're not worried because I'm pale, are you? We've been over this. The pale skin is not a bug, it's a feature."

Simon Dale snorted softly and dug into the basket of fries that graced the middle of the small, battered table they were sharing. He dipped a fry in the bowl of gravy that had come with the appetizer, then popped it in his mouth.

"No, though I don't know why more vamps aren't into self-tanner. You'd be less obvious. No, I'm just asking because despite your triumphant ripping up of those Ptolemy last night, Lyra's been weird all day and now there's you with the moody. Well," he smirked, "I mean, I think you're moodier than usual. It's hard to tell."

Jaden's tone was acid. "Funny."

Simon grinned. "I'm here all week."

Jaden still hadn't figured out what this invitation was about. Simon Dale was hard not to like. He was a little like an overgrown puppy: amusing, slightly rude, and prone to eating everything in sight. He had also been the first member of the pack to actively seek out Jaden's company, which made Jaden inclined to like him just on general principle. But still, the offer of a drink tonight was undoubtedly about more than friendly conversation. For the moment, however, he played along.

"I'm not moody, I'm a vampire. And as for Lyra, I don't know. When I left, she was locked away nursing a headache. If you mean something beyond that, you should probably ask her."

Simon's smile faded. "I would, if I thought I'd get a straight answer. She hasn't wanted to talk to me about much of anything since you showed up, no offense." He contemplatively swirled another fry in the gravy. "I probably shouldn't have pushed it when her father tried to get her to marry me."

Jaden gagged on the small sip of beer he'd just taken, then started coughing. Simon's lips twisted into a cynical smile.

"Yeah, that was basically her reaction too," he said.

Jaden's voice sounded strained and slightly hoarse when he finally got his power of speech back. "You were supposed to get married?"

Simon shrugged. "It was more of a suggestion. A *strong* suggestion. You've seen Dorien when he wants something. If Lyra wasn't just as stubborn as he is, I'd be wearing a ring by now, barely knowing what hit me."

Jaden sat watching Simon's hangdog expression, and he wondered just how unhappy the wolf would have been about that. Something curdled and unpleasant settled into the pit of his stomach. He tried to remind himself that wolves' ways were much different from vampires', that Lyra was likely to end up with some wolf or other eventually.

Since he now knew he was sitting across from one of the prime candidates, that didn't work.

"I'm not really sure how you win over a woman like Lyra," Jaden said. His guard was up immediately. If this was about fishing for information on the direction of Lyra's affections, he wanted no part of it. Simon's laughter did little to ease his tension.

"You and me both. But even if I knew, trust me, it would never have worked anyway. Lyra and I...it's just never been like that. I mean, I thought about it back when we were teenagers. I'm not blind, and I'm not stupid. But it wouldn't have worked out. We're good as friends. More than that, not so much."

Jaden managed to relax a little at that, though the words sounded so rehearsed that he wondered how many times Simon had repeated them to himself, trying to become convinced they were true. Of Lyra's disinterest Jaden had no doubt. But Simon struck him as a little too protective, and a little too interested, for a guy who wanted to be a platonic friend. Still, Jaden didn't plan to argue Simon out of his stated position. It worked just fine for him.

"At least you've stayed friends," Jaden said. He had no idea how Simon had managed all these years. He would never have been able to spend so much time with Lyra without touching her. He hadn't even two nights here without his hands on her. More would probably have driven him permanently insane.

Simon considered while he ate another fry. "I would have married her, though, don't get me wrong. Dorien's my Alpha, so going against him is usually a bad idea. And Lyra and I go way back. Friendship isn't such a bad place to start, you know? But we wouldn't have made each other happy in the long run."

"How so?" Jaden asked, genuinely curious. On the surface, if he put his own feelings aside, Simon would seem to be a good fit.

"She wants all of this," Simon said, gesturing around him with a small half smile. "Lyra was born to lead the Thorn. She loves it. She loves the people, the place, everything about being a werewolf except for some of the, uh, gender-specific issues." He eyed Jaden. "She might have mentioned those. Or not."

Jaden shifted uncomfortably. "I heard about that.

Elsewhere." Simon looked relieved to not have to go into them.

"Anyway, she wants it, and maybe she'd change a few things here and there, but she loves it for what it is—a scrubby wolf pack in the middle of nowhere."

"You don't like it here?" Jaden asked. It seemed a rather harsh assessment. Most of the wolves seemed perfectly content in their little forest oasis. They came and went during the day, working here or in other surrounding towns, then returning to be among their own. There was a rhythm and a flow to life here that Jaden found comforting after so many years of upheaval. But he knew very well that some would find it stifling... especially a young wolf like this who had never been out in the world.

"I don't know," Simon said, running a hand through his hair. "Yes... and no. When you're born into this, you don't get a lot of choices, you know? Most of us just grew up here. We're expected to stay here. And it's great if you want it! But it's always the same. Nothing ever changes. And I just—"

Jaden found himself offering a sympathetic smile. "Believe it or not, I know exactly how you feel." Simon had unwittingly just described Jaden's mortal life. He could look back on those emotions now and see them as what they were: the natural growing pains of a young man who wanted to make his own way in a place where he was expected to do things the way they had always been done.

Jaden certainly had managed to escape all that in a big way. Though even in that, he'd never really had a choice. He'd just been jerked from one predetermined path to another with no warning. And there had been no going back.

Simon smiled, tipped his beer in Jaden's direction. "Thought you might. You've got that long-wandering look about you. How'd it turn out for you?"

"What, wandering?" Jaden asked. Simon nodded, and Jaden searched for an appropriate answer. It wasn't a question he got much. Or ever.

"I suppose I'd have to let you know when I'm done wandering," he finally said, and Simon chuckled.

"Fair enough. I'd like to know, though." His face fell a little. "The only wandering I'll be doing is vicarious. I'm on my way up in the pack guard. Maybe if I get a scar or two I'll find a woman. Could be worse."

It surprised Jaden to see his mortal self reflected so strongly back at him tonight from a werewolf. He understood, more than he could express. And that understanding made him want to help if he could. He was tired of wandering, himself. But most people didn't have an eternity in which to do it.

"Maybe you can come out to Massachusetts once I go. I can convene a vampire forum on how to bag hot women, just for you."

Simon grinned. "It's not a bad idea. If you're serious, I'll see. We don't usually get too far outside the territory, but Dorien seems to like you, so . . . we'll see."

He looked intrigued by the possibility, at least, and that was something. Jaden found it nice to be in a position to offer help to someone else for a change. With that done, though, he wanted to get on with this. Simon wanted something. And even though he doubted she would appreciate it, he wanted to get back and check on Lyra. The look of her this evening nagged at him, worried him.

"All right. What's this really about, Simon?"

He saw the truth, which Simon had managed to dance around for an hour now, in the way the wolf dropped his eyes. Jaden's instincts had been right: this was not purely a social exercise.

"Um. Good food and beer? New friendships?"

"Try again. I appreciate the effort, but I have things to do. Thanks, though," Jaden added, and meant it. "I know the only reason I'm not in pieces by now is because of Dorien, but you've been convincingly friendly. My usual reception isn't half as pleasant."

Simon glanced over at a table of six wolves who had been busy glaring at Jaden ever since they'd come in. He looked unimpressed and turned back to Jaden.

"Actually, you're doing pretty well for our first vamp in, well, ever. You've won over a few. Honor counts for a lot around here, and last night showed you have some. Word spreads quickly. Those guys over there are buddies of Eric's, though, so you can forget that. They hate anyone Lyra likes, and she seems to like you. Which I guess brings me to my point...because believe it or not, I've enjoyed this too. You're a lot more likable than I'd figured on."

Jaden smiled faintly. "Why do I feel like I'm not going to like what's coming next?"

"You don't have to like it. You just need to listen to it," Simon said, his own expression suddenly deadly serious and his voice dropping low enough that anyone else in the bar would have a hard time hearing.

"Go ahead." No, he was most definitely not going to like this, Jaden thought. And he wasn't disappointed.

"I'm telling you this for Lyra because she won't listen to me and you seem like a cautious sort of guy. That's good, because you need to be careful, Jaden."

His back was up immediately. "In what sense am I not being careful, Simon?"

Simon looked mildly exasperated. "This isn't to get in Lyra's good graces, Jaden. She and I are...it's just not happening. I meant what I said. But there's been some talk. Just gossip, mostly. People around here don't have anything better to do. But some of it has some basis. I mean, what exactly were you two up to last night, out so far by yourselves?"

"We were...walking," Jaden said lamely. Simon just looked at him.

"Yeah. Well, I think you know how believable that is. And the night I chased the vamp out to Grant Park? You and Lyra alone, once again. I know you were wounded and all, but at first, it looked like—"

"It wasn't," Jaden said quickly. This was rapidly turning into an interrogation, and he didn't want to answer these questions. Especially not from Lyra's best friend. Apart from the danger involved, it was also the very definition of "awkward."

Simon looked skeptical, but he let it go. "Well, whatever it actually is, I can tell you how it *looks*, and it isn't something that's going to fly around here. So I'm telling you, if you give a damn at all what happens to her, you should cool it with the alone time and the long moonlit walks, okay? Eric's got people watching you two. If he keeps looking, I'm guessing he'll find enough to take Lyra down without ever laying a finger on her."

Watched. That knocked the wind out of him for a second. He should have figured. But he'd been too wrapped up in Lyra, too focused on the outside threat of the Ptolemy searching for him to consider that Eric might be seeking to use Lyra's association with him to his advantage. Of course Eric would use it if he got a chance.

Just how he would use it, of course, was something he hadn't been quite clear on.

"So...if he did find something, some supposed evidence that Lyra and I had been, ah—"

"Hooking up?" Simon was half jesting, but there was something in his expression that warned Jaden away from saying anything more specific that might confirm the truth.

Simon steepled his hands beneath his chin and blew out a breath, seeming to search for the right words.

"Understand something, Jaden. Lyra wants Alpha. Maybe her getting it is a long shot, but she's tough. It's a real shot. More, it's what she has *always* wanted, ever since she was a little kid beating up the boys at the park. If it comes out that you two are more than friends, it kills all of that for her, even just having a chance to lead. Life as she knows it would be over."

"You want to be a little more specific?" Jaden asked quietly.

"Permanent exile. The pack would formally disown her. Everything and everyone she's known would be taken from her, and if she ever showed her face on our territory again, she would be killed. No other pack would have her either. She would be what we call a ghost wolf. A shadow of what she was...and could have been."

The truth of what Lyra had risked by giving herself to him finally hit Jaden in full. And it landed like a ton of bricks.

No wonder she'd disappeared on him tonight. No matter how much she'd wanted him, acting on it had probably made her think a lot about the Pandora's box she'd opened.

"Don't you think that's a little harsh?" he managed.

"It doesn't matter what I think," Simon replied. "Vampires were our enemies for centuries. Things have been quiet for a long time, and what with you coming here, it makes me think that our interactions with vampires could be on their way to changing too. But allowing our kind to mate with yours? There could be no children, I don't think, and even if there could, what do you even do with half-breed monsters like that? Whole bloodlines could end that way. And there would always be the worries about vamps just taking over outright. The rules are going to stand, Jaden, now and for a long time, I think."

He paused, took a drink, and looked pointedly right into Jaden's eyes. It surprised him—the wolf saw a great deal more than he'd expected.

"Sorry to be the bearer of bad news. But I see the way you look at her. I'm not the only one. And you needed to know."

Jaden exhaled. He must have been holding out a little hope after all because this was definitely what it felt like to have that sort of hope kicked out of you.

"What if someone wants more? What if she wanted more than the rules allowed for?"

Simon simply raised one brow and shook his head. "Lyra understands how it works, believe me. Nobody gets everything they want. Not here or anywhere else. That can't be news to you."

No, it sure as hell isn't. Jaden passed over his beer bottle for the glass of water that sat beside it, enjoying the cool sensation as it ran down his throat. He was dimly aware of the fact that he was parched, thirsty for something more substantial. Something dark and rich, and forbidden in this place.

The entire room suddenly felt far too small, the scent of wolves going from tolerable to oppressive in an instant. If he'd been under any illusions that Lyra would ever entertain being more than just a temporary lover, they had since vanished like so much smoke.

Yet when she sauntered into the bar, looking larger than life and impossibly gorgeous, every sense honed in on her until she was the only thing in his universe. When her eyes connected with his, it was as though someone had shot several thousand volts of electricity through his system. His mouth watered. His fangs lengthened and sharpened, a natural response to his most basic instincts where she was concerned.

No caution. Only need.

Simon's words only barely penetrated his Lyra-induced haze. "Alone together too often...need to listen to me before you do something stupid..."

Jaden would have warned him, if he'd been able to speak. As it was, she'd nearly reached the table by the time Simon realized they had company. To her credit, the only indication she gave that she'd heard anything was the single, reproachful look she gave Simon before turning all her attention on Jaden.

She didn't see the way Simon flushed and looked away, but Jaden did. *The poor sod's in love with her and he doesn't even know it.* Jaden couldn't conjure up much sympathy though. At least Simon had a shot. He was, after all, the correct species. But Jaden's problems loomed larger at the moment.

Like how to throttle back on his feelings for Lyra, which seemed to have taken root in deep, fertile, and delusional soil.

"Hey," she said. She still looked too pale, with dark circles shaded under her eyes that shouldn't have been there...that he very much wished he hadn't put there. But she also looked like she had pulled herself together, which was something Jaden was beginning to find he could count on with Lyra. Even when she was down, she wasn't out. Not for long.

It was a strength he could appreciate.

"Hey," he replied, wondering what had brought her after him.

"My father wants you back at the house. Something about your Jedi mind trick. I told him he can't learn to do it, but..." She trailed off, shrugged. "He's the boss, and I guess he wants entertaining. Can you come?"

Jaden realized this was the first time she'd asked him something instead of issuing a direct order. Whether or not the motives were sincere, he liked it.

"Sure, I think we're about done here." And he was glad, after watching Simon go all lovesick...not that he was entirely unfamiliar with the sensation where Lyra was concerned. Still, it was as he'd figured. "We're better as friends" sounded all great and selfless, but wasn't holding up when faced with the woman herself.

Too bad for you, Simon. At least for now, the woman is taken.

The thought, hot and possessive, came out of nowhere. And ill-advised or not, Jaden knew it was true enough.

He stood and let his eyes roam the length of her, from the tall boots and tight jeans to the long fitted T-shirt that made him want to build a shrine to whoever had first thought of adding Lycra to cotton. Her hair was partially tamed, pulled back in a ponytail and yet still managing to explode in wild curls.

"Let's go, then," Jaden said, before inclining his head toward Simon. "Thanks for the drink, Simon. I appreciate it."

"No problem. Hey, Lyra. I got optimistic and bought us concert tickets for after the Proving. Hard Reign. You in?"

He seemed ridiculously hopeful, but Lyra seemed to tighten up, her shoulders going rigid. Jaden had never seen her deal with another wolf as a superior dealing with an inferior, but it was fascinating. And gratifying, on some level. He wasn't exactly a paragon of manners, but he understood when he was being deliberately excluded. Simon was trying to add a lesson onto his lecture: *I'll be here, and with her, long after you're gone.*

Maybe he didn't like Simon much after all. And Lyra, at least right now, seemed to share the sentiment.

She stared down her nose, looking Simon dead in the eye. Jaden was surprised to see the flash of warning in Simon's eyes, surprised it took him so long to stand down. But in the end, he did, slowly dropping his head so that the back of his neck was bared to Lyra. It was a reluctant sign of submission.

"You think that fixes this?" she asked. "Do you even understand why I'm upset?"

"I understand plenty," Simon said, lifting his eyes to hers. "More than you these days, seems like." He stood, pulling his jacket from the back of the chair. He nodded at Jaden.

"Good seeing you. Remember what I said. And for Fenrir's sake, watch it."

Simon left, Lyra watching him head out the door with barely another look at her. Her face fell into much sadder lines once he was gone. She was the only one Jaden currently felt sorry for.

Deliver me from lovesick werewolves, unless they happen to be pining over me. Jaden followed Lyra outside.

The night was fragrant with the green scent of spring. Frogs sang somewhere nearby, making the silence between them marginally less oppressive. After they'd gone a few steps, with Simon nowhere to be seen, she turned to look at him.

"I changed my mind about tonight," she said, her chin up but not quite able to hold his gaze. "I want to train, I just—"

"I know," Jaden said. "I just had a crash course in a particular section of The Rules According to Werewolves."

She didn't look the least bit surprised, merely resigned.

"I figured," she said, glaring into the night. "I don't know what's gotten into him, but I knew he was up to something tonight when I heard he'd invited you out. I'm sorry. He means well, but it doesn't always translate." She sighed. "Not even to me. But maybe it's best. More believable when it's not me stammering about it."

"You regret it, then," he said quietly. Her lack of response, the way her cheeks colored, was answer enough, though her eventual answer was a little less definite.

"The answer to that is more complicated than you'd ever understand," she said.

"Try me," Jaden offered, but she shook her head.

"I just want to get back to what we're supposed to be doing," she said. "What happened, all of this...it's too much. I thought I could handle the whole 'in the moment' thing you talked about, but I can't. I'm not built that way."

He could accept that. He could respect that. Even if he didn't like it a damn bit.

"Then just promise me something, all right? I felt like we were at least getting to be friends, before...well, before. If nothing else, I'd like to pick up where we left off with that."

Lyra smiled, but it looked sad and wistful in the darkness. "I'd like that too," she replied. "Deal."

They shook on it, but even now, Jaden felt the hot snap of connection as soon as their skin touched. He didn't fully understand it, but nothing would ever make him stop wanting to explore it. And though she managed to shutter her expression quickly, he saw from the way her eyes went to burning embers that Lyra felt it too.

Even if she wanted—even if she needed—to deny it existed.

chapter EIGHTEEN

JADEN DIDN'T HAVE much to offer as a token of goodwill. He wanted Lyra to be comfortable with him again, and he wanted to try to get back on some kind of even footing, to repair whatever had been broken. He'd spent a full week now trying every rusty tool in his limited arsenal to fix things between them, from charm to humor to a simple willingness to let Lyra set the parameters of their faltering relationship.

In the end, he only had his fallback position, which was better than nothing.

He cooked.

Fragrant steam rose from the soup he'd thrown together. He stirred the pot, tossed in a pinch of salt or another herb, and then stirred some more. A cutting board on the counter sat covered in the remains of carrots, potatoes, celery, garlic, and a few onions. At his elbow rested a glass of B positive he had pilfered from the county hospital last night. The rest of the bag was staying cool and, he hoped, inconspicuous behind Dorien's beer in the garage fridge. Jaden took a sip of the blood, put down the glass, and then sipped from the ladle he dipped into the kettle.

The end product might not be as satisfying as the B positive, and he might not technically need solid food anymore, but Jaden knew he would never stop enjoying all the flavors he'd grown up with. His mother had often made something similar when he was a child. He hoped it set Lyra, and himself, at ease.

"Hey. I'm going to run out and grab some burgers. Do you need—oh. *Oh*. You cook?"

Lyra.

He felt her presence in the room as though someone had flipped a light switch on inside him. Jaden paused in stirring the soup, an odd tingling sensation suffusing him from head to toe. It wasn't the return to even footing he'd hoped for, but he seemed to need this feeling like he needed the air he breathed.

She stood just inside the archway leading into the kitchen, looking around at the scattered remnants of his soup-making extravaganza. He drank in the sight of her as though it had been years, not hours, since he last saw her. She looked as beautiful as she always did, but with a return of the caution he'd seen in her when they first met.

Patience, he reminded himself. He didn't know why it was so important to him that she relax around him, but it was.

"You don't have to stand there," he said. "Come in and sit. The soup will be ready in a minute. I'd rather it had simmered all day, but this is as good as it gets for spur of the moment."

She seemed to startle a little, like she'd forgotten she

wasn't alone. Then her eyes met his, and he felt that bright burst of connection. A silent song that insisted this she-wolf, and no other woman, was for him. He didn't see how it could be, but there it was.

"I didn't know vampires cooked," she said. She seemed a little dazed as she watched him.

"I'm a man of many talents," he replied.

"No, but I mean, you actually *cooked*," Lyra said, moving into the room. She bypassed the table, however, and came to stand beside him, peering into the pot. Then she looked up at him, her expression one of wonderment. He suddenly felt incredibly self-conscious. Maybe it had been the wrong thing...it had been a long time since he'd had to think about such things.

"It's just soup," he said.

Instead of answering him, she leaned over and inhaled deeply, closing her eyes with an expression of bliss that tugged at him.

"Nobody cooks for me," she said. "This house is like the land of processed food products. Dad and I have been eating out of boxes and cans for years, except for maybe burgers. And eggs." She paused, then smiled. "Thank you," she said. "This is the sweetest thing. Just—thank you."

Her grin was so genuine, and so infectious, he found himself returning it. Before he could think better of it, he reached up and moved a stray curl out of her face, running his thumb over her cheek. She was very still, closing her eyes for just a moment in what he hoped was pleasure. At least she didn't move away.

Whatever gulf had opened between them, he badly wanted to bridge the gap.

"You're very welcome," he said softly.

He had to force himself to stop there, to stop from gathering her in his arms. Knowing she would back away from his advances was hell, even when he could feel that she was as drawn to him as he was to her. Understanding the rejection didn't make it feel any better. And as he'd expected, she opened her eyes, blinked as though trying to wake herself up, and moved back out of reach. Deliberately, he turned and ladled some of the soup into a bowl for her, found her a spoon. She accepted both, took them over to the table, and began to eat while Jaden went back to the stove to clean up. He worked quickly, efficiently, and gave her the time to decide where and whether to begin.

Finally, she spoke.

"This is fantastic soup," Lyra said. "It's perfect. I had no idea vampires bothered to cook."

"This one does, at least. I enjoy it," Jaden said. "I always have. I don't get a lot of dinner guests, I guess, but it helps me clear my mind. I'm glad you like it. My mum used to do something like it. Speaking of, where's the amazing Dorien Black? I haven't seen him since I got up."

She stopped and looked at him intently for a moment, her spoon perched in midair halfway to her mouth. He wondered what had caused her sudden pause.

"It's poker night. I will guarantee he'll inhale the leftovers, though," she said, not sounding particularly unhappy that he wasn't there. *Good.* Neither was he.

"You've never mentioned your parents before. I almost forgot you had them," Lyra said, and then he understood what had caught her interest.

Jaden lifted an eyebrow. "Well, I didn't hatch out of an egg. Of course I had parents."

"What were they like?"

Jaden hesitated. It wasn't something he talked about. His past was his own...and really, most of his acquaintances didn't give a damn anyway. Having something important to him disregarded and mocked, as had often happened in his days as a fledgling, tended to make a man keep things close to the vest. But if it kept her here, looking at him like this, then he would try. For her.

"All right, if you're that interested. I grew up on a farm," he said. "In Somerset. We were respectable, though not enormously wealthy. The land was ours, and Father made sure his sons learned to work it, along with the rest of our education. Father was an eminently sensible man. Used to drive me mad."

"Harrison," Lyra said, a smile touching her lips. "That's your last name. I wondered."

Jaden executed a small bow. "And my first. You're speaking to James Dennis Harrison III, English farmer turned creature of the night. Biter of necks, herder of cattle, cooker of soups."

"Not to mention trainer of werewolves," Lyra added.

"Mmm. Not only am I talented, my titles are many and varied," Jaden said, turning to wipe down the counter. He'd been wrong. Lyra made it easy to talk about... natural. And he couldn't help but be flattered that she was interested. A vampire wouldn't have been. For most of his own kind, family and mortal life was very, very old news, and unworthy of conversation.

"What made you change your name?" she asked.

"You leave one life behind and take on another. It seemed appropriate to leave the name as well. Especially since, for a long time, my father wasn't very pleased to be sharing it with me." He tossed the towel on the counter, then went about throwing the vegetable scraps into the garbage as he worked... and remembered.

Love could surmount many things, but becoming a creature of the night was a hard one.

"I'm sorry. He was upset, then, when you turned," Lyra said. She sounded hesitant, but he didn't want her to be. That old wound had long since healed.

"It's all right," he said, turning to look at her. "He came around, eventually. It was hard for him on quite a few levels. I was the oldest son, after all. I was supposed to follow in his footsteps. Sort of threw a wrench in things, my becoming an immortal bloodsucker."

Her ensuing smile, always a little bit wicked, was something he didn't want to lose for the time he had left with her.

"What about your mom?" Lyra asked, her interest apparently piqued. "Was she okay with it?"

"No," he admitted, "not really. But she never stopped pestering me to come home." He smiled at the memory. "Always talked about fixing up a room in the cellar and keeping a few extra cows on hand so I could be, as she put it, a respectable vampire. She didn't like the idea of me biting people. It offended her sensibilities. I think she decided she'd raised me better than that."

"You loved them," Lyra said, stirring her soup while she listened to him. He was surprised that she sounded surprised.

"Of course I did. Very much. Not all of us had bad beginnings, you know. I just picked the wrong night to visit the tavern. A pretty barmaid wants to get friendly in the stables, you think you've hit the jackpot, and then, poof, life as you know it is over and you've got to find a new way. Before that, it was all very...normal. I would have had a good life. Inherited the farm, married some lovely country lass, had nine or ten children. Not so bad."

And that, Jaden realized as the words left his mouth, was the wound that remained, even after two hundred years. He had wanted all that. He still wanted all that. And there wasn't a damned thing on earth that could give it to him. For all the darkness and danger in his past, not to mention his present, he had very simple desires. Sadly, his life hadn't been simple in a very long time.

"It sounds nice, actually. I think normal's probably good, if you can get it." She laughed softly. "Not that I would know much about it. I was born a werewolf. Not exactly a normal beginning. It was happy for a while, though," she said. "Then my mom died. Not quite as happy, but we managed."

Jaden nodded. "Hunters, you said."

"She went out for a run one night and never came home. They found her body the next day. That's why it's so dangerous going out by yourself. But she did her own thing. The people who knew her still laugh about how stubborn she was."

He smirked. "Imagine that."

"Yeah, shocking, right? Obviously I was adopted." Lyra smiled, seeming to enjoy the comparison.

"Anyway, I was pretty young. Three. So I don't remember much about it. Afterward it was just my father, and he was always there. Even when I didn't want him to be, so I guess he was doing his job." She shrugged, her smile fading. "Sometimes I wished he would remarry. I would have liked it, I think, if she'd been the right kind of person. But he never got over her."

"And you decided you didn't much want a mate to worry over," he guessed, and saw immediately that he'd hit the mark. She flushed lightly, then began poking at her soup, stabbing so hard he wondered if she would crack the bowl.

"It isn't that. Exactly. I don't know. I mean, I definitely can't take one before we settle on a Second. And then after, well... I'll be busy, hopefully. I won't have time for any of that. Anyway, I can take care of myself better than anyone else could."

"You might be able to, but that doesn't mean you should have to," Jaden pointed out. "You might like having someone around to care for you."

Lyra took another bite of soup and propped her head on her fist, watching him. "Is that how the vamps do it?" she asked. "Hook up and then stay eternally mushy over each other? Because I know enough wolf couples who can barely stand one another, not that it..." She trailed off, her thoughts seeming to vanish into the ether for a moment before she came back.

"Not that it matters with the bond," she finished quietly.

"Um," Jaden replied. "Actually, a lot of vampires don't bother. Eternity is a very long time to spend with one person."

"Ah," Lyra said, and he wished he could take the answer back, truthful though it was.

"Well, I won't have to worry about that. I get one lifetime, that's it." Her smile was weak, though, and he wondered if they were having similar thoughts.

Yes, she did have only one lifetime. And he would be walking the world, looking and feeling much the same, when Lyra Black was nothing but dust. Even without all the other roadblocks they'd had put up between them, that one would be tough to surmount. Tough, but not impossible.

But it was a moot point, and Lyra knew it. Even if she should change her mind someday, Jaden knew he wouldn't make the short list. Or any kind of list.

She stood, picked up her now empty bowl, and took it to the sink to rinse it out, near enough for him to touch. She couldn't quite lift her eyes to his when she spoke.

"I've got some stuff to do. I'll catch you back here in a couple of hours? The night is young and all that."

"I'll be here," he said, trying to sound as casual as he could, though he knew he would think of nothing else until she returned.

"And thanks again for the soup. Really," she said, this time looking right at him. "It hit the spot. And besides that, it was . . . sweet."

That last word made him laugh, though not at her. "Not an adjective usually applied to me, but I'll take it."

A soft smile, slightly puzzled, touched her lips at his words. "You should. Have it applied to you, I mean. I know it's none of my business, but whoever hurt you, those other vampires I guess, must be the most worthless bunch of bloodsuckers going. They're probably ones we used to war with."

"I think your pack has warred with just about everyone," Jaden said, unexpectedly touched. "But thank you. And as to the other," he lifted one shoulder, nonchalant, "they'll get theirs eventually, I expect."

"Well, if and when it does, I would love to get in on that action." Lyra said. She started to walk away, paused, and then turned to look at him. "So . . . we're good, right?" she asked, and he couldn't ignore what she meant. She wanted to know if he was ready to forget what had happened and move ahead.

Since the answer "No, but I'm going to try, eventually," wouldn't be acceptable, he told her what she wanted to hear.

"We're good," Jaden agreed. But as she graced him with one last smile and headed out the door, he couldn't help imagining what it might be like to share a life with her, short though hers would seem in comparison to his own. She was a warrior of a she-wolf, brazen and bold, but unexpectedly naïve and charming at times. He would love to show her the world she had tasted so little of, to show her there was more than just duty to the pack.

Pipe dreams, Jaden thought as he tossed the ladle into the sink, where it landed with an irritated little clank.

Just then the phone started to ring. At first he ignored it, assuming whoever it was would leave a message for Dorien. Instead, when the answering machine picked up, he heard a voice no one in this town would recognize but him.

"Jaden, I know you're in there. Pick up. We need to talk."

With a final, resentful look at the pot of dinner that had accomplished everything he'd hoped and nothing he'd wanted all at the same time, Jaden lifted the phone to his ear.

He was certain some fresh hell awaited him. Just what sort was all that remained to be seen.

chapter NINETEEN

LILTING HARP MUSIC drifted through the dimly lit little store on the square called Moon Magic. Crystals hung from the ceiling, their facets glinting as they turned lazily on long bits of clear floss. A woman sat behind a long glass counter, her nose firmly planted in a battered paperback. He caught a glimpse of a blond ponytail and a pair of cat's eye glasses when she gave him a half wave that indicated she had no interest in bothering him if he didn't bother her.

Suited him just fine, considering who he was meeting.

Jaden wandered to the baskets of tumbled stones and plucked up a large chunk of tiger's eye, rubbing it in his fingers while he looked around, wondering what sort of trouble Damien Tremaine was so intent on bringing him.

A small stand of necklaces caught his eye, the polished stones in the pendants gleaming in the soft light. He walked to them, wondering whether Lyra might like one of them, and whether she would accept it or wrap it around his neck. No doubt she would think such a gift would violate the terms of their latest truce. Not that it stopped him from considering the purchase anyway.

Lost in thought, Jaden barely registered the sound of the small silver bell above the door announcing another customer. Only the voice, speaking almost directly in his ear, brought him back to reality.

"I don't really think any of those are your style."

Jaden looked up with a jerk and found himself confronted with a familiar, and generally unwelcome, countenance.

"Damien," he said. "There you are." He looked around, saw that it was just the two of them in the store apart from the still disinterested clerk. "You're going to get yourself killed just wandering around here like this, you know. They're going to smell you!"

Damien smirked, and Jaden wondered whether there was much more to him than the aristocratic brat he projected. Generally, he thought not, but he put up with the mouthy Shade because Ty seemed to like him.

"I'm a Cait Sith standing beside another Cait Sith."

"Lilim, now."

"Whatever." Damien rolled his eyes. "We both have that cat smell thing going on, and you seem to have inoculated the general populace somehow. Nobody's going to bother us for the amount of time I'm here."

"And again, why *are* you here?" Jaden asked, eyes narrowing. "You usually bring trouble with you."

"No, I participate in trouble, I don't bring it. Usually," Damien replied. "This is a special case, though. I am announcing the *approach* of trouble so that you can get out of here before it shows up to skin you." He glanced around critically. "Of all the things you could have gotten yourself tangled up in, Jaden, I don't know why you picked this one. When Ty told me you were here I had to pick my jaw up off the floor. Wish I'd known, or I could have gotten you out sooner. I was here not long ago."

That, more than anything else he'd said, piqued Jaden's interest.

"Why—"

"Shade business. And at this point, it's irrelevant. You need to skip town." Damien lowered his voice further and leaned in. "The borders of the territory are crawling with Ptolemy. Getting back in was no picnic, but I can get you out. Whatever you think you're doing here, this place is a lost cause. When the Proving happens, the Thorn is going to fall, and hard."

Jaden could only stare blankly at Damien for a moment. "Ptolemy," he said.

Damien's lips thinned with irritation. "Yes, genius, Ptolemy! Here! All the way around the territory! Do you want me to draw you a picture?"

"No, no," Jaden murmured, trying to wrap his head around what this meant. "But...I was attacked by a single vamp one of the first nights I was here. Moved like a Ptolemy, though I wasn't sure if it was one of yours, some lowblood with an ankh in his mark, you know?"

Damien looked irritated. "You really think we're still taking contracts on you, Jaden? That's insulting."

Jaden regarded him coolly. "Tell me you wouldn't do it for the right price."

"I wouldn't," Damien said flatly. "Though you're making me want to reconsider that decision. What else? I can see there's more."

"Yeah, a couple nights ago. Four Ptolemy. Lyra and I

managed to take them out. I assumed at that point that I'd been followed from Tipton. But they didn't make it back, so..."

Damien gave a small but perfectly audible groan. "Overly simplistic, Jaden. You'd think your luck thus far would have taught you that. This isn't about you, per se, though the queen following you here with an army is almost believable. From what I hear, Arsinöe's rants about you, Ty, and the Lilim in general are rather gloriously unhinged. You might have wanted to play it a bit more low key with that patrol."

"Hard to do when you've got four vampires determined to either get you in a restraint collar or take your head off altogether."

One corner of Damien's mouth quirked up. "You've got a point."

"You know, we should go someplace else to talk about this," Jaden said, realizing all at once how exposed they were for such a conversation. If the clerk was listening to this...

Damien waved the comment away and jerked his head toward the blonde, who was now bobbing her head in time to silent music. Only then did Jaden notice the earbuds.

"The teenaged wannabe Wiccan isn't interested, trust me. Look, Jaden, I don't know what more to say about it, apart from 'take off while you can.' "

Jaden thought of Lyra, and of the wolves who had come so far in accepting him among them. "I want to know what's going on. And I'm sure you know."

Damien lifted an eyebrow. "Oh? You think I'd take a contract on you, but you're going to believe me?"

"I don't have a lot of other options right now," Jaden replied, and saw Damien's blue eyes flash.

"Flattering. But honest. All right. Think about it, Jaden. Think back on the lazy, scheming Ptolemy as they were when you served them, most wanting to be waited on hand and foot all the time because damn it, they *deserved* it. Now imagine all the servants' chambers, the cages, the dungeons, empty, with nothing but sad piles of empty collars to remind the highblood pricks of how marvelous they once had it. What good is being one of the glorious Ptolemy if you don't have anyone to kick around? They're still persona non grata with the Council, and the other dynasties are steering very clear at the moment. Won't last forever, but it could be a few centuries before people get over it."

"So she's humiliated. We knew that. It's why she'd been picking off some of the Cait Sith who come into Tipton to join the Lilim. I assumed she was trying to rebuild a little of what she'd lost in the slave labor department."

Damien shook his head. "No. Arsinöe is never going to get all of you back, and she knows it, her little revenge hunts aside. She's killing most of the cats she catches anyway." He paused, winced. "In some creative ways, too, from what I understand. I think it's safe to say she's looking for new blood. And with the rest of our kind, lowblood and highblood alike, casting a wary eye on them, what is a despot in need for cheap muscle to do?"

Jaden watched Damien for some sign that he was joking, or going somewhere other than the obvious with this, but he could see none. "Wolves? They're seriously going to start on the wolves?"

Damien shrugged. "I'm not sure she would have thought of it herself. She hates wolves as much as anyone, at least in theory. Who sees them anymore? But that's the problem. The packs have been flying under the radar for a long time, Jaden. They've rebuilt since we used to fight them so long ago. Look around. They're more disciplined, stronger. Brighter, shockingly. A force to be reckoned with, too, if they pulled together a bit more. If you think about it, it was only a matter of time before a wolf with a little power and a big inferiority complex headed in our direction."

Jaden made a disgusted noise. "Our? This is why you were here a couple of weeks ago. What, is one of the Thorn working for you?"

Bloody Shades, he thought. They seemed to have their fingers everywhere, and they never caused anything but problems. Damien, as usual, looked unperturbed.

"One came to us. Drake was intrigued, naturally. Can't beat a wolf for raw muscle. But the apprenticeship didn't work out. I tried to warn him that any wolf who would come to us probably liked killing a little too much. We require finesse, you know. Anyway, didn't last. But he did a job that brought him some attention from the Ptolemy, and it got someone thinking. Unfortunately. And the packs are so loosely knit, not to mention none of them like one another all that much, that it isn't like anyone will rush to the Thorn's defense when they vanish and the Ptolemy suddenly have a bunch of pet wolves."

"So they'll just swoop in and, what, round them up?" Jaden asked, feeling slightly ill at the thought. All he had been through with the Ptolemy for so many years…no one else should have to experience that.

"I doubt it," Damien said. "Arsinoë operates with charm before force, and I'm sure she'd prefer a period of buttering them up to inspire loyalty before she really has to crack down on these new…pets. Something is in the works, though. With the number of Ptolemy just beyond the borders of Thorn territory, that's obvious. Beyond that, the Shades, unfortunately, are in the dark as much as you are."

"Who sold them out?" Jaden asked. But the moment he asked the question, he knew. It had to be Eric Black.

Damien pinned Jaden with a cool stare. "You know, you're very interested in these wolves, Jaden. It's disturbing. Now do you really need more information to get you to go? This is a death trap. I didn't think you liked those."

"Have you told Ty about this? The Dracul?"

Damien hissed out an irritable little breath through his nose. "Yes and yes. Both instructed me to come and get your ass out of here before all hell breaks loose. And by the way, Ty also mentioned that if you ever turned off your phone for two weeks again, he was going to shove it up a certain orifice from which it would be difficult to extract." His expression quickly went from irritated to confused. "And just out of curiosity, what *are* you still doing here, Jaden? I heard something about a she-wolf and a necklace, but this isn't exactly a vacation spot…" He trailed off, and Jaden remained silent, but something in his expression must have given him away. Damien wrinkled up his nose as though he'd smelled something foul.

"Oh, for the love of—you know what? I don't want to know. Really? I just—*really*?"

"I don't know what you're talking about," Jaden snapped.

"Good, because I'd rather not discuss it. The thought of the wolf stink alone…" Damien shuddered. "Whoever she is, forget her. You aren't going to want to be here when the queen arrives to start buttering up the befurred masses.

She'll take her time, I imagine, but it'll all end the same. And I'm sure your presence will not be appreciated."

"I'm not going anywhere," Jaden said flatly. "I'll tell Dorien, the Alpha, what's going on. This can all be taken care of before anything actually happens."

Damien stared at Jaden as though he thought he'd lost his mind. "He's not going to believe some vampire."

"Yes, he will. He likes me. And I work for him... after a fashion." Jaden explained the situation as quickly as he could to Damien, whose expressions ranged from disbelief to disgust. When he'd finished, the Shade simply stared at him for a long moment.

"You've completely lost it, haven't you?"

"Why, because I'm doing something decent for a change?" Jaden asked.

"No," Damien replied, glowering. "Because getting involved with wolf politics is madness. Even a worse idea than getting involved in dynasty politics."

"That's what you do for a living," Jaden pointed out, his blood starting to simmer.

"Yes, but I'm an expert at meddling, and I'm paid very well for the trouble. I wouldn't touch this mess with a ten-foot pole, though. Does Ty know that's what you've been up to?"

"Ty isn't my keeper," Jaden shot back. "No one is. If you want to run off and tattle, Damien, go right ahead. I've got things I need to take care of."

Damien's brows shot up. "Oh? In a hurry to get yourself killed, I guess. If one side doesn't destroy you, the other one will, Jaden. These wolves are hardly worth your time. They're all miserable beasts, one's the same as another... pretty twist of tail or not."

Jaden's hand shot out, fisted in Damien's shirt, and he had him dangling above the ground in seconds. Damien looked more irritated than intimidated.

"Oh, this helps. You're welcome for the information. Jackass."

"Thank you," Jaden gritted out. "Really. Now stay out of my way." He let go, turned on one heel, and was out the door before Damien hit the ground. Damien watched him go, an expression that was a mixture of pity and amusement on his handsome face. He looked sharply at the clerk, ascertained that she was still oblivious, and pulled out his cell phone.

"Ty? Damien. Yes, I found him. No...no." He looked toward the door, where Jaden had just slammed out into the night thinking he was going to save the day.

"It's complicated, naturally. And if you want him, you're going to have to come down here and haul his ass home yourself. I've done my good deed for the decade." He ended the call, then cocked his head at the start of a strange sound outside. Then he closed his eyes with a resigned sigh when he realized the source of the racket.

The distant but unmistakable sound of a full-blown werewolf fight. And he'd bet money it had something to do with Jaden.

The poor bastard should never have killed that patrol, Damien thought. Should never have presumed to come here in the first place.

Whether Jaden liked it or not, the end of the Pack of the Thorn had already begun.

"I need a bloody vacation," Damien growled, and vanished out the back of the store and into the night.

chapter **TWENTY**

JADEN DUCKED out the door of the shop and headed down the street, his body on autopilot, instinctively heading in the right direction while his mind whirled with the information he'd just been given. He needed to get to Dorien, and to Lyra, before Eric and the Ptolemy could do anything. Hopefully nothing was planned until after the Proving, but he could take no chances.

He strode down the sidewalk, so focused he didn't notice the men walking straight toward him until it was far too late to do anything but try and absorb the blow.

A huge, thick male body slammed into him, the force sending Jaden stumbling to the side as he tried to stay on his feet. Not often taken by surprise, it took him precious seconds to figure out what was even going on. By the time he got his bearings, two other wolves had gotten him by the arms.

One of the first rules of combat with a wolf had always been don't ever let them get a hold of you. But it was far too late for that now. Grips like iron vices encircled his upper arms. Immediately he began to thrash, hiss, and spit, but it did no good. He was being dragged backward, toward the green at the center of the square. He could hear a deep voice bellowing.

"Wolves! Wolves!"

Howls began to rise around him. Jaden tried to shift into a cat, but they had him sequestered too well. He dangled helplessly for a moment, his legs caught just as effectively by his captors as his arms had been, before giving up and shifting back. Finally, the men dragging him stopped, and he heard a soft laugh.

It was no surprise to look up into the face of Eric Black.

"What the hell is this?" Jaden asked. He could see wolves gathering all around him, running on four legs and then switching to two as they came together to see why the cry had been raised. There was curious murmuring that ran through the crowd, an electric sound. They all knew something big was coming, but no one knew what.

Least of all Jaden.

"Eric," he growled when the man didn't answer him. This time, the large wolf looked at him, a threatening gleam in his eye.

Dimly, he heard a voice calling his name.

"Jaden. Jaden? Jaden!"

The click of boot heels resonated on the concrete, and there was Lyra running toward him. Her eyes were wide, and Jaden realized he'd never really seen her look frightened before. The fact that her fear was on his behalf didn't give him much confidence in what was unfolding.

He caught the way Eric looked at her, and alarms sounded in his head.

"Lyra, don't—"

"Grab her," Eric said. Seeing a couple of Eric's thugs put their hands on her was worse, somehow, than being caught himself. Lyra was more stoic about the current situation than he had been, likely because she knew these people, but her fury was evident. She held herself as regally as a queen.

"Let go of me. I demand to know the meaning of this."

"You're going to," Eric said flatly. "Where the hell is Dorien. On his way? Good. He'll hear me." His voice rose again.

"Wolves of the Thorn," he cried. "We gather tonight to decide the fate of one of our daughters!"

Lyra knew what was happening a split second before Jaden did. He saw the realization dawn, all the color drain from her face. This sudden turn of events could mean only one thing, he realized. And the knowledge was accompanied by a sinking feeling deep in the pit of his stomach.

Eric knew. Somehow, he knew that he and Lyra had been together. And he was going to cast her out, just as Simon had warned him. How he'd found proof, Jaden didn't know. But he must have, somehow. His shoulders sagged.

These bloody wolves were all far too interested in one another's business.

Dorien shouted as he approached, then burst through the front of the large circle that had gathered in the square, surrounding them.

"What is the meaning of this? Eric, damn it, this time you've gone too far! Get your hands off my daughter, now!"

"It's Lyra who's finally gone too far. She's bonded with

this filthy bloodsucker, and she still thinks she should lead the pack!"

The crowd went into an uproar, but all Jaden could see was Lyra. That single word spoke volumes, slammed into him with all it might mean. Her beautiful face, usually so full of light, told the truth. Bonded, he thought. How could he not have known? Suddenly everything, her odd behavior after their lovemaking, her cautious reengagement with him, made sense. But why hadn't she just told him?

He supposed he was living the answer to the second question right now. Still, something so important…he wished she had trusted him with it. *Bonded*. But what exactly did that mean, when he'd seen no marks on his own body…how did she know?

More important, how did she feel?

Her eyes met his for a single instant, and he felt her pain slice through him like the edge of a knife. And he knew—she might feel for him, but this, all of this, was not what she had wanted. How could it be? Yet some part of him had hoped that after all this time, he might actually be someone's first choice.

A fool's wish.

At first, Dorien was incredulous. He barely glanced at Lyra and Jaden, instead striding up to growl, red faced, at his nephew. His voice was quieter, but Jaden, and he imagined most of the other wolves here, could hear him perfectly.

"You'd better have some damned good proof to back up what you're accusing her of, boy. This is my daughter."

"I know," Eric said flatly. "And I do, Uncle. Have a look." His voice raised. "Everyone look at what your would-be Alpha has been doing!"

Jaden was disgusted. "Why don't you just brand her

with a scarlet A, you pig? You say you don't want to be seen as savages? What the hell is this?"

Eric rounded on him as he stepped to Lyra. "Shut up," he snapped. "You've got no right to speak here, just like you had no right to touch her. You disrespect my pack, our traditions, our laws, everything with what you've done. You think I'm happy to lose my cousin to this? It's a blight on our line!"

"Actually," Jaden growled, "I think you must be dancing with joy on the inside."

"Think what you will," Eric sneered. "I have no use for vampires. Our kinds don't mix. And now *this*."

He reached for Lyra. She didn't struggle but merely stood there, a mixture of defiance and resignation, while Eric extended his claws and tore through the sleeve of her shirt. Gasps rose from the crowd as the fabric fell away and revealed a delicate band, lighter than ink but too dark to be imagined, encircling her arm.

The mark was like nothing Jaden had seen before, and he strained forward, trying to get a better look at the band. But he was quickly jerked back, and he whipped his head around to glare at his captors.

"Watch it," he growled.

Dorien's voice, now strained, drew his attention back to the scene unfolding before him. The Alpha stood in front of his daughter, disappointment etched so deeply into his face that Jaden imagined some of the lines would stay permanently. And Lyra, who he had once thought would spit in the face of anyone who crossed her, could barely meet his eyes.

She was losing everything. Because of *him*. Something deep within his chest constricted and began to ache.

"Don't punish her," Jaden said. "Blame me. She didn't know. Neither of us knew."

A little of the fire flared in her eyes as she lifted her head to look first at him, then at Dorien.

"I take the blame for my actions. What's done is done. I have nothing to say in my defense. Just..." She trailed off, her voice softening. "Don't hurt him. Do what you like with me, but don't hurt him. His intentions were... his heart was... in the right place. He didn't understand. I did. Blame me."

Eric crossed his arms over his chest. To Jaden he looked like some tribal chieftain, and he knew he had not truly appreciated what an ancient and closed society the wolf pack could be until now. This all had the feel of a ritual that had been played out many times before, whenever a wolf ran afoul of the pack. A casting out.

And from the heartbroken look on Dorien's face, Jaden knew the man would do nothing to stop it. Whether he couldn't, or just wouldn't, was irrelevant.

"Lyra," Dorien said quietly. "I knew there was something, but you were so close. You know there's nothing I can do. Why?"

She tipped her head up to look into Dorien's face, and Jaden saw a single tear slide down her cheek. Jaden held his breath, barely realizing that he was, waiting to hear what she would say. But he knew that what he hoped, what he needed, to hear was something that might never fall from her lips. And certainly not here, in full sight of her pack.

Even as they cast her out.

"Does it matter?" she asked quietly. "It comes to the same thing. I'm sorry, Dad. We didn't mean for it to go so far."

Dorien shook his head as cries began to rise from the pack, demands for justice to be meted out on both Jaden and Lyra. Not all the wolves, though, Jaden saw, looking around. Not even most. He saw everything from sympathy to sorrow to shock reflected back at him in the glowing eyes of the pack. Lyra was well loved. It shouldn't have surprised him. But none of them would go against the laws they had always lived by, the laws that had protected them from destruction more than once. He was just an interloper, a thief.

A vampire.

He caught sight of Gerry, the leader of the pack guard who had been kind to him fairly quickly. The man shook his head sadly as their eyes met, and then turned away. Suddenly, Jaden realized Simon was nowhere to be seen. He had known, Jaden thought. He'd warned him. But it had already been too late.

All eyes were on Dorien as he approached Jaden. He didn't struggle, knowing it was better to face whatever the Alpha was going to dish out without fear. Inside, however, nerves jangled. He had no idea what to expect.

"I trusted you," Dorien said. Jaden could hear the storm beneath the calm surface of the Alpha's voice. "You were supposed to help save her. And now I've lost her forever."

"I fell in love with her," Jaden said. He felt Lyra's shocked gaze on his face, but he couldn't look away from Dorien. If he had to be subjected to this, if she did, he would say his piece.

He saw surprise, anger. "Love doesn't matter."

"The hell it doesn't," Jaden said, his voice carrying over the crowd. "She's waited her entire life to be seen for who she is, instead of just a token of power. She was brave enough to reach for what she wanted, and open minded enough to see me as a man instead of just a blood-sucker. She is exactly the sort of woman your pack should be holding up as an example. This isn't the damned Dark Ages anymore, Dorien. Those battles are over. The rest of the world has moved on, and yet here we are. You're going to give up your daughter, make her a pariah, for acciden-tally bonding with a man who loves her. Who would sup-port her, *and* this pack. I would accept you, even though you're not my kind. You're really going to disown your only child because you refuse to accept me?"

Eric curled his lip in disgust. "We have laws for a rea-son, vampire. We had chaos once, and it almost destroyed us. The Thorn is moving forward. Letting in the vampires jeopardizes all of that."

"Then why are you talking to the Ptolemy?" Jaden asked, and saw Eric's face darken with fury.

"The Ptolemy? This is the dynasty that's been hunting you here? Why would I have anything to do with them? One vampire is the same as another. I wish they'd gotten you. It would have saved us all of this."

"You could have saved yourselves all of this anyway, if you'd open your eyes. I know you've had contact with the Ptolemy, with Queen Arsinöe. With the House of Shad-ows. You'd align with them and still throw Lyra out for touching me. How does that make any sense? The queen will destroy you a lot more effectively than I ever could!"

Eric walked up to him, bared his teeth, and slashed him across the face with his claws. The pain was sharp, but brief, as his head rocked to the side. He heard Lyra's furious cry.

"Eric, don't!"

Jaden saw the blood spatter the ground, but he could already feel the flesh knitting together.

"Don't accuse me, vampire," Eric growled. "All your wishing I would destroy my pack that way won't make it true." He shot a heated look at his cousin. "Some of us actually care about preserving what we have, instead of trying to change everything."

He turned away, and Jaden was left to glare after him. Unlike the mark on Lyra's arm, there was no proof that Eric was in league with the Ptolemy except for the word of a Shade, another vampire who had doubtless skipped town at the first sign of trouble. Maybe there was more they could do, if the Thorn would even allow his kind to help. But he and Lyra would have to deal with the problem at hand first. And he could see already that for Lyra, this would be nothing less than devastating.

He would get her out of this. And then he would do what he needed to make her see that even if he wasn't the future she'd wanted, he could provide her with far more care than she would ever have gotten from any wolf.

"Dorien, don't do this to her," Jaden said, a final effort to convince the man even though he could see the time for convincing had long passed.

"I'm the Alpha," Dorien said with a shake of his head. "Some things can't be changed. No matter how much I wish they could be."

"Then you're nothing but a fool, after all," Jaden snapped, finally understanding what Lyra had been up against her entire life. Even if she hadn't bonded with him, someone would have found a way to stop her at the Proving. She'd never had a chance. He credited Dorien for trying something unconventional instead of forcing her to bend, but Jaden doubted the man would ever buck the system again. No change would come here without a violent upheaval, and he hated to imagine what that would be.

Dorien didn't lash out at the retort. He seemed as though he'd barely heard it, moving in a daze to stand beside his nephew. The heir apparent.

"Wolves of the Thorn! Choose the fate of my—" His voice faltered for a moment, and Jaden thought he might stop and reconsider, despite everything. But after a deep breath, the Alpha pressed on.

"Choose the fate of my daughter!"

Silence ensued for several seconds, and Jaden felt a glimmer of hope that a handful of the bravest would take up her cause, would demand she be allowed to stay. But then the chant started, low and soft, like the rhythmic beating of a drum.

Lyra looked at the ground, then lifted her head to hold it up, a final act of defiance as she was cast away.

Ghost wolf… ghost wolf… ghost wolf… ghost wolf…

The chanting rose, crested like a wave, echoing into the night sky like some dark song. When Dorien raised his hands, it died away. He nodded to the wolves holding her, and they released her, stepping back. Pain echoed through every word Dorien spoke.

"Lyra Black. You are cast out of the Pack of the Thorn as of this night, cast out of our pack, our territory, our world, never to rejoin our kind. You are a ghost to us, a wolf only in the form you take, not in the life you've chosen to lead. And you are no longer my child."

Jaden heard Lyra's sharp intake of breath, as though she'd been slapped.

"Dad," she said softly, pleading. But Dorien turned

away. And the anguish Lyra felt tore through Jaden as though it were his own, screaming out of the night and nearly taking him to his knees. The shock of Dorien's decision made him stumble, and he found himself jerked upward by the men who still held him.

Eric looked on approvingly, though Jaden supposed he couldn't say the wolf looked pleased. He'd expected more gloating... but maybe that would be saved for later, when he could laugh with his cronies about how easily he'd won after all.

"What about the vampire?" he asked Dorien quietly. "Shall I kill him, or would you like to?"

Dorien shook his head. "Let him go. He defended the pack once, despite everything." He looked directly at Jaden, his eyes burning with emotions Jaden didn't even want to guess at. "Consider this a debt repaid, Jaden of the Lilim." He stepped closer, leaning down to speak directly in Jaden's ear.

"Take care of her, damn you. It's the least you can do."

Then Dorien rose, motioned to the wolves behind Jaden, and Jaden found himself released. Lyra stood alone, looking around as though she didn't quite know where she was. He hesitated, but finally he went to her. What point was there in hiding it now? She would need someone. Whether she liked it or not, she would need him.

He took her hand, and she didn't resist. But it felt cold and lifeless in his.

"Go," Dorien said, and turned away. He began to walk, and didn't stop, pushing through the crowd so that it swallowed him up and he vanished from view. The fact that he couldn't watch his daughter go said something. But it would have said more if he hadn't let it happen at all.

Lyra looked at him, her eyes shining with unshed tears. Her voice was so soft as to be barely audible.

"Help me do this," she said.

He nodded. He would walk through fire for her if she asked. One day, maybe she would see that.

The crowd before them parted, clearing a path out of the square. Jaden tugged at Lyra's hand and got her to start moving. *You can do this*, he willed her silently. *You can do this. Just a few steps more.* He didn't know whether she could sense any of his thoughts, as his kind could do while in their feline forms. But she did come with him, putting one foot in front of the other.

The wolves were silent as the outcasts passed by, and as they passed, each wolf turned his back. The powerful symbolism affected Jaden in no small measure. This truly was meant to be the end for her. He hoped he could be enough to get her through the aftermath. No matter how strong she was, this wound would take time to heal, if it ever did.

They finally passed the edge of the crowd and continued down the deserted street toward the house that was no longer Lyra's. Jaden wanted to retrieve his car and get out of town as quickly as possible, partly because when he looked over at Lyra, what he saw worried him deeply. She was obviously in shock. She looked as white as a ghost, and her eyes bore a glassy cast. He had never seen her anything but strong. This was not a Lyra he was quite sure what to do with—she had never accepted his comfort, had never needed it. But she clung to his hand as though it was the only thing keeping her afloat.

He would take her to Tipton, and to Lily, Jaden decided. After that, they both could decide what to do next.

"Come on," he said, urging her to move more quickly. "We need to get to my car and get out of here." He was suddenly uneasy. They were being watched. He could feel the eyes on them, and seconds later, he picked up the scent.

It seemed they'd be leaving Silver Falls in a bigger hurry than he'd thought. And he could guess very well who had provided them with an escort like this.

Don't accuse you my ass, Eric Black.

"Shit," Jaden said. "Run."

The urgency in his voice seemed to snap her out of her fog, at least enough to move. They dashed forward, Jaden shifting smoothly into his faster form. Lyra must have done the same, because seconds later he had a sleek wolf running alongside him. They headed down a side street, and Jaden knew they were being pursued. He pushed his body to the limit, faster and faster, until his feet barely seemed to be touching the ground. There was the sound of vicious laughter behind them, close. Still, he and Lyra managed to stay just ahead, winding down streets and dashing through yards until they reached her street. He could see his 'Vette shining beneath the streetlight. They were so close—

He realized all at once that Lyra was no longer at his side. Jaden skidded to a halt, spun around, and saw that Lyra had decided to confront their pursuers on her own. She stood, splay-legged, in the middle of the empty street, hackles raised, growling low in her throat at a small group of beautiful, pale-skinned Ptolemy women emerging from the darkness. One, a beautiful blond courtier Jaden remembered lusting over for a time several years ago, strolled to the front of the group, hips swaying. Her smile was cruel.

"Oh, leaving so soon? Come here, doggie. Let's play."

Jaden ran to place himself in front of Lyra and shifted into a man again. He could see they all recognized him, not that it would make any difference in their fun. The blonde hissed at him.

"Traitor," she sneered. The others took up the chant, spitting the word at him.

He could feel Lyra standing behind him, but he stayed where he was.

"It's a she-wolf," one of the others snickered. "Interesting company you're keeping these days, Jaden." She looked at her blond companion. "Remember how he used to stare at us? Such a pretty cat. Shame he's got dirty blood. I almost feel bad, seeing what he's been reduced to."

The blonde—Jaden remembered her name as Carissa—shrugged. "Kill the wolf. Arsinöe wants Jaden. There are many of us here," she said, turning her attention back to Jaden with a smile. "You'll never get out."

"I'm really not in the mood for this," Lyra said, her voice hard. "Turn around and leave, or lose your heads. Jaden and I are out of here either way."

Amazed, Jaden watched Lyra stride past him to face Carissa head-on. The vampire was too stunned by the she-wolf's audacity to move right away, which he supposed Lyra had counted on. By the time Carissa thought to react, it was too late. Lyra had her by the throat. The tips of her claws dug into tender flesh, and if Carissa's wide eyes and lack of breathing were any indication, Lyra had a hell of a grip.

Lyra bared her teeth and looked at the others. "Leave us or her head comes off. Then yours."

He wasn't surprised to see the uneasy glances exchanged

before the lot of them slinked off back into the darkness. These were no hardened hunters, just courtiers in town for some fun. He was sure they'd decide not to mention this unpleasant incident to anyone else and find a different way to amuse themselves. Once they were gone, Lyra hurled Carissa to the ground where the vampire collapsed, gagging. She would heal soon enough, though, and from the look in her eyes she wouldn't slink away quite so easily.

"Come on," Jaden said. "In the car. Now."

"You got it," Lyra said. There was a deadness in her eyes that chilled Jaden to the bone. In this state of mind, he felt sure she would have gladly leaped into a sea of Ptolemy, fighting tooth and claw until she was overwhelmed. He recognized the symptoms—he'd been there before. Right now, she didn't care about anything, least of all herself. But she couldn't stay numb forever. And he wanted to be well out of here when she started to fall apart.

Jaden pulled the keys from his pocket, and they got quickly into the Corvette. As soon as they were inside, he locked the doors. A quick glance at the street showed him that Carissa had already vanished. He doubted she'd gone far, though. All the more reason to burn rubber out of here.

"It's going to be all right," he told her as the engine growled to life, as much to convince himself as to convince her. Lyra didn't look at him, just stared straight ahead, expressionless.

"Just drive," she said.

So he did, pushing the pedal to the floor and roaring off into the night.

chapter TWENTY-ONE

By the time they made it to Tipton the next night, Lyra was fighting to maintain the eerie calm that had stolen over her after her father had turned his back on her. She knew Jaden was worried, but she didn't want to talk about it. Talking about it would make it that much more real. So she had spent most of the two nights of their trip sitting quietly in the car, or pretending to sleep so he would leave her alone.

She wished she could really sleep, but that had proven elusive. Every time she lay down, the entire terrible scene played over and over in her head on an endless loop. While Jaden had slept the day away in their hotel room, she'd taken his cell phone down to the lounge and tried to call her house, over and over again.

No answer. Just her father's gruff and grumbly voice on the answering machine. Eventually, she'd realized she was just calling back to hear his message and stopped. She tried Simon, both on his cell and his house phone, but got no answer there either. It was as though they had dropped off the face of the earth.

Or she had.

So she'd eaten some fruit from the continental breakfast, which she hadn't really wanted and had barely tasted. And then she'd gone back up to the room, and while Jaden slept peacefully on one of the two beds, she'd curled into him to take what comfort she could. By the time he'd awakened, she was back on her own bed. He'd seemed a little puzzled—Lyra wondered whether he sensed that she'd essentially stolen comfort from him. In truth, she had no idea how to ask for it when he was awake.

Jaden had humbled her with the words he'd spoken in front of her pack. She was grateful, too, that he didn't seem to expect her to return them—the words or the sentiment. She didn't know how she felt, or how she would feel once the full import of what had happened sunk in. She didn't even know if the bond mark she wore on her arm would matter to her anymore, because right now, she couldn't seem to feel much of anything but an ache that echoed all the way down to her soul.

After a lifetime spent pushing against boundaries that often refused to give, she was finally, completely, free to do what she liked. But with her entire life, all her dreams, crumbled around her, Lyra no longer knew what she wanted.

Tipton was quiet when they arrived at the Bonner Mansion, which was now the seat of the Lilim. The town had seemed sleepy at the best of times, from what Lyra remembered of her trip there, but on a Tuesday night around midnight, there was only the occasional car on otherwise empty streets. Jaden pulled around into the little parking lot beside the house, which Lyra had learned had functioned as the county historical society for quite a few years prior.

Jaden turned off the engine and sat quietly for a moment, waiting, she supposed, for her to show some sign that she was coming out of the wraithlike state she'd been in since her expulsion from the Thorn last night. Lyra tried to meet his gaze, but she had to look away. He saw too much. Her defenses were low, and she could no longer be sure what would come tumbling out. The worry, stress, and little sleep had taken their toll. She was in the same clothes she'd left Silver Falls in, rumpled and weary. Her eyes felt dry and irritated. Her hair was clean, thanks to the hotel's complimentary toiletries, but it was pulled into a careless bun.

She didn't know what she looked like, though she doubted it was good.

At this point, she didn't care.

"Lily and Ty are good people," Jaden said. "They won't ask too many questions, and they won't be offended if there's something you don't want to answer. But…pretty soon you should start talking to someone, Lyra. Even if it isn't me."

She nodded. Then a sliver of terror managed to penetrate her little cocoon. Would he expect her to stay with him? If she stayed with him, he was going to see her break. She was supposed to be strong, independent. If he offered his shoulder, she might have to take it. Then he might see that she really was just as weak as her kind had judged her to be.

But alone…being alone actually scared her worse.

"You'll stay with me, Lyra. At least at first. I can sleep on the floor if you want, it doesn't matter. But I'm not letting you out of my sight."

She was torn between relief and annoyance at having the decision made for her. She didn't *really* want to be alone right now...but she also didn't want to be told what to do. Confused, exhausted, she focused her ire on Jaden.

"You're not my boss. Don't push me around like one," she grumbled.

Jaden glowered back at her. "I promised I would take care of you, and that's what I'm doing. You do need some care, Lyra, even if you don't think so. Last night was a hell of a night for both of us, so quit being a stubborn ass about it and just...accept it, okay?"

He sighed and shoved a hand through his hair, and Lyra felt the guilt creeping in. He'd been wonderfully accommodating. And she'd been either catatonic or prickly. It wouldn't kill her to be gracious, she thought. None of this was his fault, unless she counted his being too appealing as a mark against him.

"I'm...sorry. I'll stay with you. Thank you."

She knew she sounded stiff, but she couldn't help it. She thought she might actually sleep, at least, because her body was finally going to give her no other choice.

"Let's just go in," he said. "They're expecting us."

Lyra was glad about that. She just wasn't sure what to expect herself. She slid out of the car and walked beside Jaden to the house, a beautiful old Victorian. Lights glowed cheerfully in the windows, melting away just a little of the ice that seemed to have frozen into a hard ball right at the center of her. With that melting came a wave of yearning for home. That was something she knew she was going to have to learn to deal with. Jaden slowed, and she could feel him looking at her. Her feelings must be written all over her face.

"Lyra—"

"Hmm?" She couldn't look at him. She just wasn't ready to see what might be in his eyes.

He hesitated. Then gave up ... for now.

"Nothing."

The heavy front door swung open as soon as they got halfway up the steps, and a woman Lyra remembered very well came rushing out to throw her arms around Jaden. Lyra watched him accept the embrace and felt an unexpected twinge of jealousy. She was well aware of who this was, and Jaden had said enough that Lyra knew she was married. But still ... didn't she have her own man to paw at?

Lyra looked the leader of the Lilim over while she waited for her to stop fussing over Jaden. Lily MacGillivray had been a beautiful woman when Lyra had met her months ago. The change in her, though, was remarkable. She'd gone from beautiful to drop-dead gorgeous. And the tall, dark vampire lingering in the doorway with the intense expression ... she remembered him, too, and he was almost—but not quite—as good looking as Jaden.

Lily and Ty were definitely vampires, with all that untouchable perfection. But at least they seemed friendly. Well, Lily did. And after a moment, Lily turned her oceanic blue gaze on her. The sympathy Lyra saw reflected back at her was almost too much for her to deal with. Pain, bright and sharp, sliced neatly through her haze.

"Lyra," Lily said, striding forward to stand before her. She stood probably a head shorter than Lyra, but still managed to convey a sort of regal grace. She wasn't exactly imposing, though. No one who wore her emotions on her face so unabashedly could ever be imposing. In this case, Lyra counted that as a good thing.

"I'm not sure you remember me, but I'm Lily."

"I know who you are," Lyra replied, and then offered what she knew was only a small, weary smile. "Thanks for having me. Congrats on the whole dynasty thing."

"Thank you," Lily replied, her answering smile full of warmth. "And you're more than welcome. Anything you need, I want you to let me know, okay? I know what it's like to have your life turned upside down."

"I bet," Lyra replied, looking up at the impressive façade of the house again.

"Come on in, please," Lily said, laying a hand lightly on Lyra's back and guiding her inside. Lyra allowed it, glad to have someone pilot her body around for a little while since her mind kept trying to check out.

"Let's get you settled in. I'll show you where your room is, and then you're welcome to rest or join us. Whatever you're comfortable with. And don't worry that you won't be treated well. I've got no problem with werewolves, and my people aren't going to either."

"Trust me," the man in the doorway said, "she read everyone the riot act. If anyone had a problem before, they'll be keeping it to themselves now. Lily's got a mouth on her when she feels like using it."

His silver eyes glinted with humor, and an obvious love for his wife. Lyra had to admit, Lily and Ty made a striking couple. As she passed him, he nodded at her.

"I'm Ty MacGillivray. I remember you too. I'm sorry your troubles have followed you so long," he said, his voice touched with a lovely, lilting brogue.

Great, more kindness, Lyra thought. Her eyes watered threateningly. Fueled by her fatigue, no doubt. Still, she managed a smile as she walked into a beautiful, high-ceilinged entranceway with a wide staircase directly ahead. Lily started toward the stairs.

"You'll be staying up here," she began, but Jaden's voice, rough from the trip and his own stress, cut in.

"I already told you, she's staying with me. I'll take her up to my room."

Lily narrowed her eyes and turned around to address him. She kept her voice reasonable, but Lyra could hear the irritation beneath.

"And I thought I told you that Lyra can make her own decisions on that. I'll give her a room. If she wants to stay with you later on, that's up to her. She's a big girl, Jaden."

It was interesting to hear herself argued over, but all Lyra really wanted was to get upstairs and fall into bed. She must have looked it, too, because no one argued with her when she spoke up.

"I appreciate it, Lily, but I'd just as soon room with Jaden. I need to get some sleep. And anyway," she muttered, embarrassed by Jaden's obvious pleasure at her decision, "I'll never hear the end of it if I don't."

That was as close as she was going to come to saying she needed him near her right now, in case she started to fall apart and she couldn't put herself back together. It would be a lot better than simply crumpling up in front of Lily and whoever else lived here.

Lily's expression was kind when she looked between Lyra and Jaden. She nodded. "Okay. I understand completely. Jaden can get you settled. Obviously I'd like to hear about what's going on, and maybe talk about what you want moving forward, but that can happen whenever you're ready."

Lyra nodded, grateful that Jaden had pegged Lily

and Ty correctly—they wouldn't press her. At least not tonight.

"I think," she said quietly, "I'll be turning in, actually. I don't mean to be rude, but I've barely slept. But wake me up if, you know, anyone comes looking for me."

She knew how pathetic it sounded, but she couldn't give up on the faint hope that her father would change his mind, that the pack could be swayed. That she could somehow go home.

"We absolutely will," Lily said. Lyra took some solace in the woman's calm strength, which seemed like a beacon in the miserable storm her life had become.

"I'll show you where you'll be staying," Jaden said, slipping his arm around her waist. Lyra let him, mainly because her legs had gone wobbly and weak, and she wanted to make sure she actually made it up the stairs. She didn't want to lean on him—but it was hard not to when her body refused to have it any other way.

Lily watched the two of them go up, and Ty came to stand beside her as they vanished around the corner and onto the second floor. Jaden's room was on the third level, where he preferred it, so Lyra would be well tucked away from the curious eyes of the rest of the Lilim and Cait Sith if she wished to be.

Ty looked in the direction they had gone, and moved behind his wife to wrap his arms around her. She leaned back into him, comforted by his strength. He rested his chin on the top of her head.

"You've a good heart, Lily."

She gave a short, humorless laugh. "For what it's worth. I don't know if I'm ever going to understand the way your world operates, Ty."

"Our world," Ty said gently. "And the wolves are, in some ways, even more rigid than our kind. Some of that is the vampires' fault. And some of it just *is*. We're changing. Maybe they will too."

"They have a big, unpleasant change coming if Damien was telling the truth." Lily shook her head. "The Ptolemy are like a vampire wrecking crew. They destroy everything they touch."

"They didn't destroy us. Their time is coming, Lily. They'll meddle in one thing too many, and it'll bite Arsinöe right in the ass. You'll see."

"I hope so. She didn't stay down for long the last time. And with a pack of wolves at her disposal, she could make a lot of trouble. It doesn't help that the Council is afraid of her."

Ty rubbed his chin against her hair. "She's very old, very clever, and very powerful. But she's afraid of you, my lovely Lily. So we continue to build, and we wait for the right time to stop her permanently. The rest will stand with us, when it's time."

"I hope so. For now, I just want to be of some help to poor Lyra. She's lost everything," Lily said. She knew how it felt to be alone all too well. But it hadn't been quite as blood-soaked as Lyra's separation from her pack. Her human best friend hadn't deserted her, though Bay was still getting used to hanging around with a bunch of vampires. And she had Ty, one of the greatest gifts of her life, greater, even than the gifts her blood had given her.

"I don't know about that," Ty said. "Jaden seems to want to be something to her, that's certain."

"It's good to see him attached to someone," Lily admitted. She'd seen the way Jaden looked at Lyra. His heart was right in his eyes. "But a vampire and a were-wolf...it seems like that comes built in with a whole lot of issues. And that's even before her specific baggage, which is probably considerable."

Ty chuckled. "I wouldn't have expected him to choose someone without issues. Jaden never does anything the easy way."

"Yeah. I guess you weren't kidding about that," Lily said, though she didn't see much humor in it. She loved Jaden like family. And she knew firsthand that even impossible problems could sometimes be gotten around. But this...she just wasn't sure.

"Jaden will be down before long," Ty said. "There's a lot to talk about."

Lily nodded. "We'll wait in the kitchen. Jaden's most comfortable in there." She gave his hand an affectionate squeeze, and the two of them headed to the back of the house.

chapter TWENTY-TWO

THE DAYS immediately following her expulsion from the Thorn were a blur.

Lyra woke and slept, ate little and moved even less. Her pack, her father, had declared her a ghost wolf, and that's exactly how she felt. She had no interest in anything. She didn't want to die, but she wasn't quite sure how to go about living, and there didn't seem to be any energy in her reserves to figure out a solution.

Jaden watched her like a hawk, the concern etched ever deeper onto his preternaturally beautiful face. At first she found it as frustrating as she did reassuring. It wasn't simply that she could see his worry...she could feel it whenever he was near, flowing from him and into her, upsetting the comfortable cocoon of numbness she had settled herself inside. What did he want from her? Didn't he see she *needed* space even if she wasn't sure she *wanted* it? And yet he was always there, waiting with his steady, reassuring silence. He pushed food at her and made sure she ate enough to keep going, prodded her with suggestions to get up, to bathe, to re-engage.

She hadn't been ready for those things. But that didn't stop him from trying.

She watched sunrises and sunsets, wandered like a wraith through the mansion when the sun shone and stayed curled in the secluded cave of Jaden's room at night. She didn't want to see anyone. They might want to talk about what came next.

And for a woman who had lived her entire life with a single goal in mind, those conversations frightened her most of all.

She'd known, however, that the fugue state she was in couldn't last. And finally, after six days of wallowing in the depths of herself, she surfaced.

She awoke not knowing what time it was, her eyes opening in the darkness that she'd made sure was no indication of what time of day it was outside. Lyra blinked, then gently lifted her hands to rub the sleep from her eyes. Something was different.

She could feel again.

Lyra breathed in deeply, as though she was awakening from a long and unpleasant dream. She felt...grimy. And wrung out. But sadly, that was an improvement. Slowly, she raised herself to a sitting position in the midst of the tangle of covers she'd spent many of the last days burrowed in. As her eyes adjusted to the dark room, she could see the Spartan trappings she'd become accustomed to: the long, low dresser, the simple nightstand and lamp, the battered and ancient chest that squatted at the foot of the massive four-poster bed that had been her nest.

Then she looked down and saw the figure on the floor. He

slept, perfectly still, on a featherbed that had been dragged in here by a couple of nervous-looking vampires. She had some vague memory of gazing blearily at them from beneath the covers while they worked. His slim figure was curled into a loose fetal position, one arm tucked beneath the shaggy head and the other pressed against his chest. In the silence, Lyra could hear the soft and steady sound of his breathing, occasionally punctuated by a light snore.

Jaden.

Feelings she had buried rushed back to the surface all at once with a painful swiftness, but for once, she welcomed them. Images flickered through her memory, of being watched, cared for, looked after. Loved.

He loved her. Even when she had done nothing to encourage it, or to reward him, he'd stayed by her side. And what she felt in return, flooding her until it felt as though she might burst with it, was both painful and beautiful. In all this darkness, she would never have expected that he would have been her light. Yet here they were.

She steeled herself and sat up, slowly swinging her legs over the side of the bed. Her body felt odd, rusty from disuse. She lowered her feet to the plush Oriental rug that covered the floor and then stood, swaying unsteadily in the darkness. Nothing stirred. Lyra decided that no matter what hour of day it was, she had enough time to at least get a head start on her plans.

She had mourned enough. And Lyra found a piece of her that thrilled, just a little, with the knowledge that in this new life of hers, she could count on someone to stand beside her.

Whatever there was to face beyond the smoking ruins of her old life, she would not be facing it alone.

She finally knew what she wanted. And since she did

everything the hard way, she'd had to go through hell to figure out that the right thing had been staring her in the face—or brooding in her basement—for weeks. He was the only one who'd ever accepted her just the way she was, who'd supported her dreams without questioning her ability to achieve them. And in return, she'd pushed at him and run from him and pretended that she would have been able to let him go. He'd been endlessly patient. She'd been a fool. But Lyra was going to have all the time in the world to make it up to him. So she would give Jaden the only gift she had, the only one she could give.

To get moving, and begin again. With him.

Jaden awakened to an empty room and the faint sound of laughter. There was something familiar and wonderful about it, and he let himself drift for a moment, listening as he stretched languidly, allowing himself the time to wake up fully.

Then he realized why he recognized the sound.

Lyra.

He was on his feet in an instant, slamming out of the room and rushing into the hallway. It was empty, but the sound of voices was clearer. Lyra was downstairs, engaged in what sounded like animated conversation with Lily. The relief surged through him, threatening to take him to his knees. He'd begun to think the Lyra he'd known was gone, replaced by a shell that would never do more than drift from place to place.

He should have known she'd be stronger than that. But what she'd been through wasn't something most would ever have to experience, and something even the strongest people would have a hard time dealing with. He had managed to keep his family, after a fashion, once he'd been turned. Losing them had been hard, one of the hardest things in his long life, but he'd known they cared up until the end.

Lyra would get to live with the knowledge of her rejection. But he swore he would be there to help her deal with it, whether she wanted him or not. Her mark meant something to him, even if it was never more than an unfortunate reminder to her. The strange irony was that she wore the mark, but he was the one who felt the bond most deeply.

Jaden rushed down the stairs, taking them two at a time, before leaping the last few and heading into the parlor, which Lily had recently redone to her taste and often spent time in. The sight that greeted him as he hit the doorway stopped him in his tracks.

Lily and Lyra both turned to look at him, but all he could see was his woman. Lyra reclined comfortably on a leather couch, her legs loosely crossed. She wore the jeans she'd arrived in, long since cleaned, and a light-colored button-down shirt he didn't recognize. Her feet were bare; her hair fell in loose coils over her shoulders. Though she still looked a bit too thin, a bit too pale, like she had just recovered from a long illness, the blush of health had returned to her cheeks. The look in her eyes, luminous in the candlelight that Lily often preferred here, was pure pleasure. Her smile, however, was unsure.

"You slept in," she said.

He shoved his hair back from his face, flustered by his overwhelming desire to rush in, gather her in his arms, and cover her in kisses. Somehow, he doubted she was ready for that.

"I—yeah, I guess I did. Now I wish I hadn't," he said,

and finally managed to walk in. He looked to Lily, who looked like a cat who'd caught the canary.

"Lyra and I were just discussing some of her options. She thinks she might like to stay on, if I can find her something to do."

He looked at Lyra, who nodded. "As long as you'll have me."

Jaden wasn't sure whether she meant the Lilim, or him personally. But from the way she shifted nervously and nibbled her lip, he thought—he hoped—it was both. Lily stood, an empty mug in her hand, and Jaden saw she was still in a rumpled pair of oversized pajamas.

"I think you two probably want to talk," she said. "I'm going to go get some more coffee." Then she grinned at Lyra. "I'm actually kind of glad that vampirism didn't kill my coffee addiction. We'll talk more later, okay? But I'm glad you're back. And trust me, I'll be glad to have you here. We all will."

"Thank you. For everything," Lyra said, and Jaden could hear the emotion in her voice as Lily glided past him, sliding him a knowing look on her way by. He didn't miss the fact that she shut the door behind her.

Lyra stood the moment the door was closed, and Jaden took a cautious step toward her. One. Two. But she showed no sign of bolting.

"I have a couple of things I want to say," she said. "So hear me out, okay?"

He nodded. "All right. But after that, you're going to let me say my piece too."

"That's fair," she said, though she looked like she might be dreading that part. He wasn't sure why, but he hoped she would be pleasantly surprised.

"First, I have to thank you," she said. "You've been taking care of me when I couldn't take care of myself. Nobody's ever done that for me. Not that I can remember, anyway. I was always supposed to be self-sufficient, and strong, and—"

"You're all of that," Jaden said. "What happened to you—"

"Nope, not finished," she said, holding up her hand. "I didn't know how to lean on someone. You didn't give me a choice, and I'm so glad you didn't, because alone, I don't know what I would have done. I don't know how I would be right now. Or *if* I would be right now. You gave me something to wake up for, and you kept pushing at me to do it. That means more than I can say."

"You're welcome," Jaden said, taking a step closer. Her words were a balm to him, healing wounds he hadn't even realized were there.

"Second, the fact that I'm bonded to you."

"It's not your fault," Jaden rushed out. He'd done a lot of thinking, and he had no interest in pushing her about it. That didn't mean he wouldn't keep trying to win her over, but as far as he was concerned, the bonding thing would not be an issue until she wanted it to be.

Lyra glowered at him. "You're seriously ruining my planned speech, Jaden. Give it a rest for a minute, will you?"

So happy to hear the snap in her voice, he fell silent.

She took a deep breath, and then plunged ahead. "I want to honor it. And...I know how to seal it. If you want that."

He stopped, taken completely by surprise. "You... how..."

She dropped her eyes. "The day after everything happened between us, I went digging in the histories the pack keeps. There was something there." She paused, then recited:

> *When werewolf's bite the vampire takes*
> *The wolf will bear the mark that mates*
> *And vampire's kiss will seal their fate*
> *To bind, stop time,*
> *Both day and night are thine*
> *Eternally entwined.*

She raised her eyes again to meet his, and he was arrested by all he saw there.

"I want to be with you," she said. "If what I read is right, it's possible. I won't age, I guess, and you... I'm not sure what will happen to you, except that you'll be saddled with me." She gave a short laugh. "The one example of this I know about didn't really last long enough for them to record all of the pros and cons. So we're an experiment. I don't know what I've got to give... but whatever there is, it's yours. If you want it."

He could barely speak, could barely breathe. She stood, waiting, but he was afraid that if he reached for what he wanted so desperately, she would vanish. Just like everything else he'd ever truly wanted. But when he took another step toward her, closing the distance between them, she remained very real.

"Are you sure?" he asked hoarsely. "It's fast, Lyra. I don't want this to be because you feel obligated, or afraid. I want you to be sure. I've got time."

She reached out and took his hands, the warmth of her

being flowing through her hands and making him feel sun
kissed. He looked for any sign of indecision on her face,
but there was none. Only acceptance. And if not love, a
promise that there could be, in time.

"I realized a little while ago that even if things had
come off just the way I thought I wanted, I wouldn't have
been happy. The thought of you walking away doesn't
work for me, Jaden. I would have gone after you, or tried
to keep you around, have it both ways. This was always
going to happen. Because I need you more than I need
anything else. I would have liked to figure it out in a less
earth-shattering way, but… well, that probably wasn't
going to happen, either. I can be kind of hard-headed
about some things. You may have noticed."

It was hard to think, much less speak, when he was
finally hearing the words he'd never thought to hear.
Not from anyone, but especially not from Lyra. But he
couldn't quite let himself believe that for the first time, he
was getting exactly what, and whom, he wanted. Needed.

Loved.

His voice sounded hoarse and strange to his own
ears. "But if your father comes for you? What if the pack
changes their mind?"

"They won't," Lyra said, her eyes hardening. "But
even if they did, it wouldn't change how I feel about this.
I put my life on hold for too long thinking I could change
the way things were. And they cast me out for something
that's really no one's business but mine. I'm ready to live
my own life, wherever that takes me. Us."

"And… how do you feel about… us?" he asked softly.
There were three words he longed for. He had given
them to her. And he hoped, in time, she would return

them. When she spoke, they weren't the three words he'd wanted, but they were ones he would certainly accept in their stead for now.

If she was serious, they would have plenty of time.

"I want you," Lyra said. "I choose you. I'm already yours. I want you to be mine."

"Then come with me," Jaden said, and he laughed from nerves and excitement. "Come with me before you change your mind."

"I'm not going to," Lyra said, and her smile was beautiful. It was everything.

As Jaden led her from the room, he felt himself flooded with a strange emotion, one that was vaguely familiar though it took him a moment to recognize it.

He wasn't sure, but he thought it might be happiness.

chapter TWENTY-THREE

LYRA BARELY REGISTERED the walk from the parlor up to Jaden's room. She felt like she was floating, anchored only by the rapid fluttering of her heart. But she no longer had any doubts. Being with Jaden felt right. She wanted to join with him, fully. And when it was done, she planned to tell him what was in her heart.

That would be the right time, she knew. And since she'd never said the words to any man, and never planned to say them to another, she wanted the timing to be perfect. It was amazing, how quickly doubt had fallen away once she'd seen his face.

She loved him.

Even with all the uncertainty before her, knowing that, accepting that, was all that seemed to matter right now. His love was the one thing she had been able to depend on through everything. And in return, she would give him whatever she had to give.

Right now, that amounted to her body, and her heart.

When he opened the door to the bedroom, Lyra eyed the mass of blankets and sheets in the middle of the bed with a wrinkled nose.

"We should probably burn those," she said.

His laugh was music.

"Later. The featherbed is comfortable, I swear."

Jaden closed the door, plunging the room back into darkness, though her wolf's eyes adjusted quickly. Even in the absence of light, Jaden was beautiful, she thought. And the way he was looking at her made her feel more precious than gold. It was an unfamiliar feeling, but one she savored.

Jaden's eyes sparked that amazing blue and began to glow softly as he approached her. His expression held so much longing that it took Lyra's breath away. Why had she been denying herself this, she wondered? All this time, he had been hers for the taking, and she'd wasted it. No longer.

"I wish I hadn't fought it," she whispered, at a loss for the words that would properly express her regret.

"Don't," Jaden said. "It wouldn't have meant anything to you if you hadn't. And I wouldn't love you if you didn't fight." He lifted his hand to stroke her hair, her cheek, his eyes drinking her in with a thirst unlike any she had known. His words washed through her like moonlight.

"Be with me," she said, her voice a plea, a sigh. "Please."

"Your wish," he murmured, his breath feathering her face, "my command."

His mouth claimed hers in a series of teasing kisses designed to heighten her already fathomless desire. Jaden's hands dropped to her shirt as he continued his sweet torment, lifting the fabric gently to expose bare, creamy skin. She shivered in the cool air as she helped him, then tugged at his own top. It was gone in seconds, his motions quickening as need sparked and caught fire.

"You're cold," he murmured, pulling her to him. His own skin was far cooler than her own, and yet it had the opposite effect, sending heat coiling through her. His hands slid up her back, unfastening the clip of her bra to send that sliding to the floor. She closed her eyes and exhaled, half sigh, half moan as her bare breasts pressed against his skin. The nipples quickly pebbled into tight, sensitized buds, and every movement he made as he shifted against her was exquisite torment. Jaden's hands slipped down to cup her ass and pull her into him.

He was already rigid through the fabric of his jeans. Instinctively, Lyra arched into him, trying to get closer to his heat. She heard his shuddering breath, and he skimmed his lips down her cheek, her jawline, awakening thousands of tiny nerve endings that danced and quavered.

"Beautiful Lyra," he murmured. "I can never get enough of you."

"Don't try," she replied softly. "I'm here. I'm yours. Take as much as you want... there will always be more."

His laugh was like dark velvet. "You don't know how badly I've been wanting to hear you say that. Mine," he sighed. And then again, with dark possession that made her tremble with need, "Mine."

It was a word she'd once feared but now knew could be the sweetest heaven when the one possessing was also willfully possessed. She belonged with him. And she was so tired of fighting it when he was all she wanted.

They came together more eagerly now, mouths and tongues tangling in an ancient dance as they fumbled with their clothes. Lyra's hands roamed over his silken skin, unable to get enough of him, wanting to touch him everywhere. As incredible as the first time had been, she knew this would be more.

She pulled away only for a moment to drop onto the bed, landing amid the pillow-soft bedding to watch Jaden immediately come after her, on all fours, his ebony hair falling into his face and looking for all the world like a fallen angel. When she reached for him, he pushed her back gently with a small, wicked smile.

"Mine," he repeated. Then his mouth was on her, and she forgot to breathe as he began to claim her in earnest. He trailed a hot path down her body, beginning at the neck, where he kissed and nibbled down the long curve. She could feel the tiny points of his fangs graze her skin, a decadent reminder of what he was—and what he could do to her.

What he *would* do to her.

Knowing what lay ahead fueled the fire burning deep within Lyra, as did Jaden's talented mouth as he suckled her breasts, drawing the tight buds between his teeth and lavishing them with attention. Lyra writhed beneath him, wanting more, restlessly urging him on with her body when words failed her.

He delved lower, swirling his tongue in the indent of her navel before sliding lower...lower...

Lyra cried out when he laved the throbbing bud of her sex in one long, hot stroke of his tongue, her hips jerking off the bed as everything inside her tightened with exquisite anticipation. She looked down to see his dark head between her thighs, and the sight alone was enough to push her even closer to the shimmering edge.

She wanted...yes, she wanted...

With only a few rhythmic laps of his tongue, Lyra

came with a sharp cry, her body bowing upward. And still he tormented her, wringing every ounce of pleasure from her until she was shaking. Even then, she knew he was nowhere near finished. Nor did she want him to be.

Her breath came in short gasps as Jaden rose over her, her dark god of night. Their eyes caught, held. And in his, she saw the truth of his feelings for her. They were as real as the heart that beat against her chest, and her own heart sang in response. She had only a single word, ragged and broken as she lifted up against him.

"Yes."

He was inside her in one long, hard stroke, filling her completely, stretching her so that each shift as he settled sent sensation shimmering over her skin. His beautiful face contorted as he moaned, the sound welling up from the depths of him and reverberating through her, making her hot, making her impossibly, deliciously wet. Lyra's hands went to the sharp juts of his hips, wanting to feel the flex and release of every thrust. He began to move, slowly at first, then faster as the passion took them.

In the darkness, Lyra clung to him as she felt the magic coil outward from the very center of her, intensifying sensation, binding them together as a single being. She heard his shuddering breaths as he began to feel it, rippling over skin, urging him to pump deeper, harder. The bed rocked beneath them, and the soft, guttural sounds Jaden made at the apex of each thrust were driving Lyra slowly wild. She gave over to the instincts, to her wolf, letting her claws lengthen, her teeth sharpen. She wanted only this vampire, both man and cat, and she told him so with her words, her mouth, her body.

She could feel him tensing, the air itself taking on

an electric charge that would soon demand release. And everything inside her was winding tighter and tighter, until something had to let go.

They came together, Lyra slamming into him on a blinding flash of light as he went rigid, emptying himself into her with a shout. They clung to one another as the climax crashed through them, fusing them as one. Words echoed in her head, a chant.

Eternally entwined... eternally entwined...

"Your bite," she whispered in his ear. "Now..."

She heard him gasp a word of praise to the gods above, and it made her smile even through the incredible sensations flooding her. He sank his teeth in, and she felt the night burst around her as though she were at the center of a supernova.

For the first time Lyra truly let go, swept into the sweet darkness of the man she loved, feeling herself changing as invisible bonds wrapped them together, gossamer threads as strong as iron, as unbreakable as forever. He drank, shuddering with pleasure, and then lifted his head to kiss her lips, letting her taste what she had given him.

The words rose in her mind, and she opened her mouth, glad to finally give him this gift, the only one she had to give.

"Jaden," she murmured. "I—"

But she stopped and stilled as a terrible pounding began at the front door, and she heard her name being called in an anguished voice she was stunned to recognize.

"Simon?"

Jaden stilled above her, then sighed.

"That doesn't sound good," he said. "We'd better go see."

chapter **TWENTY-FOUR**

SHE THREW ON CLOTHES in the darkness, then headed for the door.

"What do you think *he's* doing here?" Jaden asked. He sounded angrier than she normally heard him, but she didn't blame him. The thought of seeing Simon, or any of her pack again, gave her a sick feeling in the pit of her stomach. Not even her oldest friend had stepped up to defend her. It wouldn't have made any difference, but the support would have given her some small comfort.

Instead, she had left the pack without a soul to speak for her but the man beside her. And she wasn't going to forget it. Jaden, however, seemed worried as they stepped out into the light of the hallway and hurried toward the stairs.

"Whatever he says, don't let him guilt-trip you into anything," Jaden growled. Lyra looked over at him, surprised, as someone opened the door downstairs. She heard gasps and worried voices, and the sick feeling intensified.

Something had happened, she knew it. And if it had to do with the Ptolemy...

"Why would I do that?" she asked.

"Because you care," Jaden replied. "That's fine, but remember how quickly they cast you aside. Whatever has happened, you're not going to go rushing off to save the day with Simon. We're a team now."

She glowered at him, but as they came around the curve of the staircase and she saw what was waiting for her at the bottom, her irritation was quickly forgotten. Dull horror replaced it as she took in the sight of the man, or rather the shell of the man, Simon had dragged in. Every last bit of glow from what she had shared with Jaden vanished.

"Oh no," she breathed. "Dad."

She flew down the last few steps, then stopped short as she watched a group of unfamiliar vampires, all dark and somehow feline, take Dorien's unconscious form and lower it to the floor. Lily was there, dressed now, and cast a single worried look at Lyra while issuing orders like a seasoned general.

"We need to change the bandages and see about cleaning out those wounds. Put him in the gold room on the second floor," she instructed the group of vampires. Newly minted Lilim, Lyra guessed, from the deference they showed Lily. There were nods, and they gathered to prepare to lift him back up. Lily instructed Ty, who was coming toward them from the back of the house, to call Vlad Dracul for his doctor. Lyra had heard the name in passing once or twice, but she wasn't sure why more vampires would be required.

"He has an excellent doctor among his people," Lily explained when she saw Lyra's puzzled look. "I'll get a local doctor if I have to, but considering how fast we all heal, it can get sticky with the explanations. And the Dracul can get here quickly if they need to."

"They need to, then," Lyra said as she rushed to her father.

What she saw shocked her.

Dorien Black was less a man than a crisscrossing roadmap of wounded flesh. He had been bandaged in some places, but it seemed there had just been too much area to cover. Some of the bandages looked fresh, others were crusted with blood from areas that were still oozing. His face was white, covered with long, curved scabs. There was a faintly bluish tint to his lips, and the soft breaths Lyra could hear were distressingly shallow.

She had never seen him look so vulnerable.

"Dad," she whimpered, her hands fluttering helplessly over wounded flesh. But he wasn't there...she could feel it. Dorien was either deep inside himself, or nowhere at all.

"Let us take care of him," Lily said. "We can at least get him cleaned up and looked over while we wait, and then I'm sure you'll want to sit with him. Whatever was done to him it's more than what we can see. He shouldn't be unconscious." She pushed her hair behind her shoulders and motioned for the gathered Lilim to lift Dorien to take him up the stairs. It took a lot of effort for Lyra to step back, but somehow she managed. She heard Lily's muttered curse.

"What a mess. Jesus."

Lyra felt Jaden's hands on her shoulders, shelter from another storm if she needed it. She nearly turned into him for comfort, except for the sight of the haggard man who was nearly unrecognizable from just a week before.

"Simon," she breathed, and rushed to him, finding herself quickly enveloped in the warm and comforting embrace of her friend. He squeezed her tightly, nearly taking her breath away with the force of his hug. Then she understood exactly how bad it was. Simon was right on the edge of breaking down.

She pulled back when he released her. He was unmarked, but for a long red scar that curved from the top of his right ear down his cheek. His eyes were haunted, and he was just as pale as she was. Dark circles beneath his eyes made him look like he'd been punched.

"What happened?" she asked.

"That's what I'd like to know," Jaden said, his voice like ice.

Lyra turned to see Jaden watching the two of them with poorly disguised jealousy. She stepped away but could see the damage was already done.

If relations between he and Simon were going to improve, it wouldn't be anytime soon. She wondered how much convincing he needed to believe she wouldn't leave him. Then, right on the heels of that, she realized that she now had as long as it took.

Despite everything, that knowledge gave her strength.

"You were lucky you got out when you did," Simon said, then closed his eyes and shook his head. He looked so defeated as he stood there, so unlike the man she'd known for most of her life, that it scared her more than most things could. He had been there. If he thought there was no hope...

"Was it the Ptolemy?" Jaden asked. "Have they moved in this quickly?"

"Ptolemy?" Simon asked, looking puzzled. "No, those

haven't been seen since that group attacked you. No, this is all Eric."

"What's all Eric?" Lyra asked, her stomach doing a slow, sick roll. All those years suspecting her cousin would do something terrible. And now to have that come true . . . she should have done something, stopped him long ago somehow. But it was too late.

Simon laughed, a hollow, mirthless sound. "Eric Black is Alpha now. He challenged Dorien right after you two left, saying he should step down since his daughter's actions had ruined his credibility. Dorien had to accept. There was nothing anyone could do."

"But . . . I thought Dad left," Lyra murmured. She could never forget the sight of her father's back walking away from her for good.

"He didn't get far. And, as you can see . . . it didn't go well."

"How?" Lyra asked. "How could Dad not have beaten Eric? No one could beat my father! There wasn't another Alpha in the country who could take him on. This makes no sense, Simon."

"Poison," Jaden said quietly, and all eyes turned to him. He looked up, met Simon's weary gaze. "That was where the Ptolemy came into all this. They provided some of that damned poison. Dorien would be a lot easier to beat if his wounds didn't heal."

"That's right," Simon said. "It was some kind of poison, though I didn't know where it had come from. Are you sure?"

"I'm sure," Jaden said flatly, and Lyra thought of the long, thick scars on his back. He, of anyone, would know.

"Eric got you, too, I see." Lyra sighed. "Simon, I'm so sorry."

He shrugged. "I tried to help Dorien when I saw what was happening. It was the least I could do. I think it may have helped Eric decide not to kill your father outright, though. The crowd was not exactly... with him. Though he has enough supporters to stay in place, for now. I've been taking care of Dorien all week, but the wounds aren't healing, and he got sicker and sicker. When I was asked to find you, I had to bring him with me. He kept asking for you."

Lyra felt the unwanted sting of tears and tried to blink them back. She was just starting to get her feet back under her, and she felt as though the world were tilting on its axis and trying its best to knock her off.

"I'm glad you brought him to me," Lyra said.

"We'll do all we can for him," Lily added. "And you, if you'd like to stay. But as far as the affairs of your pack, if you're looking for someone to overthrow this Eric, I'm afraid that's not something I want the Lilim involved with. We're just finding our footing as a dynasty, the Vampiric Council is watching us like hawks, and I'm coming to find out that your kind likely wouldn't appreciate the meddling."

"No, no," Simon said, eyes widening. "I wouldn't want you to think that. And I wouldn't ask. It's not your job to fix what's happened. But like I said, I was asked to come find Lyra." He looked Lyra in the eyes, and she knew what was coming before he even said it.

Please no, she thought. *Not now, after all this.*

"The pack is restless, Lyra. Eric knows that they'll never see him as legitimate the way things went down, and he's a man who values his control. There was a big outcry over Dorien... and over you. So Eric sent me here.

To ask you to come back and compete against him in the Proving, and settle this the right way."

"Bullshit!" Jaden snarled, surprising Lyra with the heat in his voice. "You were there, you saw what they did. The whole damned pack turned their backs on her. And now they want her back because they don't like the alternative? They don't deserve her. They do deserve what they get."

"Jaden," Lyra said gently, putting her hand on his arm. "I broke pack law. A big one, and a very old one. I'm not sorry I did, but did you really expect that they would all just turn around and go against the law, not to mention their Alpha? It's the way the wolf pack operates. Strong leader, loyal followers. And with the Thorn, strict rules."

"Don't tell me it didn't hurt you," Jaden said. "Don't make excuses for them either. I can understand the bloody cultural differences, Lyra, but you were banished and not a one spoke up. They have no right to ask you to come back and put your neck on the line for them!"

"Maybe not, but she's our only chance. And if Eric did get that poison from the Ptolemy, then there's more trouble waiting in the wings. You want to condemn an entire pack because of hurt feelings, Jaden?"

Simon's cool, disaffected tone surprised Lyra as much as the depth of Jaden's fury.

He rounded on Simon, fangs bared in his anger.

"It's easy for you to stand here and ask her to do this. You didn't see what it did to her. You didn't sit here and worry she was going to stay a zombie and never snap out of it. I blame every damn one of your pack, and Dorien most of all. This is his only daughter. He should have known to value her more than he did. Would he have come looking for her if everything had stayed the same?"

"That's between him and Lyra," Simon said. "I'm sure he'd be happy to talk about it, if he ever wakes up."

"Don't you dare make light of this," Jaden growled, stepping closer to Simon. "This is Lyra's life."

"It is. And last I checked, you didn't run it." Simon was starting to bristle, and Lyra worried that in seconds she could have a full-blown fight on her hands. Both men had been pushed too far recently. And they both wanted very different things from her, which she had no idea how to reconcile.

Lyra sighed, the weariness and depression she'd just emerged from threatening to return and settle back around her like an old coat.

"Don't. Don't fight on my account," Lyra said. "This is something I've got to think through. Which means neither one of you is going to be satisfied right now." She looked at Jaden, who turned his attention back to her with a warning glint in his eye. It was amazing how quickly his calm strength had deserted him in the face of her old life. She knew he felt threatened. But right this second, she had more pressing concerns than assuaging his fears.

"I want to see my father," she said.

He nodded, though his eyes were troubled. "I'll come with you," he said.

Lyra shook her head gently. "I need to see him alone."

She saw the hurt and hated that she'd caused it. But there were things she needed to say to her father in private, in case he never awakened. Things she only wanted him to hear.

"Simon, let me show you to a room for the night. You look exhausted," Lily was saying as she led Simon away. He sounded grateful when he accepted, though he cast a long, searching look over his shoulder toward Lyra.

"I'll be up if you want to talk," he said.

"As will I," Jaden said. And despite the anger she could feel radiating off him, he leaned in and placed a soft, gentle kiss on her lips before turning and walking away, leaving in the direction Ty had gone. It had been meant as reassurance...and as a show of possession to the assembled.

Only Jaden, she thought ruefully, could make her feel flattered and pissed off at the same time.

Then she was alone, left to ascend the stairs in silence toward what she knew could be another good-bye. She didn't know exactly what she was going to do...she'd been honest about that. But what she knew in her heart, and what she dreaded telling Jaden, was that no matter what, the pack was her family, they were in trouble...

...and if they needed her, she would answer their call.

chapter TWENTY-FIVE

Y OU'VE GOT TO RELAX, Jaden. She's not going anywhere tonight."

Jaden turned to glare at Ty, stopping in his tracks
from where he'd been pacing in Lily's parlor. He'd been
incredibly happy in this room not two hours ago. Now, he
thought his head might burst into flames.

"She's going to help him. Them. Miserable creatures,
too timid to speak their minds and far too invested in
playing follow the leader. How can she help them?"

Ty leaned back on the couch, his silver eyes intent
and unblinking. "You're right, in a way...but so was she
when she said you still don't really understand the way a
pack works. As monarchial as we are, there's a lot more
open dissent among vampires than you'll ever find among
wolves. They work as a unit, live as a unit. And ever since
the humans hunted them nearly into the ground, they're
very invested in protecting what they have. That includes
not allowing their women to mate with men who can't

give them children, and who might just take it upon themselves to either drain the pack of blood or drain a bunch of humans and then blame the wolves."

"It's bullshit," Jaden snapped. He hated it when Ty gave him one of his reasonable lectures. He was never in the mood. And Ty never cared.

"I didn't say it wasn't. Probably it made more sense a few centuries ago, when packs were smaller and a lot more exposed to danger. More vulnerable. So they need some better leaders who are willing to change things."

Jaden glowered. "Like Lyra, you mean."

"Sure. Sounds like many of them recognize it, even if they're not willing to openly advocate for it. That's a flaw in their system, Jaden, but one that can be corrected with time and encouragement."

"And my woman risking her life."

That broke Ty's calm façade a little. "Yes," he said solemnly. "And that. But you can't make the decision for her."

"The hell I can't."

Ty snorted. "I'm going to bet Lyra would have a different opinion on that."

Jaden resumed pacing, his hair hanging in his face. "Tynan, Lyra is not bloody William Wallace of the Wolves, okay? She's not going to go leaping in there with her face painted blue howling about freedom. She's got a decision to make about whether to head back into that hornet's nest and do what she set out to do in the first place. But it's different now. She's got to worry about the Ptolemy, who have their fingers in this for sure. She's got to worry about her psycho cousin, and that little shit Simon, who I don't trust as far as I can throw, and she's got to worry about—"

"You," Ty supplied, taking a sip from a glass of bright red liquid that sat by his hand. He cocked his head at Jaden, giving him the appearance of a quizzical cat. "Tell me something, Jaden. You love this woman."

"Yes," Jaden said, and the truth of it reverberated through the deepest reaches of his soul. "With everything I've got."

"And you trained her, from what you told me, for just this thing, right?"

"I did."

"And were you confident in her ability before you were both tossed out on your ears?"

"Absolutely," Jaden said, not sure where this was going.

"Then why have you got your knickers in a twist so badly? If she decides to go back, with you, I'm assuming, then nothing has changed except maybe you'll have a few more wolves on your list you want to beat the piss out of. If you know she can do it, then just...support her. Take it from a guy who's married to the descendant of a demon queen. Lily's got me beat in the scariness department, and I've made my peace with it."

The truth came tumbling out before Jaden could think better of it.

"But what if she doesn't love me? What if she gets hurt, or bloody *dies*, and just slips away from me? I can't lose her, Ty. Even if she never thinks of me as anything but a soft place to land, an acceptable fallback position, I can't. Because I love her...too much."

Ty's hawkish features softened with understanding, and Jaden felt the knots he was tied up in loosen, just a bit.

"Have you said any of this to her? Hell, never mind, of course you haven't. Has she ever told you she loves you?"

"No," Jaden said, stopping to shove his fingers through his hair. "Not yet. I've thought she might say something once or twice . . . but no. She cares, at least, or she wouldn't have finished the bond."

Ty's eyebrows raised. "Finished it? I didn't know there was more to be done."

"It was only half done before. Just on her end. I had to bite her . . . you know . . . among other things. But she's the one who knew how to do it. And she's the one who asked to seal it." He smiled, feeling like an idiot, ranting one minute, blushing like a schoolboy the next. Thankfully, Ty didn't press him for details.

"It was her idea to bind herself to you for the rest of her life, and you're worried she doesn't love you," Ty said blandly.

"Well, I . . . yeah," Jaden replied, beginning to feel more than a little foolish.

"I'd like you to think about that for a minute, dumbass, and then get back to me on how well it makes sense."

"But what if she—"

"Honestly, Jaden, Lyra chose you. The first time, and the second time. She could have left. She could have told you to piss off. Instead, this woman who you have described to me as a prickly pain in the ass has thrown herself at you and demanded to be taken as your life mate. And you're worried she feels nothing."

Jaden paused. "I've been a fool."

Ty sighed, but his smile was affectionate. "Yeah, but I went through it not that long ago. Just be careful not to hang on too tight, Jaden. You wouldn't have fallen in love with her if she weren't strong. So let her be. She'll need you by her, whatever she decides."

Relief washed through Jaden, a cool and soothing balm to a soul that was ragged-edged with nerves and worry. Ty was right. He knew Ty was right. The truth had been there in Lyra's eye for a while now, not to mention in her voice, in the way she touched him. Still, he wanted to hear her say it. As soon as she felt comfortable doing it. And he planned to spend a lifetime—lifetimes now, thanks to the bite he'd given her—making her so. They had time, if they could get through this mess with the Thorn.

Jaden sighed, stuffing his hands into his pockets. "But what if this is some kind of trap for her? What if the Ptolemy are waiting with Eric? I know her father's in some sort of coma, but this whole thing doesn't feel right. Too abrupt, too odd."

Ty frowned. "You don't believe Simon? Isn't he a friend of Lyra's?"

"Yes. No. I don't know. The little bugger has a thing for her, and she doesn't see it. Or she just ignores it."

"That's a separate issue," Ty said. "Try to remember that. And I can already tell that Lyra isn't the sort of woman who would get this far with you and then change her mind. Wouldn't worry about it."

"Yeah," Jaden said. Something about Simon and his story was niggling at him, though he couldn't put his finger on what. Probably some stupid little thing. He'd go wait for Lyra, and then maybe his head would be clear enough to recall.

"Thanks, brother," Jaden said, meaning it. "I needed that."

"I'm always here for that, or a good kick in the ass, which works just as well sometimes," Ty replied with a smile. "Go on. Her father's in bad shape. She'll be needing you, trust me."

Needing him. Hadn't she said as much?

Jaden left the parlor and headed for the stairs, exponentially calmer and ready—almost ready—for whatever Lyra decided. And then, he would try like hell to support her as best he could . . . as long as she stayed by his side.

Lyra was still at Dorien's side as the sun began to rise.

She rested her head on the covers beside his arm, willing this poison to work its way out of his system. Jaden had poked his head in a while ago, noticeably calmer. She needed o remember to thank Ty for that, since she was sure it had been his influence. Jaden was quiet, but still waters ran deep. He was no exception.

He'd said that Dorien would likely never look the same if he pulled through. Many of the scars would remain. Lyra didn't care . . . Dorien was her father, and despite what had happened, she still felt a terrible and deep love for him when she looked at his pale, almost fragile form laying so still in the bed.

He'd also said that he would be waiting for her in their room, and that he was all right with whatever she decided as long as he could stand by her. Lyra smiled as she began to drift off, thinking that she wouldn't have it any other way. What a gift, to have a man who didn't always feel the need to stand in front of her . . .

"Lyra."

Simon's voice slipped through her haze, and she lifted her head. He stood in the doorway of the room, the oddest expression on his face. It bespoke some incredibly strong emotion that might have been love . . . and was almost hate.

A chill slipped down Lyra's spine, though she admonished herself for it immediately. This was Simon, her best friend!

"Did you come in to take a shift?" she asked, standing to place her hands at the small of her back and stretch. "I want to stay, but there's no change at all. He's quiet. And I'm beat."

"You can't stay," Simon said, not moving a muscle and continuing to stare at her. "It's time to go."

"Go? Go where?" Lyra asked, feeling the first tickle of fear at the back of her throat.

He looked wrong somehow, like someone had taken her childhood friend and put someone else in his skin. Someone dark.

"Home, of course," Simon said. "We have a deal, Arsinöe and I. We'd already agreed that if she helped me take Alpha, she'd have the full use of the pack and all its resources. But once she figured out Jaden was in town, she sweetened the pot a little: I give her Jaden, I get you."

"Me," she murmured, trying to get her head around what was coming out of Simon's mouth. "But you don't want me."

"More like you didn't want me," Simon replied, his voice queerly flat. "What was I supposed to do, beg you? You were what I wanted. You, and to get the hell out of that Podunk town. Remember when we were sixteen and we used to talk about going to Europe, checking out the Thorn's ancestral grounds, poking around all of the old lore..."

"We were just kids," Lyra said. "It was a great dream, Simon. We could still do it. But things got in the way..."

"Yeah, with you they always seem to. School, playing werewolf ice princess, and then that *cat vamp*," he spat in disgust. "You're lucky I'm willing to overlook that half-mark you've got."

He must have seen her surprise, because he smirked. "You and your cousin aren't the only ones who can access the histories, you know. I can deal with the mark. I can deal with the fact that you screwed him. But trust me, I'll enjoy giving him to Arsinöe. She's got a lot of plans for him. When they're finished, I'm thinking that mark may fade right away. Jaden certainly won't be around to get in the way anymore."

As she watched him, listened to the unfamiliar cold-ness coming from her childhood friend, Lyra felt some-thing inside start to ache.

"Don't do this, Simon. I loved you. We were friends. Why would you do this to me? To the pack? To my *father*?"

"I told you how I felt. I wanted out. I wanted more than I was ever going to get pigeonholed into a second-rate position in the Thorn. If you haven't noticed, Lyra, there's not much room for upward mobility in our little pack. My bloodlines were only good enough for your father when he was getting desperate. You should have seen the faces when I won the Proving," he said with a smile. "The Dales weren't supposed to be Alpha material. Guess they were wrong. But if it makes you feel any better, this is your fault."

"Mine?"

"If you'd consented to marry me when Dorien tried to force it, I could have been Alpha and avoided all of this. I still would have taken it."

"And then handed us over to the Ptolemy," Lyra said, the ill feeling in her stomach intensifying until she thought she would keel over from it. "Gods, Simon, what are you doing? Do you know what they do to their servants? What they'll do to *you*?"

"Not to me," Simon said. "To the others, maybe, but not me."

Lyra could only stare at him for a moment, astounded that she hadn't seen this side of Simon before. Either it hadn't been there until recently, or he'd just hidden it away until presented with the right opportunity. Hidden it under a mask she'd believed in.

"So everything you told me was a lie," she said, her voice a hoarse whisper. "My father...Eric..."

"Yeah, well, if you thought they were going to postpone the damned Proving just because princess Lyra got booted, you're wrong. It was two nights ago. Didn't you notice the full moon? No, never mind, you were probably too busy pouting and pretending your whole fucking life was over. And your pathetic father, so surprised to see me win. Actually said he was proud of me. Must have been a new feeling for him." His voice turned vicious, ugly. And unrecognizable as the boy she'd once known.

"How?" she asked softly.

Simon shrugged, his eyes feral. "I could have done it myself. Not that the Blacks ever gave my family credit for anything. *She* sees it. My—our—new queen. She was looking for strength, not just my damn pedigree. I've waited my whole life to be first in line, to get what I wanted instead of just the scraps you and your family left behind. And you know what? It was *easy* for me. A couple of Ptolemy in the woods for the Proving to clear the way, a little of Arsinöe's poison for Daddy, and I'm right where I belong." His lip curled. "Where you could have been, if you had the guts to do what it takes to get what you want."

Lyra felt sick. Simon's words had sliced her open as effectively as any knife.

"And Eric? Was he even helping you?"

At that, Simon actually laughed. "Like I needed a Black to take over? To try and push me out of the way? No, Lyra. You're not listening. You never did. *I did this.* Your prick cousin was so upset at the Proving I thought he was going to sit right down and bawl. I would have liked that, actually. I thought about killing him, but Arsinöe likes the look of him, gods know why, so he's being... taught to obey. He likes rules so much, he'll get the hang of it." Simon smiled, and it was a horrible thing. "You bought all the crap I told you about him, didn't you? I whispered in a lot of ears, and he never knew where it came from. Dumbass. Those stories must have just killed that prude every time he heard one. The women, and the kinky death sex. I had a lot of fun with that."

Every revelation was a new punch in the gut, and there was no question Simon was enjoying her reaction. That he was preening over it.

"You know the only twisted thing about Eric is that he's probably still a virgin," Simon snorted. "He had a stick up his ass, but he was never any danger to you."

"You were," Lyra said, taking a step back. Her heart began to pump more quickly, adrenaline rushing through her system. "Were you ever who I thought you were, Simon?" It infuriated her and made her feel so incredibly sad at the same time. Especially because in Simon's sad smile, she saw a ghost of the boy she'd adored.

"Sometimes," he said. "But you only saw who you wanted to see. Nobody ever really saw me. I tried to run with the Shades, but I couldn't be what they wanted either.

I've got so much anger in me, Lyra." His face twisted into something almost unrecognizable. "So much anger. I don't even know where it comes from. But you can make me feel better. You always do. Even when you're being a selfish bitch." He pulled something thin and silver from his pocket, and Lyra recognized it immediately: one of the collars the Ptolemy had used on their cats to keep them animal.

He would use it on her.

"I've got another for Jaden, and a sack to throw him in. Pretty fitting for vamp trash."

"Simon," Lyra said slowly, moving away from the chair toward him. "You know I'm never going to accept this. I'm going to fight you tooth and nail, fang and claw, until one of us kills the other."

"No," Simon said confidently. "You'll submit. Arsinöe's going to help me with that too. As long as I give her Jaden. It's amazing, how bad she wants this cat. The one downstairs, too, but she's waiting on him. Said one at a time is less conspicuous."

Lyra glanced at her father, still and unconscious, and then looked back up at the monster who had fooled her for so many years. Horror and sadness faded, consumed by a black rage unlike anything she'd ever known. It looked as though she would be having her Proving here and now. And with the sun just breaking over the horizon, she would be doing it just as she'd once wanted: on her own.

Except now she found herself wishing, desperately, that Jaden were by her side.

chapter TWENTY-SIX

JADEN DRIFTED, as he always did when the sun rose, in a place somewhere between sleep and waking. As the sun went higher, he would sink deeper, sometimes dreaming, sometimes simply existing in his own darkness before the moon rose again.

His body relaxed as his mind slipped away, peacefully floating.

Then the noises began.

He heard them from far away at first. A shout. The sounds of feet moving, scuffling. A snarl. Lyra's voice crying out.

Lyra's voice.

Jaden struggled upward, fighting the currents his body had become accustomed to for so many years. He clung to his consciousness by a thin thread, using it to pull himself out of the dark. He strained, forcing it long after he should have let go—the sun had to be in the sky by now. Beads of sweat appeared on his brow...he could feel each cool bead form and roll.

And slowly, the voices grew louder.

"I'll never let you take me, you son of a bitch!"

His eyes flew open in the darkness of his room. Jaden tried to get out of bed, but his movements were sluggish, like trying to walk through molasses. Still, he managed to get one foot down, then the other, and push onto his feet. He stood there for a moment, swaying, his body feeling as though it weighed a thousand pounds.

There was a crash, then a masculine shout.

"Stop fighting me, Lyra! There's no one here to hear you!"

Simon.

Anger sparked and began to work its way though his blood like wildfire, warming limbs cold and heavy with sleep. He righted himself and began to move more quickly. Still, he opened the door to his room cautiously. There weren't many windows here, only at the end of the hall, but he would have to be careful not to step into a pool of sunlight.

Sunlight. How the hell was he even up?

Jaden didn't have time to ponder. There was another crash on the floor below. And as he thought of her, Jaden could feel the adrenaline pumping through Lyra's veins, taste the metallic tang of fear on his own tongue. She was scared for her life.

"Don't make me do this, Simon!"

Laughter. "You can't hurt me, Lyra. Your father was right. You didn't have a prayer against the rest of us. And especially not me. I know you too well."

"You don't know shit about me!"

"I know that if you have a choice between getting in this collar or me taking your father's life, you'll take the collar."

Then Jaden was running, his feet barely touching the floor as he leaped down the stairs, barely registering the light streaming in the windows on the east side, the halls illuminated in a way his eyes had not seen in well over two hundred years.

All he could think of was Lyra. And as though she had felt him thinking of her, she cried out his name.

"Jaden! Can you hear me? Help me!"

He burst into the room as Simon was circling her, laughing.

"Like calling a vampire for help after sunrise is going to do anything for you. Nice one."

"It was, actually," Jaden growled, and both heads whipped toward him at once. Jaden saw immediately what was happening. A dagger, long and smeared with crimson, extended from Simon's hand. And Lyra was trying to keep between Simon and her father.

The relief on her beautiful face was all he needed to see. Though the sheer terror on Simon's was a bonus.

"Would you like to take him out, or shall I?" Jaden asked.

Lyra sank to the floor, and he finally noticed the spreading red stain on her shirt. She shook her head. "You're going to have to take it."

Simon's final seconds were consumed with a single sight: a pair of feral cat's eyes lighting with a bloodlust so dark and elemental that he knew there would be no defense against it. He flung up his hands and screamed as the cat leaped.

And Simon Dale knew no more.

It seemed to take days instead of hours, but by late afternoon, Lyra stood in the place she'd never thought she would see again: home. And in the basement where Jaden had spent so many days was Eric Black, tied and beaten, but with a fire in his eyes that told her he'd be all right.

Lyra quickly severed the bonds holding him, seeing the shimmer of silver in the rope. A clever way to hold a wolf, but easily undone with help, she thought, wincing only a little at the sharp pain in her side where Simon's poison-dipped blade had pierced her. The wound had been cleaned and bandaged as best she could, but it burned. Jaden had assured her it would subside before long.

He had slipped back upstairs, into the dark and shut-tered house, once he'd checked the rest of the basement. Lyra could barely think of him without her heart feeling like it might burst out of her chest. When she'd needed him most, he had been there. He'd saved her.

And strangely enough, having been saved didn't piss her off at all. It made her feel safe, secure . . . loved.

The thought of having a man to count on, to have her back in a fight, turned out not to be so hard to swallow after all.

And the fact that he'd asked, very politely, if he could take Simon out didn't hurt. The memory, despite the terror she'd felt at the time, made her smile. Only Jaden would decide to get proper at a time like that.

Gods, she loved him. And she would have told him already, if he hadn't been busy alternating between plotting to take out the entire house of Ptolemy and marveling at the sunshine the entire way here. His wonder at the first touch of light on his skin in centuries had been a precious gift to see.

The poem had been right, though she'd had to remind him. *Night and day are thine.* She'd gotten his life span. He'd gotten her ability to walk in the sun.

They were stuck with each other now, both officially freaks of nature, even for the world of night. And she couldn't have been happier.

"Are you okay?" Lyra asked Eric as she pulled the gag out of his mouth. He looked at her warily as he flexed and moved muscles that had to be stiff and sore from being bound.

"Yeah. I actually preferred the days. This is like storage. At least it's quiet and I'm not in that damned collar. Nights were…" He trailed off, then shook his head. "Did you kill Simon?"

"Yeah. Well, Jaden did."

His eyes darkened. "Good." He stood up, and Lyra watched him, realizing she didn't really know her cousin at all. She'd spent all these years believing the worst of him, things that weren't remotely true of anyone in the pack except, perhaps, Simon himself. The thought of him made her nauseous. The thought of how long he'd deceived her made her feel worse. But she knew that eventually she would mourn, if only for the idealistic dreamer of a child he'd once been.

"I take back what I said about your man," Eric said, looking over his shoulder at her. "I only had a couple nights of the Ptolemy. He had, what, a couple hundred years? No thank you." He paused, then looked away. "I was wrong. Blind. You were never the one who didn't deserve to be here."

It was a big admission. And Lyra felt she owed him one in return.

"And I…apologize. For all the terrible things I said about you," Lyra said. He looked back at her sharply, as though he thought he hadn't heard her right. She nodded.

"I bought a line of bull without knowing you. That's on me. Maybe we'll get along, maybe we won't, but I'll make that up to you, Eric, if I can. If you'll let me. You're my blood. I'd like to get to know you as my cousin instead of just a rival."

The flicker of surprise and cautious pleasure on his face told her she'd done the right thing. He might never be her cup of tea...but then, Mr. Law and Order might not be so bad either. At least now, she would have the opportunity to find out.

"I'd like that," he said. "I think...after all this...I'm going to have to reassess some things. I hope you'll come back to us, Lyra."

Lyra found she didn't have an answer for that. Not yet.

"We'll see. Come on," she said. "Jaden's upstairs looking for Arsinöe."

"He won't find her," Eric replied, following her up the stairs into the kitchen. "The woman has some serious protection around her. She wasn't spending her days in town. None of them were. Simon made a big deal out of the fact that he'd hooked a big dynasty to help give the pack a leg up. I don't think the pack was too nuts about it. Or him. He started to get seriously strange after you...after I, um..."

Lyra raised an eyebrow. That, he was perfectly allowed to feel like an ass about. Forever.

"You know you have my apology. And for what it's worth," Eric said quietly, "it turns out the pack wasn't too pleased about that either. You should know that. They followed the law, but invoking it hasn't exactly made me popular."

Jaden reentered the kitchen, silent and graceful as a ghost. He didn't look happy.

·

"Not here," he growled. "I thought this would be it. I could put a stake in her and end one very big problem for our kind."

Eric stared at Jaden for a moment, as though only just realizing something. "You're out in the day *how*, exactly?"

"Long story," Jaden replied.

"We'll find her," Lyra said. "Though . . . if she's as powerful as you say, killing her might create more problems than it solves. Especially because everyone's going to suspect it was someone attached to your dynasty."

Jaden shook his head. "Doesn't matter. Not right now. All that matters today is that she won't be coming back here. The woman's got a sixth sense about places where her neck's at risk."

Eric looked between them, and Lyra realized how beat he looked. "Gods, Eric, I wasn't thinking. Go home. Though if you'd stop and tell Gerry about Dad, that would help. Jaden and I will be over to tell him everything. Soon."

He looked relieved, and exhausted. "I can do that. And . . . thanks. To both of you. I didn't realize—" He stopped, then smiled. At that moment Lyra recognized a young version of her father, handsome as sin with that smile. Maybe now he would do it more often.

"Just thanks," he finished, and made a point of shaking each of their hands before vanishing through the door, leaving Jaden and Lyra alone in the darkened kitchen.

"I'm sorry she wasn't here," Lyra said. She loved the way he looked, so darkly romantic. She just wished she could remove some of the care from his eyes. But when he turned them on her, glowing a soft blue in the semidarkness, she changed her mind. All of that feeling— relief, care, longing, and most of all, love—was for her.

She couldn't wish to change that precious gift.

"Are you all right?" he asked softly, moving toward her.

Lyra nodded, stepping forward as well and sliding into his arms.

"How about you?" she asked.

"Well, so far I've gotten rid of the biggest psychopath in the pack of the Thorn and seen the sun for the first time in a couple hundred years. Also, I have my arms around the woman I love, so . . . not bad for a day's work."

"I love you, too, you know," Lyra said. Jaden went very still, and the hope in his eyes tugged at her heart. He'd been through so much. Lost so much. Lyra felt humbled that he was still capable of this kind of love, that he would give it to her. Nothing else could be nearly so important. She'd been so worried about shaping her own destiny she'd nearly missed the best parts that fate had sent her.

She just wished it hadn't taken her so long to figure it out. But she would spend the rest of her life appreciating it.

"I'd like to hear that another thousand or so times, if you don't mind," he said. Lyra smiled and lifted her mouth to his for a gentle kiss.

"I love you. I love you. I love you," she said, punctuating each proclamation with a kiss. "There's a start for you."

"A start," Jaden murmured. "That's what we have now, isn't it? The only question, love, is where you want to go from here."

She knew she would need to think that through. That they would need to talk about what each of them wanted and needed. Even if she was allowed to return here, would she want to? Lyra no longer knew. There would be a lot to sort through, a lot of things that needed to be said between her and her father regardless. But none of that mattered right now . . . because she had the most important thing right here in her arms.

"I'll go anywhere," Lyra said, "as long as you're with me. How's that for a start?"

"I like it," Jaden said with a slow smile. "But we'll have to make our home somewhere, eventually."

Lyra pulled him close, her mouth a breath away from his, and told him what was in her heart.

"I already have."

Epilogue

One month later

THE SLEEK GRAY WOLF stood in the middle of the circle, her final combatant stumbling away before flopping on the ground. From her teeth dangled a moonstone pendant on a chain, her family talisman, and the treasure to be sought beneath the full moon of the Proving. Her breath came in short, quick pants, adrenaline rushing through her system as the crowd of familiar faces erupted in wild howls all around her.

It was over. She'd won.

Lyra shifted, dashing on long legs into the embrace of her dark-haired mate, who lifted her up and spun her around, a huge smile on his beautiful vampire's face before letting her father have a turn. Dorien Black's eyes glowed gold in the night, beaming with pride. Things had

changed between them since his brush with death. A little
sadder. A great deal sweeter. And far less concerned with
tradition when it was clear there was a better way.

"I still owe you a boon," Dorien said, reluctantly letting go of his daughter so that she could return to Jaden.
"Name it, boy. I owe you more than I can say."

Lyra looked up at her mate, a smile curving her lips.
She'd told Jaden to expect this. And despite the warmth
with which her pack had accepted him, a thing that still
touched her deeply after all that had happened, she knew
that Jaden's request would make some waves. Good ones,
she hoped. It was long past time for the old divisions to die.

"I've something in mind, actually," Jaden said, his
eyes glittering in the dark. "But this isn't really the place."

"Nonsense," Dorien blustered. "No better time and
place than now. I've learned that the hard way."

"Well," Jaden said, exchanging a glance with Lyra,
"remember why we pretended I was here the first time?
Ties between the Thorn and the Lilim and all that?"

"Mmm. Yes," Dorien said, finally sounding wary. Lyra
laughed softly. This was only the beginning. She wasn't
the only one who was interested in shaking things up in
the world of night, apparently.

"I know someone who's looking for a few good, strong
guards," Jaden said. "So tell me . . . which of your men and
women might be interested in spending some time with a
dynasty of vampire cats?"

Beneath the full moon, the Thorn celebrated the selec-
tion of their new Second and future Alpha. And Lyra
Black, the leaping cats and wolves of her mate's mark bared
proudly, danced in the arms of the vampire she loved.

Acknowledgments

Deepest thanks are due, as always, to the group of people who push me, support me, and make my writing shine. Selina McLemore. Seal of Awesomeness. 'Nuff said. Latoya Smith, for her almost terrifying organizational ability and for e-mails that always make me smile even as I am being assigned more work. That's talent. Kevan Lyon, for being the best. agent. ever. My husband, Brian, for being a rock. Thank you for knowing how I get at the end and never fleeing in terror. My mom and dad, for love and sanity checks. The sisterhood, Cheryl, Marie, Cindy, and Linda, for being my friends (not to mention being as warped as I am). And finally, my readers. What an incredible group you are. You make the journey worth it, every time.

Can a vampire's vow of eternal
protection stop an ancient evil?
Or will it unleash one
unsuspecting young woman's
dark destiny?

———————

Turn the page for an excerpt
from the first book in the
Dark Dynasties series.

Dark Awakening

chapter ONE

Tipton, Massachusetts
Eight months later

TYNAN MACGILLIVRAY crouched in the shadows of the little garden, listening to the mortals rattling loudly around inside the stuffy old mansion. He tried to concentrate on the scents and sounds of the humans, hoping to pick up any subtle change in the air that might indicate a Seer was among these so-called ghost hunters, but so far all he'd gotten was a headache.

This small-town gimmick was a long shot, and he knew it. But he'd been everywhere in the past eight months, from New York City Goth clubs to Los Angeles coven meetings. Anywhere there might be a whisper of ability beyond the norm. In all that time, he had found not the faintest whiff of a Seer or even a hint of anything paranormal at all. Just a bunch of humans playing dress-up, trying to be different.

He wondered how they would feel if they walked into an actual vampire club. Most of them would probably be too foolish to even be frightened for the few seconds their life would last in one of those places. But they might note that there wasn't nearly as much black leather and bondage wear in undead society as they seemed to think.

Ty got to his feet, all four of them, and arched his back, stiff from keeping so still in the bushes all night. His cat form was the gift of his bloodline, though it was of dubious help in places like this. The house he was staking out sat just off the town square, and there were only a few scrubby barberry bushes for cover. His fur was black, yes, and blended into shadow, but dog-sized cats didn't exactly inspire the warm cuddlies in passersby.

Hell. It's no good. Ty gave a frustrated growl as he accepted the fact that this trip was just another bust. He'd been reduced to combing psychic fairs and visiting what were supposedly America's most haunted places, hoping something would draw out the sort of human he so desperately needed to find. But soon, very soon, Ty knew he would have to return to Arsinöe with the news that the Seers had, in all likelihood, simply died out. For the first time in three hundred years of service, he would have to admit failure.

And the Mulo, the gypsy curse that was slowly killing those he was charged with protecting, would continue its dark work until there was no one left who bore the mark of the Ptolemaic dynasty, the oldest and most powerful bloodline in all of vampire society, begun when Arsinöe's life was spared by a goddess's dark kiss. No other house could claim such a beginning, or such a ruler. But if things continued, the other dynasties, eternally jealous of the Ptolemy's power, lineage, and reach, wouldn't even have a carcass to feed upon.

The invisible terror had attacked twice more, both times at sacred initiations of the Ptolemy, both times leaving only one vampire alive enough to relate what had happened. Or in the case of the first atrocity, one nearly-turned human woman. Rosalyn, he remembered with a curl of distaste in the pit of his gut. They had brought her back to the compound, bloody and broken, taking what information they could before finally letting her die a very human death. He doubted she had known how lucky she was.

Ty, used to fading into shadow and listening, knew that all in the inner circle of Arsinöe's court agreed: it was only a matter of time before the violence escalated even further, and the queen herself was targeted.

Without their fierce Egyptian queen, the House of Ptolemy would fall. Maybe not right away, but there were none fit to take Arsinöe's place, unless Sekhmet appeared once more to bestow her grace on one of them. If the goddess even still existed. More likely there would be a bloody power struggle that left but a pale shadow of what had been, and that petty infighting would take care of whoever the Mulo had left behind, if any. And the Cait Sith such as himself, those who had been deemed fit to serve only by virtue of their Fae-tainted blood, would be left to the dubious mercy of the remaining dynasties that ruled the world of night.

He could no more let that happen than he could walk in the sun.

Ty pushed aside his dark thoughts for the moment and debated heading back to his hotel room for the night, maybe swinging by a local bar on the way to get a quick nip from one of the drunk and willing. Suddenly a back door swung open and a woman stepped out into the crisp night air.

At first he stayed to watch because he was merely curious. Then the moonlight caught the deep auburn of her hair, and Ty stared, transfixed, as she turned fully toward him. Utterly unaware of the eyes upon her, she tipped her head back, bathing herself in starlight, the soft smile on her lips revealing a woman who appreciated the pleasure of an autumn night well met.

He heard her sigh, saw the warm exhalation drift lazily upward in a cloud of mist. For him, caught in some strange spell, it all seemed to occur in slow motion, the mist of her breath hanging suspended for long moments above her mouth, as though she'd gifted a shimmering bit of her soul to the night. The long, pale column of her throat was bared above the collar of her coat, the tiny pulse beating at the base of it amplified a thousand times, until he could hear the singular pulse and pound that were her life, until it was everything in his universe. Her scent, a light, exotic vanilla, drifted to him on the chill breeze, and all thought of drinking from some nameless, faceless stranger vanished from his mind.

Ty wanted *her*. And though a certain amount of restriction was woven tightly into the fabric of his life, he would not deny himself this. Already he was consumed by the thought of what her blood might taste like. Would it be as sweet as she smelled? Or would it be darker than she appeared to be, ripe with berry and currant? Every human had a singular taste—this he had learned—and it spoke volumes about them, more than they would ever know.

She lingered only a moment longer, and her heart-shaped face, delicately featured with a pair of large, expressive eyes he was now determined to see close up, imprinted itself on him in a way he had never before experienced. Ty's mind was too hazed to question it now, this odd reaction to her, but he knew he would be able to ponder nothing else later.

Later. Once he had tasted her.

When she turned away, when the burnished waves of her hair spilling over the collar of her dark coat were all he could see, Ty found he could at least move again, and he did so with the ruthless efficiency of a practiced hunter. Like a predator that has latched on to the scent of its prey, his eyes never left her, even as he rose up, his feline form shifting and elongating until he stood on two feet among the straggling bushes.

He breathed deeply, drinking in that singular scent with anticipatory relish.

Then Ty turned up the collar of his coat and began the hunt.

Lily rounded the corner of the house with a sigh of relief.

Probably she should feel guilty about bailing on the annual Bonner Mansion ghost hunt. Bailing before anything interesting happened anyway—so far, all she'd seen was a bunch of overly serious amateur ghost hunters who thought every insect was a wayward spirit. Oh, and that couple who had set up camp in a closet with the door shut, she remembered with a smirk. Whatever sort of experience they were after, she was pretty sure it wasn't supernatural.

Why she'd even let Bay con her into this was a mystery; their weekly date to watch *Ghost Hunters* didn't translate into any desire on her part to *actually* go running around inside a dark, musty, supposedly haunted house. Thank God the hottie from the Bonner County Paranormal Society had shown up when he had. Lily wasn't sure which had made her best friend's eyes light up more: the tight jeans or the thermal-imaging camera. Either way, she wasn't even positive the group had heard her when she'd claimed a brewing headache as an excuse to leave them there, but Bay's grin told her she'd be thanked for going at some point in the near future.

She lifted her wrist to glance at her watch, squinting at it in the darkness, and noted that it was about quarter to twelve.

"So much for another Friday night," she muttered. Still, it didn't have to be a total waste. Maybe she'd get crazy, stay up late with some popcorn and a Gerard Butler movie.

Wild times at Lily Quinn's house. But better, always better, than running the risk of sleep. She didn't need a silly ghost tour to scare her. Nothing could be scarier than the things she saw when she closed her eyes.

Lily crunched through dead leaves, then stopped, frowning at the unfamiliar view of bare trees and, a little farther off, the wrought-iron fence that bordered the property's grounds. Despite the reasonably close proximity to the town square, the Bonner Mansion sat back a ways from the road, and the historical society had managed to hang on to a portion of the original property, so there were still grounds to the place. But there was, as a nod to modernity, a parking lot.

And it was, Lily realized, on the *other* side of the house. She tipped her head back, closed her eyes, and groaned.

Her impeccable sense of misdirection had struck again.

After a moment spent silently cursing, Lily shoved her hands deeper into her pockets and set off on what she hoped was the correct course this time. Directional impairment was one of her defining features, right along with her inexplicable aversion to suitable men. If she could only find a well-educated, Shakespeare-quoting bad boy who still had a thing for sexy tattoos and maybe a mild leather fetish, she might at least have a shot at avoiding her probable future as a crazy old cat lady.

A long shot, maybe. But a shot.

At least it was a beautiful night, Lily thought, inhaling deeply. The smell of an October night was one of her favorites, especially in this part of New England. It was rife with the earthy, rich smell of decaying leaves, of wood smoke from someone's chimney, and shot through with a cleansing bite of cold.

Lily looked around as she walked, taking her time. In the faint glow from the streetlights along the road, this place really did have a haunted look about it, but not scary. More like someplace where you'd find a dark romance, full of shadows and sensual mystery.

She huffed out a breath, amused at herself. She taught English lit because she had always liked the fantasy of what could be, instead of the often unpleasant reality of how things were. Speaking of which, it looked like a little *Phantom of the Opera* might be in order for her Friday night movie. Even if the ending absolutely refused to go the way she wanted, she thought with a faint smile, no matter how many times she'd willed Christine to heal the dark and wounded Phantom instead of wasting her time on boring old Raoul.

It would have made for one hell of a love scene—

There was a sudden, strange tingling sensation at the back of her neck. Lily felt the hairs there rising as a rush of adrenaline chilled her blood. Someone was behind her. She knew it without seeing, felt eyes on her that hadn't been there a moment before.

But when she whirled around, stumbling a little in her haste to confront whoever was behind her, she saw nothing. Only the empty expanse of lawn, dotted with the skeletal shapes of slumbering trees, an empty bench, and beside her, the dark shape of the house. Nothing.

Nowhere even to hide.

Lily felt her heart kick into a quicker rhythm, and her breath became shallower as her eyes darted around, looking for a shape, a shadow, anything that would explain her sudden, overwhelming certainty that she wasn't alone.

Stupid, she told herself. *You're walking through a horror movie setup, and it's just got your imagination running, is all.*

Lily knew that was more than likely it, but she still wanted to reach her car and get out of here. Soothed a little by the thought that there were a whole bunch of people inside the house who would hear her scream if anything did happen, she turned to continue making her way out front, casting a lingering look over one shoulder.

Though the moon rode high in the night sky, nearly full, and the air was still rich with the very scents she'd just been enjoying, all her pleasure had vanished in favor of the insistent instinct that had kept humans walking the Earth for as long as they had: flight.

"Hey, are you all right?"

She gave a small scream before she could stop herself, jumping at the sudden appearance of another person in front of her when there'd been no sign of another soul only seconds before.

He raised his hands in front of him, eyebrows lifting in an expression that plainly said he was as startled as she was. "Whoa, hey, don't do that! I'm not a ghost or anything. You can start breathing again." One eyebrow arched higher, plaintive. "Please?"

It was the faintly amused concern he put into that last word that finally got her to draw in a single, shuddering breath. But she still shot a quick look around, gauging distance in case she had to run.

"Look, I'm sorry," the man said, drawing Lily's full attention back to him. "I needed to get out of there for a few. Too many people, not enough ghosts, you know?"

"I . . . yeah," Lily said, still trying to figure out how she should deal with this. Had he been inside too? She wasn't sure. . . . There'd been a cluster of people, and not everyone had shown up at the same time. It was certainly possible. But when she looked more closely at him, she was sure she would have remembered if they'd crossed paths.

"Let's start over," he said.

This time she picked up on the lilting Scottish accent in a voice that was soft and deep but with a slightly rough edge.

He extended a hand to her. "I'm Tynan. MacGillivray."

Yeah, it didn't get any more Scottish than that. Lily hesitated for a split second, but her deeply ingrained sense of politeness refused to let her keep her hand in her pocket. Tentatively, she slid her hand into his and watched as his long, slim fingers closed around it.

"I'm Lily. Lily Quinn," she said, surprised by the sensation of cool, silken skin against her own. But at the point of contact, warmth quickly bloomed, matching the heat that began to course through her system as she finally noticed that Tynan MacGillivray was incredibly good-looking.

Not handsome, she thought. That was the wrong word for what he was, though some people might have used it anyway. He was more...compelling. She let herself take in the sharp-featured, angular face with a long blade of a nose and dark, slashing brows. His mouth held the only hint of softness, with an invitingly full lower lip that caught her attention far more than it should have, under the circumstances. His skin was so fair as to make him pale, though for some reason it only enhanced his strange appeal, and was set off further by the slightly shaggy, overlong crop of deep brown hair that he'd pushed away from his face.

It was his eyes, though, that Lily couldn't seem to avoid. Light gray, with a silvery cast from the moonlight, they watched her steadily, unblinking. She wanted to believe he meant her no harm. But there was an intensity in the way he looked at her that kept her off balance. *I should get moving, get out of here*, Lily thought, feeling like a deer that has picked up the scent of a predator.

But she was caught by those eyes, unable to look away. She shuddered in a soft breath as he stepped in closer, never letting go of her hand.

No, she thought, her eyes locked with his, her legs refusing to move. But then, right on the heels of that: *Yes*.

"Lily," he said, his voice little more than a sensual growl. "Now, that's a pretty name. Fitting."

No one had ever said her name quite like that before, savoring it, as though they were tasting it. Desire, unexpected, unwanted, but undeniable all the same, unfurled deep in her belly. She tried to think of something to say, something that would break this odd spell she was falling under, but nothing sprang to mind. There was only this dark stranger. Everything else seemed to fade away, unimportant.

"You're shivering," he remarked. "You shouldn't be out here in the cold all alone."

"No, I...I guess not," she murmured, mildly surprised that though she was shivering, she hadn't even noticed. She certainly wasn't cold anymore. And for some reason it was difficult to hang on to her thoughts long enough to form a coherent sentence. "I was...just going to my car."

His eyes, she thought, caught up in a hazy rush of desire that flooded her from head to toe, banishing any awareness of the temperature of the air. His eyes *were* silver, she realized as they grew closer. Silver, and glowing like the moon. Strange, beautiful eyes.

"Why don't you let me walk you?" he asked.

The words barely penetrated her consciousness. After struggling to make sense of them, she found herself nodding. Car. Walk. Yes. Probably a good thing. "Yeah. That would be great."

Tynan smiled, a lazy, sensual lift of his lips. It seemed the most natural thing in the world that, despite what each of them had said, neither of them made a move to go. Instead, he trailed his free hand down her cheek, cool marble against her warm flesh, and rubbed his thumb slowly across her lower lip.

Lily's lips parted in answer, and her eyes slipped shut as a soft sigh escaped her. She'd never felt such pleasure from such a light touch, but all she could think of, all she wanted, was for it to continue.

"Lily," he purred again. "How lovely you are."

"Mmm," was all she could manage in response. She turned into his touch as his skilled fingers slid into her hair, as he let go of her hand to slide his around the curve of her waist as he stepped into her. It was like drifting in some dark dream, and Lily embraced it willingly, sliding her hands up his chest and then around to his back, urging him even closer.

She wasn't sure what she was asking for—but at Tynan's touch, something stirred inside of her, some long-dormant need that arched and stretched after a long sleep, then flooded her with aching demand. She turned her face up to his, a wordless invitation. His warm breath fanned her face, and even through the strange haze that seemed to have enveloped her, she thrilled a little at the ragged sound of his breathing, at the erratic beat of his heart against her chest.

"Lily," he said again, and this time it was almost reverent.

He bent his head to hers, and Lily's lips parted in anticipation. She had never wanted a man's kiss so desperately; her entire being seemed to vibrate with desire. Her breath stilled as she waited for the press of his lips against her own. But instead of taking what she offered, Tynan's mouth only grazed her cheek, and his long fingers deftly cupped her chin to turn her head to the side.

Lily made a noise then, a soft, frustrated moan that drew a chuckle from her tormentor.

"Patience, sweetheart," he admonished her, his gruff brogue more pronounced now. "Too fast and you'll spoil it."

Tynan trailed soft kisses along her jawline, the relative chill of his lips against her warm and sensitive flesh a shocking pleasure. Lily writhed in his arms, wanting to be closer, wanting some nameless *more* that she couldn't identify. But Tynan seemed to be relentlessly controlled, the uneven intake of his breath the only clue that he might be as close to undone as she. Lily heard his voice then, seeming to echo right inside her head.

Let me taste you.

Powerless to do anything but obey, Lily let her head fall back in submission, baring her throat to him, willing him to touch more, take more. In some dim recess of her mind, it occurred to her that this entire situation was madness at best, suicidal at worst. But the harder she tried to hang on to any rational thoughts, the quicker they seemed to evaporate. And wasn't it so much more pleasurable to just give up, give in? As though Tynan wanted to illustrate just that point, he nipped at her ear, flicking his tongue over the sensitive lobe.

"Please," Lily moaned, moving restlessly against him, not even sure what she was asking for. Then he was drawing her hair away from her neck, tugging her head to the side to gain better access. He forced the collar of her shirt down, baring her collarbone to the cold night air. Lily allowed it all, her only desire to feel his lips on her skin again, to give him whatever he wanted. All the world had vanished except for Tynan. She could feel his hands shaking as his handling of her roughened, and she sensed his need was even greater than her own.

Suddenly he stopped, going stock-still as he expelled a single shaking breath. Lost in the deepening fog of her sexual haze, Lily gripped the thick wool of Tynan's coat harder and made a soft sound of distress. Why had he stopped? She needed . . . she *needed* . . .

All she heard was a softly muttered curse in an unfamiliar tongue.

Then, a ripple of air, a breath of chill wind. Lily slowly opened her eyes, only barely beginning to register where she was and what she had been doing. Her hands were fisted in nothing but empty air. She blinked rapidly, taking a stumbling step backward, feeling a crushing, if nonsensical, sense of loss. She turned in a circle, knowing that he had to still be here. He couldn't have left. It was impossible for a man to vanish into thin air.

But whoever—or whatever—Tynan MacGillivray was, Lily was soon forced to acknowledge the truth.

He was gone.

When a dangerous assassin
meets a beautiful female
vampire on the run, the Dark
Dynasties' most closely guarded
secret will be revealed.

———————

Turn the page for a sneak peek
at the third book in the
Dark Dynasties series.

Shadow Rising

chapter **ONE**

A
RIANE."

She stood at the floor-length window, staring out at the rolling ocean of sand that had been her home since before her memories began. Not a breath of wind moved the gossamer curtains that she'd drawn back, though she had opened the window wide in hopes that some air might clear her head.

No such luck. All she'd found was the crescent moon hanging above the same beautiful and barren landscape that she looked upon every night. Nothing changed here. Nothing except her. Not that the implications of what she was about to do didn't make her heart ache. But she had no choice.

Life eternal notwithstanding, this place would kill her, or at least the best part of her, if she stayed much longer.

"Ariane, please look at me."

With a soft sigh, Ariane turned away from the window and looked at the man who had entered the shadowed room. She had lit but a single candle, not wanting the harshness of the light, and it played over his concerned face, over features that were as hard and beautiful as chiseled stone.

Sariel. There was a time she would have been honored by a visit from him, and to her chamber, no less. He had been the leader of her dynasty since it began, or so she understood, and his word among the Grigori was law. Ariane respected him, deeply. But Sariel was content with all the things that made her restless. He could accept that her dearest friend had vanished without a trace, where her every waking moment had become a nightmare of worry and dark imaginings. And she knew already that while he cared, while some effort was being put into finding the missing Grigori, he didn't remotely understand.

"I appreciate your concern, Sariel. But I'm fine. I didn't expect to be chosen," Ariane said, hoping that she was concealing her bitterness well enough.

Sariel approached, shutting the door behind him. To anyone else, even their own kind, Ariane knew he would have been incredibly intimidating. The men of the Grigori dynasty of vampires, particularly the oldest ones, all stood nearly seven feet tall, broad chested and well muscled, with skin like pale marble. But in the dim light, he looked so like Sam that she could feel nothing but the same dull ache she had felt for a month now, ever since they'd all realized he was not simply traveling, but gone.

Sariel's face belonged on a statue dreamed up by a Renaissance master, but his beauty, like all their beauty, was cold. His white hair, the same shade as all Ancient Ones had, was an oddly attractive contrast to a youthful face. It fell to his shoulders with nary a wave to mar the gleam of it. His eyes glowed a deep and striking violet, a shade they all shared, in the dim light.

"I know you had your hopes up, Ariane," he said, his normally sonorous voice soft. "You don't have to pretend you didn't. If it helps, you were strongly considered. But the others felt that ultimately, Oren was the better choice." He paused. "If Sammael can be found, he will be. I realize he is important to you, as he is to us all."

Ariane sighed and turned away, back toward the window and the beckoning night whose call she had always been forced to resist...until tonight. She didn't really expect a vampire like Sariel to understand how much a simple friendship meant to her. He seemed above such things, beyond them, and completely self-contained. What would he know of the longing for a simple connection to another person? The frustration pushed her to finally vent a little of all she had bottled inside.

"Yes, Sam is important to all of us," she said. "But of everyone here, I am closest to him, Sariel. I think you know that. I don't understand why we're sending only one of our own to search for him when he could be hurt out there. He could be *dead*."

It was her greatest fear, and Sariel was as dismissive as she'd expected he would be. He simply didn't give in to his emotions, Ariane told herself. He was strong, unlike her. She was weakened by her attachments and her most private dreams. In those dreams, which she had never shared with a soul, she was happy, fulfilled, even loved—and far away from here.

An opulent palace could still be a prison, a lesson she had learned well.

"Ariane," Sariel said, affecting the air of a parent lecturing a willful child, "your concern is admirable, but if Sammael is still alive, he shouldn't be difficult to find. We are adept at seeking as well as watching, as you know." He paused. "Tell me, little one, is this about my brother? Or is it about your desire to get beyond these walls?"

Anger roiled deep within her at his suggestion. Of course she wanted to get beyond these walls! But her own needs paled in comparison to Sam's... wherever he was. If only he had been the one to take her out into the world so long ago, instead of Illura. He might have held his tongue, might have kept the incident to himself.

She might not be an outcast among her own, condemned to lifetime upon lifetime of existence in the desert, never to be free.

Finally, she managed to speak, her voice steady only through the strongest effort.

"Sariel, I swear that I'm only concerned about Sam. But since you brought it up, you're obviously aware of how stifling my situation is. In all these hundreds of years, I've been out exactly once. *Once*. Do you know how that feels?" She waved her hand before he could answer. "No, of course you don't. You're one of the Ancient Ones. If you want to go out into the world, you go. But I..." She trailed off, wanting to make him understand how she felt about her life. "I can only sit here. Wander the grounds. Try to enjoy the little bits of life that the humans who are brought here carry with them before they're taken back."

"The palace is huge, as are the grounds," Sariel pointed out. "Everything you could want to do is here, or could be brought. We're not beholden to the same rules as the others. It's why this place is hidden, why we are hidden. You know that. The vampires accept us as their own, and it's important that they continue to do so. The less they know about us, the better."

"But we *are* vampires," Ariane snapped, exasperated by the same old conversation. "Aren't we? We don't walk in the day. We drink the blood of humans to survive. We are the *same*!"

"Yes and no," Sariel replied, his expression guarded. "We carry a responsibility the others do not. We are the oldest by far, though that, too, must stay hidden. Especially now, when things have begun to shift. We are watchers, *d'akara*. We do not interfere. Sammael understood this. But you…"

He trailed off, letting Ariane dredge up those awful memories herself. The memories were never far from the surface, but they had been much closer lately, emerging in dreams. It was always this way during times when she felt helpless, powerless. She was never sure whether the dreams were a warning to stay out of the affairs of the world, to be happy with what she had here…or whether they were meant to spur her to leave this place and, in some small way, rectify the wrong she had seen that day so long ago.

Sam's disappearance had forced her to choose. One more thing to be grateful to him for—he had made her choice shockingly easy. She would never just stand by again. And though she knew she had to hide her resolve from Sariel, he would discover it soon enough.

"I was young," Ariane said, trying to keep all anger from her voice, her face. "I can't be the first Grigori to have had…difficulties…with seeing such senseless violence."

Sariel's indulgent smile made her want to scream.

"No, you're not, Ariane. But the degree of the reaction is what had us all so concerned. You do remember."

Of course she remembered. Weeks confined to her chambers, unable to focus, to stop seeing what she had been forced to stand by and watch. Weeping so long and hard that the tears had turned to blood. Sariel seemed to take her silence as acknowledgment.

"I understand the compulsion, you know. We have all felt it, the desire to shape things to our will instead of watching events unfold. But that is not our place. We must detach from instinct, leave our humanity behind. Living as we do and trying to exist any other way is madness."

"But Sam also—"

"His name is Sammael, *d'akara*. Show his name the respect it deserves."

Ariane's mouth snapped shut at the steely command. It was worthless to argue with him, and she should have known better. He demanded respect, but he called her *d'akara*, "little one," as though she were a child. She was fast and strong. She could speak a multitude of languages, debate music and philosophy and art. She could fight more nimbly than most of her blood sisters and brothers. And for what had she learned these things? To sit here and rot while fate was allowed to claim another innocent?

No. Not this time.

"Sammael, then," Ariane allowed, trying not to say it through gritted teeth. "He said it was important to remember how to feel for the mortals. To not just watch, but be able to understand. He's an Ancient One, too...do you disagree?"

Sariel's expression shifted quickly from insincere warmth to genuine displeasure. He was a sight to behold when angry, so Ariane counted herself lucky that he hadn't yet hit that critical point.

"Sammael has an...unnatural affinity for the humans. Always has. I've indulged him, but humanity is like a troop of bellicose monkeys. Understanding them is simple enough. It was a defective design, I've always thought," he said with a small, cold little smile. Ariane never knew what to make of him when he said things like that. It was as though he had never been human, though more likely he had no recollection of what it was like after so long.

Neither did she. But from the little she knew, that had been due to decidedly different circumstances.

"In any case, Ariane, this is not the way to allow you to try again. It's too delicate a situation, and time is of the essence. One day," he continued, stepping closer, his eyes glowing softly in a way that might almost be called warm, "I will make sure you get another chance to keep our watch. You have my word on this, *d'akara*."

She stayed still, though his nearness had begun to make her uncomfortable. The visit itself was highly unusual. Sariel's interest in her well-being was even more so. She couldn't recall him ever paying much attention to her...though Sammael's disappearance, and her connection to him, seemed to have remedied that in spades. She should have enjoyed it. And yet somehow, his interest in her provoked nothing but a faint revulsion.

Another sign she was finally ready to go.

As though he'd sensed the direction of her thoughts, Sariel murmured, "I have no idea why your beauty has escaped my notice for so long. All these centuries, and you and I have never truly spoken."

"No, this is true," Ariane agreed with a small nod. She hoped he didn't reach for her...then what would she do? Running was always an option, but a very poor one when your pursuer was a seven-foot-tall vampire. And no woman in her right mind would reject a man like Sariel. Of course, she wasn't in her right mind at all these days. She couldn't be, to have planned such a course of action.

To her relief, Sariel seemed to realize that his sudden attentions had taken her by surprise. He came no closer, but the keen interest in his gaze was unmistakable.

"I would like to see you, Ariane. To spend some time with you. Tomorrow night, perhaps? We should get to know one another, after all this time."

It was all she could do not to sob with relief.

"Of course," she replied, and even managed a small, demure smile. "I would enjoy that."

Her answer seemed to satisfy Sariel, and he nodded.

"Good. I'll send someone for you then." He turned, strode toward the door, and then stopped just before leaving, looking back at her. "Don't worry about Sammael, *d'akara*. If he lives, he'll be found, and he would not be so easily killed. Trust me...I've known him a great deal longer than you have."

Ariane nodded. "Then I'll just keep hoping for the best," she said.

When the door shut and Sariel was finally gone, she expelled a long, shaking breath, her legs going wobbly. She bent at the waist, placing her hands on her knees and breathing deeply, trying to regain her balance. The visit had rattled her even more than she'd thought. Why had he really come? Was he worried that she might do exactly what she was planning? And if he was, had he seen that he was right?

She didn't think so. But then, there was no real way to know. Even she didn't fully understand the Ancient Ones and their gifts, and she was probably closer to Sam than anyone. Still, the man was good at keeping secrets, especially his own. And whatever Sariel had come looking for, whatever he had seen, nothing had changed. For once, she had a choice, and she chose to act. It was terrifying, yes.

But Ariane had faith it would also be freeing.

When she thought enough time had passed, Ariane moved to the bed and pulled a small beaded satchel from beneath the mattress. The bag held the handful of things of any importance to her. A sorry commentary, she supposed, on a life that had lasted so long and yet meant so little to anyone. She slung the satchel across her body with its long, thin strap, then moved to the window, her diaphanous skirt swirling gracefully about her legs.

She flipped a small latch, and the two panes of glass swung outward, revealing a gateway to the night. Ariane paused for only a moment, steeling herself. She had no desire to look back, to take in the pretty room that had been her safe haven for so long. She feared doing so would lessen her resolve, and she would need all her nerve and more if she really wanted to find her friend. Not to mention evading her own capture. The Grigori did not take kindly to deserters. If she ever returned here, she doubted Sariel would be inviting her to his chambers again.

Not in the short space of time before she vanished forever.

No. That isn't going to happen. I can do this. And if finding Sam doesn't sway them, then I'll stay gone and stay on my own. Make a real life. Somehow.

Reassured, Ariane stepped onto the slim window ledge, glad that she faced the desert and not the courtyard. Her only witness was the moon. She closed her eyes, breathed deeply, and summoned the gift that she had been able to use all too rarely. She felt them rise from her, sliding through her flesh as easily as water flowing into a stream. Her wings.

Ariane extended them, allowing herself only a moment to turn her head and admire the way they shimmered in blues, lavenders, silver...twilight colors. And gods, but it felt good to free this part of herself. She lifted her hands to her sides, like a child balancing herself on a beam, or a dancer ready to begin.

Then she leaped into the darkness, and in a flutter of wings, was gone.

THE DISH

Where authors give you the inside scoop!

From the desk of Sherrill Bodine

Dear Reader,

One of my favorite things about writing is taking real people and mixing and matching their body parts and personalities to create characters who are captivating and entirely unique. And of course, I always set my books in my beloved Chicago, sharing with all of you the behind-the-scenes worlds and places I adore most.

But in ALL I WANT IS YOU, I couldn't resist sharing one of my other passions: vintage jewelry.

Thanks to a dear friend I was able to haunt antique stores and flea markets all over the city, rescuing broken, discarded pieces of fine vintage couture costume jewelry and watching her repair, restore, and redesign them. She gave these pieces new life, transforming them into necklaces, bracelets, and brooches of her own unique creation, and it was an amazing thing to see.

I just knew my heroine, Venus Smith, had to do the very same thing, and thus her jewelry line, A Touch of Venus, was born.

And of course it seemed only fitting that Venus's designs end up in Clayworth's department store, the store I created in my previous book, *A Black Tie Affair*, which is a thinly veiled Marshall Fields, Chicago's late great iconic retailer. Of course, the most delicious part is that Clayworth's is run by Venus's archenemy, Connor Clayworth O'Flynn, the man who betrayed her father and ruined his reputation. And yes, you guessed it—sparks fly between them, igniting into a fiery passion.

But this book isn't just the product of my imagination. Readers have been so kind, telling me the most amazing stories that have transported me to fascinating places, and I want to take all of you with me!

When someone shared with me the legend of the "Angel of Taylor Street," I fell in love with the story and couldn't resist using it myself. The Angel of Taylor Street was a person or persons who for decades did good deeds for strangers without ever asking anything in return. I changed the character to the Saint of Taylor Street in ALL I WANT IS YOU, and now it's an important part of Venus and Connor's story.

But that isn't the only one. Did you know there's a private gambling club hidden beneath the parking lot of an old Chicago restaurant, one that's been in business since our gangster days? I didn't either, until someone tipped me off. Of course it is the site of a fabulous adventure for Venus and Connor. It is just a hint of Chicago's inglorious past, but this time it has a positive spin—I promise!

I hope you'll enjoy Venus and Connor's story in ALL I WANT IS YOU. Please come visit my website at www .sherrillbodine.com. I'd love to hear from you!

Xo, Sherrill

Sherrill Bodine

♥ ♥ ♥ ♥ ♥ ♥ ♥ ♥ ♥ ♥ ♥ ♥ ♥ ♥ ♥ ♥

From the desk of Kendra Leigh Castle

Dear Reader,

"Dogs and cats living together...mass hysteria!"

I heard the voice of Peter Venkman in my head a lot as I was writing MIDNIGHT RECKONING, the second book in my Dark Dynasties series. That's because his little quip there is the basis for the story. Well, maybe not the mass hysteria part. But I did want to see what would happen when one of my cat-shifting vampires met a gorgeous woman who wasn't just out of his reach, but out of his species entirely. This is a tale of cat vamp meets werewolf, and relationships don't come with more built-in baggage than theirs.

I love a good star-crossed relationship, as long as it works out all right in the end (I still suffer traumatic flashbacks from *Romeo and Juliet*), but writing one turned out to be more difficult than I'd imagined. I'm perfectly happy to torment my characters from time to time, but the deck was so stacked against these two that even I was sometimes left wondering how they could possibly work things out. You see, Jaden Harrison and Lyra Black are natural enemies. In their world, vampires and werewolves don't mix, period. While the vampires rule the cities, the wolf packs keep to more rural areas, and the enmity between the races is strong despite years of relative peace between them. The wolves think the vampires are arrogant, worthless bloodsuckers; and the vampires think the wolves are wild, unruly, violent beasts. Each race steers clear of the other, so the chances of

Jaden and Lyra ever meeting were incredibly slim. But they did...and it left quite an impression.

If you've read *Dark Awakening*, you'll remember the beautiful she-wolf who stalked off after Jaden insulted her. What she was doing in a vampire safe house was left a mystery, but in MIDNIGHT RECKONING, you'll discover that Lyra has much larger problems than one rude vampire. She's the only child of her pack's Alpha, and the natural choice to fill his shoes when he steps down. There's just one problem: Lyra is female, and werewolf society is patriarchal, with some archaic notions about a woman's place that would horrify most twenty-first-century women. But this is Lyra's family, Lyra's world, and rather than desert them she's determined to make them see her value. She wants to win the right to lead at the pack's Proving...but to do so, she'll need to learn to fight in a way that evens the playing field. Finding someone to teach her seems hopeless as the clock ticks down, until a chance encounter with an unpleasantly familiar face leads to unexpected opportunity...and a very unlikely teacher.

The wolf and the cat together are a volatile mix of confidence and caution, brashness and reserve, unrestrained ferocity and quiet intensity. Their interaction is frowned upon, and a relationship between them is strictly forbidden. But a blue-eyed Cait Sith is hard to resist for even the most stubborn she-wolf, and it isn't long before both Lyra and Jaden start to wonder if there might not be a way around the traditional "fighting like cats and dogs" arrangement. That is, if the forces working against them from within the pack don't end Lyra's chances, and her life, first.

How Lyra and Jaden find their way to each other, and whether Venkman was right about canine/feline love affairs being a harbinger of the apocalypse, is something you'll have to read the book to find out. But if you're a fan of the sparks that fly when opposites attract, you'll want to come along and visit the Pack of the Thorn, where a vampire cat without a cause has finally met his match.

Enjoy!

Kendra Leigh Castle

♥ ♥ ♥ ♥ ♥ ♥ ♥ ♥ ♥ ♥ ♥ ♥ ♥ ♥ ♥ ♥ ♥ ♥

From the desk of Rochelle Alers

Dear Reader,

You've just picked up a very special novel, one that has lingered in my heart for ages.

SANCTUARY COVE, the first book in the Cavanaugh Island series, not only comes from my heart, but connects me to my ancestral roots.

Set on a Sea Island in the Carolina lowcountry, SANCTUARY COVE envelops you with the comforting spirit of a small town, where the residents cling to old traditions that assure a slower, more comforting way of life. Drive slowly through quaint Main Street, and you'll sense a place where time seems to stand still. Step into Jack's Fish House and be welcomed with warm feelings and comfort food. Sit quietly by the picturesque harbor and listen to the natural ebb and flow of nature.

The Cove draws recently widowed Deborah Robinson into its embrace, offering a fresh start for herself, her teenaged son, and her daughter. Her grandmother's ancestral home reaches out to her, filled with wonderful childhood memories that give Deborah the strength she needs to face her future.

When Dr. Asa Monroe arrives at the Cove, he's at a cross-roads. The loss of his wife and young son in a tragic accident has devastated his world, sending him on a nomadic journey to find faith and meaning. And as he spends the winter on the Cove, he discovers a world of peace that has eluded him for more than a year. When he meets Deborah, he realizes not only that they are kindred spirits, but that fate might grant him a second chance at love. When friendship gives way to passion, Deborah and Asa find their greatest challenge is hiding their love in a town where there is no such thing as a secret.

The residents of the Cove are loving, wonderful, and quirky, just like the relatives we love even when they embarrass us at family reunions. So come on home and meet Asa, Deborah and her children, and a town full of unforgettable characters that will make you laugh, cry, and long for island living. Sit down with a glass of lemonade, put your feet up, and let life move a little slower. Enjoy the magnificent sunsets, the rattle of palmetto leaves in the breeze, and the mouthwatering aroma of lowcountry home cooking. If you listen carefully, you'll even hear a few folks speak Gullah, a dialect that is a blend of English and African.

And don't forget to look for *Angels Landing*, the second novel in the Cavanaugh Island series, coming in the fall of 2012.

Read, enjoy, and do let me hear from you!

Rochelle Alers

ralersbooks@aol.com
www.rochellealers.com